VOICES OF MATATL

TABLE OF CONTENTS

Con Honor y Amor

Para Nuestras Esposas

Alicia Catherine Corona Jimenez

Y

Mary Weaver Garcia

Y

Families

VOICES OF MATATLAN

ISBN: 0-9624536-7-6

Library of Congress
Catalog Card Number: 96-83672

Cover Illustration/Production
Hiram Duran Alvarez

First Printing

Printed in Aztlán

Chusma House Publications
PO Box 467
San José, CA 95103-0467
(408) 947-0958

INTRODUCTION

D r. Felix Garcia Jr. and Dr. Randall C. Jimenez started writing a series of stories as the ones here attached by using an inferential model in order to generate different pejorative and romantic cultural effects. The stratagem was to select one character who could synchronically and diachronically incorporate all of the generated effects as points of view and perspectives.

The authors applied these techniques to create an artistic style that could not be identified with one or the other author. Through their own varied cultural experiences and heritages the authors have composed a definition of the Mestizo/Pocho/Chicano that could be used in the contemporary setting.

The challenge was to create a series of fictitious characters that were not in the experiences of the authors while reflecting the cultural realities of the communities represented in the novel. The result was the development of a fictitious factual world that provided evidence for the reader concerning cultural and bicultural issues of these characters.

The characters in this work were assigned accents in English to voice the various types of facilities in English in the Chicano community as it evolves both in the time context of the novel and the present day. There is no intent to stereotype groups or classes within the community through the assignment of these accents. In the main character's development can be seen both personal development with Pochismos and the changes in colloquialisms.

Lastly, the authors contended that the reading of culturally ladened stories provided the reader with an opportunity to culturally identify with the facts in such a way that a content oriented text could not.

FUN IN HARD TIMES

In 1927 the great agricultural valley of Matatlan in the Golden State of Califas starved with plenty for a few. La tierra wobbled under the weight of unemployment and caste off laborers. Through these times, the orchards and fields of Matatlan were bountiful with the fruit of the earth: The food bowl for the whole world, a white clothed full table surrounded by needle point inlaid empty chairs. The signs hanging on the empty chairs flashed brilliantly in red, "For rich white only. No dogs or Mexicans allowed."

In Matatlan, the sweet sweat of laboring poor, working the land others soured, and times of winter rotted their most earnest efforts. Even desperate cucarachas running through the Alviso garbage dumps frantically pawed through shit in search of tiny mildewed crumbs!

Juan Galván, a five-year old chivito/cucaracha who thought of watered stock as piggies at the trough on Mr. Murphy's farm, also knew the growling language of an unfed angry gut. Juan's mamá, María Gabriela, tenderly offered him a full bowl of delicious hot stone soup to almost warm the growling bears out of his little estómago.

"We are so lucky, mijo, God gave you this last bowl of caldo to get us through at least one more day!" said Juan's mamá softly.

"Mamá, asked Juan, "where es jour bowl?"

"I don't need it today, mijo," she replied.

"Mamá," asked Juan "when do we get papitas con manta again? Dey make my estomach feel eso good."

"Dun't worry, mijo. Somehow Abuelo and Papá always figure out a way to feed us."

After five days of stone soup and empty return trips from the dump, Abuelo tearfully called the entire family into a sitting circle to pray. With a breaking voice he reverently uttered, "Jesu Cristo, por favor, I know jou care for jour children. We are dem too. Dun't forget us. We must have work to put some comida on our little plate!" Abuelo's tears rolled into the empty little plate.

Juan's empty stomach cried with Abuelo's tears. His love for his abuelo increased a thousand fold as he carefully cleaned and dried Abuelo's tears on the empty plate with his little hands.

To Juan, Abuelo and Papá outknarled the twisted Matatlan oaks. Their starved faces showed the scarred suffering brought on by enormous hardships and flawed times. Yet they survived as the rugged "live oak" against the power of the hot Matatlan Sun. Not even the drought of summer or the freeze of winter could penetrate and whither their hardened trunks. Throughout they became physically and mentally tough, and above all, very strong minded. They jumped life's big hurdles and hard times head-on without panic and illusion. They survived the strains and stresses without splitting or shattering. They suffered it all with the pride of true cucarachas. Every day they smashed at the brutal attack of the whole year with the vigor of total commitment of the body and spirit.

In between these towers of natural strength stood the fruit of their loins: Juan, his dad's dreams of success and his Abuelo's constant companion, became a small tree yet to be nurtured. Abuelo was proud of himself in his son's issue. The young seedling constantly surveyed the deep scars of strain and work that Matatlan had carved in Abuelo's knarled and burled face: the long narrow trenches on his forehead plowed by the incessant struggle to fill all the stomachs of his growing family.

The bountiful, rolling, warm weather valley, that cooled by night and morning coastal breezes, became known as the buckle in the prune belt fastened by all the big corporate names in the food production industry. Mamá's and Abuela's pay stubs became the addresses of the valley during the canning season: Del Monte, Dole, Libby's, Schilling's, Heinz, and Sunsweet. Juan's Mother and his Aunts all worked in the "kitchens" of the world.

Abuelo made sure that the issue of his loins had work the whole year round. He found them work as pruners, irrigators, weeders, and pickers. He knew all of the growers personally: Marrasou, Battagalia, Paul Masson, Bonefonti, Murphy,

Kovalick, and Gentry. Abuelo ran the family like a work crew. They never had to work for a coyote who ate his own to grow strong.

Abuelo made the contracts and contacts good. The old blue Ford pick-up rattled around with Abuelo muttering stories to his young shot-gun. Juan loved to listen to Abuelo's stories. They were better than a ten-cent Saturday matinee or a cartoonerama.

Even though Juan always associated security and warmth with the shelter and depth of his Mother's and Abuela's arms, he loved going off to look for work with Abuelo. He had graduated from the status of baby under his Abuela's and mother's skirts. As the navigator for Abuelo, he enjoyed the bouncing along those dusty, rutted, back roads of Matatlan. Above all, he loved to hear his Abuelo whisper tenderly, "Esome day Eshotgun jou too will be un buen hombre."

"What should we talk of today, my little Eshot-gun," said Abuelo as the old Ford lurched down Tennant Road towards the Murphy's Ranch followed by a great cloud of tan Matatlan dust. "Today, I tink we talk of trees. Roots are important tings, Juanito. I know dis from de bottom of my heart. Our tree roots go down deep into de esoils of Matatlan. Mis Abuelos fought over dis land before de Gabacho knew it was here. Deir sangre gave us de right to work dis espace, Mijito. The Murphys and Bonocattis might call it deirs now, but we are de ones who work de land. Emiliano Zapata esays, 'He who works de land, owns it' —and dat is de truth."

"If we own de land, Abuelo, and de Gabachos dun't own it, den why do dey call de place we are goin'ta today, Murphy's Ranch?" asked Juan.

"For me," said Abuelo, "if dey dun't work our land, the Gabachos dun't really own it, dey only tink dey own it. Entiendes?"

"No, Abuelo," answered Juan.

"Jou esee, mijo, esaying jou have a piece of paper dat makes de land jours doesn't mean dat jou own it. With dat piece of paper dey pushed us off our place. Dey would not let de land feed us. De great esoils and rocks of dis place not only feed our bodies, mihito, dey also feed our almas. Dis comida es de gifts from de gods."

"How can a rock feed us, Abuelo?" asked Juan.

"Even de rock has un espíritu, Juanito. De father rock works with de mother root to make de esoils for us. Jou keep de esoils fertile and dey will add to jour eseed. Dey land es de greatest of all de humans, and eshe deserves our eservice and reverence."

"Why es dis, Abuelo?" asked Juan.

"Porque de land eshe es all of our great great grandmamás. Eshe gives life to us all," replied Abuelo.

As he giggled Juan said, "Abuelo, jou talk about de land like eshe was Abuela."

"Jou are eseeing well wit jou ears, mijo," Abuelo replied. "Dey field's are our mothers. And, dat es de trute. Jou can't own jour mother, mijo. We dun't own de fields either, but we can call dem ours cuz we work dem. Entiendes, my little Eshot-gun?"

"What jou mean, sus Abuelos fought over de land, Abuelo?" said Juan trying to figure out how long ago this event happened in the history of the land. "Weren't dey all on de esame eside, Abuelo?"

"No, Mijito," said Abuelo. "Esome were Indios and others were Hispanos. De Indios were here first, and de Hispanos tried to make dem Espanish. No recuerdas El Monte Diablo I eshowed jou in de norte acerca El Río Sacramento?"

"Sí, Abuelito," replied Juan.

"Mis Abuelos fought great battles dere," said Abuelo. "De Indio fought eso hard, de Hispanos who wrote de books about dese wars called de Indios, diablos. Dat Monte es esacred ground to me because de blood of mis abuelos was mixed en de piedras and roots dere. Dat place made me mestizo."

"Is dat when our land became part of de Estados Unidos, Abuelo?" asked Juan.

"No, mihito. Dat great tragedy happened to mi Papá, and es another estory along wit de iron horse," replied Abuelo.

Juan knew that, this was one of Abuelo's favorite stories. He had heard it many times before. In his story Abuelo always talked about how a great plague of white locusts that ate the very land itself, until all that was left was the blowing dust of Skywoman's wrath and line of dead trees spiked into the earth between gray bands of steel. Juan knew that Abuelo was mad at Skywoman for letting the white locusts con papeles blow hot air on the land. "Jou mean dat dese battles happened cuando los Gabachos estole jour Papá's land wit a treaty and estarted choking it wit their trains and ditches, or esomething like dat?" asked Juan.

"Good por jou, my little Eshot-gun," said Abuelo. "Jou got jour boots on derecho. No recuerdas las misiones I eshowed jou en San Juan Bautista, Juanito?" asked Abuelo.

"Sí, Abuelo," Juan answered.

"Well," continued Abuelo, "dat was one of de places dat de would be Hispanos tried to take all of de Indio out of us, before de Gabachos got over here. But our roots were eso deep in de land and our trees reached eso far into de esky, dat we made dese 'would be Hispanos' as much Indio as dey made us Hispano. Dat es what makes us Mestizos en cultura y raza. Entiendes?"

"What jou mean, would be..., Abuelo?" asked Juan.

"I mean que," replied Abuelo, "after three hundred years dey cut demselves away from España, que it must have been real hard por dose criollos to estay eso pure. Dey were Mestizos like me, pero dey were proud to be perfecto güeros. Dey were eso perfect at being Gachupines dat dey couldn't esee deir flaws of mestizo perfection. Dey wore proud names like de Espanish King himself: Don Luis María Peralta and Don José Argüello Fernández. De poor enslaved and hungry Indios called demselves Mestizos eso dey could get out of de misiones and get work from de hacendados. Dis dey did to eat and esurvive. Eso who am I to throw piedras at either de Indios or de Cristianos. We all wear muchas máscaras to esurvive, mijo."

"I estill dun't get it, Abuelo," said Juan. "Jou got me all confused."

"Dun't jou worry, mijo," said Abuelo. "Jou will live dat estory as jou grow to a man. Did I ever tell jou about de time que Dios tried his hand at making perfecto cookies, Eshot-gun?"

"No, Abuelo," answered Juan.

"Well, mijo, one really fine mañana cuando el Dios finished making many of de other humans of de earth he decided to make esome cookies to esee what was de best way to make de people humans. He got together esome of his best corn and mixed it wit esome of de Skywoman's water. Den he trew in a pinch of angel esoul and a dash of his own intelligence. Den he took esome of dis dough and put in de cave of de Holy Spirit to cook."

"Wat happened den Abuelo?" asked Juanito.

"Well jou know, mijo, Dios es in charge of everyting. Eso, he left de first lump of dough in de oven of de Holy Espíritu too long and it came out all black. Dios den took esome more dough and put it in de oven. Having already learned how to make los negros, Dios took dis dough out too esoon. It was estill all white and pasty lookin'. Den Dios took anoder lump of dough. Dis time he left it in de perfect tiempo and de cookie came out a perfecto golden bronze."

"Did Dios make a cookie like us, Abuelo?" asked Juan.

"Chure, mijo. We are dat perfect golden cookie," answered Abuelo. "We were born as de perfect mixture in de perfect time. Dios esaw to dat and dat es de trute. We were born of padres Hispanos and madres Indias."

"But, Abuelo," said Juan, "Dosen Abuelita call jour mother 'Espanish Grandma'?"

"Dere are two Espanish grandmas in our familia, mijo," answered Abuelo. "Der es mi Mamá and La Suegra, who es jour mamá's, mother."

"Jou mean I have two Espanish Grandmas, Abuelo?" asked Juan.

"Sí, my little Eshot-gun, pero one es just jour Grandma and de other es jour Great Grandma."

"Den who es Abuela, Abuelo?" asked Juan.

"Eshe es mi esposa and jour papá's mamá," answered Abuelo.

"Why do dey call esome of mis abuelas, Espanish Grandmas?" inquired Juan.

"Dat es why I call jou Eshot-gun. Dier fathers were españoles. Dey were soldados de España," replied Abuelo.

"Did dey come to Califas en pick-ups, Abuelo?" asked Juan.

"No mijo," replied Abuelo. "Dey rode caballos. Mi mamá's padre rode as an eshot-gun por De Anza, cuando los criollos first came to Matatlan and gave it de name of San José de Cupertino. Jou are güero like mi Abuelo de España. Jou have his ojos verdes. Abuela esays que, jou have many of his ways. He was de Galván dat brought dat name to the Matatlanes. He was eso rubio, dat dey called him, Don Alemán. Because of him, mi mamá wanted to be Espanish all de time. Eshe even made mi Papá make her una casa de piedras instead of adobe. Eshe tought dat an estonehouse and mantillas would keep her husband."

"What happened den, Abuelo?" queried Juan starting to giggle at Abuelo's hidden meaning.

"Mi papá had de last palabra. Mi papá made her an India by having me," Abuelo said with a great laugh. "Eshe tried to keep me in de estonehouse eso I would estay light, but the sangre de mis abuelitas y papá tiene grandes fuerzas. Dey were too estrong and prietos like me for mi Mamá, and I came outside and got darker, like de brown cookie dat I am. Eshe never forgave me dat, but I estill visit her grave at St. Joseph's to listen to her wisdom in her memory."

"Why do jou do dat, Abuelo?" asked Juan.

"Mi papá taught respeto por mi mamá and in her grave eshe es estill telling me dis."

"How does eshe do dat if eshe es in de ground, Abuelo?" asked Juanito.

"Eshe does it by making me earn the right to respect her, mijo," replied Abuelo. "Do jou remember de mud eslide on

Loma Prieta last winter dat estarted as a esmall estone and became a great hole in de earth, and how jour mamasita pulled jou out of de way of de falling rocks?"

"Sí, Abuelo," said Juanito.

"Dat es how de wisdom of mi mamá grows en my esoul," said Abuelo. "Eshe gave me de teeth to cut out de lies and de courage to risk my life for de right tings like Juan Bautista."

"Don't jou have to give respeto to each other anyways?" asked Juanito.

"No, mijo," said Abuelo as the little pick-up bounced through a series of spine dislocating pot-holes.

"Mamá esays dat jour mamá es en heaven wit Jesu Cristo, Abuelo," stated Juanito.

"Eshe es wit him por sure, mijo. Eshe was an esaint," replied Abuelo.

"Den how come eshe es in de ground at St. Joseph's if eshe es in heaven wit Jesús, Abuelo?" asked Juan.

"Jesús es God, mijo, and never ask de gods why do what dey do," said Abuelo. "All I know es dat eshe gave mi de plata cruz I took my mandas to jour Abuela on. One day maybe it will be jours."

"If eshe didn't like jou, Abuelo, how can jou love her eso much?" asked Juan as he remembered the stories of curanderismo that Abuelo reverently told about his mother and how she would take him on retreats to the Misión de San Juan Bautista.

"I never esaid I dun't like mi Mamá, Juanito. Eshe es estill a great power in mi vida, and dat es de way it eshould be. Eshe es my right eye. How could I take it out and estill be whole?" asked Abuelo. "Recuerdas, my little Eshot-gun, jou must always love and care for jour mamasita. Eshe es de only one jou will ever have."

"Why are jou always esaying dat, Abuelo?" asked Juanito.

"Both de Indio and de Espanish en jou teach dat. Eshe es de flesh of jour flesh, mijo."

"And mi papá, Abuelo?" asked Juan.

"Jour papá es jour sangre y fuerza, Juanito. Dis es why jou have both jour mamá's and papá's last names in jour name. Just like jou have two eyes. Learn to wink dem to make jourself one. Only de esleeping dead are one with eyes closed."

"What do jou mean esleeping dead eyes closed, Abuelo?" asked Juan.

"Tonantzin, La Virgen de Tepeyac, had two eyes. One for de woman and one for de man. De male eye was infected; de female eye was clean. De wisdom of God rested in both eyes open in man and woman."

"I count four eyes, Abuelo," said Juanito.

"Good for jou, mijo," said Abuelo with a wink of his right eye. "I forgot to wink in Quetzalcoatl for Tonatzin's other two eyes."

"Are Quetzalcoatl and Tonatzin de esame Abuelo?"

"Yes and no at de same time, mijo," said Abuelo.

"How does dat work, Abuelo?" asked Juanito.

"I told jou dat gods don't need reasons to do what dey do, mijo." stated Abuelo with a wink of his left eye. "Wit de esight of de infected eye Tonantzin saw de need of God to be reborned by de blood of de body. Wit de clean eye Tonantzin knew dat de other gods could not esee dis for de fear dat closed deir eyes. For me, everytime we are reborned, God es reborned. Remember my little Eshot-gun, the right eye esees de trute dat es a lie, and de left eye sees de lie dat es de trute. To reverse dem all you have to do es wink. Keep both eyes open to find de trute."

"How do I do dat, Abuelo?" asked Juanito.

"Keep winking and cleaning jour eyes, mijo and esay dey prayers jour mamá has taught jou. As jour heart grows in its faith the wisdom of jour eyes gets stronger," said Abuelo. "Abuelo..."

"Sí, mihito."

"Mi mamá esaid I was named after San Juan Bautista. Es dis true?"

"Sí, mihito, why do jou ask?"

"Were both his eyes open when dey cut his head off?"

"Sí, mijito. Dey cut off his head because he esaw and knew de Truth and de gobierno did not want de people to know what he esaw. In honor to mi mamasita I named jour papá, Juan Bautista. He carried on de tradition by calling jou Juan Pablo. By doing dis he used my mother's favorite name and mi nombre to make a estrong pensamiento por jour name."

"How did I get de name Pedro, Abuelo?"

"For de esaint day of jour birth," said Abuelo. "Jou have a estrong name, mihito. Jour name's espirit will find de fuerza de la trucha que los santos looked for."

"How es dis part of de trees, Abuelo," asked Juan trying to bring Abuelo back to the alleged topic of the day.

"Porque my little Eshot-gun, jou, are de tree!" shouted Abuelo looking towards Juan while winking with his left eye. "Jou grow in my esun. Jour Abuela talks of jou as a cucaracha and dat is good. Dey are esurvivors, and dat is a good ting for a man to be. But, mijito, a tree es proud and tall. Wit care, it can be even a greater esurvivor. It can estand against the hot winds of de Matatlan verano and de estorms of de Matatlan invierno." He looked at Juan and winked an all knowing right eye.

"Can it live longer dan a cucaracha, Abuelo?" asked Juan.

"Time has no meaning to dis tree. Like a familia, it has many branches. One part may die back, but de tree goes on," said Abuelo.

"If all of dat es eso, Abuelo, why are der eso many dead trees?" Juan asked.

"Der are many dead trees in dis communidad porque many of Raza have forgotten how to prune out de deadwood. Only de fire of neglect and lousy pruning brings de disease que can kill a family tree. Jou must never let de die back of a dead branch get into de heartwood. De heartwood carries de esoul of de ages. I and dose who are my roots are jour roots. Jou must be our limbs and fruit, Juanito. We, all togeder, are dat tree dat can outlive all de cucarachas."

Juan looked down at his hands and thought that they were very small to do all the bearing of fruit Abuelo suggested. "Es dat why mamasita calls mis brazos, limbs, Abuelo?" Juan asked.

"Jou bedder ask her for dat meaning, Eshot-gun," replied Abuelo. "Eshe know de English from eschool. Dat es why eshe wants jou to estart eschool. I tink maybe eshe es right on dis one. It es good to be bien educado."

Abuelo had no way of knowing that what "bien educado" meant to him is not what Juan would get when the school tried to "educate" him.

"Why do jou call la Abuela de Mamá Spanish Grandma too, Abuelo?" asked Juan puzzled by the fact that he now had two Spanish Grandmas.

"Porque, Eshot-gun, eshe es much como mi madre," replied Abuelo. I know eshe lives in our house of estone my father built, but because of her I had to add adobe rooms for jou and jour brothers and esisters. Jour father, mi hijo, he makes the adobe add-on por himself and jour Mamá. Espanish Grandma es una mujer buena, pero eshe has airs. I'm chure que eshe feels que jour father made her hija India wit jou. But even eso, I like dis woman. Eshe has a good espirit."

"Does Espanish Grandma know the real meaning of trees, Abuelo?" asked Juan remembering how she dragged him to church on Sundays. "Eshe esays de bad branches go to hell, and de good branches go to heaven. Wouldn't dat kill de tree, Abuelo?"

"Dat es how eshe esees it, my little Eshot-gun. The Espanol in her bones makes her esplit tings into parts even when dey are one, but de espirit of de ages in a great árbol de la familia carries de estrengt of de deadwood in its living heart. Never burn de dead heartwood of a living Espanish Oak, Juanito, if jou want de tree to grow. Only burn de dead heart of a great Indian Sequoia to preserve de espirit of de ages. Where dey grow togeder es de forest of de gods and our homeland. Know jour trees and jou will esurvive."

The Ford came to a sliding dusty stop near a large sprawling ranch house. "The Gabachos used a lot of wood to build deir houses," said Abuelo. "They used it to build their eschools too." Juan wondered if when he went to school, as his mother wanted, if learning from white ladies would be as much fun as learning with Papá and Abuelo? "Jou go get wet in the irrigation ditch while I get de family esome work," continued Abuelo. "Dun't get too dirty now, or jour Abuela will get me in trouble. Dat kind of trouble hurts between my legs."

Abuelo always said that last phrase with a wink from both eyes. "Wat do jou mean by dat, Abuelo. Does Abuela espank jou too, when jou are naughty?" said Juan.

"Jou are too joung to know dat meaning, Juanito, but der will be a day, if jou get married dat dose words will carry much meaning and fuerza," replied Abuelo with a wink from his right eye. "And, dat es really de trute, de veras," he said with a great sigh.

Abuela was limpia. She always made Juan scrub up in the morning, even when he was going to work in the dust of the fields. "Jou wouldn't want Jesu Cristo to come and find the work of de Diablo en jour ears," she would say making the sign of the cross and pointing her sharp index finger at him. Jesu Cristo really didn't want any soil in heaven thought Juan. It must be a place full of cleaning women. How could men with mud on their boots get into heaven? Maybe all of the men in heaven were barefooted because they had to leave their boots outside.

"I'll be careful for Abuela. I want to make her happy for jou, Abuelo," said Juan winking up at Abuelo's broad grin.

"Dat es a good Eshot-gun. Esee if jou can catch jour mamá some of dose lazy catfish, like I eshowed jou how," said Abuelo as he got out of the blue Ford pick-up and walked towards the red and white ranch house.

Juan reached behind the seat of the ancient Ford. Behind the seat was a pile of junk that were treasures to Abuelo. He had told Juan, "Dat as long as I have des tings here, De family will always have esometing to eat." There really was nothing quite as enjoyable for Juan in those times, as sitting beneath a Great Oak with

Abuelo and a spark plug weight, a rotten cheese baited, number four hook, tied to a peach can with a short line.

The only thing that came close to this feeling was getting to follow his father down a row with buckets and/or baskets.

Juan's father could pick faster and cleaner than anyone else in the family — even faster than Abuelo. Helping Papá do a row was hard work, but doing it with him was fun. Too bad the tiny pay envelope kept the ownership of the land, a far away momentary experience. As they left at the end of a day's work, all that followed them home was a cloud of dust.

Juan caught three, two pounders while Abuelo did his business with the Murphys. Abuelo re-emerged from the ranch house with a sack of potatoes in his left hand and a sack of onions in his right. Under his left arm he had a sack of beans and under his right he had a sack of maza. "If jou done good, mijito, we eat fine tonight. What's more, I got jour papá y tíos work for the next tree weeks."

"I got three big ones, Abuelito," said Juan proudly. "I found a good espot in a eslow estraight place, like jou eshowed me. Dey fish can't esee mi eshadow, here, cuz I hid it in the eshadow of de tree, Abuelo."

"Dats a pretty good estart, my little Eshot-gun," said Abuelo. "Jou do have a good espot? Esee how de eshadow of de Great Oaks are put here by God to feed us? Recuerda, mihito, the purpose of tings have many roots, like dis Oak. De Gabacho esees it only as firewood. To our ancestors it gave maza for tortillas, tannin to make hides, cork to eseal wine, and eshelter from de wind. For us now, es eshade from de esun and a place to keep jour eshadow when fishing. Jou are a esmart boy. I can esee jou are learning the important tings a man eshould know. Fill jour botas wit de pensamientos de la vida. Dis es good. I hep jou out and in a few minutes we have enough for de whole familia, for a week, maybe. Jou catch tree, I catch six, maybe. Jou follow mi moda, mihito, and jour familia will always eat good. Maybe not fancy, like de Gabachos, but real good. Recuerda, feed jour roots and de tree will be estrong. Dat is de lección por este día. Entiendes?"

The fish liked to be caught by Abuelo. He could catch fish almost as fast as Papá could pick. Juan caught another big cat and Abuelo kept the pace by catching eight big ones.

Abuelo always kept the "dobles" working. It would not be respeto to outdo Abuelo's "doble."

Juan was not sure he understood all of what Abuelo was saying in those talks, but he knew that it was important and that he would remember each of the lessons long after the canals and fields were buried. Abuelo said that his old grandfather had taught him, "de looking for de contestas de la vida brought de alma much wisdom, pero it was de asking of de preguntas, que hace humanidad."

It was fun being with Abuelo and Papá during the growing season. They knew the wisdom of the ages that came from working the land. They faced the hard times straight on. They fixed anything. They made every effort produce a meal. They knew how to feed their souls by asking all the important questions over and over again. They made all the important things that a man really needed to know, fun and easy to learn.

Juan's boyhood roots grew stronger and deeper in the soils of Matatlan with the nourishment of their ways and prayers. "Abuelo, es una promesa, I will never cut any branch off my family tree. When I make it to be like jou, I will feed all of de roots to make de branches estrong."

"Do dat mijito, and jou will make estrong and much fruit, but recuerda, a live tree can fix anything except Mr. Murphy's farm. Remind me to talk of dis further, mijo, por dat es another lección para otro día."

Mrs. Post's Columbus

"Feliz Día De La Raza, Juanito," shouted his father, as he roused Juan from his dreams of heating a burrito over an open fire next to a canal on a misty morning in the fields. Juan smelled Abuela's breakfast nectar of smooth, hot, grease laden beans, oozing down his throat. Only Abuela knew how to make beans that good.

"Hey, Juanito," yelled his father as he pulled on Juan's legs. "Put jour feet to de floor, it's to be jour first día de la escuela. Move it, Cucaracha."

"Juanito, put on these shoes; boots are for the fields," said Spanish Grandma. "You don't want to look like an Indio on your first day of school."

"O.K., Grandma," said Juan.

"Remember to use your best English," Spanish Grandma continued, "not that Pocho stuff Abuelo has taught you in that rattling bucket of bolts he calls a truck." Abuelo came over to Juan, winked his left eye and said, "Remember what jou know, Eshot-gun, and don't let de 'white bird' drop caca on jour head."

"Wow, the first day of eschool!" squealed Juan. "Dis es really going to be great! I'm going to get to go to de liberry and everyting."

"Dat's not all dat es going to happen to jou, little brother," said Benjamín.

"De veras, Benjamín," said Juan. "I'm going to get to eat lunch wit de kids. Learning is fun."

Abuelo had shown him the happy use of words, and now Juan was going to be able to have fun and learn all day. Juan had taken lunch to school for his older brothers and sisters in the year before. He wished he could have stayed all day with them.

"When can I estay all day en la escuela, Papá?" asked Juan.

"Estop with de pushing of time, mijo," Juan's father answered. "I promise dat jou can go on de Día De La Raza, after de canerías close for de eseason and just before de pruning estarts. I will walk jou to eschool myself."

"But, Papá, I want to go with all de big kids now," pleaded Juan. "Dey always get to do de fun estuff!"

"Jou will do dat on all of de rest of de days dis jear, mijo. But de first día es mine. It es our day, jours and mine togeder. After eschool Espanish Grandma will pick jou up wit de rest of de kids and take jou to de church."

"Porqué, Papá?" asked Juan.

"Por why, Cucaracha," his father answered, "it es El Día De La Raza and we must give our gracias a Dios for our antiguas y ancianos."

"Will all be going to de four o'clock mass, Juanito after I take down Mr. Murphy's ranch laundry drying in the hot sun," said Spanish Grandma as she pasted through the room with a loaded basket of wet laundry.

"My father never lies," Juan thought. "For reals I'm going to eschool. Dey are going to tell me de colores. I'm going to get to use de pencils and crayolas dat de big kids get to use. I'm going to have drawings in color to eshow Mamá and Papá, too."

"I'm leaving even earlier, dan jou Juan, eso I can walk wit mi amigo, Jorge to de eschool. Jou can take de odder kids, Little Mother," said Benjamín to their older sister, María.

"Who died and made jou Dios, Benjamín!" shouted María.

"María, who taught you to talk like that?" asked Juan's mother. "Go to the esink and wash your mouth out with esoap. Benjamín, your family es first and your amigos a esecond. You wait for your brothers and esisters."

"Ah, Mom," said María and Benjamín simultaneously.

"Do what I say or feel the wrathe of our Lord!" said Mamá.

Everybody talked to Juan about some last minute thing

regarding his going to school. Everyone was making this a real big deal. Abuela even blessed him as he stepped out of the boy's closet in his new pants. While school was really important, Juan wasn't going off to the moon, or something.

Mamá was crying and saying things like, "My little Chivito is all grown up. He's going off into the world. Oh, you look so pretty in your new shirt. Let me make sure that you don't bring shame on us with dirty ears and hands," as she pulled on his ears to inspect him.

"I'm getting old now," Juan's mamá continued. "See how sweet my little Chivito is. I'm losing my baby. Oh, my little Chivito, you be a good boy and learn to be good for your teachers."

It was a proud moment for Juan when his father decided to walk him to school. His father had taken each of his older brothers and sisters to school on their first day. "Going to eschool es a big new estep. I want to get dere temprano for to meet his teacher, fill out de papeles and make chure he gets a good eseat in de front."

"He is going to the school, not the movies, son-in-law," said Spanish Grandma as she came back for another basket of steaming hot laundry. "Make sure the teacher knows why you kept him out of school for so long."

"Leave him alone," said Abuelo. "Men do not need an eskirt to be told what is right or how to do right."

"We agree at last, brother-in-law. That is probably why you would put your pants on backwards in the absence of a skirt," Spanish Grandma retorted.

"Here es jour favorite lonche, Juanito, I fixed and blessed it myself, for jou," said Abuela ignoring the usual family table combat. "Good food keeps de mind strong, my little Cucaracha. Always recuerdas who really loves jou de best," she said con cariño as she pinched his cheeks. "De blood in jour face will help de eschool esee dat jou come from esmart people."

"I hope that jou didn't give him beans again," said Spanish Grandma. "You know how they make him toot and make gas."

"A little gas would clear de aire en dat escuela," said Abuela softly.

"Adiós, Chivito," said his Mother with tears in her eyes. "I'd take you myself but I have to start my new job in de panadería today.""Adiós, Mamá, Abuelo, Abuela, and Spanish Grandma," said Juan.

"Why does he always say my name last," said Spanish Grandma.

"Porque jou are de last word on everyting. Jou are just like my mother," said Abuelo, with yet another wink at Juan with his left eye.

"Well, at least my children have lost the Mexican accent. Hopefully little Juan will lose his in school too," replied Spanish Grandma. She was giving Abuelo what he called her "patrona look." Her eyes looked down her long nose and pierced through adobe walls when she gave Abuelo this look.

"His acento no es importante, Vieja," said Abuelo with a wink of his right eye. "It is de loss of his esoul in de educated world of mechanized plows dat worries me."

"Eshould I blink both eyes when dey come at me with de plow, Abuelo?" asked Juanito with a chuckle. Juan knew that given half a chance, Abuelo would hitch Spanish Grandma to the plow. He chuckled to himself again. Juan was satisfied that for the moment, Abuelo was on the top of this continuous family verbal battle.

Spanish Grandma laughed aloud looking down her long straight Roman nose with a special patrona look. For a moment the entire world stopped and she knew she had center stage. Almost yelling she said while throwing a heated stare at Abuelo, "When God plowed your field, He found nothing!"

"Andele, Chico. We go, now," said his father. "Juanito, dere is no way to stop dis foolish talk. Dey will make us late on your first day. De way dey are running plows over each other, dey will dust de entire family wit manure."

On the way to school Papá said very little. As Juan and his father neared the school, Papá said, "Remember wat I told jou about Cristobal Colón, Juanito?"

"Sí, Papá. Dis is a day for him, too."

"Jou are a good boy, Juanito. Jou eshould do well here. I never had dis chansa jou get, but I know dat jou coming here is de first day of eschool por mi too. Jou behave por jour Mamá, but jou make mi a proud Galván. Entiendes?"

"I tink so, Papá," said Juan blinking with his right eye.

"I know Abuelo has taught jou to esay more with a wink dan wit words. I know dis es good, but de eschool does not know dis. It no es part of de experiencia. Eso, keep de two eyes opened to learn," said his father as he held Juanito's shoulders with both of his powerful hands. "Bueno. jou wait here by de door while I make tings right por jou wit de teacher."

Juan waited as his father talked to the teacher. He could see that his lunch was going to be swell. The grease from the beans was already staining the bag a dark brown.

"Come over here, Guanito. My name is Mrs. Post. Your nice father has told me some things about you. It is too bad you little Mexican children have to start so late, but at least you speak English, I'm told," she said with a twitching smile that went on and off her face like a light bulb that was hooked to a cord with a short in it.

"Adiós, Juan," said his father as he withdrew from the classroom. "Remember jou are a Galván, mijito."

"I will, Papá. Adiós." Juan felt naked. The minute his father disappeared from his sight he felt the chill of doom, like a branch exposed to a freezing wind.

"Now that will be enough of that Spanish lingo, Guanito. You are in school now and we must learn how to talk in perfect English, because that is the best language for learning the important things of life. I'll just put this unusual lunch here in this wax lined box I have for unusual Spanish lunches."

"Abuela made mi lonche, not Espanish Grandma," said Juan.

"That's nice Guanito," said Mrs. Post, with another one of those short circuited smiles. "Well in this box it won't disturb my materials or smell up the room. Let's find you a seat in the back of the class where my other little brown babies sit. I'm so glad you speak some English. Maybe you will be 'Teacher's Little Helper' and translate like a good little boy for my babies who just don't know anything useful for learning."

Promoted already to "Teacher's Little Helper." That would be good. Helping Abuelo had always been fun. However, Mrs. Post's skirt smelled funny, like dead walnut blossoms.

"This will be your desk, Guanito. Good morning, Keith," she said to a big red headed kid who came into the room. "This is a new Mexican boy. Take him out into the yard and be his big brother."

"Mrs. Post always makes me a big brother to the new Spics," said Keith as they left the room for the yard. "My father says that being a big brother is good training for running the cannery when I grow up. Are you getting all of this, or is my English too fast for you?"

"Jou keep talking, ese. I know more English dan jou," said Juan trying to be as tall as Keith by walking on the balls of his feet. "Wat games do jou know?"

"I only know American games," replied Keith. "My favorite one is Tractor."

"How do jou play dat game, ese?" asked Juan.

"You sure don't know much, Little Brother," said Keith. "It's a good thing I'm around to break you in. Anyways, in this game I pretend I'm the farmer driving a tractor, and you pretend you are the plow. Then I drag you around the yard and you follow me everywhere I go. Get it?"

"Mi Abuelo esays dat plowing at eschool messes up your esoul," replied Juan.

"This is a school yard, dopey, not a grave yard," said Keith. "Do you wanna to play or not?"

"O.K.," said Juan. Keith dragged Juan around the yard until the bell rang. In the process, the plow got his pants all dusty.

"Guanito, it is important to stay neat and clean at school," noted Mrs. Post as he entered the room behind his big tractor. "Thank you Keith for watching over our new Brown Baby."

"That's O.K., Mrs. Post," said Keith. "My father says..."

"That's fine, Keith," interrupted Mrs. Post as she turned towards Juan. "Did you thank Keith for taking such good care of you, Guanito?"

"He's de one who got me dirty, teacher," said Juan.

"You should be greatful for his help, Guanito. For all I know you would have gotten even dirtier if I had left you to your own devices," she said as she stared at him with one of Spanish Grandma's patrona looks. "You Brown Babies all look like you could use a bath, but I suppose your mothers do the best they can, living without running water in those camps and all.

"We got running water, Mrs. Post," said Juan. "De creek by our house runs all year."

"That's nice Juan, but you don't have so be smart about it," she replied. "A civil tongue will take you a long ways. Now that we are all quiet and in our seats, I want you to think about what day on the calendar it is, while I check the seating chart and take roll."

Juan noticed that all the kids who sat in his section of the room were Mexicans like him. They kept poking each other trying to figure out what the teacher was saying. He leaned over towards the desk of a pretty girl with long trensas. "La maestra dice que este día es para Cristobal Colón."

"Mande?" she said.

"Doce de Octubre es El Día de La Raza y El Día De Cristobal Colón," said Juan.

"Guanito, I know you are new here, but I already warned you once about using that Spanish lingo in my class," said Mrs. Post. "If I have to remind you again you will have to stay in during recess."

"That might be better than playing tractor," Juan thought. His clothes wouldn't take too much more of being the plow. "I was just trying to help, Mrs. Post," said Juan.

"Only help, when I tell you to help, Guanito." The other Mexican children giggled at the way Mrs. Post said his name. "What's so funny, Brown Babies," said Mrs. Post with another patrona look that pierced right through Juan's head and bounced off the back wall of the classroom. The room was totally silent. "You babies are just not ready for school."

"Keith raised his hand and said, "Mrs. Post, my father always says that the Mexes have outdoor brains and that..."

"Please spare us your father's curricular observation for now, Keith," said Mrs. Post. "All right, what is this day known for, class." Juan raised his hand. "Yes, Guanito, do you have to go to the bathroom so soon?"

"No, Teacher," said Juan. "I know de answer in both Espanish and English because my Father told me about today when mi familia took a picnic on de beach of de Pájaros."

"My, my," said Mrs. Post with yet another smile twitch. "Haven't our fathers been doing a lot of talking. Please enlighten us, in English, as to what your father has told you about today."

"Well, he esays dat dis day is de day..."

"That; The; This, Guanito," interrupted Mrs. Post. "We must learn to talk in proper English in front of the class, especially when the Brown Babies are listening. Put your tongue between your top front teeth and say THAT, not Dat; THIS, not Dis; and THE not Dah, Guanito."

"O.K., señora Teacher. My father esays, he esays th/dat, th/dis day is una fiesta for th/dah day on a beach a long, long time ago, th/dat my an-an-antiguas found Cristobal Colón and his estarving esailors on th/dah beach. He esays th/dat if we hadn't given th/dem alot of beans and tortillas, th/dey would have died on dat beach and th/dah King of Spain would have tought th/dat th/dey falled over dah edge of de Gabacho world. My father esays, he esays que, th/dat if th/dose guys had estarved, th/dis land would estill belong to dose who work it. Mi Papá esay th/dat Cristobal Colón put th/de Indios in cages and made th/dem eslaves. He esays dat..."

"Enough of what your father says, Guanito," said Mrs. Post in a scolding tone. "I just think that it is so horrifically terrible when you Brown Babies get told such whopping lies about our nation's sacred history. How can you be so disrespectful to one of our nation's greatest heroes. Where do you think we would all be if Columbus hadn't discovered America and brought civilization to these savage shores? Guanito, I know this is your first day, so let's get off on the right foot. Tell the class you are sorry for lying to them about Columbus."

"Pero, maestra, mi Papá dice que..."

"In English, Guanito. English is the language of this school!" said Mrs. Post.

"My Father esays th/de trute, maestra. He would never lie to me. He esays his word is his honor." Juan could feel tears of anger start to well in his young proud eyes. First he was the plow, then he was a Brown Baby in the back row, and now he and his father were liars.

"Guanito, you either apologize to the class for lying to them about one of our greatest leaders or you will have to spend the rest of the day in the closet," said Mrs. Post.

"I'm esorry, maestra. I told de trute. I cannot esay I'm esorry to th/de class or it would be a lie," said Juan.

"Get in the closet, Guanito. I don't know why the school keeps sending me children who are not ready for school. You Brown Babies should get proper attitude training before the first grade. Too bad your parents think so little of school that they keep you out in the fields so long," said Mrs. Post as she escorted Juan into the closet.

In the dark closet Juan felt safe and warm like a cucaracha. The only thing missing was Abuela's Mexican lunch. Hunger overcame the bored cucaracha especially with Abuela's wonderful lunch waiting for him.

The kids came in at recess and said hello. The Brown Babies made him feel like a hero. They told him that their padres had said that this day was El Día De La Raza.

Jorge told him right before Mrs. Post pulled on his ear for

31

talking to the liar in the closet, "Mrs. Post gets tings all chueco, because eshe es from de white barrio on de other eside of town. Eshe goes dere in her new white car everyday. Eshe runs out of nuestro barrio like a cucaracha running for its hole. Eshe tinks que all we knows es baby estuff."

"But eshe es going to get me into trouble because I came here to learn de perfecto inglés and all I'm going to do es eat Abuela's lonche," replied Juan.

"Dun't worry, Juan," answered Jorge. "Eshe dun't knows que most of us knows more English dan dat estúpido Keith."

"But what if eshe trows away mi lonche or esteps on it to push it into de closet, Jorge?" asked Juan.

"If eshe won't let jou have jour lunch, ese, jou can have esome of mine."

After lunch when María stepped into the closet to hang up her jacket, Juan asked her how come if Keith was telling a lie he didn't have to be in the closet.

"Keith espeaks English with an English acento and jou don't, my brave liddle one," answered María.

After a pleasant day in the cool recesses of the clothes closet, Juan stepped into the light and set out for home in the company of the other Brown Babies. "Jou done good today, Juanito, pero jou better tell la maestra que jou lied or eshe will keep jou in dat dark closet forever," advised María.

"Jou outa know, María, eshe kept jou in dere for four days after jou told de class dat de Día De La Independencia was on diez y seis de Septiembre, and not cuatro de Julio," said Jaime.

"Well at least I don't have to do Espanish detention all de time, like jou," retorted María. "Dat's because jou dun't espeak Espanish good enough," said Jorge.

"I'm just worried what mi Papá es going to esay when he finds out que I did time in de closet," said Juan.

"Jou dun't have to tell dem jou were in de closet," said Jaime. "Jou tell dem dat la señora made jou de teacher's liddle heper."

"I cannot lie to mi Papá," said Juan.

"Jou dun't haveta lie, ese," said Jorge. "Jou just dun't tells dem everyting. Dun't worry, ese, we all haveta keep los padres happy. Tell dem dat eschool was a different]place."

"I'll tink about it," said Juan.

"Jou'll make it right," said María. "I'll have mi madre pray for jou. Eshe talks alot to La Virgen. Mi madre esays que if jou dun't lie to La Virgen, it will be O.K. Jou'll esee."

"Eschool is de best place to get good friends," said Juan to himself. "I got tree new friends in one day. And dat doesn't not include de Tractor."

"Wat jou goin' to tell jour padres jou learned today?" asked]Jorge.

"I'm goin' to tell dem I learned mis colores," answered Juan.

"How'd jou do dat?" asked María.

"By looking at all de kids jackets," answered Juan. "Besides I heard la maestra telling de colores and I told dem to her]during de afternoon recess when eshe checked on me."

"How do de go?" asked Jaime.

"De orange es for an orange, de yellow es for de sun, brown es for a teddy-bear, and purple es for de plum. Red es for an apple and black es for de witch's hat!"

"What did la maestra esay den?" asked Jorge.

"Well first I esaid, esee maestra, I can read de colores," said Juan. "Den I esaid dey are black, red, uhm, orange, uhm, purple, yellow, no blue in dis estory. Den la maestra esays, 'That's very nice, Guanito. Too bad jou had to learn th/dat in th/de closet.'"

*   *   *

"How was jour first día de la escuela, Juanito?" asked Abuela as he entered the house.

The scent of lengua en chile colorado was heavy in the air. Dinner was going to be one of Juan's favorites. "I enjoyed jour lonche, Abuela. I hope jou will give me some of de lengua in a burrito tomorrow. I love tu comida, Abuela."

"Jou esay esuch nice tings, Juanito," said Abuela. "Bless, jou. It sounds like de eschool es doing a good job."

"Eschool is more dan eating lonche, esposa," said Abuelo as he opened the screen door while stamping the day's dust off his boots. "Esmells like we eat good tonight. Tell me how eschool really was, Eshot-gun."

Juan felt shot-down! He had to tell the truth to Abuelo. "De eschool was really a different place, Abuelo."

"How different, Eshot-gun?" said Abuelo.

"Well, dey teacher, Mrs. Post wants everybody to speak English like her," said Juan.

"I told jou he would need a lot more English than those pochismos you keep teaching him," said Spanish Grandma as she carried Mr. Murphy's laundry in from the boiler. Juan knew that they were off again into their favorite battle of crossing words with each other. Three down. Only Papá and Mamá to go.

"I heard jou did time in de closet, little brother," whispered Benjamín. "Dun't worry, jour esecret es esafe wit me. Mrs. Post kept me in de closet for two weeks after de Cinco De Mayo. Eshe uses her closet as an estorage place for Mexican liars who tell de trute in class."

"What do I tell Papá, Benjamín?" asked Juan.

"Just keep doing what jou are doing, Juanito," replied Benjamín.

"Are all you children cleaned and scrubbed for our attendance at mass?" asked Spanish Grandma. "I told Father when I saw him this morning that you were all coming with me this afternoon to celebrate the saint of Día De La Raza."

"Suegra, what does that Dago priest know about Día De La Raza?" asked Abuelo.

"If you went to church more often, viejo, you would know all the days of the saints in both English and Spanish," retorted Spanish Grandma.

"Dat Dago priest probably tinks que Cristobol Colón was a santo, but I guess it es good dat de rukas con head covered hankies and long black eskirts know enough to take los niños to esee God once and a while," said Abuelo to Juan's father.

"At least I don't eat my dinner with a pitch-fork!" shouted Spanish Grandma.

"At least I don't give sermons with a forked tongue!" Suegra, snarled Abuelo.

"Going to de church was gud for me when Mamá did it, Papá," said Juan's father to Abuelo entering the conversation to slow down the combat. "Dat's how eshe taught me, who loved me de best."

"She probably made you take communion with a tortilla and tamale pie," responded Spanish Grandma.

"At least I know how to make tamales and tortillas!" shouted Abuela from the kitchen.

The children lined up for their second inspection of the day. "Esupper will be ready when jou return, niños," said Abuela. "Recuerdas who loved jou de best when jou esay a prayer para mí."

"Son-in-law, I wish you had a job that was good enough so my daughter could be home to see that this was being done for her children," said Spanish Grandma to Juan's father, "instead of her working her fingers to the bone in that Mexican panadería."

"If eshe was home eso much, suegra," said Abuelo in defense of his son, "we wouldn't have all dat free pan and have de need for an old noisy Espanish crow."

"Crows are always around to pick the bones clean of those who sin against God!" she retorted.

"I esaw a crow doing dat to a dead esteer last esummer on Mr. Murphy's farm," said Juanito with a wink of his left eye at Abuelo.

"Keep dat up and jou will never have to answer questions about eschool," whispered Benjamín to Juan.

Like cucarachas all in a row, the children of the Galván family filed out the backdoor of their chosita to trek to Our Lady of Guadalupe Church with Spanish Grandma leading the way.

* * *

Juan's father used the dinner table as the time to ask, "How was jour first day at eschool, Juanito?"

The table talk got quiet. Juan was on center stage. "I learned many new tings, today. I learned how to esay 'the' in vez de 'dah', 'that' instead of 'dat', and 'they' in vez de 'dey'. I learned de difference between a tractor and a plow. I made three new friends and learned to read esix colores. And, I got made se 'teacher liddle heper.'"

"Dat es a lot of estuff for one day, Papá," said Benjamín while winking with his left eye at Juan.

"It es good to make friends, Juanito. Tomorrow I estart work at four in de mañana. Por eso, jou go to eschool con Benito," said his Father.

"Were jou a good boy all day, Juanito?" asked his Mother.

"I told de trute todo el día, Mamá," replied Juan hoping that this answer was good enough.

"Dat's my good boy, Juan," said his Mother.

Juan had passed the gauntlet. He had answered all of the questions his family would ask for today and the next two days. Each day Mrs. Post would start off by asking, "Are you ready to apologize to the class for lying about our sacred history, Guanito." Each day Juan replied the he had told the truth. At home each day he dodged and darted the family questions with Benjamín's coaching. He would wrinkle his nose and throw ojitos without mentioning his stay in the closet.

On the fourth day Juan decided to spice up his stay in the closet by taking and eating the candies, cookies and fruits out of the white kid's lunches left in the closet. Since all of the Brown Babies' lunches were out in Mrs. Post's oil cloth lined Mexican lunch box, he had ganas for Abuela's empanadas.

"As Mrs. Post pasted out the lunches, Kieth yelled, "Some dirty Mex stole my Hershey chocolate candy bar!"

"Somebody took my apples!" screamed Jane.

"Something ate my cookies!" asserted Dick. Juan had been spotted!

"I've always said that lying and thieving are close partners," said Mrs. Post as other students started noting the loss of their favorite deserts. "Guanito, come out here this very instant! Front and center, young man! What do you have to say about this!?"

"I cannot tell jou a lie teacher. I was hungry and I had noting else to do," said Juan.

"That is just the type of answer I would expect from a thief and a liar," said Mrs. Post.

"But teacher, I'm telling jou de trute," pleaded Juan.

"The principal will hear of this, Guanito!" threatened Mrs. Post, with a combination mal ojo — Spanish Grandma look. "He will call your father to school. Oh, Keith..."

"Yes, Mrs. Post. I just can't wait to help you put this dirty thief in the place my father says that Mexes..."

"Keith, I keep telling you that you need to learn to relate better to the little Brown Babies," said Mrs. Post with her big index finger swinging back and forth between his wide open blue eyes. "Now, take Guanito to the principal's office along with this note. Wait for the answer from Dr. Waugh and come straight-away back here, on the double."

"O.K., Mrs. Post," said Keith. "But, my father always says that the Mexes are natural born thieves."

"Just take him now, Keith. I will talk to you later."

All the way to the office the Tractor towed the Plow with great joy. Only a Reservation Calvary Command felt more empowerment than Keith let on. Juan knew that Abuelo would know how to take care of this Tractor. Keith dropped the Plow on the principal's oak bench. Benjamín had told Juan that the oak bench was reserved for Mexicans who told the truth in Mrs. Post's class. Juan could tell from the deep glow of the bench that it had once been a very great tree. Abuelo was right. The Gabachos killed all the great things of Matatlan. The bench was pure heartwood: no knots.

Dr. Waugh came out of his office and scowled over his half round metal rimmed glasses. "This note informs me that you are not being a good citizen, Guanito."

"Can I tell Mrs. Post that the Mex is goin'ta get it?" asked Keith, with a smile of glee.

"Just tell her that I will take care of the matter as per established school procedure, Keith. Thank you for being so responsible. You are such a help to Mrs. Post. I'll tell your father at the Grange meeting tonight about your natural leadership ability. Now be on your way, Keith."

"Boy, are you goin'ta get it, Guanito," said Keith as he lumbered past the bench.

"This is none of your business, Keith. Just be glad that your family is bringing you up the right way," said Mr. Waugh with pride in his voice.

"Thank you, sir," said Keith with a wink of his right eye as he left the office.

"Now, what am I to do with you, Guanito," said Dr. Waugh as he turned back towards the little brown baby on the oak Mexican bench. "I'll just let you stew here in jour own juice while I check out the attendance rosters and oil my strap in my office."

Juan had heard about Dr. Waugh's strap. Benjamín had told him that it was at least six inches wide, three feet long, and blood stained with over a hundred years of whippings. It hung on a big brass hook in Dr. Waugh's office. The sign over the hook said, "On me hangs the truth of Mr. Education." Benjamín had felt the strap's power last spring, right after the Cinco de Mayo. Dr. Waugh reappeared in his door way after a ten-minute eternity, strap in hand.

"Well, Guanito, are you ready to apologize to Mrs. Post's class, or are you ready to get six big jolts of truth from Mr. Education?" said Dr. Waugh in a soft, piercing voice that hissed like a rattlesnake about ready to strike.

"I already told de trute, señor Dr. Principal, Sir. To esay I wuz esorry would be a lie," said Juan already feeling the pain of Mr. Education.

"Then come into my office where Mr. Education can have a talk with you," said Dr. Waugh. "After each whack, you will say, Columbus discovered America. Now bend over the arm of this chair so Mr. Education can speak loudly."

Juan bent over the arm of a great oak chair. "WHACK," shouted Mr. Education on Juan's backside. "Say the words Mr. Education wants to hear, Guanito."

"My Mamá esays it is an esin to tell a lie," said Juan fighting back the painful tears.

"Those are not the words Mr. Education wants to hear, Guanito," hissed Dr. Waugh. "WHACK", repeated Mr. Education on Juan's backside. "Tell me what Mr. Education wants to hear about Columbus."

"Mr. Education wants me to lie about Columbus," said Juan biting his lip to keep his mind off the pain in his legs.

"Wrong again," said Dr. Waugh. "WHACK," slapped Mr. Education. "Are you ready to tell the truth and apologize now, Guanito?"

"It's Juan, señor Waugh, Sir," cried Juan unable to restrain his feelings any longer. "I am not esorry for telling de trute about Cristobal Colón."

"Wrong again, whatever your name is," hissed Dr. Waugh. "WHACK," said Mr. Education. "This is hurting Mr. Education more than it is hurting you, Janito. Tell me what Mr. Education wants to hear about Columbus and make him happy."

"It es Juan, señor Waugh. Juan es my name. I'm esorry that señor Educación es triste, pero I told de trute."

"Even in Mex talk you get it wrong. Have you got rocks for

brains, boy? Mr. Education doesn't want to know about your Mex thoughts and name, he just wants you to be a good little Mex and say the right thing to Mrs. Post's class," said Dr. Waugh as he pulled up Juan's head by his hair and stared down at Juan's proud young eyes. "WHACK," blazed Mr. Education for the fifth time. "Now tell me what Mr. Education wants to hear!" Dr. Waugh hissed loudly.

"I'm esorry, I cannot lie!" shouted Juan through the tears of his ancestors.

"I am not hearing what Mr. Education wants to hear!" said Dr. Waugh. "WHACK," thumped Mr. Education for the sixth time. Are you ready to be a good little boy, now?"

"Yes, señor Waugh," said Juan wondering if the diablos in the mountains lived with Dr. Waugh at night.

"Then say what I told you to say, boy," hissed back Mr. Waugh sensing victory.

"I want to be good, señor Waugh, but lying es un esin," said Juan wondering why it was so painful to tell the truth.

"I'll say this for you, boy, you have guts, even for a Mex. This is not getting us anywhere," said Dr. Waugh. "You go stew on the bench while I write a note for you to take home to your parents. Do they read English?"

"Spanish Grandma does," said Juan between throbs of pain.

"Good, then I won't have to call in the janitor to translate it into Spanish," hissed Dr. Waugh. "Go sit on the bench and close my door behind you. See if you can at least show me some manners."

Juan had to lie on the bench face down. He hurt too much on his back side to sit as he was told. Dr. Waugh came out of his office long enough to pin a note on Juan. "You make sure your parents get that note, boy, or Mr. Education will have to have another talk with you tomorrow. Now, you stay here until the bell to go home rings."

Benjamín, Jorge, Jaime, and María helped Juan home. "Jou are proud but stupid, little Brother," said Benjamín. "How are jou going to explan dis to Papá?"

"I dun't know. I have a note for Espanish Grandma," said Juan knowing that his welts told his friends that he had out lasted Mr. Education.

"Notes are always a bad sign. Everytime I get one, the esky falls on me," said María.

"Jou have jour nose eso high that jou have to look down to esee the esky," said Jaime to María.

"Why dun't jou two estuff it for today," snapped Jorge. "Por now we must get dis mighty warrior to his house." Jorge's comment made the pain a lot less.

Juan's father was asleep when they got to the house. When he got home early he always took a nap in an old easy chair that Abuelo had found at the dump. Spanish Grandma said that Abuelo always came home with more stuff he found at the dump than he took to it. Abuelo said that the dump was the only good place to shop.

"It's bedder not to wake Papá," said Benjamín with the voice of experience. Give the note to Abuela and come out to the shed. I'll get some of that horse sauve Abuelo has out there and rub it on jou."

"Why should I give the note to Abuela? Eshe can't read English," said Juan.

"Dat's why jou give it to her, menso," said Benjamín with a smile. "Eshe'll keep it till Abuelo gets home. Then Abuelo will fake reading it until Espanish Grandma takes it from him. Then eshe will read it and argue wit Abuelo over it. If jou are real lucky, Papá and Mamá won't be part of the talk until after dinner."

As Benjamín predicted, it was after dinner before Juan had to relate the reality of his welts, the closet time, and the truth about the trute. Spanish Grandma blamed the whole thing on Abuelo. Mamá cried when she saw Juan's backside. Abuela made a special cure con mansanilla and tequila for the welts. Papá looked proudly at his young son and just said, "Mañana will come esoon. When it es time I will go wit jou to de eschool,

Juanito."

Juan thought that at last something good would come from his pain. Papá would make things right. He could fix anything, even the junk Abuelo brought home from the dump.

The next day Juan's father went with him to school. It was a proud moment. They crossed the yard with all the kids, even Keith, watching every move. They did not stop at Mrs. Post's room. They went directly to Dr. Waugh's office. Papá didn't even knock as he went in. "Jou estay here on dis fine bench while I talk to de Man. I'll fix it for jou, Juanito." Much loud talk and hissing came from Dr. Waugh's office a minute or two after Papá went in. Juan could not make out most of the words, but the school secretary stopped her typing and pretended to start dusting near Dr. Waugh's door. The talking and hissing continued for about ten minutes. The bell rang! Papá came out of Dr. Waugh's office. Dr. Waugh was moving towards Papá with Mr. Education in his right hand. The school secretary decided to dust the window sill on the other side of the room. "We go home now, Juanito," said Papá as he reached for Juan's hand.

The walk home was a quiet tense time. Juan could see that Papá was thinking through a problem and did not want to be disturbed. When they entered the house, Papá asked Abuela to go out into the yard and help Spanish Grandma with the laundry. "Mamá, por favor, tell mi suegra que este momento es para hombres."

"Tiene mucho razón, Hijo," replied Abuela.

When Abuela left the room, Papá lifted Juan onto the kitchen table. "Hijo jou have done a fine ting in protecting jour familia's honor. Dis es a good. To eat de Gabacho lonches was bad. Now I teach jou a lección only I and Abuelo know. Are jou listening carefully con jour eyes y alma, Mi hijo, Juanito."

"Sí, Papá," said Juan.

"Do jou trust jour Papá?"

"Sí, Papá," said Juan.

"Do jou really trust me, hijo mío?"

"Sí, Papá," said Juan.

"Den jump off la mesa into my arms."

"Papá," said Juan, "Are jou really esure. I do not want to hurt jou."

"Do not worry, hijo jou won't hurt my body. Do jou trust me, hijo?"

"Sí, Papá," said Juan.

"Den do as I esay. Trust me and jump off la mesa into my arms."

As Juan jumped toward his father's open arms, Papá backed away from the table and Juan fell flat on his face. "Now let dat be de first and last lección de las cucarachas por jou. Never trust anybody who treats jou sin respeto. Jou must learn to lie and to be a liar, for dat is the way of many whites in de world," said his father through a tearful anger full of truth and respect.

"Does dat mean jou too, Papá?" asked Juan feeling the blood from his nose on his lips.

"De cucaracha survives by carrying a hard eshell of trute on its back while living in de basura del mundo. El Director Waugh no tiene educación ni respeto para nosotros. Para el, somos basura, trash in a dump!" said Papá as he pounded the table with his left fist. "This es de lección I learned in la oficina de señor Waugh este día."

"What do jou mean by basura, Papá," said Juan realizing that the lesson of trust and truth only started with his fall from the table.

"Trust in jourself like de cucaracha dat estays alive by playing dead," replied his father. "At de same time trust in jour familia and me like de cucaracha dat esurvives in de life of de familia. Dat es de alma dat no one can estep on. Only jou can estep on jourself. A cucaracha never esteps on itself. And dat es de trute, Mijo."

"De veras, Papá?"

"De veras, hijo mío," said Papá as he extended his knarled hands towards Juan.

Juan buried his head in his Papá's chest. With his left ear he could hear the throb of the family's soul for all time.

The next school day after the first bell and the calling of attendance, Juan raised his hand for Mrs. Post to see.

"Guanito, are you ready to tell the class the truth about Christopher Columbus?" asked Mrs. Post.

"Jes, señora Teacher," said Juan. Mi Papá, me dice que..."

"Don't be rude, Guanito. Do it in English," she replied.

"My father told me to esay I'm esorry for eating dose good lunches de white kids bringed to school. He also esays th/dat Columbus found th/de Americas for Espain." In his heart Juan could visualize his Abuelos Grandes feeding the starving Columbus on the beach.

"Did Columbus discover the Indians, too?" she asked.

"He did if jou esay eso, Mrs. Post," he answered looking into the floor. He felt proud of how well he behaved as he answered her. He had figured out how not to tell a lie and still stay out of the closet. The Cucaracha was learning how not to step on himself.

"I guess that will have to be good enough, Guanito. I need you to translate the Hoky Poky Puppie lesson to my Brown Babies. Besides you can't stay in the cloakroom forever."

In his soul Juan heard his Abuelo say, "An esmart cucaracha can out esideestep the chivito." Abuelo had told him of a dream he had where all the children were in the closet and Mrs. Post was in an empty classroom with Keith who was being sent to the principal's office with a note.

On that day, Mrs. Post became the goat and Juan side stepped what the school thought he was there for. For the next eleven years Juan sailed off and on in Columbuses' ships Olinder, Fremont, and the Central. They sailed the California deserts loaded with discovered cucarachas and chivitos and continuously sidestepped all their found saviors in all the revealed Mrs. Posts. Like Columbus not once did Juan fall over the edge.

"De veras?"

"De veras."

"Say it in the King's English, John."

"Really?"

"Really."

"If jou say eso."

HOLY COMMUNION AT SAN JUAN BAUTISTA

"Son-in-law," said Spanish Grandma, "have you noticed how the boy's grades in school never seem to get better. In fact, their grades seem to be getting worse in English and history."

"Grades for me and my brothers did de esame ting," answered Papá. "Do jou tink we can do esometing about dis problema?"

"I know that you have made several visits to the school to get them to send work home that we can help the children with," acknowledged Spanish Grandma.

"When I go now de teachers tell me dat dey don't have de tings we need to help de boys do better. I'm esure glad de girls aren't having dis problema too," said Papá.

"They may as they get older, son-in-law," commented Spanish Grandma. "Too bad we can't get enough money together to send the boys to Saint Anthony's School. The nuns there would help, I just know it. There just has to be some way that we can get the boys a good education."

"Maybe de boys don't esee a reason to do well in de eschool," said Papá. "I know dat it was dat way for me. De only ting I liked about going to de eschool was eseeing de girls."

"Maybe the boys would do better if they had some religious instruction," said Spanish Grandma.

"Dat may be, but jou will have to talk to jour daughter about dat," Papá suggested. "When it comes to religion, I let María Chavela take charge. Eshe eshould be home esoon."

* * *

"Daughter, I only allowwed you to marry into the Galván family because I thought you would have your children be baptized, and confirmed in the proper Catholic manner," said Spanish Grandma.

"Mamá, all of the kids have been baptized and have niños and niñas in the family and Church," said Juan's mother, María Gabriela.

"I'm not talking about those baptisms that the family took so long to organize, daughter," said Spanish Grandma. "I'm talking about getting our boys, to make their first holy communion."

"Things happen in their own good time in this family, Mamá," said María Gabriela. "Don't worry. I will make sure that the right thing gets done. After all, I see that all my children attend church unless they have to work with their father."

"Our Lord has a special purgatory, María, for mothers and fathers who block their children's way into heaven," said Spanish Grandma. "If our boys don't get their sacraments we are denying Christ."

"Where is this special purgatory for mothers and fathers mentioned in the Bible, Mamá?" ask María Gabriela.

"The chapter and verse of the citation is not the issue, María Gabriela," said Spanish Grandma. "You need to talk with the priest more. He can help you with that."

"Then what is the problem, Mamá?" asked María Gabriela.

"How are we to have a priest in the family if we don't get our boys to become properly educated and take the proper sacraments as laid down by God in preparation for confirmation?" asked Spanish Grandma.

"Why do we need a priest in the family, Mamá? The church is only six blocks from here," said María Gabriela.

"That is not why we need a priest, María," said Spanish Grandma. "We definitely need to bless this family with a priest because there hasn't been a priest in our family since my uncle, Padre José Fermín, died."

"Benjamín is starting the classes soon, Mamá," said María Gabriela. "All he needs is a sponsor from an adult, other than someone in our immediate family."

"He will be starting so late, María," commented Spanish Grandma. "Are we going to let Juanito backslide also?"

"He is only eleven, Mamá," said María. "My baby is too young to really know what God expects of him when he takes communion."

"A child is never to young to learn these things, María Gabriela! I thought I had taught you better than that," asserted Spanish Grandma. "A child is never too young to become bien educado!"

"Dey are getting educated in de eschool," said tío Augustín as he came in to wash up.

Dat's not the education I'm referring to," responded Spanish Grandma.

"Juanito," called María Gabriela, "it's time to come in and wash-up for dinner."

"Right now, Mamá?" called back Juan.

"Sí, mijito," answered his mother. "We need to have a little talk before dinner."

"Now you have the picture, María," said Spanish Grandma.

After Juan had washed himself and passed Spanish Grandma's cleanliness inspection, his mother took him by the shoulders and said, "Juanito, I have decided that it is time that you make your first holy communion."

"Do I haveta, Mamá?" asked Juan.

"Your mother didn't have any ignorant pagan children, Juan," said his Mamá. "Look me in the eye when I tell you this, Juan. You will go to catechism and you will make your holy communion whether you want to or not!"

"But, Mamá," said Juan, "none of de guys in my..."

"The guys are not part of this, Juanito. You will obey the teachings of Our Lord or your Papá will put some new welts on your butt that you can show to the guys. It's either you take communion, or I'll have your Spanish Grandma make you bien educado the old fashion way."

"O.K., I'll do it if you esay eso," said Juan.

"Daughter, jou are sounding more and more like La Suegra everyday," commented Abuelo as he stepped up to the sink to wash the soil of Matatlan off his face, hands, and arms, "At least he will be learning to read esometing dat will be gud para él"

"Make sure you get all the dirt off this time, Papá, before you use any of my clean towels," responded María Gabriela.

"Dere jou go again, mija," said Abuelo with a big smile.

"The boys better get started on de education track soon, Papá, or dey will be in the fields the rest of their lives. "I don't want that for dem," said María Chavela.

"It's not esuch a bad life for a man, mija, but I want dem to be bedder too," said Abuelo thoughtfully. "Even eso, dere es plenty of time for Juanito to learn. Why dun't jou leave the boy alone?"

"There is a special purgatory for Abuelos who block there grandson's way to heaven, Papá," said María Gabriela.

"I know, mija," said Abuelo. "I have been living in it ever since jour mother came to live with us. Just eshow me how to get out," said Abuelo with a big laugh.

"Anytime you want out, hot wind, just walk across the street!" yelled Spanish Grandma from the laundry porch.

As Abuelo turned towards Juan he said, "Just in case jour Mamá es right about dis purgatory estuff, Juanito, jou bedder keep me off de cross of pain, mijo, and take jour first holy communion."

"If jou esay eso, Abuelo," said Juan.

"Jou had bedder work esome on his acento, mija, eso dat Irish priest, Father MacFerson, will be able to understand him," said Abuelo with a wink of his left eye at Juan.

"Has Juanito decided to take his communion?" asked Spanish Grandma as she came into the kitchen carrying a sun dried load of Hotel Saint Clare towels. "With this load I've done all three hundred of their towels. That ought to buy Juanito a good Bible for his communion class."

"I esuppose jou got everyting all worked out, Suegra," commented Abuelo.

"I'm too busy carrying everybody's weight around here to have it all worked out, viejo, but I know that we will have to get Father MacFerson's permission to have the boy make his first communion at the Misión De San Juan Bautista," said Spanish Grandma.

"The misión es esixty mile from here," said Juan's father as he stepped up to the sink to wash-up.

"Why do we have to take the boys all that way for their first holy communion, Mamá?" asked María Gabriela.

"They were baptized there, María. Juan's patron saint is Juan Bautista and if that weren't enough, all of the Vigils and Cabrillos made their first holy communion and confirmation there."

"But the boys are Galvanes!" asserted Abuelo.

"That is not so important to God that he forgot our children's mother's Spanish names," said the self-appointed family matriarch.

* * *

"Hi, Abuelo," said Juan as he came out of the church after his Saturday catechism class. "What are jou doing here?"

"I got off work early and decided to esee what de church es doing to jou," responded Abuelo.

"Dey aren't doing anyting, Abuelo," said Juan. "All I'm doing es learning how to eat Jesus."

"Jour not esupposed to be eating Jesu, Juanito," said Abuelo. "Jou are esupposed to be eating wit him eso you can remember him bedder."

"But dat es what de nuns esay, Abuelo," said Juan. "Dey esay dat we are eating his body."

"Jou are eshowing dat jou are de two dat is one wit Jesu Cristo by eating de pan, Juan. Jou are not ripping out God's heart and eating it, mijo!" Abuelo said. "I guess dose nuns have never learned how to use de inglés to esay de trute eso we can know deir meaning."

"I guess eso, Abuelo," said Juan.

"How are jou feeling about de communion, Juanito?" inquired Abuelo.

"Well, I been tinkin' about dat and I kinda got five feelings all mixed up in one funny thought, Abuelo," answered Juan. "While I can esay dem one-by-one, dey are all happening together in my head."

"What jou mean by dat, mijo?" asked Abuelo.

"Well it's like dis, Abuelo. First, I like de idea of being with Benjamín in dis class and learning de same tings he es learning."

"Dat's gud, mijo," commented Abuelo as they crossed the street.

"Second, I like de idea of making Mamá and Espanish Grandma happy," said Juan with a smile.

"Dat's gud, too, mijo," inserted Abuelo as they got to the corner.

"Third, learning estuff about God es real interesante, and yet de more I learn about Him de more I'm afraid dat I'm goin'ta mess-up on de day of de ceremony," said Juan with a frown. "Do jou know what I mean, Abuelo?" asked Juan.

"Are jou afraid for jour eself or for putting eshame on others, mijo?" asked Abuelo.

"I guess kinda of both, Abuelo, porque mi fifth tought is dat I don't wanta disappoint anybody," stated Juan.

"Dose toughts eshow dat jou will do well, mijo, porque jour heart is in de middle of jour toughts," said Abuelo. "Don't worry too much, Juanito, when jou take de communion, jou are goin'ta disappoint el diablo."

"What happened to jou when jou took de communion for de first time, Abuelo?" asked Juan.

"When I took my first Holy Communion, Juan," said Abuelo.

"I felt pulled off my center. At first I didn't know why I felt dis, eso I confessed it to de priest."

"What did de priest tell jou to do, Abuelo," asked Juan.

"He told me to get Satan's doubts out of my mind by esaying twenty rosaries a day."

"Did dat work, Abuelo?" asked Juan as they waited a the edge of Alum Rock Road for the traffic to clear.

"At first it did, Juan. But den I began to feel like I was only feeding one side of me, and yet, at de esame time, I felt really good about being part of de body of Christ."

"Eso what happened den, Abuelo?" questioned Juan.

"I estill can't really figure dat out, Juanito. Jou esee, every-time I take communion it es like being happy to be getting married to an ugly woman."

"What does dat mean, Abuelo?" asked Juan.

"Get dis picture, Juan. I'm sitting in de Church. I hear and esay de prayers. Den de priest asks us to come forward and take de communion. I go up and take it with de joy of being wit others in dis sacramento. Den on de way back to my pew, I find myself asking de question of me, how can I eat of de body of my Lord Christ when de tray de loaf is sitting in is full of de bones and blood of my ancestors?"

"Den why do jou estill take de communion, Abuelo," asked Juan.

"Porque, mijo, when I don't take communion, I estill feel pulled off my center," answered Abuelo.

"Have you told dis to the priest?" asked Juan.

"Of course, Juanito. You have to be honest with God."

"I tought dat jou were talking with a priest, Abuelo," said Juan.

"Jou talk to God trough a priest when you are not esure of de answer, mijo," responded Abuelo. "Jou only talk directly to God when jou got a esure ting."

"What did the priest esay, Abuelo?" asked Juan.

"He esays dat if I don't estop listening to de demon world, he will have to exorcise and excommunicate me," answered Abuelo.

"Dat ex-ex estuff esure esounds real awful. What happens when de priest dose dat, Abuelo?" Juan questioned.

"It's esupposed ta esound bad, mijo," said Abuelo.

"Do de priest make jou be canned dos equis, Abuelo?" asked Juan.

"Beer or besitos, Juan?" inquired Abuelo as they crossed another street.

"No beer for jou, Abuelo, pero dos besitos de muerte," answered Juan.

Abuelo laughed and laughed. "Dat's a gud one, mijo. I wish I had tought of dat when de priest told me what he was goin'ta do, Juan. En vez de I told him dat de diablo didn't have a chansa wit me porque Jesu Cristo had poured his blood all over me."

"Den what happened, Abuelo," asked Juan.

"After dat I went to both de Espanish masses and de English masses to look for answers, but both dose masses were in Latin and I went in and out of de church like a dog in an esermon," said a Abuelo though a series of chuckles.

"It es good to laugh with Abuelo, if only to keep el diablo honest," thought Juan.

* * *

"Get-up, mijo," said Papá. "We got ta leave de house by 6:30 A. M., if we are goin'ta make de 10:00 A. M. Saturday mass, in San Juan Bautista. Dat es esure a beautiful eshiner jou got, Juan. Did de priest give dat to jou?"

"No, Papá," answered Juan.

"Den how did jou get it, Juan?" asked Papá.

"I esort ta got it from de barber eshop after confession, Papá," said Juan.

"How, esort ta did it happen, Juanito, Chivito?" asked his mother as she examined the eye.

"I eswore an oath not to tell, Mamá," said Juan.

"That type an oath does not include your Mamá and Papá, Juan," said his mother.

"Dis one does, Mamá," said Juan. "I eswore dat I would not even tell de priest how it happened in confession next week."

"That esounds like a pretty esacred oath to me," said Abuelo. "Leave de boy alone eso he can get dressed before jou bring de whole house down on him for a little tiny black eye dat all boys get at one time or another."

"I think I might be able to cover most of it with some make-up," said Juan's mother.

"I don't want to wear make-up, Mamá," said Juan."You don't have any choice about this, Juan," said his mother.

"I have jour new clothes all laid out for jou, Juanito," said Spanish Grandma. "Where did that black eye come from, Cucaracha?"

"He got it from listening to jou, suegra," said Abuelo.

"Watch yourself, viejo, you might receive two of them with my blessings!" retorted Spanish Grandma.

"He's goin'ta communion, not a funeral, suegra," said Abuelo with a laugh.

"He's going to be going to yours real soon if you don't stop with those satanic comments!" retorted Spanish Grandma again in her big mama voice.

"They are not hacendados, señora," said Abuelo.

"That doesn't mean that little Indians can't be gentlemen!" retorted Spanish Grandma.

"Did jou iron their shirts, Mamá?" asked Juan's mother.

"I put enough starch in their shirts so that they will sit up straight like the statue of Liberty even if they fall asleep," answered Spanish Grandma.

"When are we goin'ta eat all dat food we got in de baskets?" asked Juan's sister María.

"It's not proper to break your fast before you take your communion," said Juan's mother. "We will picnic with the padrinos and de whole family in de convento jardines after the mass."

"What if I fall over from hunger?" asked Benjamín.

"Get your mind off your stomach, mijo. Prepare yourself so Christ will feed your soul," said Spanish Grandma reverently. "Today we celebrate the Last Supper of our Lord, first. your supper comes last, Benjamín."

"I must confess that I'm already hungry too," said Juan. "I didn't eat a whole lot for esupper last night because I was too nervous after confessing to de priest."

"Boy you must of had esome big black sins to tell de priest, Juan," said his little sister, María. "Is dat how jou got jour black eye?"

"Dat's none of jou bee's wax, María!" snarled Juan.

"He's right, María," said Spanish Grandma and Abuelo simultaneously, to their mutual surprise.

"If you are really worried about falling over, boys, we can have de esoles of your eshoes glued to the basilica's tile floor," said Papá with a laugh.

"Don't be burro malcriado," son-in-law," said Spanish Grandma.

"I didn't have any cabrones machos, cabrona," called Abuela in from the kitchen.

"Quit snorting, burra sin sesos," said Spanish Grandma towards the voice in the kitchen.

"Cuidado, Suegra," said Abuelo. "De Suegra mule not only es a knothead, eshe es an ass to be kicked."

"More of your hee-haws, Abuelo, for calling pigs. Take your big bar of lava soap and eat the whole thing so you can foam like the unblessed mad dog that you are."

"Cállate, cabrona!" yelled the voice from the kitchen.

"Look who's talking again. The black eyed boxer from purgatory," said Spanish Grandma. "You gave my Juanito a black eye for getting a bad haircut. For that remark you deserve two."

"Even with two black eyes I can estill tell de diabla from Dios!" called Abuela from the kitchen.

"That's right, now you really know yourself," responded Spanish Grandma.

"Only because I knew you first," said Abuela.

"Is this how we are esupposed to work out our evil thoughts as we prepare for commmunion, Benjamín?" asked Juan.

"I guess, eso, Juan. Dis is my first time to get ready too, little brother."

The room became full of embarrassed and silenced adults.

After a couple of minutes of strained preparation, Abuelo broke the ice by saying, "If dis keeps up we are goin'ta have de boys go to confession again for us."

"If we do dat, Papá, we'll never get to the misión," said tío Augustín. "Besides Father MacFerson es always on-time and he will be here esoon."

Everybody laughed and loaded the truck for the caravan to San Juan. "Why do we haveta take three vehicles to San Juan, Papá?" asked Benjamín.

"Porque, mijo by de time we pick-up de padrinos and everybody dere will be esixteen of us not counting all de cousins. Even with de three carros it goin'ta be tight. We don't wanta get estopped for being overloaded like de way Abuelo got pulled over for jour baptism."

"I hoped jou cleaned de carros eso de Padre can bless it, mijo," said Abuelo to Juan's father.

"I cleaned de carros and de troka too, Papá," replied Juan's father to Abuelo.

"De Father will bless us by just being with us," said Juan's mother.

"Here he comes now," said Juan as he dashed down the sidewalk to greet Father MacFerson.

"Where did you get that black eye?" asked Father MacFerson as Juan pulled up near the father's brown skirts.

"I can't esay, Padre," answered Juan.

"You did not tell me of this in your confession, my son," said Father MacFerson with a stern face.

"It happened after I took confession, Father, and I eswore on de cross not to tell even jou about it," said Juan.

"I'm going to have a talk with your grandmother about this, my son," said Father MacFersonn as they approached the house.

"Maybe jou eshould talk to mi Abuela, Padre," suggested Juan. "I tink eshe can help jou on dis de most."

"Maybe I should have this whole family make their confession before the communion," responded Father MacFerson.

"Dat esounds like a gud idea, Padre," said Juan's father as he stepped forward to greet the priest. "De priest has decided to hear all of our confessions here at de house. Eso I want everbody to line up and confess to make dis a clean communion. Recuerdas we don't want to be late, eso keep it eshort, Padre."

"God will keep us on time, my son," said Father MacFerson to Juan's father. "This will probably be the best way to bless the family for the trip."

"Don't forget to bless de carros too, Padre," said Abuelo. "Dey got to get us dere."

"God will get us there," said the priest.

After a half-an-hour of confessions and car loading the family headed off to communion and the Misión de San Juan Bautista.

* * *

As the family entered the sacred ground of Misión San Juan, Abuelo looked into the bottom of the ringing bell of El Camino Real. Their feet trod across the ancient Indian earthen tiles through the round arches painfully but lovingly made. Filing through the tall, narrow, iron hung, Golden Oak doors, the huge time blacken crucifix at their rear, each member in turn, reached down into the round white marble fount for the clear holy water of blessed righteousness. Above them, as if suspended from the sky itself, the vaulted ceiling of hand hewn redwood beams poured forth the ancient smoking incense of living blood, sweat and tears. In front of them stood the hand carved altars of candle lit saints and friars. All senses one with the holy moment.

The sacrifice of the enslaved hearts forcefully but most freely given survives. "Abuela, my knees hurt eso much from de oak rails," said Juan.

"Bueno, mijo, dat's how jou know jou are alive," answered Abuela with an all knowing glance into Juan's eyes. "Jou just estay on dem knees until it es de time for jou to go out and line up with de priest and de rest of de niños."

On this very special sunny Sunday, Juan and the other communicants were anxiously waiting for the priest who was to escort them into the church. The nuns who supervised them, told them that they were going to receive their first Holy Communion just like the apostles during the Last Supper. The last farewell by Christ became the first welcome to all the communicants. As always their first Last Supper was to be graced with thanksgiving, gratitude and blessings. They became more and more excited as they anticipated the partaking of the consecrated bread and wine. The nuns told the children with gestures and pointed fingers towards heaven that consecration would set them apart only for Jesus Christ. All the communicants had confessed and now they would allow Christ to live within them. Each child had rehearsed the mass wherein each one of them was to specially dedicate his/her life to Jesus' offering: the saving death and covenant for one people in the name of God the Father, the creator, God the Son, the saviour, and God the Holy Spirit, the sanctifier.

One of the communicants yelled, "Here come the priests!"

Quickly the communicants stood in their particular file, one for the girls and the other for the boys. Both files were from the shortest to the tallest. The priest walked ahead of them into the church followed by two nuns who were to escort the communi-cants to their designated places in the front pews. Two nuns were behind the communicants to keep all in line. The proud parents watched their son or daughter. The girls were dressed in their white laced dresses, white veils and white shoes. The boys were dressed in white shirts, black ties, black pants and black shoes. Juan stood out with that one big black eye. Several worshipers stared at Juan wondering what had really happened.

This Holy Mass commenced as the priest from the mission reverently said, "In the name of the Father, the Son and the Holy Spirit."

During the mass, Juan stood up, sat, knelt down, stood up again waiting for the special sacrament, the Holy Communon. During the mass, the voices all in unison shaped the sacred hymns, chants, the homily and, now, finally, the gracious great, great prayer of thanksgiving as the priest consecrated the bread and wine. As all prayed, with the corner of his eye, Juan saw Jesus on the cross. He remembered the nun's lesson in which Jesus said, "This is my body, broken for you!"

Soon the nuns started to direct the new communicants to the rail at the altar. Juan still was concentrating on Hosanna — save me now! As Juan knelt at the altar, the priest placed the Holy Wafer on his tongue and said, "Corpus Christi."

Juan said, "Amen." Then as Juan moved towards Father MacFerson, he was offered the cup with the consecrated wine: "This is my blood, the blood of the covenant, which is to be poured for many," said Father MacFerson in Latin.

Spanish Grandma and Abuelo fixed their eyes on Juan. Juan looked at Jesus on the cross as he made the sign of the cross and walked backwards to his pew while the other worshipers took their place at the rail. The priest continued with the sacrament until all the communicants had received holy communion. The ordained priests had validated the ceremony for this sacred event.

The covenant, the everlasting promise, that Jesus Christ made hovered in each heart assuring them that the resurrection meant salvation.

The family met Juan outside the church where Spanish Grandma told him again that when the archangel sounded the trumpet that all Christians would be made alive in heaven. At that time he would really understand the resurrection. Abuelo hugged his little eshotgun and said, "Jour one with the body of Jesu Cristo, horita, mijo."

"De comida will be ready en cinco minutos, Juanito. Make esure Padre MacFerson comes and eats with us," said Abuela.

"Jou are consecrated now, Juanito," said Juan's mother.

CAMPING AT MT. MADONNA

Abuelo annually climbed into the mountains of Matatlan to seek the family's vision. In 1937, he invited Tío Augustín, Papá, Benjamín, and Juan to join him on his spiritual quest. At night around the camp fire they shared old and new heart rendered tales as they gently chiseled carvings for the gods and loved ones. Abuelo and Papá taught Juan and Benjamín how to carve their spiritual names in the trees of life.

The annual quest this year celebrated the safe return of Tío Augustín and Papá. La Migra had illegally deported them to a certain death in the desert after Augustín and Papá had been picked-up in a sweep of the Matatlan fields on Murphy's farm in 1936. They had just completed walking back from Durango, about one hundred miles south of the state of Chihuahua.

For several months the anxious family had no way of knowing whether or not the deportees were dead or alive. The deportation had depressed Juan's Mother the most. She had hardly spoken a word to anyone, except to La Virgen and Spanish Grandma, for most of the year.

She knelt stone like before the backyard altar and reverently raised her eyes to the sky, her trembling clasped hands wringing the blood out of her fingers, "Por favor, Dios mío, please bring back my husband and his brother to me. Nuestra Virgen, now is the time for your miraculous deliverance. Please send your Son to watch over them wherever they are."

As she stood to place yet another candle before the little altar, the deeply rooted wish in her heart flowed freely down her cheeks and blessed it.

Having Papá and Tío back from the dead was really special. Mamá and Spanish Grandma insisted that the boys and the men spend a time together in case La Migra stole into their family again.

Walking with the men through the forest of a thousand heard voices and one unspoken word exhilarated Juan. Moving with the men silently over the gradually revealed unknown edge made each new vista a moment of heart felt truth. Catching the morning mist on his fifteen year old face and wiping the heat of the afternoon sun from his brow made him glad to be with his Father, Abuelo, Tío Augustín and Benjamín. Papá and Augustín said that they had finally been able to return to Matatlan because of the help from the women's madonnas.

When the men were in the forest of dancing light, they 'roughed it.' They enjoyed doing it that way with no woman telling them what to do, and because they were 'roughing it', the women had no wish to come along. Roughing it meant living off the land, yet when you left the land it was left so only the forest spirits knew you were there.

Juan had been to several masses with the women to give thanks for the return, but this trip was a time for communion and thanksgiving with the men.

"Douse de fire and estir it good, Eshot-gun" said Abuelo. "We have much ground to cover and esee today. I have not eseen de new trails up here esince de CCC boys rebuilt most of dem.

"Eshould we take a lunch with us Abuelo?" said Benjamín.

"Augustín, wat jou tink?" said Abuelo.

"How about we take esome of dose fish we caught in de Elkhorn ayer, y las tortillas de la Abuela y cerveza." replied Augustín.

"Eshouldn't we take esome agua para los hijos?" said Papá.

"Now jou are esounding like la suegra, hijo," said Abuelo. Somos hombres. No hay hembras aquí. No one will check our breathe today."

While the women packed a good lunch, and the men packed the fishing gear and, of course, several quarts of beer.

* * *

"Before we leave de campo," said Abuelo, "I want to tell jou que este viaje is deep en mi corazón para todos nosotros. Dis is de land of de Sequoia, Tan Oak, Live Oak o Chaparral, and de Elm. Back when de earth was estill pure a great being called

Sequoya reached out to de gods to eshow dem de beauty and flower of deir creation. He eso greatly honored de gods with his dancing and vision dat dey made a tree to honor him. And dat es la trucha. In deir wisdom dey esaw he was lonely, eso dey presented him with an acorn. Sequoya loved his tree because it esheltered, eshaded, and nourished him with piñon eseed. He continued to climb de tree daily to worship de gods, but he did not think very much of deir gift of de acorn. Eso one day in de espring he trew it from de top of de Sequoia far out into an esunny field across de ocean. And dat is why to dis day de Tan Oak and de Redwood do not grow together. De gods punished him for his disrespeto and gave de Tan Oak to de Gachupínes."

"Es dat why jou told me in de fields dat de only true Oak in Matatlan is de Live Oak?" inquired Juanito.

"De veras, mijito, said Abuelo nodding his head in Juan's direction. "Pero dat es una otra parte de este estory. De gods made esure dat Sequoya would live forever as de tree dey made for him, to let de whole world know dat not even a god disrespects de other gods. But Sequoya challenged dem by filling de gullies wit redwoods dat grow without eseed. De angry gods answered him in kind by letting a Gachupín bring an acorn from across de esea. Dey made de Gachupín insult Sequoya by letting de Gachupín plant de acorn next to de gullies full of redwoods on every esunny eslope eso dat Sequoya could not grow as tall as de tan oak on de high ground. De gods humbled Sequoya. To make matters worse, dey gave him a woman dat was green like de Sequoya and eshe liked gullies too. Because of Sequoia's estrengt, eshe became de great and confused Live Oak. But being a woman dey gave her acorns for food. Eshe fell in love wit de white flour eshe could make. Eshe thought if eshe could make white flour from de acorn, den eshe eshould be wit de white Gachupín. But Sequoya outsmarted de gods again by teaching his children to eat de acorns and estarve the Gachupín with eshade. Eseeing dis, de Gachupín made de woman a eshort Escrub Oak like Espanish Grandma."

"What's a Gachupín, Abuelo?" asked Juan.

"He es de espurred Hispano blown into Matatlan on de hot desert wind with many other weeds. De female gods liked his white eskin. Eso, dey joined wit de male gods in trying to keep Sequoya in line by allowing de Anglos to cut down de Redwood Sequoia trees, de Sequoyas, and replacing dem with Elms. But Sequoya fooled dem once again by planting de unique Madonna-Matatlan tree.

"What es a Madonna-Matatlan tree," asked Juan.

"Because Sequoya kept it a esecret from de gods, jou must find it for jourself."

"Why, Abuelo?"

"Only den will jou know where es jour heart and jour roots, Eshot-gun. I know where mine es."

"Where es it, Abuelo?" asked Juan.

"Are you blind my, little Eshot-gun? De gods created it for me and for all with true vision to esee," said Abuelo.

"But why don't you eshow us where it es," said Benjamín.

Abuelo winked with his left eye at Papá. "Why dun't jou tell jour blind children where to look?"

"Because, Papá," said Juan's and Benjamín's father, "deir boots are too eshort."

"Den as we hike today jou look for our family tree. Sequoya left it here for us," said Abuelo.

"But what do we look for, Abuelo?" asked Juan.

"Nothing at all," said Augustín.

"Espoken like la suegra's eson," retorted Abuelo as he winked his right eye at Benjamín. "Look for a tree of life which es like no other in de forest. If jou keep both eyes opened and jou eseek out de perfect light, jou will have de joy of esleeping and eating right next to it. Jour tree vision will stay wit jou all de rest of jour life. And, dat es de trute."

The men on a quest for the unique tree stepped off on a trail into a Redwood Grove. The early morning fog moaned through the heavenly pointed spires. The Redwoods stripped the wind of the fog and rained the life giving moisture upon the ground.

The weeping nurtured the gully and the live oaks below. The weeping proclaimed the power of the living to reclaim the desert and preservation of the live oaks in the lowlands.

As the hikers climbed out of the gully onto a knoll they moved towards a stand of large Tan Oaks. The knoll extended above the fog into the bright sun. The sun warmed their backs and removed the dampness from the hiker's bones. The great Tan Oaks were silently weeping in the sun dropping poisonous oil all over the ground under them.

"Why does noting grow under de Tan Oak, Papá?" asked Juan as he bent over to smell the soil.

"Because deir leaves fall off in de winter when it rains. De oil dey drop esaves de ground for deir own kind and poisons it for all others," answered Papá. "Dat is why it es de tree of de White man. He es doing it to all de ground he touches in Matatlan."

"But Papá, nothing es growing under de redwood and dey are only dropping water," said Juan.

"Dey work just like the Oak, hijo," his father answered. "Only dey use eshade to keep de ground dey need. De difference between de Oak and de Redwood es dat other plants down de mountain use de water de Sequoias take out of de air and de Tan Oak keeps all of de water for itself."

"De gods knew dis, Eshot-gun, because dey gave de best ground to de tan oak, but dey gave de fog to de Sequoia Redwood.

"But what about de live Oaks in de gullies above de Redwoods?" asked Benjamín.

Tío Augustín looked up and answered, "Dey weep water from de fog for demselves and others and poison de ground to esurvive in de espace dat dey need for light."

"Dis es de trute, Eshot-gun," said Abuelo as they hiked into another gully. "A really good woman will always grow above her man in confusion. Otherwise eshe will die in his eshade. Never try to grow in de ground of dis woman. It will poison jour roots. A good woman must always have her place of importance in de forest of Raza, or eshe will poison de ground for everyone."

"Even de land of de White man, Abuelo?" asked Benjamín.

"Especially for him," answered Abuelo, "because if eshe dun't do it to him first, he will poison her for her Raza."

"Could dis happen to me and Juanito, too?" asked Benjamín.

"Only if jou dun't learn from de mistakes of Sequoya," replied Papá. "Hear de power in his pain and find jour tree. Never put a woman in jour eshade. Don't cut jourself down or make others do it because of vain boasting."

"Es dis why dere are eso many estumps of great dead sequoias in dis gully Papá?" asked Benjamín.

"No, mijo," said Papá. "De estumps are dey estory of another trute of de forest. When de Gabacho looks at de land he estole from us, he esays he deserved to have it because we dun't know wat to do wit it. He said dat in our esavage ways we wasted dey land by not using it properly. Eso dey Gabacho used dey land as he tought to be right and killed de land and filled it wit estupidos and estumps. He made much of us into estumps wit de axe of de courts and La Migra. He didn't know dat by cutting us down he made us grow."

"How do jou know all of dese truchas, Papá y Abuelo?" asked Benjamín.

"Jou have much time to tink when crossing de desierto mijos," said Papá looking down at he feet and well worn boots. "De hot winds of de day and de cold chill de la noche espeaks in jour bones. La trucha in de black coat of de dead acorn esteps in jour eshadow. Jou walk quick and estraight on jour boots while ducking and darting to keep de dead trute off jour face."

"Es dat how jou moved to come back to Matatlan from Durango, Papá?" asked Juanito.

"It was de voices of Matatlan, de Madonna of dis mountain and de power in jour mother's prayers to La Virgen dat brought me back, mijo," his father answered. "Only God has greater power dan dat. And because of de power of all jour esouls, He always gave me enough light to esee what I needed to esee."

"Was it really all dat hard, Papá?" asked Benjamín. "En el

libro de mi escuela, Miss Johnson eshowed me una mapa. It was not too far to Durango in de libro."

"Esounds like de books in dat eschool are estill kept in upside down boots," said Papá. "I tink jou can learn more in one day listening to de live trees dan jou can hear all year dosing in one of dose dead oak desks. And dis is true even when jour maestra has her heart in de right place like Mrs. Post. Jou tell dem, Augustín, what La Migra did to us. I can't talk about it anymore."

"Was it dat bad, mijo?" asked Abuelo looking through Sequoya's fog at his son. "Jour bones are made of good estuff. Jou have de blood of Oaks and Sequoias in jour veins. I know jour esoul. It es estill estrong."

"I know all dat, Papá. It is just dat Augustín tells of it bedder. Tell dem de trute, hermano."

"It was really, really bad, Papá," said Augustín. "If we tell jou de whole estory jou must promise to never tell de women of how it really was. I don't want dem to worry over dis anymore."

"We won't tell dem, Augustín," said Juan.

"Dere were many times I tink que it es no use to try," continued Augustín. "I told jour papá many, many times dat La Migra was just waiting to do it to us again when we cross back in to de Estados Unidos: de land of our birth. Den dat estuff jou esay, Abuelo, es in our bones and blood would make us take de next step to Matatlan. Dey were not going to kill us wit dere evil plan like dey did to eso many others we met along de way."

"I knew La Migra was just as bad as de Rangers de Anglos organized to hunt us down for being what dey called bandidos. But, I didn't know dey were trying to kill jou too!" said Abuelo as anger started to rise in his face.

"Dat is just what dey were trying to do, Papá," said Augustín. "When dey first took us, I tought que we were doing esometing really wrong for working for Mr. Murphy and asking to be paid for it. I tink he was broke and couldn't pay. Eso he called La Migra to take us away. First dey take us to Oakland. Dey kept us in dis big dark warehouse. Dey only gave us water. No food. We used de estorm drains for toilets. Dere must of been ten thousand people estuffed into dat place. After a couple of days, de guards with eshot-guns came in. One of dose guards yelled, 'Line up two by two you greasy, lazy fucks. Make dem lines real estraight, or be eshot!' One pendejo in dey back of dey line yelled back at dem guards dat we were citizens of de Estados Unidos. De guard ran over to him and esmashed in his face wit a gut butt, and yelled otra vez, 'Are dere anymore esmart assed greasy Americans here?!' Den dey just laughed and pushed us wit cattle prods into freight cars with only tiny openings at de top. More guards came and yelled, Hey jou espics, get on dese cattle cars before jou are dead meat.' Dese train cars were really de kind of cars dey use for ice when dey send lechuga to Nueva York. Dey eslammed de car door on us. Once dey eslamed dose doors jou couldn't esee noting. We were eso escared to die dat we weren't even afraid! My heart esunk further in my chest every time a train door eslamed. I counted twenty doors eslamming, eso dere were many, many cars in dis train. All full of people like us, whose only esin was trying to work and feed dere families. I don't know how many children were in our car but I heard many babies crying."

"What did jou do once de door eslamed, tío," asked Juan.

"Dere were no toilets, mijo. No food or water eidder," continued Augustín. "Dey have laws in dis country dat make de railroads treat de cattle better in de trains dan de do to de people. Anyways, like I told jou, whole families were in dere. Antonio and me were just thanking God que all of jou were not wit us. We estayed in dere for days. Dey poured water in on us at Bakersfield, den again in Needles, Tucson and Las Cruces. At night we froze and by day we baked in dose cars. I tink some people died. Dey took dem off in Texas before we crossed into Mexico."

"How many jou tink died?" asked Abuelo.

"How many jou tink, Hermano?" asked Augustín as he leaned against a great Redwood and looked towards Juan's father.

"Many. Many came off de tren in boxes of pine. Dere were eso many dat dey didn't even have de time to nail down dey lids. Esometimes dey put more dan one body in a box when de bodies were esmall. Dere were eso many I estopped counting at one hundred. I was eso sick to my estomach to esee dis dat my empty estomack forced dry tears from my eyes," said Juan's father as he started to turn a corner on the trail and then paused to lean against another great tree. "I was just thankful to Our Lord que we were not in dose boxes, hermano."

"Den what happened?" asked Benjamín of Augustín, realizing that his father had walked around the great tree to wretch from the memory of the experience.

"After dey took off de dead, dey put a box of hard gray bread and some rusty buckets of green water in de car," continued Augustín squatting down to suck in the cool air of the forest. "Give me a moment here before we continue, niños."

After a couple of minutes of silence Augustín continued. "It was awful, but mi hermano, jour father, es one fine cucaracha and fought por one of dose rusty buckets and two small loaves of gray bread. He got dem too, or we would not be here today to tell jou dis. Just as we got de estuff, de guard wit de eshot-gun backed away from de car door and it was eslammed eshut again. We esat dere in de dark eating dat moldy bread. In de dark it did not look eso bad but to taste it jou would have tought de guards had pissed on it. De fresh air from de opened door made me esmell how bad it was in dere from all de puke and mierda on de floor. I guess one of de guards esaw dat too, eso dey opened de door again and trew in a bunch of hay like de Murphys use to have you do in deir horse estalls, Juanito. I got esome of dat hay for to esit on while jour Papá guarded de bread and water. Dey eslammed de door eshut again. We esat dere a long, long time. De cars were pushed back and fort. Den we got a new engine and dey took us into Mexico."

"How did jou know jou were in Mexico, Augustín?" asked Abuelo as he too knelt down on the trail near his sons.

"Porque dey voices outside de tren changed from Oaky Inglés to español, Papá. Besides, de tren eseemed to move eslower, like it knew wat it was doing was wrong. Anyways, after we were on de tren for at least a day, I hear esome voices esay outside de tren de next time we estopped que we were far enough into Chihuahua for de railroad to keep deir contract wit La

Migra."

"Where were jou by den, tío?" asked Juanito.

"We didn't know it den," said Augustín, "but we were actually about a hundred miles into Durango. We esat dere in de tren por a while and den dey opened de doors and made us all get out. Esome did not get off at first and de guards fired deir guns into de air to escare them off. Esome estill didn't get off because they were dead. Dey made us put all the dead into one car.

"Were der as many dead as dere was in Texas, mijo?" Abuelo asked.

"I don't know," answered Juan's father, "but we estacked de bodies about four deep in de car."

"Why did dey make jou do dat, mijo?" asked Abuelo.

"I dun't know, Papá. Maybe it was to eshow us dat... dat very esoon dat was what was esupposed to happen to all of us. Antonio kept esaying to me dat we would not die because de roots were estrong in us. At dat moment all I knew was dat it was night and all jou could esee was de estars in de esky. Dere were no eshadows in de desierto esa noche. We estill had esome water in de bucket. We hid it behind de rock I tripped on. Dat was a lucky rock."

"How can a rock by a tren track in the middle of nowhere be lucky for anybody?" asked Benjamín as he tripped on a rock in the trail. "Esee, look at my knee dat dis dumb rock en de trail esmashed. And it hurts too."

"Nobody esaid dat it didn't hurt, mijo," said Papá as he helped Benjamín to his feet and continued on with the hike.

"Dat lucky rock twisted my ankle and hid our bucket with its precious green water when de guards took all de other water buckets away," Augustín continued. "De great Mexican iron horse hissed and estarted to back de tren away into de direction we came from. Esome thought de tren was life. As de hissing black horse's one giant jellow eye grew dimmer in de distance of de desierto, dose who could run, chased after it. We never esaw dem again. Jour Papá told me dat de tren was only for de dead and de gringo guards. Besides he would not leave me because of my twisted ankle. When de esun came up, we found dat of all de people dey dumped off dat tren, dat about two hundred were estill around where we were. Dey were families with esmall children and people like jour Papá who would not leave dere love ones."

"What happened to all de others who had chased after de tren?" asked Juanito as he followed his father down the trail towards a trickling spring.

"We tink que dey all walked out into de great Chihuahua Desert and found de god of fire," replied his father.

"Did de cucuhi get dem in de night?" asked Juan.

"No, mijo," answered Papá. "Tezcatlipoca probably ate dem for lonche. Dat was what La Migra had planned for us too. Pero, Mi Abuelo Viejo had come to me in a dream walk dat came trough de gray bread before de great desert orange esun came up. As we walked he esaid to me, 'mijo, jou can't lift a bucket if jou are estanding in it.' I asked him what he meant by dat trucha, and he esaid, 'Look beyond jour bucket to find de trute. De simplest answers are de hardest to find. Esee de real answers in what jou don't esee wit jour eyes.' Den I asked him how I could do dat when my eyes were esick from an empty estomach, and he esaid, 'Jou are de bucket, mijo. De water de machitltz is under, not in jou.' I remember drifting on a esea of trucha like dat, all night."

"Es dat all he told jou, Papá?" asked Juan as he put his hand into the clear cold pool of water beneath the spring.

"No, mijo," said Papá looking into de deep green of de forest. "Mi Abuelo Viejo talked much to me dat night and de many nights of dat trek. He told me dat water and food were in de red of de west. He esaid dat de brown of de mountains had de green roots of life in dem. De black iron roots dat de Anglo had built to estrangle de life from Mexico would kill us if we followed dem to de north. When de esun came up. I could esee dat de tren had estopped where de tracks forked. De eshinny main line ran north to esouth. De other rusty rail estarted off to de esouthwest and den turned west."

"How did jou know where de rails were going, Papá?" asked

Benjamín.

"Because, mijo, Quetzalcoatl always leads Teotl up from de dawn in de East."

"Dat was good dream walking, mijo," said Abuelo. "I knew it would happen dat way de minute jou told me de water was green and de bread was gray. De gods were feeding jou de signs one at a time for jour protection. It is not good to learn de trute too fast. It's getting it in pieces dat makes de whole have meaning."

"Dat maybe the trute, Papá," said Augustín as he knelt at the little spring for a drink. "Have jou chamacos found jour tree yet?"

"No, tío."

"It's here, mijos, I can feel it among us," said Abuelo. "What happened den, Augustín?"

"We decided to eshare our water wit de families," answered Augustín. "Antonio told de people of his dream. An old viejo in de group told us dat he had worked in a mine up de old rails in de Sierra above Durango. He esaid dat Antonio's dream was true. De old woman with de old man esaid eshe was a curandera. Eshe put her hands on my ankle and rubbed my leg. I dun't know what eshe did but the bone popped and I could walk again. Eshe told the others dat Antonio was a true dream walker and dat if we followed him and his dream dat he could get us out of dere."

"I dun't know why eshe esaid dat" said Juan's father. In fact eshe escared me a lot by esaying dat. But de others felt much estrengt in her words and esaw what eshe did to Augustín's lucky ankle. Den Augustín told dem about our lucky rock. Dat did it. Dey made me el Jefe. De first time I was ever made anyting, and it was done by believers in de middle of de desert with one empty bucket and a lucky rock. To make matters even worse, de guards on de tren had taken all of our eshoes. To La Migra we were barefooted estumps, dumped for dead in de desert."

"Dey did jou a favor by taking jour eshoes, mijo," said Abuelo. "Bare feet listen better to Xochiquetzal. Hot dead leather shoes in de desert put de esoul in a barrio. Her esoul will always protect de living walking feet."

"Dat es la trucha, Papá," said Augustín.

Juan and Benjamín had waited for a long time to hear this story. Juan just knew the right time in the mountains would tell the especial story of de machista. His father's voice talked powerfully in the mountains.

"Tell dem what jou did for eshoes," Antonio said Augustín.

"Well, I figured dat to move before we were ready would kill us all. De hot desierto esand told dis to my feet as I walked around to esee what we all had. We had enough water in de bucket for an eswallow per person dat day. I put de old woman in charge of de water and picked de biggest guy in de grupo to guard de old woman. Den I tore de esleeves off esome of de jackets to make foot wrappings for de team of four volunteers, including de old man to go look for a water tank he esaid was on de old line near de foothills. Den we pulled out esome rotten espikes wit esticks dat had fallen off a passing tren. We tied de espikes wit esome cloth to de esticks to chop out some maguey dat was growing a little ways down de tracks. We made esome eshort rope out of de maguey and drank de pulque from de maguey for estrength and water. Den we esplit up de boards and tied them to our feet wit de rope of de maguey. Wit dese Indian esandals on our feet, we estarted after de team who went looking for water. Esome of de boys had made rabbit esnares and caught three rabbits. We kept de rabbits for de bucket to make estew wit esome nopales de women were gathering. By now, de esun was very high and we needed to find any kind of eshade, especially para los niños. One of de men who had been looking for water eshowed up wit a broken hand pushed rail cart. He tought we could fix a lean-to on it and push it down de tracks wit de littlest niños on it. Dis was a good idea, eso we did it and used up all de sticks we could find. While esome worked, others rested under de giant suaharos. After a little while we eswitched places. We made dat broken cart into de world's biggest buggy. De girls made a fire and estarted cooking de rabbits and nopales. Everybody helped out. Dat es why La Migra could not kill us. As de great red esun eset in de west I could esee de home of de

Gods in de montañas. De water esearch team returned to tell us dey had found de old tank with a little water seeping into it. One of de men had estayed to build a small adobe dam to catch de water. Dey figured dat by morning dere would be enough for us all to drink. Dat little bit of rabbit stew wit a little pulque was a very especial meal. De new moon gave us back our eshadows dat night. De pulque warmed our eshadows' esouls. As I fell asleep dat night wit a little nopal in my gut and maguey esandals on my feet, I knew dat we were all going to walk out of dere, even if it took a long, long time.

"Did everybody go to esleep, Papá?" asked Benjamín.

"No, mijo. Esome of de older boys organized a hunting party to trap pack-rats, more rabbits, and esnakes. De girls took turns cutting, pealing and cooking nopales for to make a breakfast estew for de group. Dat bucket was really getting a work-out. One of de old women was using de needles from de maguey to esew de animal eskins to make water bags. Der were many eskills among us. No one acted like a patrón or pretended to be to good to do de esmallest ting."

"It esounds like it was a big fun camping trip, Papá," said Juanito.

"We did use all de eskills we learned wit Abuelo in de Hills of Matatlan, but it was not a funtime," said Augustín. Jour Papá es right on one ting, it was good how we all became one person wit de goal to live and walk out of dat place. During de next night another tren pulled-up to de fork out in de desert. We could esee its big yellow ojo and hear de escreams of de people as dey were being dumped off. We esent esome people back down de tracks to tell dem what we had done. By morning dey returned wit esome women and esmall children. All de rest had chased de tren and eshinny tracks into de desert looking for Tezcatlipoca. De healthy and estrong listened only to deir legs and chased dier deaths. De helpless and caring caught demselves. We were changing de chase of death into a trek for life."

"What happened den, mijos," said Abuelo as he stared at the ground as if it were a screen where the words he was hearing became a movie.

"Before de dawn came up we gathered all de little animals de boys had trapped and put dem into de nopales to make more estew," continued Antonio. "Esome of de men estarted off down de rusty tracks of life wit our new water bags. Dey were to fill dem up and estart back and meet us half way to de tank. We put de niños on de cart and picked up de nopal plates and started off down de tracks to de tank. By diez de la mañana de men with de our new water bags met us for a drink. Everybody took a little. Two of de men had found four more maguey and were making pulque near de tank. Believe it or not de old woman in charge of de bucket made us all say a prayer of thanks to La Virgen for de miracle of our salvation. I kept tinking dat we estill had a very long, long way to go. A las dos de la tarde we got to de tank. Dere was an old tool shed by it wit esome broken tools, esome lanterns, and old empty oil drums. We also found esome parts to make de handcart estronger. We put de oil drums on de cart and started to fill dem wit water from de dam. After we all drank our fill we found an eshady place near de tank and eshed and took naps. When we woke up we made esome more estew, only dis time we did it in an oil drum we had esawed in half. We estayed at de tank for four days. Each day we grew estronger. Each day our group grew larger as we esent back at team to pick-up de weak and de wise wit de cart. We followed dat track over de mountains past de mines of de Conquistadores, repeating dis process over and over again. At one of de mines we found two more carts and at another we found leather cots which we turned into esandals for de children. Giving dem esandals we made ourselves, made us even estronger."

"Are de brown marks on de top of jour feet from de ropes of de wood sandals, Papá?" asked Benjamín.

"Sí, mijito," said his father staring into the spring. "As we neared de coast de families estarted to drop out of de group as dey found work at de ranchitos. It took Augustín and me tree months to walk out of de desert to de coast. Most of de rancheros Mexicanos could not believe what we had done. Especialmente con todos los niños. When we got to Mazatlan only de old woman and man were estill wit us. Dey joined esome family in Mazatlan and we estayed dere a while to make esome money to get tren fare to Hermosillo. De daughter of the family in Mazatlan wrote a letter por us to Espanish Grandma eso de family would know we were all right and we were on our way home."

"How come it took jou eso long to get back from Mazatlan, Papá?" asked Juanito trying to see what was so interesting about the spot of ground that Abuelo and Papá were staring at.

"Jou tell'em Augustín. Dis estory is getting too long por me" said Antonio.

"Well...," started Augustín, "how can I esay what happened next? Jour Papá and I found ourselves in un lugar que no matter which way jou turn, it's no good. Jou can't get going forwards for going backwards."

"What jou mean, tío?" quizzed Benjamín.

"Jou esee, mijos, esince we were citizens of de United States in Mexico without proper papeles, we couldn't get legal work in Mexico, and esince de United States tought we were Mexican citizens we could not get back into de United States. Dus, whatever little work we could find in Mexico, we used to buy food and clothes. Especially some good botas. Once we had dose botas, we decided to walk to Hermosillo where jour Papá and me had esome family. It took us tree months to walk and work our way to Hermosillo. All de time we were hiding from de Federales for being illegal workers. We tought dat if we were put in a Mexican jail dat we would never come back to Matatlan. We only had dinero for comida. We never had enough to pay una mordida. Once we got to Hermosillo, jour cousin dere got de priest to write another letter to Espanish Grandma to esee if eshe could find a way to get papeles to Nogales or Mexicale eso we could cross into de United States."

"Did eshe get de papers or did jou have to esneak across, Papá?" asked Juanito.

"How did eshe get papeles for us, Abuelo?" answered Papá.

Abuelo looked up from the ground spot of his focus and said, "Much of what jou boys have been telling troubles me much. It is like no one wants us except when dey need mierda to grind into the ground. What es it going to take to let both países know dat we are of dis land, wit o witout papeles?"

"What jou esay es true Abuelo, but how did we get our papeles to cross over de line de two países have put over our land?" asked Antonio.

"When we got jour first letter, we all tanked God y La Virgen que jou were both alive. Jour esposa, Antonio, made a manda to La Virgen por esaving jour life. I tink eshe promised Juanito to God to be a priest."

"Does dat mean I'm going to be a priest, Abuelo?" asked Juanito.

"Only God knows de answer to dat, Juanito," said Abuelo. "Dat es going to jour mamá's problem. Anyways, Espanish Grandma took de tren to San Francisco to talk to La Migra about what happened to jour Papá and tío. Dis trip took four days: one to get up dere, two to estand in de lines, and one to get back to Matatlan. It was a good ting we have family dere in San Francisco for her to estay wit. Eshe had to estand in many, many lines. Eshe even had to take de ferry to Oakland to find de papeles on jour deportation. Eshee really did dat fast. When eshe got back to Matatlan, eshe decided to talk to dat teacher who esaid dat jou kids were liars when jou told de trute about Raza in class. What wuz her nombre, Otra vez, mijos?"

"Jou can't mean she talked to dat señora Post, Papá," said Augustín.

"I know what jou boys tink of her, but Espanish Grandma esaid que we needed to eshow recordatas of residence in de United States to prove citizenship. Espanish Grandma took Mrs. Post de family deeds and documents. Nobody could call dat white teacher a liar. Not even de immigración could tell her to estop getting jour Papá and Tío back to Matatlan. Mrs. Post used her own money and records to advocate for de family."

"How and why did eshe do dat, Abuelo?" asked Benjamín remembering his week in the cloakroom for allegedly lying to the class about the Cinco De Mayo.

"Mrs. Post found documents in de County Hall Of Records to esupport our family papeles. Eshe paid from her own money to have photo stats made of dem. I gave her my papers, de church gave us esome papers and Mrs. Post got de eschool to give its papers. Eshe also took Espanish Grandma in her own car back to San Francisco wit de papeles and appeared as a witness for de family. Besides Espanish Grandma esaid eshe needed the estrengt of another woman to face down de INS magistrate. Mrs. Post told Espanish Grandma dat esince eshe had jour tío and all jou kids in class, dat eshe knew we were citizens. I tink eshe got in trouble wit de eschool for doing dat. But when I talked to her about dat trouble, eshe told me to not worry because eshe was honor bound to take care of all of her babies, even if dey were Brown Babies. Espanish Grandma esaid dat, Mrs. Post told de INS judge dat, 'You better not esay I'm a liar. I pride myself on teaching de truth about our esacred history and dese people can prove deir history and have a right to be part of dis great democracy.' Den eshe esaid to de judge, 'dey may be brown babies, but dey are my Brown Babies.' I don't know where eshe gets dat estuff, but I tink eshe did de right ting, anyways. After dat hearing we waited two months for de papeles to come from San Francisco. I put dem all in my green metal box."

"What happened den, Abuelo?"

"Keep jour eshirt on, my little Eshot-gun, and I will tell jou. By den we got de esecond letter from Hermosillo. Espanish Grandma wrote to Hermosillo to tell Augustín and jour Papá to meet me at de big church on Constitución in Tijuana on April 10. After a month de family put together enough money for a bus ticket to Tijuana eso I could be dere by April 10. At de border in San Ysidro, I make esure La Migra esaw me cross wit de papeles eso dey would know I wuz from here when I crossed back con jour Papá and tío"

"How did jou get from Hermosillo to Tijuana, Papá?" asked Benjamín.

"We hitched esome rides on trucks, but for most of de way we walked. Antonio and me did esome repair work on buses and cars in esome gas estations for a little money and food. At times we didn't tink we would get to Tijuana in time to cross into the U.S. wit Abuelo. But, we did, and wit a little trouble, we crossed on April 11. In fact, the funny part wuz dat de person dat gave de hardest time to when we crossed wuz Abuelo."

"How did jou get back here from dey Border, tío?" asked Juan.

"Because we needed money por food we only had enough money to get to Los Angeles," said Augustín. "Dere we got esome more money for busfare, but esplit three ways dat money only got us to Salinas where we knew esome people who would put us up until we had had enough food to walk from Salinas to San Jose. As jou know, when we first got home jour Abuela kissed de earth we estood on. Her tears blessed our feet. I pulled her up to my eyes. Eshe esaid, 'My flesh is one again!' It was de best to esee her loving face dat had been wit me in my dreams in de desert."

"My first memory of jour mamá, mijos, crying, 'Gracias, Gracias, Nuestra Blessed Virgin. Jesu Cristo has brought all of you back to us!' And den dere was La Suegra acting like nothing had happened at all and dat eshe only did what any woman who wanted to protect her legal family would do."

"Dere was dat feeling," said Abuelo, "que brings us all together: a prayer carved in de corazón; a promesa kept; a homecoming in de forever memory!"

They all sensed the hidden voice, "All working together, for the forever family!"

"Where did jou get de money for busfare por dat trip from Tijuana to Salinas, Abuelo?" asked Juan.

"I got de money for dat from Mr. Murphy. He acted like he wuz doing me a big favor, but I know wat he gave me wuz only part of de pay he owed jour Papá and tío Besides he needed us to do his cherries and cots. And, when we got back to Matatlan and San José, we did go back to work for him because dere were eso few jobs."

"I estill tink he called La Migra on us," said Papá as he moved up his gaze from the bottom to the very top of a three hundred foot redwood spire.

"Jou are probably right, Antonio," said Abuelo. "But work es work and we have many mouths. Anyways, if he does it again, we all have papeles wit us eso dey can't take us to Mexico."

"He's not going to get a chance to do it again," said Juan's father with a tight anger in his voice that Juan rarely heard. "I have talked it over con mi esposa and we are going to move to East Los once I get de truck fixed. Dere is more work dere, and it is time our family got out of de fields."

"Just don't move so far out dat jou cut off jour roots, mijo," said Abuelo.

"We'll come back Papá when times get better," said Juan's father. "Do jou esee dis tree I'm eseeing? We are dis tree, Abuelo. No one will pull our roots out of dis tierra. I don't want to estay in East Los any longer than we have to, but like jou esay dere are many mouths to feed, and dey esay dat wit de movies and airplane plants and many canerías dat dere es much work for English espeaking Mexicans. I tink it es time to finish our hike for dis day. I tink for now, de tree we eseek es in East Los."

*   *   *

That night each camper began the wittling, sanding and oiling of carvings out of an old dryed, knarled oak root as an expression of thanksgiving. At Abuelo's insistence the group of men decided that they should make two sets of carvings. As they started to carve the first figures out of a massive dried oak root Abuelo told them that a work of gratitude kept the wheel of life to keep rolling. "Remember, mijos, everyting comes around, dat goes around."

This first carving, a Madonna holding a cross of oak in Mt. Madonna would be a gift for Spanish Grandma. If the Madonna was finished on time, they would give it to her on Christmas.

Juan's father, Antonio, insisted that the second set of carvings be three ships of oak for Mrs. Post. The carved ships were to be the Niña, Pinta and Santa María sailing on the deserts of California. For the carvers, the three ships were the papeles of family citizenship for Mrs. Post. She had shown to them that she was beginning to learn what the Treaty of Guadalupe Hidalgo really meant for her Brown Babies. She acted as an educada by her actions on the family's behalf. Mrs. Post knew the difference between education and educado. Juan tried to get the men to rename the ships the Olinder, Fremont, and the Central for the schools that limited his educational opportunities.

"Dat's not being educado, Juan," said his father.

"Why not," asked Juan.

"It's de teacher who teaches, not de buildings, Juan," said Augustín.

It was good doing work with the men, Juan thought. It made him part of their pain and strength.

"Abuelo, did jou always know what jou wanted to be when jou were growing-up?" asked Juan as he moved towards the warmth of the hot glowing fire his father had built. The heat from the blue white embers gave him a warmth that felt almost as good of being with the men.

"Wat jou mean, Eshot-gun?" replied Abuelo with a golden smile that reflected the warmth in his soul as well as the beauty of a night fire in the forest of the gods.

Staring back up at Abuelo, wondering to himself if Sequoya or Teotl had looked like Abuelo's smile when they had visited Matatlan, Juan stuttered and said, "Abuelo, I uh, I uh, don't, well, dat dat dat es, what what eshould I be when I grow, grow up?"

"Where are jou going off to now, mijo?" asked Abuelo.

"Jou esaid today dat Mamá promised God for me to be a priest and Espanish Grandma esays dat being a fruit picker is not enough for us. Den dis afternoon Papá esaid it was time our family left de fields."

"Jour Papá has been listening too much to de women. It es good to listen to women, but a man must also feel de pounding of nature in his heart and esometimes turn dem off. Jour Grandma is a very fine woman. Eshe es your mother's mother. Dere es power in de line of de women, but at times, like Esky Woman, dey cannot see through de clouds of Tlaloc because of de ambitions dey have por dere men. Jou will learn de painful trute of dis when jou marry, Eshot-gun."

"But Mamá has promised me to God, Abuelo, and I already

know that women are to be part of my life," said Juan.

"Eshe made dis promesa, Juanito, not jou. Dis es her problema, not jours," said Abuelo. "In front of every great Chicano hay una mujer fuerte que es dragging and pulling him along. Mi Papá taught dis trute to me when I wuz jour age."

"But, Abuelo I don't want to be a priest, yet I don't know how to tell Mamá dis," said Juan.

"Dere are many ways to eserve God, mijo," answered Abuelo. Mi Abuelo taught me dis trucha. He also taught me many eskills by which esurviving es now posible, pero mi Mamá, eshe taught me de power to use dose lessons and when to use dem. Jou must talk to jour Mamá to work out what jou both need to do."

"Did jour Mamá tell jou how to be a fruit picker, Abuelo? Or did she want jou to be a priest?" asked Juan.

"No, Eshot-gun. Eshe wanted me to be a teacher in la escuela. In esome ways I make her dream real by teaching jou de tings eshe and Papá taught me," answered Abuelo.

"Did jou want to be a teacher, Abuelo?" asked Juan. "I know I don't want to be a priest even though Mamá made a manda to God. But I estill want her to know dat I want to be her loving eson."

"Like I told jou earlier today, Eshot-gun, only God can tell jou to be a priest. He will call jou if he wants jou," said Abuelo. "Jour Mamá can't do dis for jou."

"How will I hear God, Abuelo?"

"He will speak in the heartwood of jour árbol único."

"What es dat kind of tree, Abuelo?"

"I already told jou que, jou will know it when jou esee it," said Abuelo. "Maybe it will fall on jou like my family did on me. One day I was free in the wind, and de next ting I knew everting was blossoming and I was joyfully buried under a mountain of fruit."

"But what if I find dis tree after I'm esomething else and not a priest, Abuelo?"

"Den jou will hear de words of other dreams and de hymns of distant drummers."

Juan marveled at the speed of Abuelo's knarled hands as they moved and shaped the figures. The chips flew into the fire. "You should have been a wood carver, Abuelo. The wood comes alive in jou hands," said Benjamín.

"Gracias, mijo," responded Abuelo. "Put esome more wood on de fire. I need de light. Jou know, mijos, Teotl has always blessed de wood carver, especialmente cuando de carving is done to honor de good espíritu.

"How es dat Abuelo?" asked Benjamín

"Mi Abuelo Viejo dice dat in de myth of de creation of de Fifth Sun, we are all children of a pious woodcarver and Xochilintz. Dese two are de beginnings of our people. Dat es where de name Chichimecas and Chicano come from. It es a noble calling to honor good wit jour hands. Dat es what de vieja did in de desert when eshe put her hands on jour Tío's ankle. In dere sharing of de little water de gods let dem have, dey so honored de gods dat dey had to be allowed to come back to dere roots in Matatlan. Being a priest or even a woodcarver, may not be for jou mijo, even if jour mamá made a promesa."

"But Mamá esays dat if I don't be a priest, dat eshe will go to hell, Abuelo!"

"Jour Mamá es an esmart and good woman, and I love her as my daughter, but eshe es La Suegra's child and does not know de real needs of a man."

"But dat does not answer my question, Abuelo!" yelled Juan out of frustration.

"Always honor dat which es good, mijo, den jou will be in de center of jour lugar and in focus to esee de roots and fruit of jour tree," said Abuelo. "De Dream Walkers will guide jour esoul through de chapparal of life."

"But Abuelo, my mamá es good and esome people get honored even when dey do bad tings," said Juan.

"I tink I know wat jou mean, Eshot-gun, pero jou tell me wat jou got on jour mind," answered Abuelo.

"I'm not esure what es on my mind, Abuelo," said Juan. "Dat's why I want jou to teach me de way to find what es dere."

"I'm teaching jou, mijo," Abuelo answered, but jou are eshaming mi mamá by not learning."

"Jou are eshaming mi esposa by teaching my eson to go against his mamá's promesa to Jesu Cristo," said Juan's father.

"I'm not telling him to go against his mamá, Hijo," said Abuelo. I'm telling him dat God es de only one who know what es una promesa manda and what es not una manda.

"Don't make God into a woodcarver, Papá. He was a carpenter," said Antonio.

"Promesas are nails of wood, hijos, not nails of esteel," said Abuelo. "Dat es what hangs de Carpenter on de cross. De woodcarver was nailed into de log on Tezcoco with wooden wedges. Neither had a choice. It was de God/gods dat made dose promesas. Dat es de job of de Creators. How can jour esposa make a deal with Jesu Cristo to be de creator. God es in control of tings, not her. He pulls de plow. All eshe es doing es digging herself a hole. If it es in His mind He will reward her for her faith."

"But how do I tell dat to mi mamá, Abuelo?" asked Juan.

"I don't know jet, mijo, but I will pray and walk on dis very hard for jou," answered Abuelo softly.

"Now jou have kept jour promesa to jour mamá, Papá, by teaching my eson a trully great lesson," said Antonio.

"I just don't want to dishonor her, Abuelo," said Juan.

"Dat es good I tink, mijo, but what es troubling jou now?" asked Abuelo.

"Well, Dr. Waugh gots an award for being Educator of de Year in San José. Everybody in de schools of Matatlan es calling him 'Mr. Education'. Dat's not right."

"I thought dat dis wuz wat wuz troubling jou," said Abuelo. "Men who are blind to de Trute are honoring your señor Waugh, mijo. De gods and Dream Walkers are locked out of de mirrors in his soul. His time will come. Even smoking mirrors have true vision."

"How do jou know it will come, Abuelo?" asked Juan. "What do mirrors have to do wit it?"

"Porque de Walkers tell me dese tings witout mirrors and esmoke," answered Abuelo.

"How will I find dese Dream Walkers without mirrors, Abuelo, and estill honor Mamá?" asked Juan.

"Jou dun't have to look por dem or find dem, Eshot-gun. Dey will find jou!" said Juan's father. "Dey know de trute and de refleciones de la trucha."

"But how I do I esee dem when dey get here, Abuelo?" asked Juan.

"Jou are listening wit jour ears and not wit jour esoul, Juanito," said Abuelo as he continued wittling. "Let me eshow jou someting mi Abuelo Viejo eshowed me cuando I was just a little esmaller dan jou. Estand-up, Eshot-gun. It wasn't eso long ago I could look down instead of up into jour eyes. Now pick-up dat lamp next to de rock. Hold it out in jor hand at arms length. How far does de light eshow around jour feet?"

"About four feet in front of dem, Abuelo," said Juan.

"How far to each side of jou, Eshot-gun?" asked Abuelo.

"About tree feet each way, Abuelo," answered Juan.

"And how far behind jou, Juanito?" questioned Abuelo.

"About two feet, Abuelo, but what does dis have to do wit dream walking, honoring mi mamá and making life choices?"asked Juan.

"Estop asking questions like a gabacho on a quiz show and watch for de words in de wind, Juanito!" yelled Abuelo. "A good eshot-gun listens with his eyes and esmells wit his ears. Doing de obvious only works if jou understand dat life is full of places, of nothings and mirrors.

"O.K., Abuelo," said Juan softly. "What do I do, now?"

"Estand dere until jou are ready to esee wit jou heart, Eshot-gun." Juan stood there for a while as the lantern got heavier and heavier in his stretched out arm. "What es jour arm telling jou, Juanito?"

"It esays dat if I continue to hold the lamp dis way dat I will fall over," answered Juan.

"Jour arm es telling jou a trucha, Juanito. De light to jour feet must be in balance."

"Eso what eshould I do Abuelo?" asked Juan.

"What does jour arm want to do?" asked Abuelo.

"It wants to lower de lamp to my eside, Abuelo."

"Den listen to it, Eshot-gun, for jour ears are finally esilent." Juan lowered the lantern to where it hung at his side. "Wait a minute and den tell me what jou esee, Eshot- gun."

Juan waited for a couple of minutes and said, "I can esee for about tree feet in every direction, Abuelo. No, de actual frame of de light extends tree feet in every direction, and den dere es a kind of twight-light dat goes even further dan dat."

"Because, estúpido uno," said Benjamín, "de light isn't in jour eyes anymore, my little Bullet-Barrel."

"Give him a chansa to learn for himself, Benjamín," said Juan's father. "Jou didn't catch on any faster when I taught jou dis lesson tree years ago."

"I can actually esee even further now, Abuelo," said Juan.

"Bueno. Now take an estep forward, mijo. How far can jou esee?" asked Abuelo.

"De esame distance, Abuelo," answered Juan.

"Bueno. Now an estep to de right. How far now?"

"De esame as before, but jou already know dat, Abuelo."

"Just keep going as I tell jou, mijo. Now take two steps forward and two steps left. How far es de light to jour feet?"

"De esame as before, Abuelo."

"What es de lección den, Eshot-gun?" said Abuelo while still carving the figure and pointing directions with his knife.

"If I keep my light in de right place, I'll always have enough to know my choices and make de right decisions, Abuelo."

"Jou got it part right, Eshot-gun. Christ esays he es a light unto our feet. Eso de part about having enough light es la trucha. Making de right choice takes estaying in tune with jour maker. Isn't dat de trute, Antonio?"

Antonio looked up from the beautiful ship growing out of the oak in his strong hands. His golden sun sculpted face broke into a small but powerful smile. "Sí, Papá. When I've been in de center of my tree, de Walkers dance in my mind wind and all es well. Because of dis wind mind I know where we were, where we are and where we are going. All es one and right with today which es yesterday and tomorrow. In dese times I can feel Him in ethe center of my esoul carving my eseed through de chapparal from de spring of life."

"Jou were de leader de people needed in de desierto, Antonio," said Abuelo. Dat is why Xochilt use de old woman to anoint jou. Recuerdas mijos, Dios cuts down de Sequoia wit de eshade of de Golden Oak. De axe cuts dem both down. De axe in de hands of a Dream Walker cuts away de lie from de trute. Jou are de best axe que Dios has let me esee. I'm proud to be jour father and to have known jou, hijo."

"Jou are a blessing to me too, Papá," said Antonio.

As the wind moaned softly in Juan's young mind, he could hear them exhanging carvings in life and cutting out bosquejos for their eternal stories of the machistas, but he could not see their dreams for his life tree. Only the shadows of ancient ghost walkers danced for Juan. These were only male trees that confirmed part of his manhood. The Live Oaks had not yet annointed him.

In the strength of the spiring sequoias he hoped that his young dream walk in the ancient realms and quests for manhood would know at least as much as Papá and Abuelo. If they did, then things would come out of the throatwood and new burls all right.

The men had given him the solid beams of clear heartwood to form the bridges that he needed for the cucaracha's climb to survival.

The glowing embers of the fire faded red, the unconfirmed walkers danced gracefully at the edge of the living light. The carved roots of their unique tree fed the living family soul. The shaped roots formed the tree crown for survival. They all blessed the carving of Juan's unfound tree with one unique family voice that trembled from the solid living heartwood!

The unconfirmed launching of Juan's well laid keels still needed the hand sown sails to cross the seas of reality.

Confirmation In The Placita De Los Angeles

Sixteen year old Juan, feeling his young manhood, emerged from the side chapel of the Placita church into the warm winter Los Angeles sun. Concha who filled her clothes more and more everyday with her blossoming womanhood stood near the torquoise tiled plaza fountain in anticipation of Juan's smiling face.

"Hi, Concha. What jou doing here?" asked Juan.

"I was just passing by to see if the Placita would be the right place for my quinceañera," answered Concha.

"What do jou tink?" asked Juan.

"Some day I want to be married in this church, Juanito," said Concha softly. "It is where all my comadres have tied their love knots."

"My mamá esays dat dis church es de best place for a sacerdote to marry God," Juan commented.

"It's a fine place for a woman to a marry man, too, Juanito," responded Concha. "The Placita is a great little church that just speaks to me of the Everlasting. If everything works out, Juan, I'm going to make my quinceañera here."

"Do jou haveta take classes for de quinceañera, Concha?" asked

Juan.

"That's silly, Juan," laughed Concha. "Why would I have to take classes to become a natural fifteen? Anyways, why do you haveta study so hard for confirmation? Didn't you tell me that your mom and Spanish grandmother have been seeing to it that you learn everything a priest should know for years?"

"Dat's true, Concha, but de father esays that what I'm learning now goes beyond dat. I haveta pick my own esaint's name, get an esponsor and everyting. Dis bit here es what jou call a real personal commitment."

"Who's your sponsor goin'ta be, Juan?" inquired Concha. "I bet I could get my mamá do that for you."

"My mamá would never hear of dat, Concha," said Juan. "Eshe told me to ask one of my teachers."

"Did you ask anyone yet?" asked Concha.

"Sí, Concha."

"Well, who is it, Juanito?"

"It's my old high school history teacher, Mrs Marsh," answered Juan.

"Isn't that the teacher who calls you Guon, Juanito?"

"Sí, and I really hate dat, but mi mamá and Mrs Marsh go to de Society of St. Joseph meetings together and esaid dat eshe would be de best esponsor I could get."

"Does she come to your church classes, too?"

"Oh chure, esa. Eshe es en talking to Father Tesio right now. Actually dat es de best part of her being my esponsor."

"Why is that, Juan?"

"Because, esa, eshe brings me to here in her own carro eso I can fix it for to change de oil and estuff."

"Are you goin'ta haveta do that today, Juan?"

"No I did dat last week and eshe got's ta do esometing en City Hall eso I got ta take de bus home today?"

"Can I go with you?"

"You can do what jou wanta esa. Jou live next door anyways."

"Then I ride with you, Juanito."

"O.K., Conchita. But jou can't bother me too much on de bus, porque I got to estudy dis church estuff."

"Why is dat, Juanito?"

"If I don't make dis ting esoon, dey are gunta haveta commit me to Rancho Los Amigos Hospital for de cuku birds.

"Why is that, Juanito?"

"Because esa, like I keep tellin' jou, dis confirmation ting takes all kind of commitment!"

"Save some of that commitment for me, Juan," murmurred Concha sweetly.

"What makes jou tink, que jou are dat especial, Esweetums?" asked Juan. "I need to get dis confirmation eso de heart under mi lisa es for reals and always pure in Jesus, Concha."

"Didn't you do that with your first holy communion?" inquired Concha.

"Mi Mamá wants me to be a priest and de fathers want me to be a church esaint. Dis estuff es breaking en mi cabeza," groaned Juan.

"What does that breaking in of your head have to do with anything, Juan?" asked Concha.

"Jou are not havin'ta read all de estuff dey got me reading for dis confirmation, Concha," answered Juan. "I tink que dat I have read more for dis deal dan I have read de entire last two years at Central High Eschool. In fact, now dat I think on it, I'm esure I read more for today's lesson on de meaning of esantification, dan I read all dis year en eschool."

"I have a lot of homework in my classes, Juan," said Concha.

"Dat' because jou are a girl, ese, and dey want jou to be a clerk en esome oficina," suggested Juan.

"What classes are you taking in school now, Juan?" asked Concha. "Don't they still have you in math, history, and English?

"No, not anymore, Conchita," responded Juan. "De counselor esaid dat de tests eshowed dat I was real gud with my hands. Eso he put me in drafting, autoshop, and typing."

"Why did he put you in those classes, Juan?" asked Concha.

"He esaid dat en dose clases dat I would get all of the math of estraight lines, de history of de carros, and English of typing dat I would need to get into de army," answered Juan.

"That's where all mi comadres new esposos are going, Juan," said Concha, "and they look so cute in their new uniforms."

"Uniform o no, esa, Mi mamá wants dat I estay out of de army," said Juan. "Eso eshee told de father to make esure dat I could read all of de lessons to being de beginning of a real priest like eshe promised to God. Eso now I got no homework from de eschool and I haveta estudy all night and day just to make de priest tink I can read. I don't even know howta pick an esaint."

"You could pick St. Joseph for your name and patron saint, Juan," suggested Concha. "He married Mary, Juanito."

"Mostly girls pick him, Concha. Besides my Mother would estomp in my face if I tried to pull dat one. Eshe reads, jou know."

"Can you at least be my escort in mi quinceañera, Juanito, mío?" asked Concha.

"I'll haveta asked mi mamá, Conchita," said Juan.

"You can't hide in her skirts forever, Juan."

"A priest can hide en his skirts all his life, Concha."

"Do you have someone else that is better to you than I am, Juan?" asked Concha with a sparkle in her eye that stirred Juan's young manhood.

"You got to get out of here with dat estuff, little one," said Juan assertively. "I gotta get on with de tings I haveta do, vecina. If I got de time and jou estop bugging me, den, and only den, I might tink about putting on my zuit for jou and jour fifteenth cumpleaños."

"You are a big talker Juan. You don't even have a whole zuit," accused Concha.

"What I ain't got, mis carnales got. Between us we can do de whole cosa if we wanta," replied Juan.

"Den you had better get on with picking your saint so you can do mi quinceañera," said Concha.

"If I pick an esaint, Concha it will be for mi mamá and mí," said Juan.

"You are really tied to your mother's apron strings, altar boy," said Concha trying on her most beckoning look.

"Estrings are not on my mind and if dey were, what makes jou tink que I would trade de ones jou esay I got for de ones jou wanta tangle me in, Conchita?" asked Juan with a stare that attempted to melt her beckoning look.

"Juan," called Father Tesio as he walked towards the young couple, "Have jou made any progress on the picking of your patron saint?"

"I tink eso, Padre," answered Juan.

"That's what I want to hear, Juan. Your mother has been telling me of your desire to become a priest and the picking of the right patron saint is very important." Juan squirmed as Fater Tesio turned directly at Concha and asked, "Is this the young girl that your mother claims is trying to deprive the church of a priestly commitment?"

"I dun't know what my mamá has esaid to jou, padre," said Juan nervously, "but if I have learned anyting from jou, it es dat nobody but de person hisself can make de personal commitment necessary for confirmation, de priesthood or even a marriage to a woman."

"That's right, Juan," said Father Tesio with an all knowing priestly smile. "Sounds like something is sinking in to that head of yours. God does work his miracles, Juan. And, what is the young lady's name?"

"My name is María Concha Pacheco de Madera, Father," announced Concha proudly. "My mother is Francesca Dolores Pacheco de Alviso."

"I believe your mother has approached the Church about your quinceañera, young lady," commented Father Tesio. "How far is the planning coming along on that?"

"I'm trying to get Juan to be my escort," said Concha hoping for Father Tesio's support.

"As Juan stated, María Concha, personal commitment is a hard thing to give, and Juan has a lot on his mind right now," suggested Father Tesio.

"Not so much that he can't do the right thing by a girl, Padre," said a disappointed Concha with a masking smile on her face.

"Is there something you have left out of your confession, Juanito?" asked Father Tesio with a very serious accusing voice.

"No, Padre," answered Juan. "Eshe es walking in her dreams with Sequoya and dat es gud becuz I now know dat my patron esaint has got to be San Pedro."

"Why is that?" Juan asked Father Tesio with a puzzled look that revealed a lack of knowledgeable dream walking.

"Becuz my head is upside down on a tree most of de time, Padre, and San Pedro knows all about dat and how not to deny Jesus and de Trute," said Juan.

"Keep reading, Juan. You are beginning to show some promise," said Father Tesio.

"My mamá made de promesa, Padre," said Juan.

"That's nice," said Father Tesio with yet another puzzled look in Juan's direction. "Let's talk with you and your mother further on scheduling your quinceañera," said Father Tesio to Concha. "A lot of the girls today are only doing the celebration in the dance halls."

"Don't worry, Father," said Concha. "My mother would never let me do that. She wants me to do it right. That's why I need a proper escort."

"It's nice to have met one of Juan's little friends," said Father Tesio as he moved off towards Olvera Street. "I'll see you tomorrow in class, Juan."

"I've got ta go ta work after eschool tomorrow, Padre," called Juan. "I come here on my day off."

"It's good that you show enough commitment to come here on your day off, Juan, but don't put golden idols before the Lord," called back Father Tesio.

"He doesn't have to tell dat ta de whole world," said Juan

with the red glow of embarrassment rising over his boy/man face. "I need dat job in de carnecería to buy de tings I need to make my confirmation. Dat priest won't be happy until he has my blood. I'll never be ready by February de fourth."

"All he wants is your soul, Juan," said Concha. "You had better make it, so you can be a proper escort."

"Who esaid I'm your escort, Concha?" asked Juan.

"Your uncruxified soul, Juan, and if you know what is good for you, you won't try to cross me," asserted Concha.

"That's not funny, Concha!" snapped Juan. "Oh San Pedro, get me off dis cross! Why don't jou make de woman leave me alone?"

"I know when the welcome mat hs been pulled from under my feet," said Concha as she turned away and started off in the direction of the bus stop.

"Where are jou going, Conchita?" called Juan. "What have I done now?"

"Why don't you stand on your stonefilled head and figure it out, Mr. Unconfirmed Payaso!" yelled Concha to the whole plaza."

"Eslow down, Conchita," called Juan loudly. "What's dis estone head estuff all about?"

"I won't be fifteen for two months yet, señor Upside-down Rock Brains. I'll get Simon Polido. He will escort me. He's confirmed, good looking, has a car, a real suit and everything!"

"What do jou mean by everting, Conchita mía?" asked Juan with some concern.

"You are too self centered to know, Juan!" she snapped.

"Wait-up," called Juan as he ran to catch-up with Concha like a dog being jerked on a leash. "Who esaid jou were ta esee other guys?"

"I don't see you running off at the mouth to claim me, Juanito," snapped Concha with a jerk of her right shoulder.

"But jou are only fourteen, Concha," said Juan while trying to stay even with Concha.

"Years mean nothing when your heart is pure, Juan."

"Pure or not, Conchita, jou are not ready for de real life like de estar of my typing class, María Alvarez."

"I'm all de woman dat you will ever be able to handle, Mr. Unconfirmed. You couldn't get up next to María if you struck all your little keys and the spacer bar at one time."

"I could if I wanted to," retorted Juan.

"Maybe you are right about that, Juanito," said Concha. "I heard that she lets all de boys push her keys."

"Don't jou talk dat way, Conchita. Nice girls have clean mouths."

"Nice boys make the time to escort nice girls to their quinceañeras."

"Let me at least make esure jou get esafely home, Conchita," suggested Juan.

"O. K., but only so yous can get the practice you need to do my quinceañera, Juanito."

"If jou esay eso, Concha," said Juan with a wink of his left eye.

* * *

"I'm so glad that on dis day, Friday February 4, 1939, you are finally taking the beginning steps to your holy orders," said Juan's Mother as she handed him a freshly ironed shirt. "Your Grandmother would be so proud. I only wish we could have afforded her to come down here."

"Couldn't Abuelo and Abuela have driven her down from San José?" asked Juan.

"Your Abuelo's truck broke down again. It's like it knows what he wants to do," commented Juan's mother. "Well at least you will be a man of God, Juanito."

"Mamá, please don't estart all dat again," pleaded Juan. "All

I'm doing es making dis confirmation to make all de women in my life happy."

"I suppose that includes Miss Ojos Del Sol next door, Juan?" commented his mother.

"Concha es a really a nice girl, Mamá. Eshe es making her quinceañera and everyting," said Juan.

"The priesthood doesn't have anything to do with an escort to a quinceañera, Juanito. Besides a promesa to God is a promise forever."

"I didn't make dat promise, Mamá!" said Juan uncomfortably.

"Didn't God return your papá to all of us, Juanito?" asked his mother. "Do I have to pay penance all of my life because I promised you to God for your papá's return from La Migra's deportation to Mexico?"

"No, Mamá."

"Didn't you go to Our Lady of Guadalupe with me and mi mamá to pray and light candles of commitment for your papá's safe return?"

"Sí, Mamá."

"Would you have me crawling forever on bloody knees before the Holy Mother Church begging for forgiveness because my son perfers a fancy woman?"

"No, Mamá."

"Well?"

"I've never gone out with a fancy woman, Mamá."

"I can see it all now," said his mother ignoring Juan's assertion. "First it will be a fancy woman, then joy riding in those chopped jalapies, then hotsy totsy at the dance halls, loaded with reefer madness and sex starved women, and finally the Zuit Zoot pachuco will shame my house. I won't have it, Juan."

"What's dat, Mamá?" asked Juan.

"I won't have the roaring flapper twenties and the unprohibited boozing thirties in my house!"

"But, Mom..."

"No buts, Juanito, God has told me these truths in my prayers and you will not defy His will!"

"But, Mamá, Father Tesio esaid dat if I do dis it hasta be a personal..."

"I said no buts and ifs, Juanito, mío. He's an Italian priest and doesn't understand the really important things about God. Now, get dressed and do what I told you before your father breaks the car and we'll all have to walk to church."

* * *

Juan faced the church. In the center of the golden adobe wall shown the bright glorious rose window fashioned in love, the gaze that came from God. The iron hung redwood doors framed the empty tomb like vastness of the Placita Church. The sweet odor of myrrh drifted out from the distant candle lit altar. The bell in each belfry rang with holy spiritual authority: the voice of Jesus personally calling out the saints with universal and perpetual love. With every loud clappered gong, Juan's heart beat out the hymn/song that had been rooted in his family spirit.

The family and his sponsor joyously gathered around him to share in the sacred moment. They were all pleased. Juan, the first of his generation to be confirmed, shouldered the responsibility in a manner befitting an empowered Galván. Benjamin had had his chance but had failed to make the commitment again. At the doors of the church stood a priest, scepter in hand. Juan's father looked at Juan from the softest tenderness of his heart, dropped his gaze to Juan's freshly scrubbed hands and softly murmured, "Abuelo gave his mother's cruz de plata to me for the first of my sons to make his confirmation."

"Thanks, Papá," said Juan whose eyes watched the extention of his father's arms towards his hands.

"You have filled jour mother's heart with joy and pride," his father continued. "Today jou are de family's man of estrength and humility."

"Gracias, Papá," said Juan.

His mother took his head in her strong tender hands and lowered his forehead to her lips and then gently kissed him and said, "Bless you, my son." With the corner of her right eye she kept her focus on the priest in a cream white robe and purple elbe.

Mrs. Marsh stepped closer to Juan as his parents backed away to enter the church. As she handed him a white leather bound, golden lettered Bible, she stated, "Learn the truths in this Bible, Juan. I am responsible for you. I pray that you follow Christ as a saint."

María Chavela looked at Mrs. Marsh, held her hands and with a deep sigh uttered, "Thank you, Mrs. Marsh, we appreciate your personal commitment to our son." The mother's warm compassion flowed through the hands and finally to Mrs. Marsh's heart.

Concha gave him a 3X5 black zippered Testament bought with money from her baby sitting monies that she had put into the Bank of Italy for her quinceañera. "Juanito, you look so handsome, today. You look like the perfect escort for the quinceañera. The nuns told me to give you this Testament. I wrote inside that by remembering Jesus Christ you will remember me."

Juan's mother said, "It is time for you to make your personal commitment to Jesus."

"Look who's here at de very last minute!" shouted Benjamín.

Juan's sister, María, excitedly ran off to greet the advancing family from the north. "It's Abuelo, Abuela, Augustín and Spanish Grandma!" she yelled.

"I'm always announced last," commented Spanish Grandma.

"What happened, Papá?" Antonio asked Abuelo. "I thought jou esaid dat de troka was broke too bad ta make de trip to here."

"Eshe was not broke eso bad ta keep de family away from eseeing de church accept de life of a Galván," answered Abuelo. "Beside La Suegra had a talk wit de 'troka' and eshe moved it to holiness."

"Did jou get my gift, Juanito?" asked Spanish Grandma.

"I still have it for him, Mamá," said Juan's mother. "Here, Mamá, you give your gift to him."

"Thank you, María Chavela," said Spanish Grandma. "Juanito, I made this especially for this sacrament." She opened the gift and took out the delicate white elbe embroidered in gold and purple thread."

"Dis es too pretty for me, Grandma," said Juan.

"Put it on, Juanito," said Spanish Grandma. "It is your right by virtue of your Holy Communion."

"But I'll look like a priest in it, Grandma," said Juan.

"That's the point of your witness, Juanito," said Spanish Grandma. "Your confirmation is your public personal commitment to Jesus and God." She turned to Juan's mother and said, "Have you blessed him through the Holy Spirit, hija?"

"Yes, I have." answered Juan's mother.

"Juan, then this day of sanctification will be like all of us getting a glimpse of heaven!" exclaimed Spanish Grandma. "Besides, I heard that your patron saint is St. Peter. Three or four times he was a coward. Then Peter said that in the power of Christ he was redeemed. Upside down or not, that is the path you must follow!"

"Thanks for always eshowing me de way of the brave coward, Grandma!" remarked Juan.

"The faith of the brave coward is so strong, mijo, that it can never, never be denied, even when it is upside down!" asserted his mother.

*   *   *

Juan's confirmation entrusted him to Jesus Christ forever in his heart. His personal commitment and conviction converted him into a saint: so holy, so sacred and so consecrated: sacrifice and grace. He finally fulfilled his personal promise.

His personal life became a walk with God. As all the saints prayed, the virtuous vision of the Lord permeated his personal prayer. Others had different visions beyond the confirmation: his mother in blue envisioned him as a priest in black; Concha in pink, a husband in gray flannel; Spanish Grandma in white, a saint at the opened doors of heaven — a glorious Christian through the Body of Christ and the covenant. In preparation for this day he confessed both in the secular and sacred, repented in his daily life so as to bear the fruit that befitted his heart, and, finally, opened his whole heart to Jesus Christ.

His intense exaltation of the spiritual union rang lovingly: the pervasive tone of universal unity denying the ever, ever, ever possibility of divisiveness. Now he had kept his parents' promise rooted in his baptism. He accepted Jesus Christ as the saviour in his Holy Communion and finally he made his personal commitment to be a saint in the Holy Mother Church. His fellowship in Holy Spirit and body had been augmented by His grace.

The tones of grace continued to present the precious hymn of salvation. The tones rang clearly with that special righteousness like the bell that called all of His people. Juan felt His love: salvation by His grace. Jesus Christ had offered His divine favor and power freely to Juan. At one time St. Peter and St. John witnessed the sacrament, now the bishop confirmed the saint with the crisma:

Unus Pater Santus, Unus Filius Santus, Unus Spiritus Santus

As the saints walked out of the Placita Church, Spanish Grandma embraced Juan and said tenderly, "Juan, when you become a priest you serve Jesus Christ forever. When you become a husband, your wife and you offer all of your children to God the Father, the Son and the Holy Spirit. Then all of your lineage will be in His Kingdom forever. God bless you my son."

"Thank you, Grandma."

Juan's mother embraced him twice. With a sobbing voice she said, "My son, my saint, my son."

Juan returned her embrace very tightly. Her energy filled his being.

Abuelo reached out and pulled Juan into his side by the arm, looked at him and uttered, "God walks through you always,

Eshot-gun."

"Let him breathe, esposo," said Abuela to Abuelo. "In his heart he already knows who loves him de best."

"I borrowed my boss's Kodak for to take esome photos of de familia," announced Juan's father. "Everybody gather tightly together. Sister, can jou take esome esnaps of us?"

"It will be my pleasure. You have such a big lovely family."

"Thank you for taking our picture, Sister," said Juan's mother. "My husband always cuts everybody's head off when he takes the pictures."

As Concha crowded in next to the left side of Juan, Spanish Grandma called out to the bishop of Los Angeles and Father Tesio to join them in at least two of the group photos and one of each of them individually with Juan.

"I only got tree roles of film, Suegra and I wanta esave esome por de recepción," said Papá.

"These pictures are important to Juan's priestly remembrance, Antonio," replied Spanish Grandma.

As Juan's Mother crowded onto Juan's right side, Concha whispered in his left ear in a smiling tone, "The family is such a warm place for our hearts, Juan."

All the family gathered and walked as one that day.

The Placita bell rang three times.

"The joy of silence prevailed among the laughing voices."

THE ZUIT ZOOT

As Juan lovingly touched the fine worsted wool threads of his Zuit, the bright pleasant elation of his empowered manhood swelled his head. In his smoke vailed golden mirror he felt the searing flash of a silver sword slashing through his first eighteen years. Mocking perfection of group power creating ridiculed isolation: the beloved unsuitable Zuit!

The broad shaped shoulders of the glorious Zuit flawed the perfection of his young life: a unique red dawn blood in a high noon blue sky. He had worked so many long hours for three long years in the sweat shop carnerías and slaughter houses of California Agri-business to buy his perfect set of threads, that it eclipsed for him all other fashion.

Now the shine of his double soled wingtips made his feet feel fast and tall even when he was standing still. The chain draped gracefully across his loins with a dignity only a Cholo could feel. The charcoal grey flannel saco had the elegance and boldness of a restrained pride that glowed from within. The tramos were pleated and creased to perfection. The starched ruffled lisa armoured his chest with presence. His fidora lifted him to the top of the world.

They called him the spic greased cholo and all kinds of hate names from angry prejudicial consciences, but Juan didn't care. When he was draped in his Zuit Zoot, he swaggered cyclically down Brooklyn Avenue with his carnales. La cucaracha Juanito became Don Juan Galván, Mister Slick, El Chingón, the ultimate in suave, a real somebody like Don Quijote or the Anazassi, ready to take on all comers, kiva smashers, windmills, ladder choppers, and pretenders.

When Conchita María and Juan married on June 24, 1940, he was in his Zuit. His Drapes were pressed perfect for the occasion. To make sure the pleats and repleats were perfecto, Juan did the pressing himself. Nothing was flawed, only a brown duck feather sown under the penstripe to soften the shoulder pads had to be plucked out of the right shoulder. This made the kneeling Zuit his charcoal drapes excelente. "Don't pluck too many, carnal," said Ramón The Poet. "Jou don't want to be a plucked duck on jour wedding day."

Juan's typing teacher had told the principal, "The Zuit is a gang uniform. If we allow it in our school, nothing but violence will result."

The first time Juan had worn a full Zoot Zuit was to escort Concha in an early morning mass before the Virgen De Guadalupe on December 12, 1938. All his carnales had contributed pieces to make the Zuit complete for this dry run of Concha's quinceañera.

As Juan had stood before La Virgen on that early morning, he could feel that the Virgin could see the purity of his intent with or without his Zuit. However, the church and technical scientists had always questioned La Virgen's garments, too.

When he later left the church for school the pinche jefes of the school suspended los carnales in their Zuits. A Zuit that was good enough for La Virgen was better than the principal. How could he be a vato without his trapos and calcos? How could he move in quest of the perfect janilla with a chopped greña? The Zuit gave him a license to express los pensamientos con los carnales y rukas. For Juan the Zuit was not the violent gang disguise that hid and made the chuko visibly invisible. The Zuit was an identified reality.

How could such a beautiful set of threads, the glory of the carnales and the colors of the barrio be such a flaw for the family? His Spanish grandmother wanted him to bury it. His father laughed at his tacuche. Even his Mother screamed at Juan, "Burn that devilish money wasting suit!"

Abuelo, who discarded the Spanish dandy hacendado for the mestizo charro ranchero, told Juan that he liked the Zoot Zuit. "The estirring round estrut of jour walk makes jour tree bend and weave admist the wind of death." Then abuelo added, "Mijo, it chure looks bedder on jou dan my blue pick- up did on mí."

"Why es dat, Abuelo?" asked Juan.

"Dat chain jou got puts me in mind of a chain mí Abuelo had on his charro zuit. He was one fine caballero in dat suit. While dat charro zuit wit its magnificent rodear, never protected me from attack, it clothed and kept whole de alma of mis compadres. I married jour Abuela en dat esuit. Mi Espanish grandma never forgave me for dat, either. Eshe wanted me to wear de suit of her dead husband. De chain on jour loins will dull deir axes. I learned dat wit mí Abuelo's charro zuit."

"Den why did jou tell me ta get rid of it, Abuelo?" Juan inquired.

"I told jou dat porque I don't want jou ta have trouble, mijo," answered Abuelo.

"Eso why jou changing jour mind, Abuelo?"

"Jour Zoot Zuit has eso much estyle, mijo, dat I tink it es a new charro esuit por jou. If it gives jou de pride I felt in my esuit, den I tink it es what I call an marrying esuit."

Restaurants gave Concha and him the "water treatment" if he wore it. They served the zooters water and left them sitting there until the "policía" came and arrested them for loitering. The police targeted his Zuit as sedicious clothing. They swept the streets with Juan's Zuit.

The school hated it and and the school board banned it as "gang styled clothing." His autoshop teacher said, "Only "Greasers" wore clothes like that when out on a date."

To destroy his Zuit would be a disaster for the barrio. For Juan el Zuit was "La Trucha," la verdadera, the essence of his identity. How could something that felt so good and thrilled his eyes be so evil?

His carnal, Ramón The Poet, always said, "Juan, La Virgen de Guadalupe accepts mis trapos, but de Man esmashes my face, den espits on my Zuit, and finally attacks mi barrio. De Man mistreats me as a nameless máscara en mi colonia. De drapes son la última locura máscara. De Man cannot esee de old masks in his history. Los maestros want to humble our blazin' esouls de juventud and our lisas wit naked power. Los comerciantes want to drown us wit a glass of water. La policía wants to estrip our esouls and mask our realities. La conquista Europea wants to degrease us. Only los carnales en Zuits have de alma to esense de togedderness in de coro de camarada. De Zuit es an espotlight in a dirty esky: a window into de esoul of de pachuco. Por nosotros el Zuit creates in deir anonymous Madison Avenue penstripes named 'gente' en nuestro barrio. Los carnales pachucos are de forbidden binding threads in de here of naked nowhere." "Eso what dose dat all mean, ese?" asked Juan.

"It means for jou, carnal, Dat los gabachos want to eslice con tijeras blancas to cut us down in de estreets as de unsuited naked en heaven and de suitably Zuited en hell, ese!"

"I heard jou on dat, ese," responded Juan.

In 1941, when Juan defended his Zuit in the adult classroom at LACC, the pinche teacher yelled, "Shut your lying Spic mouth. What are you Spics anyway, Jap lovers? Only fifth columnists wear foreign clothes like those. You guys look like the bad guys out of a Republic Studios Serial. I guess it would be too much to ask you to read the papers. Don't you know that our country will soon be at war. Those clothes are a disgrace to our flag."

"Chale con dat malcriado," said Juan to Ramón The Poet. "What does de pinche teacher know about los drapes? Only a real Zuiter knows de difference between de war to esave democracy and de war to destroy anything dat looks different."

"Den why didn't jou tell dat estúpido pinche teacher ta estick it up his pinche white ass, vato?" asked Ramón.

"I can't esay nothin' en dat clase, mano. I'm just a Messican to dat teacher."

"But he's treating jou like eshit, carnal!" countered Ramón.

"Even if I'm a lump of eshit, I can eserve my country in whatever ropa I choose".

"Eso, carnal," commented Ramón The Poet. "Eso what es de Zuit ta jou?"

Juan thought a minute while trying to look profound in the position of the Gran Chuco. "For me de Zuit es not a disgrace to de Estars and Estripes, ese. De estripes in mis drapes honored de flag. De Zuit es my personal flag. It eshows turf to me y los hommies. In de end, any soldado knows, ese, dat he eserves his flag with his sangre y cuerpo. My bandera never changes its colores!"

"Jou'er right on de target, carnal" said Ramón. I dun't know where dey come off with dis estuff que our colores son grand deals. Do de pinche gabachos expect us to go into de estrects in esearch of rukas and jainillas with a naked body and garnished esoul? Could Don Quijote or Cuatemoc eset forth without deir coat of arms, ese?"

"No, ese," said Juan.

"En el coro de alma we know dat when we are en los drapes we symbolized de establishment of de barrio: de Capulli. It's like I esaid to de pinche cop who hassled me en coche, burning our Zuits brands jour estripes with de eswastika. Only de man who tinks he has de power to create de ultimate in pure aesthetic exaggerated fashion es a naked man."

The Zuit made dropping of high school out worth it. After all gabacho schools had constantly stuck him in menso classes and speech therapy programs all the way through school. Each teacher treated his abilty to speak Spanish like it was speech impediment. Even when the family moved to East Los the schools never seemed to notice his culture or identity as anything more than basura to be taken to the dump.

Why should such a worthy set of drapes bring on the contempt of even the adult school? Why did the wearing of the Zuit bring upon Juan beatings by organized gangs of soldiers on leave from nearby bases as well as the stationery iron cages of the L.A.P.D. (Los Angeles Police Department). Why did honoring his Zuit provide a "voluntary" opportunity to exchange the Zuit for the uniform of the American Army?

The P.D. made it clear to Juan that they were going to "volunteer" him for the army. They were going to make a patriot out of him. Juan had to pay for the privilege of living in the United States. If he didn't, they would put him in an iron cage permanently for inciting riots by wearing the Zuit. Juan couldn't understand why they just didn't let him sign-up on his own. Zuit or no Zuit, he still thought of the United States as his land. Hadn't his ancestors taught him this? Hadn't Mrs. Post proven it?

Ramón The Poet was always saying, "Dey want real bad to be de fashion of now, like us, ese."

"Eso why dun't dey just do it and be coolo like us, compadre?" asked Juan.

"Dey dun't know how, carnal. Dey look too much like Nazis. Eso dey got to estrip de estripes off our esleek brown bodies and cover los carnales con khaki green."

* * *

As Juan started to dress with his best man, Ramón The Poet, on his wedding day, he said, "Just tink, Ramón, esoon I will be turning in dis classic charcol estriped drapes for de estars and estripes of Tío Samuel, ese."

"Keep dat tought to jourself, ese," said Ramón The Poet. "Like I keep telling jou, ese. Jou dun't want ta be a plucked duck on jour wedding day, carnal."

"Dats going to be hard ta do, ese," Juan said. "Esome how I feel like dis day es like ducking into a torn curtain, carnal." "Jou just remember dat tonight when jou take off dis trapos and eshe esees jou in jour altogether zuit, ese. Dun't be like dis guy I heard about que didn't know how to act once he got his zuit off."

"Wat jou mean, ese?" asked Juan.

"Well," said Ramón as he rubbed his bigote like a poet that was about to spout la trucha del mundo, "de way I heard it wuz que, when dis guy got married, his Papá took him aside right before de went into estand before de altar. His papá asked him if dere was anyting que he wanted to know before de wedding. Dis guy, he esays que, he wuz pretty esure he got de wedding part down becuz of all of de rehearsals and estuff, but what had him worried wuz que, what he wuz esupposed to do cuando dat night when his novia estripped de Zuit off him. His father esaid dat was no problem and dat he had an easy answer for his virgin eson."

"Cut to de chase, carnal or I'm going to miss Concha's weddin'," said Juan.

"Dun't jou worry, ese," replied Ramón. "Dey wun't estart until we get dere. A funeral cannot begin without de cuerpo."

"Right, right. I forgot about dat," said Juan with the voice of nervous worldly knowledge. "I guess I'm more nervous about dis weddin' dan I tought. It's a good ting I put in a little extra estarch when I ironed my repleats.

"Jou are goin' ta need more dan estarch in jour reet pleats to get jou trough dis día, carnal," came back Ramón The Poet.

"Funny, man," said Juan as he laughed and acted like he knew what Ramón The Poet was talking about. "Eso what did dis guy's papá esay to him?" asked Juan.

"His papá dice que, ese, dat at night after de fiesta and weddin' dat cuando dey got between de esheets of dier wedding bed, all dis guy had to do wuz to estart wit de kisses and everyting else would happen like natural, carnal. Eso de guy esays to his papá what did he mean like everyting would happen. His papá den told him que dat first ting to do wit jour novia es to kiss her on her lips and esay de most beautiful thing jou can tink of esoftly in her ears. Den if jou do dis just right jour novia will esay 'lower, Cariño.' Den his papá told his eson to kiss his novia wit all de passion he could eshow on de neck witout leaving a mark, porque novias dun't like deir necks marked after dey are married. In de middle of de kissing jou esay in a soft high voice, 'I love jou, querida'. And, if jou do dis just right jour novia will esay, 'lower, Cariño.' Den jou kiss her chichis wit even more passion den jou did her neck and jou will feel de power of the thighs of la Hemacera around sides. and den jou esay again, 'I love jou, querida.' Den eshe will esay again 'lower, querido.' Den jou roll jour face softly across her estómago, kissing her all de time and den whisper in a soft esweet but passionate voice, 'I love jou, querida.' And if jou do dis just right, eshe will put her hands on jour eshoulders and esay, 'lower, querido.' Den his papá dice que nature will tell jou what ta do."

"Eso what happened to dis guy on his wedding night," asked Juan as Ramón helped him put his sacko on and mold the shoulders.

"Well, carnal," said Ramón with a chuckle in his voice, Dis guy did everytin' his papá told him to do. He kissed on her lips and esaid, 'Honey I love jou;' den he kissed her neck and esaid in an esoft voice 'Honey I love, jou;' den he kissed her chichis and esaid, in ane soft and higher voice 'Honey, I love jou;' den he pressed his face into de esoft flesh of her estomach and he could feel her young body pulsating and demanding his total attention. Eso, dis vato esaid in an even a higher voice, 'oh honey, I love jou.' And den his most loving and beautiful novia esaid almost breatlessly, 'lower, mijo.' And, do jou know what dis pendejo did, Juan?" asked Ramón the poet trying to hold in his laughter.

"Jou tell me, carnal," said Juan with a swagger and posture of worldly knowledge.

"Dis pendejo raised up into a position like he is going to do a hundred push-ups. Looks down into the moist, soft, glowing, esmiling face of his hot and willing novia and esays very slowly in his deepest most masculine low pitched voice, 'Oh Honey, I love jou.'"

Ramón doubled over with laughter. Juan laughed like he knew what Ramón was laughing about, but in all reality what the guy had done sounded plausible to Juan. After a pause for additional laughter and hand slapping that lasted for what seemed to Juan as the right length of time to show respect for Ramón's knowledge and joke, Juan said as he postured himself in front of his mother's full-length mirror, "Ya know, ese, now dat we got dis hole set of drapes together, wit everyting just right, I feel like un toreador in de perfect position ta kill de bull."

"Dats a nice illusion, ese, but all jou have es de Zuit con un carlungo ancho and a perfectly ironed cross adored, white Lisa. Concha has de esilver esword con de red passion for de kill," retorted Ramón The Poet.

Juan laughed again like he knew what Ramón was talking about. "I guess it's about dat time que we get dis Zuit over to de church," said Juan.

"If jou esay eso, carnal," answered Ramón The Poet. "I never esaw un chingón en such fine ropa who was in eso much of a hurry to getta his own funeral."

"Ponte abusado, carnal," retorted Juan. "Dat remark es puro pedo, ese. Eshe es de finest ting dat has and will ever happen for me, ese."

"Esuicide was never an option for Quezalcoatl, carnal," answered Ramón The Poet.

"It's not an option for me eidder, Ramón," said Juan.

"If you esay eso, ese," repeated Ramón the Poet.

*   *   *

On the way to the church, Juan's mother cried with joy and agony: she was gaining a daughter, but she was losing her priest. "Are you really sure about this marriage, Juanito?" she sobbed. "It's not too late in the eyes of God to change your mind."

"I've never been eso esure about anythin', Mamá. Never eso esure."

"How can you be so sure, Juanito?"

"Concha is the woman to ever make me feel like a man and to make me want to get married," said Juan reverantly.

"Is she that committed to you, Chivito?"

"I'm absolutely esure of dat too, Mamá,"

"It's not just that she has used your feminine wiles on you, mijo?"

"Eshe es eso pure, Mamá, eshe could be a nun."

"When we get to the church I'm going to need one last talk with Concha and her mother."

After they dropped Juan off at the back of the church and parked the car, Juan's mother, María Gabriela approached Concha and her maids of honor. His sisters gathered around Concha like she was a queen bee. They acted like they needed to take lessons from her on how to kill a Zuit.

"You are so beautiful, Concha," said Juan's sister, María. "I can't believe you finally got my brother to take the plunge. You even have my papá in a tuxedo."

"I still don't believe it either María," replied Concha. "You know how Juan is, it won't be a done deal until the priest says, 'I pronounce you man and wife'."

"Well I think that your white satin empire is the perfect match for my brother's Zuit," said Luz. "The train is perfect. Just make sure my brother follows you around like that train, and I'm sure you will be the perfect couple."

"Thanks for that word of advice," said Concha with a laugh. "I'll keep your brother on the straight and narrow track."

"Mamá is still trying to figure out how to do that to Papá," said María.

"Is my vail straight?" asked Concha.

"You look perfect, Concha," answered Luz.

"Concha," called María Gabriela, "I need just a short moment of your time, sweetie."

"How can I help? Has something gone wrong? Did Juan get to the church? Did he remember the rings?" asked Concha nervously. "No offense intended, but your son would forget to carry around his head if it wasn't tacked on real tight to his shoulders."

"No, it's nothing like that, sweetie, and no offense taken. He is just like his father," María Gabriela answered. "You'll have a lot of those kinds of worries if you marry a Galván, Concha."

"Then what is it? The processional is about to start."

"Since my manda to God to return his father from Mexico, I promised Juan to be a priest. Your marriage to my son will break that promise. Are you absolutely sure about your marriage to him?"

"It's all I have dreamed of for three years. I knew that he was the one for me the first day that I met him. I'll make him the best wife that you could ever imagine. I'm totally committed to him both in heart and soul."

"I guess that is what I needed to hear, my daughter!" said

María Gabriela as she wiped the tears from her eyes. "I know he loves you, dear. Just make my son happy."

"Thanks for your blessing, Mom. This is really important to me on the happiest day of my life."

Turning to Spanish Grandma who was fussing about the very last detail of the wedding dress," María Gabriela asked, "Is everything ready inside?"

"Of course it is daughter," answered Spanish Grandma. I made sure that the church has all of the proper items for the wedding ritual. I even made sure that Juan went to confession yesterday. I told him, 'Chivito, you don't want to enter into this most holy of His institutions with an unclean heart.' I bought the kids' wedding candle and it's on the altar. I not only provided Concha with her dress, I've perfected it to fit her like a glove. I gave Juan a family bible for him to share with his lovely bride on their honeymoon."

"That's nice, Mamá," said María Gabriela as she wiped her eyes once again. "Could you check and make sure the men are ready? You know how they muddle up things, Mamá."

"No problem, María. Consider it done," said Spanish Grandma as she headed towards the side door of the Placita Church.

"Is everything in readiness here?" she asked as she approached the men.

"I think eso, Grandma," said Juan. "How does my Zuit look?"

"While I do not like your suit of clothes, I suppose they are necessary, Chivito. I must admit that you look quite handsome in them, even though they are a bit garish for a wedding."

"Do you really feel dat way about dis Zuit, Grandma?" asked Juan. "Why does everyone have to make a comment about?"

"Isn't that why you are wearing it, Juanito?" she asked.

"No, Grandma."

"Then you don't need a Zuit of clothes to show off your excellence before God. He sees your soul in your blessed nakedness!"

Spanish Grandma shouted.

As Abuelo had came by to give Juan one last wink before entering the church, he could hear Cortez shouting El Requerimiento and looked upon his little Eshotgun like he was seeing another great Zuit falling into the really dry dust of the ground during the conquest of la tierra. "Eshe's got dat one right, mijo," Abuelo announced. "Did de priest do for jou as I told him to, Eshotgun?"

"What was dat, Abuelo?"

"Di he take jou and jour papá into de rectory for un tragito de tequila?"

"Sí, Abuelo. Dat's all dat es keeping my nerves from exploding."

"Dat's good, mijo. Jou esave all dat exploding movidas for tonight with jour novia," said Abuelo with a wink of his left eye as he turned to get Abuela's left arm.

"Just remember who loves, jou de best, mijo," said Abuela tenderly as she followed Abuelo into the church.

As Juan stood in the side doorway of the church shoulder to shoulder with his papá, he decided to asked his papá one last time if there was anything he should know about the wedding night.

"Papá," said Juan in a whisper.

"Relax, mijo. Jour pantalones gots both a wide cinturon and suspenders. Deir estuffed cuffs will even keep jour ankles estraight."

"I know dat, papá. Ramón helped me to make chure que dat de Zuit was perfecto. But dat es not what I'm worried about," Juan whispered.

"Dat es all I worried about when I married jour Mamá," whispered his Papá. "Eso what's got jou eso worried and in a horse sweat, mijo?"

"Es dere anyting I need to know dat maybe jou have been esaving for de last minute, Papá?" asked Juan.

"I guess I estill dun't know what jou are whispering about, mijo," said Juan's father.

"I'm talking about dis night wit Concha?" said Juan.

"We are in de doorway to de church, mijo. I tought jou and jour brother knew all about dat. Dis es really not de time to talk about dese tings."

"I know dat, Papá, but I estill need some advice and a little last minute help. Who else can I asked dis of, Papá?" whispered Juan.

"De low lit fire of de hembra will light jour way, mijo," his father whispered. "It es better if jou and Concha find each other's way. Just recuerdas que de starch in jour pantalones won't be dere to harden jou tonight. Eshe es tender, young and beautiful. Be tender to her. Dun't press her too hard, just estay hard."

Juan looked at his father out of the side of his eyes. Something his papá had said had lit up his father's face with joy. Two or three of the elderly women in the side rows of the church were giving his father the mal ojo. This seemed to delight his father even more. Juan had no idea what all the fuss was about. He just hoped that Concha's mother was informing and helping Concha more than Ramón and his father had informed and helped him.

As the organ music started the processional, Juan leaned towards his father once again and asked, "Do jou tink I picked de wrong Zuit to get married in, Papá?"

"Jou and jour best man look great, Juan, but jou, not jour zuit es getting married, mijo," his father answered.

The wedding and the fiesta went off just like the priest, Concha, and her mother had planned it. All the rehearsals and meetings with the priest paid off. Even the white satin cushion that Abuela had made served to preserve the crease in his tramos.

There were lassos and comadres for everything. It was like de whole barrio was in on the wedding. Fortunately everybody brought all kinds of food. The cake had five large four layered tiers. Tío Antonio used his connection at the Mirassou Winery to get thirty cases of champagne for cheap. The carnales pitched in for three full kegs of beer. Abuelo buried and roasted, in the old way, an entire dressed steer.

They really knew how to spend Juan's cannery savings. The pockets in the Zuit were emptied. Only a few kernals of rice remained. Everybody drank, ate and danced until all were satisfied. All went home happy. Only Juan in his Zuit and Concha in her dress seemed to want to continue the fiesta to prevent the future from happening.

Dat night the Zuit was hung in de closet next to de white satin dress. The embers of the hembra lit his face. Starch welled up from with in him. Juan got his voice lowered, but the glowing virgin only groaned with joy.

*   *   *

Those days before bombs on Pearl Harbor were a honey dew fog for Juan and his jainilla. The Los Angeles summer and fall were tall and the movidas suaves. The work in the slaughter houses and canerías refilled their pockets with just enough change to keep the glow on things. The broken Zuit still could stand tall with his jainilla leaning on them. The saddle of marriage was balanced by the romantic dances and movies that filled their minds with dreams. Concha made him taller than Don Quijote en coche. Their memory of Juan in his Zuit, Conchita in white silk satin, both in a chopped classic short, cruising Olympic Boulevard sizzled and foamed in their hearts like a freshly poured goblet of California champagne. La Reina y El Rey for the day in the peaceful hot June barrio sun drifted in their chopped short classic towards the grey storm clouds of the Goths at war.

Even finishing his high school work at LACC like his probation officer required did not push back the gathering clouds of world wrenching violence.

In the peace of those preludial months he resided in the sacred trust of her bosom. Concha loved him unreservedly. He felt that having her keep the Zuit would be a sacred act of trust. He told her, "Jou know how my familia feels about dis Zuit. Dey act as if it will make me an outsider. With jou I'm an insider."

"Juanito, mío," she replied. "Your zuit and jour carnales put me on the outside. Do jou want me to be on the outside of jour familia forever, too?"

"In my Zuit, Concha. Jou will never be an outsider with me," asserted Juan.

"I married you, not your damn Zuit, Juanito mío," Concha replied. "Your mother and grandmother will laugh at me if they find out I'm backing you on this."

"If jou don't back me on dis Concha, jou will be deir daughter without being my wife."

"Don't say that to me, Juan. You have no idea how much that kind of stuff from you frustrates me!"

"Por why are jou esaying dis, Conchita?" asked Juan.

"You are shoving me outside of the family house wrapped inside your zuit. You have wrapped me up for a burial. Is that what you really want?"

"Jou will never be alone, jainilla mía," said Juan. "Jou are my carnala. Please, keep our zuit close to jou as if it were our life."

"You're killing our love with this damn zuit, Juan! What kind of life can I have buried in your lying zuit?"

"Por favor, Quierda, drape my drapes over jour wedding dress. After I'm gone tell my mother that I bowed to her desire and burned it. Jou are my life and I leave me entrusted to jour canción."

"Our canción, Juan, is not a dress and a Zuit. Our souls are the drapes in my singing heart."

"Den I have no fear for our future knowing my lies and soul are safe in our love," said Juan as he caressed her small shapely form.

"Do really want me to swallow that line of bull, Chivito Cucaracha!" shouted Concha.

"Well dat's de logic my voces are esaying en mí cabeza,

Conchita," answered Juan.

"That's a set of voices you had better look at, Juan, because I only see bull artist skid marks and no logic."

"Are you goin' ta do what I ask or not, Conchita?"

I don't know why I love you so," she said. "You have got me all confused! If you love your damn Zoot Zuit so much, you drape your own drapes in the closet."

Before he left for the train to the induction center in Oakland he carefully wrapped the Zuit in the bridal box with Concha's dress and buried it in the back recesses of his mother's closet.

Concha shook her head in wonder at the stupidity of her beloved. "I hope you haven't buried us, by doing that Cucaracha?" said Concha in a soft intensely angry voice. Her teeth remained tightly clenched as she stared sadly out the window.

THE INDUCTION DEPARTURE

Juan had to stand in line for everything: the police station, the train, baggage check, induction, physicals, getting a job, buying groceries, giving confession, admission to city college, finding a parking space - even to pee. Life was a series of events interrupted by time waiting in a line, thought Juan.

The lines that got him to the induction center train all started at the police station where Juan and his hommies were busted for wearing their Zoot Zuits. In the police line-up he was given the choice to join the army or do time. Who would believe that such a line in the police station was the recruiting office in the barrio? Only the lines in the immigration office held more fear for Juan's family.

"My mother kept telling me to burn de Zuit, but to me dat beautiful eset of unsuitable 'drapes' esuited me perfectly," said Juan to the large silhouette of Union Station. "After I'm a war hero I'll show her how important de Zuit Zoot es to de barrio. She'll haveta believe a war hero! Mi mamsita will forgive me, anyways. After all, she didn't take losing a priest in de family all dat bad. Eshe truly loves me and wants de best for me. Besides eshe gave me my great grandmother's silver cross and rosary to protect me from de evils of war."

To Concha the lies converted the zuit into a living hell full of contradictions. She knew that Juan expected her to act as if she would protect him from everything, even the Nazis, the police and his Zuit. She knew that if she didn't protect his Zuit, he would act like a little boy lost. How could she continue to fight with him over the zuit when he was going off to the living hell of war?

"God forgive me for the living lie he is forcing me to live," Concha prayed. "Please protect him as he leaves the safety of my arms. In my conflict I must remain silent."

Silence in war: war in silence.

Now Juan was waiting in line with the entire barrio of former

Zoot Zuiters for the train to take him away from East Los to the induction center in Oakland. At first his family was in the line with him but the M.P.s stopped them from going beyond the iron fence next to the train.

"Wachate, mijo," said Abuelo, "jou bring jour flesh back to Califas. De outer rings of de great oaks are jour future. Remember me and de familia in jour heartwood."

"Why es dat, Abuelo?" asked Juan.

"It may look dead, but it es our estrength, mijo. Don't get caught in de forest fire of estupidity.

"I won't, Abuelo.

"Remember dat every year's crop of eseeds has to learn dat de estove of de real mundo es hot. Dis time es jour chansa to learn witout getting jour ass burned."

"I'll remember, Abuelo," replied Juan.

"No jou won't, mijo. Deir es too much Galván in jou. Pero jou will remember when jou esit on de pyramid de wrong way," said his father with a big laugh.

Spanish Grandma stepped foward and pushed Juan's father to her side said, "Old man, you and your son better stop already with that wood and tree stuff. What the boy needs to know is that he has our prayers and blessing from God. He is the only way."

"He already knows dat, vieja," retorted Abuelo. "I made esure jour daughter gave him la cruz de mi madre. He must do as he must. War es no estranger to our familia."

Spanish Grandma looked straight into Juan's wide open eyes and said with a tear in her voice, "The last time I saw my husband was in a train station much like this one, Juanito. He never came back to me. I will always pray that you come back to us." She took him in her arms made strong from years of scrubbing clothes on a wash board and hugged Juan tenderly.

"Gracias, Grandma," said Juan.

Papá then reached out with his knarled right hand, placed it on Juan's left shoulder and said, "De estorm jou are headed into es no dreamwalk, mijo.

"I tink que dat I know dis, Papá," mumbled Juan.

"Dat maybe, Juan. But it es hard to know de trute of hell until jou are upside down en de middle of it. Jou just remember to estep on jour enemies, mijo. Don't let dem put deir boots on jour back."

"I won't, Papá," replied Juan.

"Remember jou are a Galván," his father continued intently. "We cucarachas and chivitos can esurvive anyhing. Be esomething and esomeone dat jour madre y hermanas can be proud of."

"I will, Papá," replied Juan.

Abuela said with the wells of deep brown eyes, "Remember who loves you, Juanito. Here es un burrito de lengua dat espeaks for me."

"Gracias, Abuela, I will miss jour comida eso much."

His mother stepped out of the familia, hugged him and said, "I love you, mijo. Dis country always takes our best babies."

"Mamá..." moaned Juan out of embarrassment.

"Let me put my finger on your sweet little head like you let me do on our walks in East San José."

"Mamá..." moaned Juan once again as she ran her fingers through his shiny black hair.

"Make sure they give you a good haircut. I hope the uniform they give you fits you well. It will look much better on you than that zuit you burned for me. Make sure that they give you good food. Keep your socks dry. Remember to brush jour teeth and comb jour hair, mijo."

"O.K., Mamasita," replied Juan thinking that he wished he could tell his mother his truth: the only uniform that would ever fit him really well was his Zuit.

"He's not going away to a girl's camp, esposa," said his father.

"Tell de boy something dat will get him through de war."

While throwing a look of poison daggers at his father, his mamasita said, "Good health habits never hurt anybody, Juanito. I'm still trying to teach jour father this. Pero, mijo, jou just remember to be honest and they will treat you fair. Remember to say jour prayers and go to confession. And, Juanito, don't do anything that will let them take you away from me forever!" She pulled him back to her chest once again, wondering if her precious son would ever return.

"O.K., mamasita," replied Juan

"Benjamín leaned forward and whispered, "Juanito jou are not alone in dis. I upped yesterday for de Marines. los padres don't know yet. I'll tell dem later after dey get over jou going and all."

"Write me and let me know how it turns out, big brother."

"We'll take care of your things and Concha, Juan. Don't you worry about anything but staying alive and carrying the flag," said Ventura as his sisters started to weep.

"Can I use your radio while you are gone, Juan?" asked María Dolores. "I promise to take real good care of it."

"Jou can have it, baby sister," replied Juan.

"Thanks. I'll always think of it as yours."

"I'll light a candle to La Virgen for you, Juan, every month," said Luz between sobs.

The M.P.s started a sweep. "Ten minutes for departure, Five minutes to fall-in," shouted the station loud speaker.

"I'll bet dose guys in dose M.P. outfits use to work for La Migra," said Abuelo. "Dey push people around too good to be new at deir job."

"We are here to see Juanito off to war, suegro," said Spanish Grandma, "not make political statements."

"Who's being political?" said Abuelo as he winked his left eye towards Juan.

Francesca, Concha's mother, said, "Son-in-law, bring your body back whole to my daughter. She loves you and depends on you for a full life. War took her father from her. Don't let it take her husband too."

"Don't worry, suegra. I'll be back with bells on."

"Well, querido, they haven't left us much time," said Concha with the clear tears of true love in her eyes. "There was so much I wanted say to you. The family has said most of what I feel. I know you will laugh at me, but all I can think of right now is you looking down on me with your big brown eyes questioning and glowing. You said, 'Oh Honey, I love you.' Then I said, 'lower.' And then you said with your deepest most masculine voice, 'Oh Honey, I love you.' That was the sweetest thing that happened on our wedding night. To think it all happened because your father and carnales tried to help you out."

"I love jou, too, querida," Juan murmured.

"Love like yours makes me love you more and more, Juan." Her tears ran uncontrollably down her cheeks. She sobbed and said, "On our wedding night, all the stars in heaven were the brightest because for the first time in my life, you were mine forever. Give me a KISS and make it all right."

As Juan pulled away from her soft, shiny shapley lips, Concha whispered between sobs, "Kiss me again, Juanito. This last kiss will be our first good-bye."

"Fall-in," blared the station speaker.

He loved the softness of her big brown glowing eyes. Her breasts pressed in on his chest. This was more than enough reason to come home whole. He took her head and cradled her face in his face into his. He kissed her as gently as he knew how. "I want to kiss you lower right now," he whispered in her ear."

"If I know you the way I think I do, Juan, I'll bet that that's not all we would do," Concha responded.

Juan kissed Concha again. "That's a sucker's bet, querida," he whispered in her other ear."

"You had better stopping thinking about sucking things," she whispered in his ear. She pulled away just far enough so he could focus of the twinkle in her eye and not feel her heavy heart.

The M.P.s started their final sweep. He could no longer hold hands with Conchita and hug her. Only inductees with passes were permitted to go beyond the bars of iron. His familia, thank God, was not going. His Dad, Mom, Abuela, Abuelito, and his new wife were not getting on the train.

As he went through the gate, Juan knew that this was a turning point in his life, but at that moment he could only turn and strain another anxious look at his familia. This could be the last time he would see his Abuelito alive, but no matter what happened to Abuelito, he had told Juan that he would visit Juan's dreams many times in the war that Juan was entering by standing in line.

As America's filing young men snaked passed the large smelly, black and silver, hissing iron horse to board the train, Juan thought of his great grandfather's stories of the meaning of the train to his people. It had brought the whites faces to Matatlan and destroyed much of his ancestral culture. Many of the great acorn bearing, sacred flowered Golden Oaks of Matatlan had been sacrificed to fuel the hungry fire boxes of the iron wheeled steeds. Without the acorn the people starved and the white drivers and financiers of the iron horse continued to make progress.

Juan could see in the wheels of the great engine the honorable tears of his Great Grandfather when he would say, "The white eyes esay dey civilized our savaged living land by killing de rooted giants and by laying deir tracks upon de graves of our ancestors." Unfortunately for Juan the years of schooling and English speech therapy from the Mrs. Posts, Conneleys, and Marshes had made these stories only vague memories: flashes of light in the distant land of a small boy: the dreamwalking world of the Sequoya and the Olone/Miwok. Those memories were also filled with the summer swimming holes of the Guadalupe and Coyote Rivers. The sprawling oaks of Matatlan still stood boldly and strongly against the winter storms: the tierra of Abuelo's abuelo. As Juan stood on the platform in the long long line of patriotic and drafted youth, the stories of hissing, belching, iron horses and shining silver crosses set him and his familia wholly apart from the faceless thousands of the station. If he lived through this war he would have to take the time to find the reality in his great grandfather's words. Even his carnales and all their rayo could not take him on this quest for la trucha ruta.

The line of cars following the big northern driver railed and jerked their way through Matatlan over the graves of his people and culture to the U. S. Army induction center in Oakland, California. The newly christened induction center had been used as a holding pen when his father and uncle had been deported. From the induction center it was on to boot camp in Pittsburg, California. Camp Stoneman was out east of Matatlan. Then the trains would take Juan away from Matatlan for a long time.

As the conductor yelled, "All aboard," Juan glimpsed at the waving hands of his familia. Even with the noise of the recruits, crying rukas and the straining grunting sounds of the great iron horse, he heard "Hijo mío" and "Mi querido"! "Vaya con Dios, adiós." He waved from his closed train window. His hands could not touch their tears. Their voices, the key to his survival, would spirit him back to Matatlan.

A Camp Of Dust And Stone

Out east of Matatlan for nine months of each year was a dry hotland on the Sacramento San Joaquin River Deltas. As he quickly wiped the sweat from his forehead with his right hand to overcome the dryness, he gazed at the dry winter delta plain. The growers had drained and channeled the land to irrigate crops for a hungry nation. The Sarge told them that it was a drowned delta because the tidal lands were part of the San Francisco Bay. The land tanned by the hot sun, the trees yellowed by choking dust: a place to prepare to die.

Twentieth century technology was drowning the land and soil mining was turning the great delta bogs into dusty crop land. Only a few great Oaks survived the overgrazing and replacement by pear and walnut orchards. Juan had worked these hot, dusty orchards in the summers with his Father and Grandfathers. It seemed like the stain of the walnuts was still in his finger nails.

The new war and camp blossomed in the land full of history across the Carquinas Straits from Bencia. In 1849, the town of Bencia, the first capitol of California, became a harbor for the paddle wheelers that carried dream filled prospectors to the great gold fields in the Sierra Nevada Mother Load. In 1942, all that remained centered upon a small state historical park and a railroad bridge head.

The railroads, as newcomers in 1855, dominated the valley, gave Sacramento its economic status but strangled the roots of the land where the new camp was built. The land suffocated under the burden of this iron ribbon's stamp. Down river from the camp in the town of Martinez remained the home of John Muir, the first conservationist to get the attention of a President.

El Diablo, the great mountain manadknock dominated everything in sight. This mountain had been God's stronghold for the "peaceful" coastal Indians dancing merrily in the pages of the state school history textbooks. The strength of the never yielding mountain would not let Juan's ancestors give the land away to the death wielding invaders who took the land and destroyed this Indian paradise. The White Eyes called the Holy Mountain the Devil's Punch Bowl. The angry Miwok-Oloney nation used the mountain's great spirit to resist pacification.

Abuelito said that one of Juan's Great Great Grandfathers, Mixcoalt by name had fought the colonial efforts of Spain from the mountain fortress. El Diablo hung over the straits of Carquinas and the camp like a great gate to the agricultural heartland of Califas. Juan drew a strength from the history and roots of this place that helped him through the rigors and tedium of boot camp. The Army had used the killer railroad and bullets of steel to cut him off from everything but his hommies and his God's stronghold. Drilling in the shadow of the stronghold the hommies melded into steel jacketed killers for the red, white and blue. Rhythmic boots of war stamped the ancient land into dust.

The towns near the camp had names like Pittsburg and Port Chicago. Located as deep water ports like their eastern U.S. counterparts, Pittsburg, a sleepy little agricultural cross-roads, and Port Chicago, a Naval Weapons dump across the Carquinas from Mare Island naval base, resided as repulsive pustulent pimples on the golden land of the Oloney-Miwok. In between these forgotten hell-holes sweated Camp Stoneman.

"One. Two. Three. Four. We are civilians no more. One. Two. Three. Four. We are civilians no more." The Zooters landed in Camp Stoneman. It should have been called Camp Dust. The dust from marching Zooters stuck to Juan's body like bondo from a bad paint job. Everything about the place now was temporary and portable, even the dust moved twenty-four hours a day.

The camp was built fast, not to last. The barracks were thrown together so fast that the best part about them was the shine the recruits put on the floor. The Sarge rarely let them stay in the barracks anyway. He said, "Those barracks are your home boys. We had 'em built of cardboard so they would feel familiar ta yaal. However, for yous home boys, your living room is goin ta be six-foot deep foxholes. None of my boys are goin ta be brown-bagged and red-tagged before we leave dis here camp, unless I get ta do de baggin and taggin."

"Hey, Ramón," said Juan in a rare spare moment, "de truck dat Abuelito used to move de men en de family from field to field felt more like home dan de barracks and tents de Sarge has eshown us how to assemble."

"Dose tents esmell like a dirty gopher hole full of moldy yellow jackets," said Ramón The Poet.

"Dem tents esmell more like World War One latrine tanks," added Javier.

"Dey're eso crowded with esweating hommies dat dey're harder to walk through dan de obstacle courses de Sarge keeps making us build," concluded Juan.

"At least de esmell bedder dan dat doctor who did de physical on us in Oakland," said Eddie.

"Dat wasn't no physical, Eddie," said Juan. "All I did was cough when he said cough."

"I tink dat Doctor was passing us on de kind of cough jou made when he stuck his finger up jour asshole," commented Ramón the Poet.

"I just tink he was a pinche maricón, ese," asserted Roberto.

The hommies had found a living hell at the feet of El Diablo. The next set of recruits would have it made: they would get to train in the cardboard, slit trench dug camp that the hommies were building. Most of their 20-hour days that weren't spent building camp Stoneman, were spent marching with full packs in hot wool uniforms that fitted like a bad set of dirty gym clothes. Juan was sure that his uniform was left over from World War One like the Sarge and tent barracks.

Marching in long dusty lines, trying to look like soldiers, the hommies made excellent targets for any rifleman. When they weren't marching or building the Sarge found time for them to dig latrines, ammunition pits and foxholes. This skill was a lot more useful than marching when it came to combat.

Camp Stoneman had young men from all over the state, but people of color, except for the home boys were notable for their absence. These Crackers and Paddies weren't any better at being soldiers than the hommies, but the Sarge sure seemed to think they were. He had told the Hommies, "The only thing strong about you Mexes are your farts. In fact, your Mex farts smell so bad that they melt the creases out of my trousers." Somehow the Sarge's bombastic disdain united the hommies. They even became proud of the farts the army beans encouraged their bodies to blow and bomb. Yet this unity also separated them from the other soldiers.

The Sarge had told them that every soldier in the unit was dependent on all the other squads covering their backs. Juan wondered if perhaps it would a good idea to make an effort to know the other groups. On the other hand, it was a good feeling being surrounded by hommies who had the same sense of loss and loyalty that he did. Even so, because of ill feelings towards "Messicans" in the papers, Juan decided that there would be less trouble if he limited his contact with the "white" soldiers.

Juan's first experience of the finality and reality of war came on the day that hommies got their first 105 recoiless rifle demonstration. The idea of the weapon was to mount heavy support fire power on a the back of a jeep.

The Sarge told them, "Listen up, beaners. Use them big saucer brown eyes to feast upon the marvels of modern military engineering. This weapon is goin' ta win the war for ya. If you're lucky, you'll get to ride one of these to the front."

To Juan, the weapon looked like a tank without protective armor. It reminded him of Abuelo's story about the cucaracha that wanted to be an ant. Even before the demonstration Juan decided that only an unlucky fool would volunteer to ride the gun. The cannon mechanism was supposed to limit the recoil shock to the jeep, but everytime the cannon was fired the jeep and the crew were thrown around like rodeo riders on a brahma bull at a 4:00 P. M. charriada on Sunday.

"What these meatballs are going to show yous beaners is the art of trajectory and range finding," said the Sarge. "First they will fire a lob and then they'll shoot their own shell out of the air with a low angle shot. When yous can do that, yous gots it down. Now, watch the procedure, you're next."

"Fire." Juan watched the 105 crew ride the gun and drop the gun's point of aim to the level needed to blow the first shell out of the air with the second shell. "Fire," yelled the Sarge again. The shell blasted out of gun. As the gun recoiled it caught the edge of the gunner's helmet and ripped his head right off of his body. Juan never witnessed the perfect trajectory that allowed the two shells to hit and explode each other in the air. He was too busy watching the trajectory of the gunner's head that was still flying in the other direction. He never saw the landing of the head because his gazed became fixed upon the seatbelted headless body that was still riding the gun while squirting blood all over the rest of the 105 team. "Now let that be a lesson to yous ant brains," said the Sarge like this happening was an expected part of the demonstration, "Never buckle your helmet chin strap when your firing this weapon." Juan decided to puke on the ground instead of in his helmet. "What's the matter Guanito, is the wonderful army chow too good for your bean bag gut?"

"No, Sir, Sergeant, Sir," said Juan between heaves.

"Then climb up on the 105 and see if you can do it right."

Maybe Juan should have stayed with his Zuit in the LAPD jail. He made sure his chin strap was unbuckled, but he missed with both shots. Juan was one nervous cucaracha riding a gun. His shaking head and body, however, were still one.

The short time allowed for the young private's private thoughts were held by Conchita. He didn't even miss his mother as much as he missed Conchita. Juan never had felt before the void in his heart that Conchita's absence created. Letters from her on mail day were as precious as the thin gold ring she had placed on his finger, even if his limited reading ability made it difficult for him to comprehend them.

Just knowing that she was thinking of him made their separation more tolerable. Her thoughts for him were doves of peace in a war torn world of the stoney boot camp. Because of his limited writing ability he could not truly express to her how much he missed her. If she truly loved him, she didn't need his letters, anyways. Besides, his mother was always there to keep Concha from feeling lonely. He managed to get one letter off after the Red Cross workers told him that his Mother and Concha were inquiring about his well being.

Hi Family and Concha too,

What have you been up to? I've just completed my fifth week of bootcamp and it seems just like I just got here, even though it has been forever. For the last two months, I dug more latrines and foxholes than there are cucarachas in Califas. I saw a guy get killed last week!

I passed my marksmanship test. Ship me some salza to cut the grease in an unmarked box. The food here is lousy.

I just took my first writtens. It wasn't that hard cause I spent a bunch of nights explaining the stuff in the manual to the hommies here. The only thing that is holding me back is being out of shape. I lost twenty pounds. I've been trying to push myself as hard as I can to pass my endurance test.

Anyways, I hope to hear from you all real soon. Please write a letter. When you read this Concha, know that I   miss you a whole lot.

Love,

Juan

Juan knew the minute boot camp was completed, he would hot foot it back to Concha's soft, loving embrazos. On one of his cryptic postcards the Red Cross made him write, he told Concha to have his Zoot pressed and to make reservations at the Aragon Ballroom. Juan told Ramón The Poet, "I'm only living for and dreaming of the day when I'll be dancin' up a storm with my Angel."

"Don't dream too much, carnal, or de Sarge will be dancin' up jour ass," commented Ramón.

"Wake-up, yous Spics," said the Sarge. "This is no summer camp for girls. Today we finally got your new uniforms. The Army has decided to put the flag on you boys. I hope your brown stained assholes blend into the Red, White, and Blue. So, get on your fatigues and form a line. All I want to see are assholes and elbows."

"Boy," thought Juan, "we get to form another line."

The Sarge was always so racist in his remarks that Juan couldn't get serious over them anymore. "I heard that," said the Sarge. "This is the Army, not the pansy-ass brigade. So, move it! Move it, girls! Let's not miss our appointment with destiny. Move it Guwan. What's your brown ass need? An engraved, gold filled bad ass invitation?"

"No, Sir! Sergeant, Sir!" replied Juan with as much military bearing as he could muster. The Sarge liked to use opportunities like this to assign extra duty and push-ups.

"Then move it, pansey-ass," said the Sarge moving off to look for another target to spit at. The Sarge must have been in a good mood that instant because Juan didn't get assigned any extra duty for the first time since the Sergeant took a "liking" to him. Being the "center" of the Sarg's focus was not a good place to be.

The Sarge was a harder case than the walnuts that Juan had hulled in the orchards near the camp. His face was wrinkled and dried like a cut cot on a Matatlan drying flat. His mouth snarled like a smashed walnut shell. He walked like the L.A.P.D. bulls that hassled the cruising hommies in the shorts on Olympic Blvd. in Tortilla Flats. His shirt was starched so perfectly that his back would stay straight even if his spine were smashed by a three-point-five-rocket launcher. Plugs of tobacco fired out of his mouth like projectiles without targets. Juan always thought that in a tight squeeze the Sarge could spit the enemy to death.

The Sarge loved the word "asshole." He had a thousand stories about various situations an asshole could be found in. Whenever one of the recruits in Juan's squad had an excuse the Sarge would say, "Excuses are like assholes, everybody has one."

The Zooters in fatigues formed one of the Sarge's perfect lines and marched off to the Quarter Master's warehouse, the only place in the camp where the dust settled on everything. The Army gave the negroes the job of cleaning the warehouse, as if the Army thought that keeping the blacks in the dust pit and out of the sun would make them whiter and cleaner.

Getting this uniform was the Army way, all of the way. The Sarge always said, "There is the right way, the wrong way, and the Army way. You Mother jumpin' foul-ups are going to learn the Army way, or you won't live long enough to leave this camp!"

"Recruit," said the Supply Sergeant, "you look like a slob." Juan would have killed for those remarks if he had his drapes on, but in fatigues and in this line, being a slob seemed natural.

"The top of your body looks like an 38 regular, to me," the Supply Sergeant continued. Juan thought that the sergeant knew what he was doing, because that was his size. "We got any-more of those Reg 38's back there?" yelled the Supply Sergeant at a black private running with a stack of shoe boxes.

"No, Sergeant, Sah," said the black private. "We's all out of dem blouses, Sah."

"What we got back there, boy?" said the Supply Sergeant.

"We's got lots of dems 46 longs, Sah," replied the private while setting down the boxes on the counter. "We's got lots of 28 waist by 38 pants too, Sah."

"What size are them shoes?" said the Supply Sergeant.

"Dees here, Sah?" asked the private.

"No, the shoes that Tojo wears!" yelled the Supply Sergeant. "You still got cotton for brains, boy?"

"Yeh, Sah. I's mean, no, Sah," replied the private. "De are 11 triple E's, Sah."

"What we got in shirts, boy?"

"Same things we's got last time you asked Sergeant. We's gots a whole bushel of 17/5's and not much else," said the private. "The belts and socks are one size fits all, Sah."

"Did I ask you about the socks and belts, boy?" bellowed the Supply Sergeant.

"No, Sah, yous didn' says nothin', Sah," said the private moving off towards a huge stack of shoe boxes.

"Then shut your rubber lips, boy. I'll never figure out what Lincoln had in mind when he made it possible for you colored boys to join the Army. Well, beaner," said the Supply Sergeant, turning back to Juan. "I changed my mind. You looks like a 46 long blouse, 28 x 38 pants, a 17/5 shirt, and 11/triple E shoes. Here is a 7 and 3/4 hat," he said as he slapped a hat onto Juan's head. "Sign this requisition and the boys will issue you the set in that line over there. Next!" yelled the Supply Sergeant as Juan moved off towards the rear of the next line.

As Juan got to each new station, he handed the sheet to an out-stretched hand that grabbed the sheet and returned it with a garment that approximated the specifications on the sheet. Juan followed the line full of hommies with new folded clothes.

"Form a line in front of your bunks and prepare to become proud wearers of your country's flag," barked the Sarg. "You got four minutes to make inspection."

Juan thought the tailor in the barrio who had made his Zoot Zuit would be out of business in a day if he did things the Army way. He got his uniform and put on his socks. So far so good. He put on his new underwear. A little roomy, but his mother always bought his underwear a little big so he could grow into them. May be he would grow into these. He put on the stiff starched shirt. If you rolled up the sleeves and belted it, it would make Concha a neat shirt- dress. Next, on with the pants. The waist was perfect. Marvel of marvels at least they wouldn't fall down. The length of the trousers was another matter. If he was to grow into these, he would have to be six foot eight. Not likely to happen. Juan rolled up each leg about eight inches so he could get the shoes on.

Then came the shoes. Shoes! These weren't shoes! They were sleds. They were too wide to be skis. Maybe they were snowshoes. He slid his size eight B feet into the shoes. At least he could put them on without untying the laces. That was a nice feature. His Mamá was always yelling at him to untie his shoes before he put them on. "Jou will break down the heel Juan. If you ruin them, jour little brother won't be able to use them," she said. The blouse was something special. It was roomier than his barracks. There was enough material in the thing for his Abuela to make school clothes for all the kids in the family. By now, the muddy sweat on his forehead was allowing his cap to slide down to his ears. This must be a new look he thought. The enemy would miss him because he was lost in the uniform.

Juan stood tall in his new set of threads. He looked around at the other recruits who had finished dressing. He burst out laughing. He was beside himself with joy. Then the others started to laugh. All the hommies were wearing duplicates of his uniform. These were the saddest set of drapes you could ever have imagined.

"Attention," barked the Sarge. All the hommies tried to snap to. As they did, several of their pants fell down. "What't so funny, Guwanito. Wipe that smile off your ugly fudge face. You beaners are a disgrace to the flag you are wearing."

"Sergeant Sir, may I esay esomething?" asked Juan wishing that his tongue and brain were in another country.

"Spit it out, soldier, and it better be good. You'er supposed to be wearing the American, not Mexican flag!" replied the Sarge. "No one should represent the flag of this U.S. of A. as turd lice wrapped in a paper bag."

"Well, Sir, we really dun't wanta look like dis. De way we look es important to us, whether we are de flag or not. Dis es what dey gave us. We know dat jou will make it right, Sergeant, Sir."

"Right!" shouted the Sarge. "You Spics may be turd lice, But you are MY turd lice! No foul-up quartermaster is to stir up my turds! Those halfass clerks are messing with the flag, now. I told them that this would happen if we let the chocolate drops organize this outfit."

"We didn't organize dis foul-up Sarge, Sir," said Juan as the Sarge breathe all over Juan's face.

"Is the brown pit turd lice in my face trying to step up in the world by admitting that he is a Neegroo?" asked the Sarge.

"No, Sir, Sergeant Sir," responded Juan.

"Then keep your brown ass wiped face buttoned up, Guwanito," yelled the Sarge up Juan's nose. "Nobody messes with my flags." The Sarge pivoted upon his heels to address the line of hommies with pant clad ankles. "O.K. you horseshit, turd lice, strip to your skivvies. Return to your fatigues, fall in and prepare to assault the Quartermaster warehouse."

"Boy, dese flags are esure esweet memories in bitter times," murmered Ramón The Poet.

"I heard that, Shit Bucket," snapped the Sarge.

"I prefer de bitter memories en esweet times," whispered Juan.

"I heard that, too, Private Guano! Left, Left, Left," yelled the Sarge in Juan's ear.

The hommies turned in their new misfitted flags, but they were not issued new uniforms until boot camp graduation.

Juan saw the lack of a dress uniform during boot camp as a blessing. It was easier to pass inspection in fatigues and the uniform would be crisp and new when Concha's soft flesh would extend an embrazo.

One week before leaving boot camp the new flags arrived. For this set of flags, the Sarge pulled every string he could to make himself better than a baby-sitter for marble fudge dust covered brownies. He doublechecked every move the quarter master made at least three times. The Sarge said that he would 'make war on the Army way' if they fouled him up again. He told the hommies, "I'm madder than a wet hen with my feathers pushed the wrong way!"

The hommies, Juan included, decided that the Quartermaster used them to draw and quarter the Sarge. An ankle clad platoon was the Army's way of pulling the Sarge's pants down in front of the entire regiment. The Sarge's Spics made well dressed, "half decent flags" as they passed in review for the last time on the dust laden fields of Camp Stoneman. "Eyes right, Left, Left, Left, marble fudge, makes the score!" barked the sarge as he passed the C.O.

Dear Family and Concha too,

Every day more and more hommies show up here to the camp. The Sarge says we are the flag, but he treats us like serpents and scrub instead of eagles and Sequoias. He stomps all over us. He says that this will make us soldiers. I think he just hates Chucos and hates that he needs us to fight for this country.

You don't have to keep bugging the Red Cross to make me write. I will write that by myself when I don't have anything to say that will be censored out.

The Sarge has us marching over ground so much that we have worn the grass off the land. The laundry is so full of dust that our green uniforms are turning a funny kind of green yellow. They need Spanish Grandma up here to get things organized.

The Sarge says that we'll never get organized enough to do much more than pick Mussolini's grape harvest. But, he has never seen us fight for real. There is a rumor that we may get some leave after boot camp. If we do and I can hitch a ride to see you all real soon.

If you are reading this, Concha, you know what I wanta say. Use that fancy imagination of yours when you are thinking of what I'm thinking about you.

Love,

Juan

Marble fudge hommies covered with dust in the hot Matatlan sun in the Shadow of El Diablo. No camp guns or sarges were going to step on them. "One. Two. Three. Four. We are civilians, no more."

FOUR DAYS OF BLISS

In the damp and dreary early morning tulle fog that daily shrouded Camp Stoneman in late winter, Juan stuffed his kit with all his belongings. He thumbed the testament from Concha as he gently placed it in his bag. The Sarge had told them that not even a speck of their shadow was to remind the universe that they had ever occupied this space. He locked his bag; checked his new uniform form straight creases; shouldered his bag, and quickly marched to the sergeant's quarters at the end of the barracks to get his orders. The sergeant was busily handing out passes and vouchers to the eager soldiers through the upper half of his open dutch door.

The sergeant checked Juan out to see that he was fit to represent the U. S. Army off base. "PFC Guano, make sure of this. There will be no A.W.O.L. zooters in my platoon. Know this and know this well. Even if the U. S. Army gives up on yaal, I'll come looking for yaal. I will see yaal in the Borrego in one week. Is that bean fart brain of yours getting my drift, Guano!?"

"Yes, Sir, Sergeant, Sir," answered Juan. "I didn't know jou were goin' ta be dere too, Sarge."

"Count on it, Guano!" yelled the Sarge. "You are stuck with me for the duration of this damn war! Do you have your traveling orders?"

"I got dem in my inside blouse pocket, Sir, Sergeant Sir," said Juan.

"Then what the hell are you doing here, Guano? You don't want ta waste your seven-day leave looking at me, and I sure as hell don't enjoy looking down at your sorry asshole," snarled the Sarge.

"Right jou are, Sergeant, Sir," responded Juan.

"Then fall-in and get your mable fudge fart-blown asshole on the train!" ordered the Sarge.

"Yes, sir, Sergeant, Sir!" barked Juan as he saluted sharply and pivoted to leave the barracks.

Juan ran out of the barracks to get in line to get on the train for Oakland. From there he would change trains to Los Angeles. The snaking file of home bound hommies and Juan, clad in their new flags with brand new green currency in their pockets bragged on all of the women that would notch their guns before this leave was up. On the other hand, Juan dreamed of how he could convert his hundred dollars into a last fling with Concha before he was sent to the Borrego.

Leave at last. Even the grey clouds of cigarette smoke and GI/hommie banter of the crowded old army green pullman coach could not keep Juan's thoughts in check. The very thought of a moment with Concha in the arms of his Zuit was a visualization of heaven on earth for him. "How could the being with your one and only become so central to your own feeling of whole?" Juan asked of himself.

"Oyes, Vato, get jour feet on de earth and off jour ruka, eso we can get a card game goin', ese," said Javier.

"There will be plenty of time for cards, ese, once dis lurching bucket of bolts estarts to roll," countered Juan.

"Can't jou esee dat de married man only has eyes por his novia, ese?" asked Ramón the Poet.

For the first time the black soot belching iron horse rolled off in a direction his heart desired: home and Conchita!

The changing of trains in Oakland took forever. The beautiful orange Daylight streamliner steamed for Los Angeles before Juan could make his connections. He had to take an unnamed milk-run down the coast. He called Abuelo from the Oakland Mole so the family in San José could meet with him for a couple of hours during the layover there.

As the train pulled into the old Cahalan Station in San José, Juan peered through the dusty windows of the no name train for the first glimpses of the family. As he passed over the Stockton street tressel he spotted Abuelo's battered old turquoise blue Ford pick-up next to the freight loading docks. "Abuelo can't be too far away from dat old truck, he never lets it out of his esight when he es outside of de barrio," said Juan to himself.

"San José," called the conductor, "Change here for Morgan Hill, Gilroy, Salinas, and all points south ta Santa Paula. For the Lark and the express ta Las Angelizees, there will be a three-hour lay over. All those heading north up the pennisula to San Fran and all stations in between can stay on broad this train. We leave in five minutes."

Juan gathered up his bags and the small gifts he had purchased in the Oakland Mole for the family, checked under his seat and in the overhead rack for any miss laid items, jerked and pulled his way to the car entrance and got off the train.

"Dey aren't feeding you, mijo, jou are eso flaco," said Abuela as she greeted Juan with a warm powerful abrazo. "Why didn't you tell me jou would be eso hungry? I only brought a dozen tamales and an esmall olla of arroz y frijoles in dis cajita."

"Whatever jou brought, Abuela, es just what I need," said Juan as his eyes moistened.

"But what about jour compadres, Juanito? Dey look hungry, too. If you could estay longer, I could take really good care of jou and jour compadres, Juanito," said Abuela as she fingered the strong material of Juan's new uniform.

"We can only estay a couple of hours, Abuela," said Juan as he motioned to his six compadres to come over and meet his Abuela.

"I dun't hardly ever get to esee into jour heart for de light in jour ojos, mijo," commented Abuela.

"Where is Abuelo and Spanish Grandma, Abuela?" asked Juan trying to avoid Abuela's smiling, inquiring, sad eyed gaze.

"Dey went to get jou esometing out of dey troka. Dun't let de Army put out de light in jour eyes, Chivito Cucaracha. Dey are esuch beautiful ojitos, Juanito!" said Abuela as tears flowed freely down her cheeks. She pulled him towards her face and gave him another tender but strong abrazo. Her hug almost took his breath away.

"I'll be all right, Abuela," said Juan trying to mask the loss of breath.

"Dats what jour papá esaid when La Migra took him away from me, Chivito! I don't want ta hear any of dose mentiras de machos."

"I could never lie to jou, Abuela," said Juan.

"Dat's de way it eshould be, Juanito. Dis Army gives me eso little time to feed jou," said Abuela as she reflected on who were to feed Juan in battle.

"It's O.K., Mrs. Galván," said Ramón the Poet feeling Abuela's agony. "We got esome chits to eat here in de estation," he continued as reached into his pocket and pulled his vouchers.

"Maybe I could go to a comadre who lives about two blocks from here to get esome comida for jour beautiful amigos, Juanito," said Abuela. "Dey can't move on estómagos que dat are chewing demselves."

"Do what jou must do, Abuela," said Juan as his abuela turned and went off to get more comida for her warriors.

"Jour Abuela es real nice, Juan," said Javier. "Do jou really think eshe can get us all esome comida Mexicana? After dat boot camp eslop I could eat a thousand tamales in one esitting."

"If my abuela esaid eshe wuz goin' ta get us, comida, eshe will get us comida even if eshe has to pick de beans herself to get it," asserted Juan.

Out of the crowds of soldiers and commuters in the station emerged Juan's Spanish Grandma carrying a large bundle. "Have you been saying your prayers, mijo?" inquired Spanish Grandma.

"Sí, Grandma," said Juan as she stepped up to her soldier and used her long arms to give him a clean squeeze.

"Are these the friends that Abuela is rushing off to get comida for?" she asked.

"Sí, Grandma," answered Juan. "Amigos, dis es my Espanish Grandma, señora Cabrillo."

"I brought you a bundle of socks that you can share with your compadres," said Spanish Grandma.

"Where did jou get all of dese esocks, Grandma?" asked Juan.

"I collected them from all of my friends in the St. Joseph Society of San José. The Red Cross said that our boys need all the socks they can get," said Spanish Grandma.

"The Sarge esaid dat jou can't march in combat boots with hard esocks and frozen feet, señora Cabrillo," commented Jaime.

"We will esurely be tinking of jou when we see de other guys wit esore feet, señora," commented Jorge.

Spanish Grandma reached into the cavernous bag she called a purse and pulled out a brightly colored package. "I knitted these myself for you, Juanito. They are done in señor Cabrillo's favorite colors. They are all the rage. They are knee high, brown and gold argyles with a hidden inner stripe."

"Dese are really eswell, Grandma," said Juan. "They are too good to wear inside of combat boots. Where is Abuelo?"

"He'll be back with the comida that Abuela is rounding up for you and your friends. Those socks aren't for combat, mijo. They are 'prayer socks.' With every stitch I prayed that the sacrifice made by señor Cabrillo would bring you home to us."

"Thanks, Grandma."

"I am now making you a new suit of clothes for when you return from the war, Juan, so don't go and lose anymore weight. I'm patterning it after what señor Cabrillo called the continental cut. I'm looking for a good black worsted wool pin stripe so it can replace the zoot zuit you burned to please my daughter. Concha will be so proud of you in it."

"That will be really nice, Grandma since the only suit I have now is this uniform," lied Juan for the fifth time.

"I tought jou estill had jour zuit, carnal," whispered Ramón the Poet.

"Cállate, ese," whispered Juan with a wink of his left eye.

"What did he tell you, Juan?" asked Spanish Grandma.

"I think I esee Abuelo with de comida," said Juan while avoiding Spanish Grandma's inquiring gaze.

"It's good eseeing jou, mijo," said Abuelo as he came up to Juan and the rest of his party. "Your arms look estrong and fit. Too bad jou won't be with me to eshort hoe on Murphy's farm. With my brains and jour muscles, we could clean-up. We could harvest eso much together. Dun't let dem cabrones harvest jour life."

"I'll be all right, Abuelo," said Juan softly.

"I wish I could be with jou to eshield jour face from de anger of Huitlilopochtli!" murmured Abuelo intensely.

"I'm with my carnales, Abuelo. We can take care of anybody who wishes to harm us," said Juan.

"Cucaracha, jou are like a canning tomato dat es to green to be picked and too ripe for de pot."

"I'm not too green, Abuelo," said Juan.

"Jou are green enough to bleed red blood," said Abuelo.

"What are jou esaying Abuelo?" asked Juan.

"You are ripe for war, mijo, but too green to fight it," said Abuelo. "Eshotgun, I have long fought the war of the living and the hungry. I have eseen truck loads of esquashed tomatos rotting on the side of de road. I just know that in my heart of hearts, I will never esee in dis earth jou again."

"We better get to dis great esmelling comida before it gets, cold, Abuelo," said Juan trying to avoid the meaning in Abuelo's last comment.

"All honest tings become cold in order to provide warmth and esurvival to others," commented Abuelo as he handed the box full of hot ollas to Juan. "Before jou eat dis whole box, Eshotgun, and de black iron horse dat rips jou away from my tree and takes jou to jour novia and de cabrones war, make esure dat jou eshare one tamal with me in de front eseat of my pick-up like we use ta when jou were just a little cucaracha full of preguntas."

"Dat will be a real honor, Abuelo. I miss dose fun times a

whole lot, too. Dey were esweet moments in bitter days," said Juan as tears of remembrance filled his eyes.

"And now, Juan?" asked Abuelo. "Eshare wit dis old man's tears, a young man's memory in dis eshort forever time of loading and unloading of our family roots."

"Jou got it, Abuelo," said Juan. "Dey got me a job driving a half-track in de Army. Dose times of dirt road driving with jou are really paying off."

"Just make esure, Eshotgun, dat de check es not esigned with jour espilling blood," answered Abuelo as he hugged his Little Eshotgun. "Jou have estrengtened de humility in my root, and eshown me de pride in my tree. You are de macho of my esword. Do not draw me in anger," whispered Abuelo loudly in Juan's right ear.

"Gracias, Abuelo," said Juan.

"Jour abuelos are maza at its best, carnal," said Ramón the Poet.

The carnales ate a great meal at the station. They all put on their new soft socks. "Dis es an esweet memory in a bitter time," said Ramón the Poet.

The soldiers hugged Juan's grandparents. The station master announced the departure of the Lark Sleeper Express for Los Angeles.

"Give our abrazos to de family in Los Angeles," said Abuelo with his last hug. "Tell them dat we will be moving down dere in a few months."

"Kiss jour dear little wife for me," said Abuela with yet another hug. "Let her know who loves her de best, mijo."

"I have the sisters making scarves for you boys," said Spanish Grandma. "Make sure that you read your Bibles," she continued as she blessed Juan with the sign of the cross on his forehead. "Even if I'm always the last one, His sign is always first, Juan."

As hands waved and kisses were blown, the sleek black and silver streamliner roared out of the station into the darkness of the Matatlan night. With each rhythmic turn of the great wheels, it sped Juan to the loving arms of his Conchita.

The Lark in Abuelo's tree was singing the family's sweetest song.

* * *

When Juan awakened the next morning, the conductor was announcing the imminent arrival of the train in Los Angeles' Union Station. As agreed upon, Concha was waiting at the train station.

The Lark ground to a slow smooth stop. The soldiers anxiously got their duffle bags down from the overhead racks, stood in line and started to get off the train. Some of them started looking for their families and loved ones. Others gathered in groups to decide which spot on Olvera street they would stop in first. And still others worked their way from their seats to the coach doors.

Self appointed "hospitality ladies" in very short skirts descended on the servicemen who had already made it off the train, like flies to a pile of fresh hot dog manure.

"Get a load of dem legs," said Javier as they peered through the train windows and inched their way closer to the end of the car.

"Jou keep jour legs, carnal," said Martin. "I like nalgas puras de las rucas, not nalgas flackas de las gringas."

"Just think with de head on jour shoulders and not de one in jour pants," said Rogelio.

"Of course, little Juanito, is all gone over his ball and chain," said Jorge. "Isn't dat la trucha, married man?"

"Jour just celoso, mano," asserted Juan. "Dere eshe es horita. Hay lo watcho, carnales!"

"Dun't do anything we would do, ese," called out Ramón the Poet.

"I not getting off dis tren to write poetry, ese," retorted Juan.

Juan jumped from the second step on the platform. He heard his name. "Juanito, I'm here. I'm here!" yelled Concha deliriously.

Juan saw her and ran towards her. He dropped his duffle bag, stretched his arms towards her, held her as tightly as his heavy woolen overcoat would allow and kissed her and kissed her, "Oh, how I have missed you, Concha!"

Concha twirled in her military skirt and blazer. In Juan's honor she was wearing khaki green: the "soldier" on the home-front. She looked at Juan and whispered, "Now that you are here I'm never going to let you go. We are going to be alone for four exciting days. We will see the family on your last day, Juan. How selfish of me for not sharing you with anyone. We will be together without anyone to tell us anything. Just you and me."

"Do we have a ride home? Where es de family?" asked Juan.

"As I told you on the phone, Juan. We will see them on your last day. I'm driving," said Concha.

"What do jou mean jou're driving, Concha?" asked Juan as he wondered in what condition he would find his car.

"I've been planning this joyful adventure to continue our honeymoon for at least four more days, Juan," asserted Concha. "All you have to do is be your charming self. We are going to Big Bear in our 36' Ford. My boss loaned us his summer cabin for four days."

"But, it es estill winter. It will be cold in de mountains, Concha." Juan remarked.

"Not with me around, Juan." she laughed. "Let's get out of here, Juan. Let's go to that old cabin with the big porch. Your boots from the slaughter house are in the trunk of the car because the snow will be deep."

"How do jou know it has a big porch, Concha?" asked Juan.

"He put a picture of it on the company bulletin board when he announced that the tellers with husbands on leave could use it during the winter."

"Oh!" commented Juan with a big sigh of relief.

"How is your dear friend, the Sergeant?" Concha teased.

"Forget dat Sarge for de next four days, Conchita. Where did jou park de carro?"

"It's in the lot behind the Placita Church, Juan. I thought we could stop in the church to light a candle to La Virgen."

"Whatever jou esay, Conchita."

The young loving couple walked the one block from the front of Union Station to the Placita Church. They dipped their right hands in the font, genuflected and made the sign of the cross near the front entrance. Then they quickly strode towards the candles just in front of the statue of the Virgin. Concha took a long wooden match from the small tin cup, struck the match and nervously lit the candle. They each silently prayed as they held each other's hand.

Concha looked at the Virgin and tenderly said, "Thank you, Virgin for bringing Juan back to me. And thank you for giving me four days of leave to be with my Juan." Concha continued to pray for about five minutes. Juan remained silent throughout. Concha looked at Juan and whispered, "Let's go to the car, Juan. Our honeymoon has been sanctified. La Virgen is blessing our four days together. In this holy place before La Virgen, Juanito, I want you to remember that I love you always, Juan!"

"I love jou very much, too, Conchita!" emoted Juan.

They kissed spiritually con respeto. They stood up and walked quickly to the front door exit. They stopped, genuflected on one knee, stood up again. Juan picked up his duffle bag and quickly walked side by side with his soulmate to the car.

Four days of leave from Concha's job. The larking leave equaled four days of care free adventure that lead to a deceptive responsibility for each other's love.

"Do you have to wear that uniform the whole time, Juan?"

"I dun't have to wear it in bed, Concha, why do jou ask?"

"This is our four days, Juan, not the army's."

"Does dat mean dat jou brought my Zuit."

"Are you serious, Juan? Do you want to dampen these few

precious days with another lie? Isn't one war at a time enough for you?"

"I'm just trying to make jou happy, querida."

"Oh, Juanito, maybe I ought to do a Joan Crawford and dump your hot brain on the cold snow."

"Just get us to de cabin, Concha while I get esome of dis food you have in de back seat."

"Make me a sandwich too, Juan. I've been so excited about what we are going to be doing these next four days that I forgot to eat!"

"O.K., janilla. I hope jou didn't forget anythin' else, esa," said Juan as he opened an olla of carnitas and made her a burrito.

"Don't worry, hot pants. I've haven't fallen off any bicycles lately," Concha retorted.

"Dese carnitas look as good as de tamales Abuela made for los carnales in San José last night," said Juan chosing to ignore the challenge in Concha's remark. "Did jou make dis estuff?"

"What do you think, Juanito? I know how to make a lot of stuff, soldier boy," said Concha with a teasing wink of her right eye.

"All I'm esaying es dat dey look like good carnitas, Concha," said Juan, again not choosing to bite into Concha's double meaning.

"Then I'm glad you like them, Juanito, because I made them."

"Do jou plan ta make any estops on de way up to de cabin, Concha?"

"I want to make sure we get to the cabin before dark, Juan."

"My Abuelo always taught me dat de only light jou need es enough to esee tree feet en front of jour feet.

"When did he tell you that?"

"He told me dat on one dark night in Mt. Madonna."

"Let's stay on track until we get to the cabin, Juan."

"Whatever jou esay, querida. I'm in de dark already. I'm just happy to be with jou."

"You'll see the light in my eyes tonight, Juanito," Concha teased and laughed.

They got to the cabin by two o'clock in the afternoon. The bright late winter sun sparkled upon the deep blue waters of the mountain lake. The snow clad lakeshore and red jeffery pines added to the peaceful serenity. White sky yachts cruised across the heavens predicting a cold late winter storm. The two room cabin with the big porch and huge stone fireplace looked like it had been designed by a Disney cartoonist. The ice capped snow crunched rythmically beneath their feet as they plodded back and forth from the car to the cabin unloading the year's worth of supplies that Concha had packed for their four days.

"You had better change into your work clothes, Juan, so you can chop some wood for the fire place tinder box because it is supposed to snow tonight."

"How much wood do jou want, Concha," asked Juan.

"Enough to keep me hot and bothered, Juan," teased Concha again.

Juan couldn't get into his work clothes fast enough to suit him. The ax flew through the wood pile with the expertise of a latrine digger. The word "bothered" bothered him. Wood chopping was hot work.

"Your mother gave us some whip cream and liquor de café for an ice cold dessert tonight, Juanito," announced Concha through the window over the sink.

Love was a whole lot more than a splintered thing that night. Concha tried to plant a new tree. The creamy desert flowed and made them feel serenely secure admist the gathering clouds of the storm.

The next morning at dawn, Juan awoke to the call of his Sarge, "Get your splintered asshole out of the sack, Guano." Juan leaped to the floor before he remembered that the graceful soft form next to him was Concha and not his duffle bag. He threw on his great coat and stepped out the cabin door onto the snow covered porch. In the morning light of the receding storm he could make out the distant Mojave Desert far below on the eastside of the cabin. The blowing dust of the desert reminded him that he had only three days left in the snow covered fairy-land of mountain joy. For those next three days, Juan chopped wood as Concha planted his roots again and again.

The morning of the fifth day they dug the car out of the snow, packed the remainder of the year's worth of supplies, cleaned the cabin, and headed back to East Los and the family.

Each member of the family, including his parents and Concha's mother tried to act bravely about the shortness of their time with Juan. Only once did his mother cry uncontrollably when Juan asked how Benjamín was doing. "They are going to take both of you away from me!" she cried. His sisters and his mother made sure that all of his favorite comida was on the table at each meal. Juan figured by the two-inch expansion of his belt that he had put ten pounds on that the Sarge would take great joy in wearing off of him.

His father got up early during the morning of the day of departure for the special military train for the Borrego. "Dis war has made a lot of work for de barrio, Juan. De white soldiers tink we are doing too well at deir expense and raid us each semana de fin. I'm glad you burned dat Zuit and will be out of here before dey come back to rape our women and burn our homes dis weekend."

"Papá, dis really worries me. Are de women and Conchita esafe here?" asked Juan anxiously.

"I go get Concha at the bank and each of jour sisters at dier eschool every evening to make esure dat dey get home O.K. I even walk Concha right up to her mother's house next door. It's de least I can do por jou, hijo."

His buddies came for Juan in a cab to pick him up to go to the Union Station. There they would take the military train to the secret base in the Borrego Desert. The goodbyes were short and sad. Tears flowed once more. Juan held Concha very close to his heart and told her, "I will esee jou esoon, querida. I love jou more dan my life."

"I will be waiting, Juan. Always waiting," she replied softly through her tears.

Juan got in the cab with the carnales. The parting soldiers waved goodbye to Juan's warm caring family.

At the station, the conductor yelled, "All aboard," as all the green clad faceless soldiers filed onto the train and prepared to face a new world: to the slaughter or for the slaughter.

The lark stayed in L. A. Her melancoly song haunted Juan in the whistle of the locomotive throughout the day long trip.

LAST DANCE AT THE ARAGON

The mid summer in the Borrego Desert meant super hot dry weather. High noon meant 114 degrees in the shade on a daily basis. It was no summer camp for sissies.Learning to drive a half track when there were only a few broken down jeeps and commandered green painted farm equipment was difficult. Juan learned how to fire the B.A.R. and the 105 Recoiless Rifle without getting his own head blown off. The more he trained, the more he realized that he and the hommies like him were still green tomatos on the Sarge's barbeque.

The letters from Abuelo that the army routed to the secret base in the Borrego were full of suggestions for strategic thinking, but the Sarge said that they were not to think, but to follow orders.

"The day yous marble fudge boys start to think is the day the other side wins the war," said the Sarge.

"Don't worry, Sarge, we've kicked butt and smashed ass before," asserted Rogelio.

"The Japs and Krauts train from birth on how to slash your soft green assholes!" snapped the Sarge. "They know how to fight and die. They'er fanatics and killers."

"So are we, Sarge," said Martin.

"You candy asses still miss your mommies. You can't even smash your own ass in a latrine. You sorry butts all fight like a one-legged man in an ass kicking contest. You won't be killers until you've seen wiggling body parts in your foxhole."

"How are we goin' ta get to be killers when all de training we get is on how to put up field latrines, Sarge?" asked Juan.

"Private Guano, ass draggin', mommie suckin', bean eatin' recruits need big holes for dumpin' and reamin'. Yoal act like you'er goin' ta a dance with the Japs and Krauts. The only jitter bug you're goin' ta be doing is the pissin' jitters in your shoes with or without latrines."

"When we goin' ta get some real fighting equipment, Sarge?" asked Juan.

"When yual need it, Guano. Right now, all you brown toed assholes need is these fourteen-day passes I got you so I won't hear anymore of yoals sorry ass, tit suckin' stories.

The trainees were surprised with joy.

"I didn't hear my mouth say you were dismissed, fudge balls. Before you leave here, you are to police the area so that your mother will be happy to eat off the ground. In case anybody asks you weren't here and this place isn't here. Lose lips sink ships."

"Do we pack up all our gear, Sarge?" asked Ramón the poet.

"Any dung heap that thinks he can leave before his kit is packed perfectly stays here and digs the next group a new set of latrines. Your weapons will be cleaned and you, people, will pass a dress inspection before I cut your traveling orders. The train is leaving in three hours. If you are on it, you will get a free ride to L. A. and an extra day to find your tit and stroke your dick."

Juan made the train. No time to call home. Rogelio and Martin got latrine duty. Javier and Jorge missed the train. Ramón the poet saved Juan a window seat.

The dusty bone rattling, smoke belching antique that gave them the free ride to L. A. jerked its way into the Union Station at 10:08 P. M. Juan called Concha's mother's house from the station. Concha and his father came down to get him. They arrived home at 1:00 A.M. Concha's mother and Juan's mother had a fiesta ready when they got there.

Since Concha couldn't get away from her job at the bank except for Fridays and Mondays, Juan used his free days to cruise with his hommies and talk with his father. His Papá worked the graveyard shift at the new Douglas aircraft plant in Santa Monica. His mother was working swing shift in the Del Monte Cannery. The fourteen days were split into workdays and fun nights. One moment the hearts were together; the other moment, split.

His father told Juan about a resort down by Pacific Ocean Pier and worked out some reservations there for a four-day weekend for Juan and Concha. The guys on his Papá's shift even passed the hat to help pay for a couple of the nights. The family came up with the rest.

Juan had arrived on Monday. By Thursday he was so restless just wanting to be alone with Concha the whole day. Early that Friday Concha and Juan left for the resort in their '36 chopped Ford. Concha and Juan spent the weekend at Venice Beach just enjoying themselves to no end. Concha found a large abalone shell at Muscle Beach. As she held the shell up to her right ear, she listened to the strange echoing sounds of an altered reality. For the first time, Concha heard her heart in a different place.

Juan ran after her shapely golden form as she glided over the sand. He acted like a little boy who had found a new toy. He forgot the hot dusty and choking dry sands in Borrego: the bitter days to the slaughter and for the slaughter. The lapping sounds of the beach songs were vastly different: no more war chants; only soft melodious love songs.

The two of them threw sand at each other and then rapidly ran into the blue cold of the sparkling Pacific Ocean. The soft caress of the white seafoam salted the memory in their hearts. The time flew so fast that the secondhand did not have time to rest.

Concha whispered in Juan's ear, "I wish I could be with you here forever. You are like the disappearing snowman in the mountains. You are with me for a few days and then you are waving goodbye as you melt into the wind blown sky."

"Please don't jou worry about what es gone, I'm here right now. Enjoy de moment, Concha, as it es ours forever!"

"I agree, Juan. I never want to forget this sweet memory but my bitter tears remind me of you in a soldier's uniform. You are becoming a stranger with a hard face like an eagle from the other side of the mountain."

"Dat's one of Abuelo's lines, Conchita." retorted Juan.

"So be it, Juanito!" she snapped. "But when you left the last time, I felt so lonely that I kept looking for you everywhere I went. Yet, while I couldn't see you I could feel you out there somewhere getting ready for war."

"I pray dat I can be with jou but everytime I estart de gunfire interrupts my prayer, querida. My great urge es to take off my esoldier's uniform just to be with jou like in de old days of just last esummer." said Juan.

"Juan, while you were gone the last time, my boss got a telegram from the Armed Forces. The Red Cross notified the head teller that her son had been killed in Corregidor. For a moment I thought that telegram was for me. I saw my friend crying aloud so lonely, so afraid. The rest of us stared at each other just trying to hold back our tears. Since that day I saw your soldier's uniform very differently."

"But it es estill de esame suit of clothes, Conchita. I'm no different."

"You are so close to you, Juan that you can't feel the change I see. When I wait for your Dad to bring me home, all I hear is that soldiers and zoot zuiters are killing each other. No matter what you wear you remind me of a skull," Concha remarked with a distant look.

"De eskull of de Abalone, Concha, es its home," said Juan as he tried to bring her back to his tree.

The last day on the beach had its twist of sand blown all the way from Borrego on the Santa Ana Winds. The Día de los Muertos was approaching fast in the hot hands of the Headless Horsemen.

On their way back to her mother's house in East Los, Concha asked, "What are you wearing to our dance at the Aragon next weekend, Juanito?"

"Why do jou ask, Conchita?"

"I need to know so I can make an outfit that matches yours, Juan."

"Just wear your little red esequin dress I like eso much. Jou look like Ginger Rogers in it. Many a night I have fallen asleep while dream walking with jou in dat little dress."

"But I only wore that 'little dress' as you call it, when you were in your Zuit, Juan!" Concha snarled angrily. "Does that mean you intend to wear your Zuit?"

"Jou married me in dat, Zuit, Concha."

"I married you, Juan I would have done that even if you walked into the placita Church naked. Besides, the City Council has passed a law making the wearing of your beloved Zuit illegal."

"Eso now jou want me ta go ta de dance, naked?" asked Juan.

"Yes, if it is a choice between the uniform and the Zuit."

"Naked, I'm dead, Concha."

"Then what are you without me, Juanito?"

"I'm me, Concha."

"Then go dance naked by yourself and wrap yourself up in your arms and make love to your naked self."

"Look, Concha, all I want es to have an esweet memory of jou in dese bitter times. I want ta leave jou with a memory of me at my best."

"Don't ask me to swallow chocolate beans without sugar, Juan. Why do you have to wear that Zuit once more? Don't you know how heavy my heart is to see the way I saw you as my groom."

"I'm tired of fighting dis battle over a few lousy rags, even if dey are de most beautiful rags in de world. I'll wear whatever jou want, Conchita."

"Then are you going to wear the uniform, Juan?"

"Remember dat uniform dat escares jou was forced upon me. I chose de drapes, myself," Juan answered. "All I haveta go dancing in are my Zuit and my dress uniform, and I wanta be out of de army for at least one night of dis leave."

"That's a poor excuse upon which you wish to risk so much. What if you get caught out of uniform and they arrest you for being in a Zoot Zuit?" asked Concha.

"I don't care about dat!" said Juan. "Dey already caught me, Conchita. Dat's why I'm wearing dis uniform. Dey P. D. used it to esplit up de barrio. I'm not wearing dese khakis because I'm in love with dem!"

"Then you are fighting, as your Abuelo would say, in five directions at the same time, Juan: the battle with the barrio, the one with the army, the lie with your mother, the war with me and the one with yourself. Either way you go here, Juan, you are a skull to me, again!"

"Dat's no problema for an águila in de middle of his bowl, Conchita. Like jou esaid, anyways I go out from here, I'm a burned eskull," said Juan as he stared at the floor of the Ford.

"I just want you to be honest with me and your mother, Juan."

"Jou want honesty? Den here's a little honesty. I just want to get out of dis situation alive, Concha!"

"Are you really saying that if we burn that old Zuit that we are killing you?"

"I already told jou dat trucha, Concha."

"Then, if that dumb Zuit means that much to you, Juan, be a man of your convictions and tell your Mother the truth. If you don't, you'll have me fighting two wars for you. I'm not your Spanish Grandma at the bottom of your list."

"Will jou go out with me in de Zuit if I tell my mother, Concha?" asked Juan trying on his little boy look.

"No, Juan, I can't!" shouted Concha with her big mamá voice.

"Why not, Concha?"

"Didn't you hear what I have been tellin you, Juanito?"

"Tell me again, Conchita."

"Oh, Juan! You can be so thick at times."

"Thick roots are goodta have, Janilla."

"That's not what I'm talking about and you know it, Juan!" snapped Concha. "I'm afraid of what will happen to you if we do go out with you in that Zoot Zuit. You can't dance your way out of a war, Juan."

"But, Conchita, dat es what I am talking about. I'm more afraid of what will happen to me if I don't wear de Zuit at de dance, Concha. I'm no coward. You see, Janilla, in my Zuit, jou are my home."

*   *   *

The Sarge had told them that they were fighting a war against the aggression of dictators and facists. In his uniform he was fighting for the right to wear his Zuit. The risking of being out of uniform in order to be Concha's groom once again would have been worth it if she had felt about the Zuit the way he did. The Sarge had also told them that they were fighting this war to make the "home of the brave and the land of the free" safe for their love ones. Making Concha feel safe in the barrio, even if it meant wearing the uniform of death, was even more important than wearing his Zuit. Being her man was more important than being just a man. He was home in his Zuit, but the center of home was Concha in his eagle arms.

When the sweet memories of the barrio glowed, los carnales were in their colors and Concha cloaked him in her love. Dancing at the Aragon, even if for only one night, was a true way to honor the flag and the drapes. The four-hour dance in this special civilian place made the war go away for an evening, even though most of the hommies were in uniform.

Juan's eyes were on distant fronts although they had to look through Concha's eyes to see them. Scuttle-butt had it that those who got a fourteen-day pass went overseas almost immediately upon reporting to their next station.

For Juan and Concha the dance at the Aragon became that fleeting moment when their two hearts moved gracefully and effortlessly across the ballroom floor as if their feet rhythmically styled their own mood of the tune. Their hearts danced together: love full of the bitterness in the sweetest of times and of the sweetness in the bitterest of times: a space to be remembered always. It is a sin to tell a lie: the space and time of this very precious moment of truth.

"I love dancing with jou, querida," said Juan softly into Concha's ear. "Jou make me proud to be a man."

"That is good Juan. I'm glad I can make you feel that way. You are my man, Juanito," said Concha María. "You take care of him and bring him back to me."

"Nothing can happen to me. I'm not worth killing, querida," said Juan as he took a deep breath and filled his lungs with the sweet musty Aragon air filled with the smell of stale perfumed smoke.

"Don't talk like that, Juan," responded Conchita. "You are all that is special in the world to me. You know how Mamá fears that you will be gassed like my father. She said that the last war sent her back a half alive dead man. Don't let them do that to you, Juan."

"Are jou telling me to not come home if I'm wounded, or que dat I have esome part of me espread on de tierra de mis enemigos, querida?" asked Juan.

"I'm just saying be careful, Juan," replied Concha.

"Ramón de Poet esays que a careful esoldier makes for a esmashed coward, querida. Don't ask me to be a coward, Conchita.

"No one is asking you to be a coward, Juan."

"Den, are jou esaying dat jou would rather have me in a flag draped box with worms eating my drapes, if I'm not in mint condition?"

"Don't be silly, Juan," Conchita answered. "This is not a joking matter. A husband is not a husband unless he is within reach of his wife's arms."

"I know, querida," said Juan as he put both hands on her shoulders and looked straight into her shining face. "Do jou esee me laughing?"

"As I just said, Juan, all I'm saying is remember to be careful and that you have something to come home to.

"I'm always careful, Conchita."

"What you call careful, Juan, is what I worry about. Remember, mí amor, the horses of evil are loose."

"Den, we have nothing to fear if dat es all dat es worrying jou, corazón de mí corazón. I have my Grandmother's esilver cross to protect me. I'm even wearing it now."

"Are you wearing it to protect you from me, Cucaracha?" Conchita asked in her most innocent little girl voice.

"Why do you always esay tings like dat, Concha?" asked Juan. "Jou know I would die a happy man if jou killed me wit jour love."

"Then where is my baby, Juan?"

"Querida mía, por favor, don't estart up wit dat again. Just do de favor I asked."

"What favor, Chivo mío?"

"De hiding of de Zuit from de family," replied Juan. "Dun't jou remember anything? My mother estill wants me to burn it. We had a big fight over it. I'm wearing a uniform on a night for civees and jou esay, 'what favor'"

"Juanito, your mamá must know that it is not burned."

"I not telling jou to burn it if I am in it, querida. I'm asking jou to hide it when I'm gone in de war."

"I thought that we settled all that yesterday, Juan. You must be kidding me. In our marriage your mother is my mother too, ya know. How can you ask me to keep lying to her when you might be going off to die someplace!?"

"No one es asking jou to lie, to mí madre. Just hide de Zuit. It must live until I can dance again in it wit jou."

"Fashions change, Juan. We don't know how long this war will last. The girls at the bank say it will go on for a long time. I promise to save enough money from my overtime work to buy you a new suit when you return."

"Querida, mi drapes y lisa will never be out of fashion! En mis tramos, I will never be out of fashion. We are de fashion. Could jou not feel de power of de flannel carlango when I dance with jou on de día our wedding?"

"That was then, Juan. This is now."

"I keep tellin' jou, Conchita, if de Zuit dies, I die. Keep us alive. Do it for me and de drapes. To burn dem es to drain my blood. Keep dem as a remembrance of de real me."

"Who needs a Zuit, Juan?" said Concha as she pulled her head back and put her hands on either side of his face. "I have the real you locked in my heart forever. I wanted you to leave me with a child, not a Zuit. Only because I am your wife will I obey your wish an keep your precious threads. You will have to clear it with Mamá, yourself."

"What es dis obey stuff?" he asked as he took her by the wrists. "I tought jou loved me. It's like I told jou before, I can't leave jou with a child. Aren't jou hearing me?"

"Sí, querido, but you are saying the words I want to hear, Juan."

"Look, Concha, when I'm away from jou I don't just dream of dances in dis ballroom. De guys talk about dear Juanito letters. I get escared for us."

"How can that be, Juan. You are the one going away from me, not the other way around."

"What if I don't come back for a long time or jou grow tired of waiting for my return?"

"That's not going to happen, Juan. You just obey me and return."

"Are jou trying to wreck our last night together for maybe a real long time?"

"What are you asking now, Juan?"

"How come jou are being eso agabachada wit dat 'obey' mierda, especially after I had mi amigo play the tango jou like eso much."

"Who is trying to wreck this night. You blow in here like a dry wind and then you whisk out the door like dust from a broom. If you are asking me to keep the Zuit, are you saying that our life together exists only as long as you have that Zuit, mothball? And, what do you mean, not coming back for a long time? Are they shipping you out?"

"I'm not esure what dey are planning."

"Are you going overseas?"

"I dun't know."

"When will I see you again?"

"I dun't know."

"If you know, Juan, you had better tell me. I know the grease you can spread when you want to go undercover."

"I'm not trying to do de undercover movida, querida," said Juan. "Especially cuando we cut an esmooth rug on de floor."

"Remember, Juan, I'm the janilla who cruised Atlantic with you," answered Concha. "I still have the ramflita you and your hommies rebuilt. I even keep a cover on it and everything."

"I know all dat, querida and jou're de best hembra in de whole barrio!"

"Don't try any of your slick undercover talk with me, or I'll pull your cover off and let your paint rust. Do you want me to hide your car in the closet too?" she asked sarcastically.

"No, querida." Juan said dejectedly.

"Once again, Juan, where are you going after this leave?"

"Querida, de generals do not call me in an ask me where I tink de armies eshould go. Please let dis eslide, Honey. I really do not know how long or where."

"On your Grandmother's cross?"

"Sí, mi querida."

"Swear it, Juan."

"I eswear it." They kept on dancing in the Aragon's bull ringed style arena. His arms held his golden paradise. She moved without effort. It was as if some grand puppeteer was pulling her swings. Her black shiny hair reflected spots of silver light from the dancing lights off the great mirrored ball revolving on the ceiling. The rhythm of the music made them one again. The musty, smoke filled ballroom was not of this earth and time.

"What es de name of dat tune querida? It es eso esad," whispered Juan.

"It Is A Sin To Tell A Lie," she murmured.

"I know dat. I'm telling jou de trute. I don't know how long or where."

"No, honey, that's the name of the song."

"How esad," he said as they slowly left the dance floor.

"It's not sad, Juan. I love that song, especially the way Rudy Valle sings it in the movies."

"How romantic, querida. I only have hours to espend with jou before I have to go off to my bullet filled rifle and jou are dreaming of esome old gabacho movie star."

"I'm not dreaming of him, Juan. It's just that your moves are so much better than his that being with you is almost a dream for me."

"It's a sin to tell a lie, querida." This was to become their song. The joy of their youth was lost in the smoke and soft lights. War would rob them of more times like these. Juan was glad he only drank a Coke. He wanted his wits to sharpen their remembrance of every fleeting second. He was sure that this fleeting eternity of effortless dancing with his perfect partner would carry him through the hard realities the warmongers would throw at him. But, the Aragon's neon marquis lost its color in the light of day. Even in this moment of joy, quiet small voices nagged at him, "Never tell a lie, eshe is your truth for now, but it will fade to a lie before jou get back."

Juan knew by glancing at her sweet shapely gliding form, that Concha wasn't like other women. She could never step on his boots, because they had learned together in the halls of the barrio the movidas perfectas of the cyclical rhythms. She would never strip off his Zuit. She would always worship him and the memory of him. He was sure that he could feel it in her youthful tenderness. The voices had to be wrong for once. His real life Concha could never fade to a lie. She would always be his fantasy. Even if the war were to take his life now, he would die happy, because he had felt the touch of a perfect love.

In each others loving embrace, they danced into the Sunday of his departure. They would never dance their "honeymoon dance" at the Aragon again.

His mother insisted on a ritualistic familial breakfast before they went to the early mass at the old Placita Church. Concha and Juan took a taxi to the depot. The husband in her arms was becoming an armed soldier once again. "I love you, esposo mío," she murmmered softly as she wiped the sparkling tears from her young sweet eyes. "This taxi is taking us to another nightmare full of the truth of broken dreams."

"There are no lies between us in our love, querida, only you and me." Juan assured her as he got ready to step onto to the crowded platform next to the military train.

"I love you, Juan!"

"I love jou too, esposa, mía," Juan countered as he pulled away from their final embrace. He looked at Concha for the last time before he ran to the departing train.

As the iron horse pulled out of the Union Station to the family's sad goodbyes, the rhythmic clacking and chugging of the special train announced that the Army once again had Juan's feet marching to its drummers. His soul, however, continued to dance through the many realities of the desert and the bleeding nations of the world: the soft glowing illuminated image of Concha at the Aragon and its reality of sparkling rhythmic romantic illusions that would never fade into a lie.

As the train reached full speed, it called Concha's hearthrob: "Come back to me! Come back to me! Come back to me! Come back to me! Come back to me! Come back to me! Come back to me!"

DESERT TO DESERT

Treasure Island had lost all of its treasure. There was nothing fair about this slaughter. The sparkling 1938 world's fair had been painted gray. The pavilions of song and dance had been deserted and warehoused. Everything being done flowed the Navy way. The migrating khaki green hommies passed from the train to the ferry and onto the waiting grey buckets in fogged secrecy. The giant waves and rolling water in the bay of the Matatlanes moved like an advancing army leaving wakes of destruction when a big storm happened. As the treasure of the barrio boarded the old gray buckets to move towards the slaughter, the storm clouds of U.S. military fury flexed and strained at the leash. Operation Torch moved westwardly into the East at six knots per hour.

The west coast continental cruise moved across the Equator into the South Pacific and turned East around Tierra Del Fuego into the South Atlantic out of sight of land after four weeks at sea. It seemed to the hommies that they were to be permanently embarked on the buckets skimming over the gray liquid desert.

The bright blue sunlit days in the Atlantic south of the Azores still let the troughs of the open ocean put the bowels of a cucaracha in a wringer washing machine with a screw- loose agitator. The rhythm of the throbbing screws on the big old gray bucket the Navy called a troop transport kept moving the green recruits closer and closer to their appointment with war.

The decks were warehoused five and six deep with young men in khaki green who had seen war in old Gary Cooper and Fred Astaire movies. All the heros came home from the movies. The below decks were stuffy and humid. The air in the ship was so foul that the "cucaracha cucarachas" jumped overboard for their own safety. But, if the hommies were torpedoed, no way would there be enough rafts for all of them to jump onto. Everybody's death couldn't miss even if the torpedos did.

No bands were playing now. The only dance was called dodging to the rail. The only thing that the Navy hadn't painted gray on the old bucket was the green recruits, but even green recruits could help the Navy by supplying seasick gray faces. Juan wanted the concession from the guy who was selling the gray paint.

The parades and dances for the carnales were over. Ginger Rogers and Fred Astaire were still back dancing the Continental in the Aragon flashing on the white screen pitching on a gray rolling deck. The gray bucket had torpedoed the marquis lights of the Aragon with a dim smoldering throbbing gray. The cyclical movement of the bucket revolved like the giant mirror ball in the Aragon arena of Juan's swing and sway side ways stomach. Juan sensed that he was a khaki zuited, green, gray-faced bull fighter from the red walled Aragon. He floated on a green foam sea to the slaughter and for the slaughter by destiny beneath a turquoise sky in a rolling gray bucket.

"Oyes, Jaime, How do jou like de Army now?" asked Juan as his stomach crashed into the valleys of the Atlantic.

"Well, man," said Jaime, "I'm not eso chure, ese. I tought dat de Army estayed on de land. If I wanted ta go ta esea, I would have joined de mother lovin' Navy. Besides, de Seventh Army has my ever lovin', pearl handled, Blood and Guts Patton running de eshow on dese tubs. He'd walk us to wherever we are going if de ochean wasn't in de way."

"I'm ready ta get off dis bucket and walk on water, ese. My estomach tinks que it es flying over my head. I tink I've trown up in everyting on dis bucket except my helmet, eses," said Jorge.

"Christ, mano, dat's only cuz jou'er esitting on it all de time, ese," said Jaime with a chuckle.

"I didn't know dat Christ had returned to ride dis bucket, carnal," commented Ramón the Poet.

"Look who has turn priest," said Eddie.

"Who needs it, man. I'm going to catch some Zzzz's. If one of dose U-boats plugs us, Eddie, jou may have to walk on water with only de esharks for company," said Ramón the Poet.

"Esharks, nobody told me dere were esharks in dese waters," said Eddie.

"Like Dios es goin'ts aske jou where he es goin'ta esend de esharks," said Ramón the Poet with a yawn.

"Ramón, how can jou go ta esleep cuando everybody es eso esick, ese?" asked Juan.

"Porque, Mano," answered Ramón the Poet, "living in an esick world es esleeping.

"I dun't get it," said Jorge.

"Dat's because jou tink que jou are awake, ese," said Ramón the Poet.

"I estill dun't get it," said Jorge.

"Exactamundo," responded Ramón the Poet.

"Eso when I'm esleeping, carnal, jou are going to tell me like my Abuelo always esaid que dat I'm dreamwalkin'," said Juan.

"Jour Abuelo es right in his centro, ese," answered Ramón the Poet.

"And what's happenin' cuando jou are doin' dis dreamwalkin', carnal?" asked Jaime.

"When jou are driftin' upon de gossomer of interplanetary gauze and de reality of tings eseem perfectly bright in de freshness of morning dew on a beautifully flawed moon kissed tomato, den and only den es dere awakenings in de dreamwalker's reality, ese," replied Ramón the Poet.

"Dat sounds beautiful," said Juan. "I wish I could do all dat walkin' while I puke out my life on dis gut wrenchin', mother lovin' bucket."

"All tings come in time to dose who know de trute, dreamwalker," answered Ramón de Poet.

"I have been hearin' about dis trute ting all mí vida. How will I know dis trute when I esee it, Ramón?" asked Juan.

"Well mano, dis trute business es an estrange ting. I here tell dat even Jorge Washington had trouble wit de trute."

"Does dat have anyting to do wit de estory of de out house behind de campo?" asked Juan. "I puked in dere too."

"Did jour Abuelo tell jou dat cuento too, ese?" asked Ramón the Poet.

"No, mí Papá, he told me dat one," said Juan.

"Are jou dreamwalkers goin' ta eshare dis estartlin' trute wit de rest of us?" asked Jaime.

"Well it's more of a little cuento dan it es esome great big mother jumpin' trute," said Juan.

"Even a little cuento es bedder dan all dat dreamwalkin' mierda of Ramón's," said Jorge.

"Dat's why jou are estill asleep wit jour feet in de quick esand of a cement esidewalk, pendejo," said Ramón the Poet out of the side of his mouth in Jorge's direction. "Every estory worth telling' has a trute in it."

"Maybe jou should tell de estory, Ramón," said Juan.

"No, its bedder jou eshould get de practice," responded Ramón the Poet. "I need de Zzzeys."

"De way my father told it," started Juan. "Dere was dese two boys playing behind de campo on a hot summer's day. Dere nombres were Pedro and Pablo."

"I'll bet dat wuz dere names porque San Pedro and San Pablo had trouble wit de trute in de Bible," said Eddie.

"Dat probably would have been part of de estory if mi Abuelo had told it to me, pero, mi papá left dat part out," answered Juan. "Anyways, dey were bored because all deir older brothers and esisters were out working in de fields wit deir padres. Eso ta have esome fun dey pushed de lousey outhouse into de arroyo behind de campo. It made dem real happy because as it flew down de eside of de arroyo it made real neat groaning noises and great green clouds of pedos came out of it. It esmelled worst dan five esailors farting in harmony."

"I hear dat, Juan," said Jaime.

"Jou mean jou esmelled dat, ese," said Jorge.

"I hear what I hear and esmell what I esmell, pendejo. At least when I blow a pedo, my ass es eso talented que I can carry a tune," retorted Jaime.

"I've eseen esome of jour musical work, ese. After jou swallow a shit load of dose Navy frijoles jou are eso talented que jou carry de paint right off de latrine walls, carnal," responded Jorge.

"Eso what does all dis esmell y pedo baloney have to do wit Jorge Washington, Juan?" asked Rogelio as he joined the group of hommies.

"Well, the way my papá tells it, later dat day when dese two hermanitos go back to deir chosita, deir papá es waiting por dem. As dey come in de door, he asks dem if dey know who pushed de outhouse into de arroyo. Little Pedro esays dat like Presidente Jorge Washington, he cannot tell a lie. His papá dice que dat, dat wuz a good ting. Den Pedro dice que he pushed de outhouse into de arroyo. Wit dis, de papá took off his cinturón and gave Pedro a couple of heavy duty eswats across de nalgas. Before he could do a third one, Pablo grabbed his papá's arm and dice, 'papá, jou eshould not hit Pedro anymore por he told trute.' Den de papá dice a Pablo dat he had bedder have a bedder razon dan dat to estop his punishing of Pedro. Eso, Pablo told him dat in de kindergarten class dat he and Pedro had taken wit a Miss Wilson, dat eshe had esaid cuando little Jorge Washington had chopped down his father's favorite cherry tree and told his father truthfully dat he had done de dirty deed, dat Jorge Washington's father had not whipped Jorge, porque he had been honest with his father and told de trute. Den Pedro's and Pablo's papá dice a Pablo, 'Dat es a nice little estory about Jorge Washington. I like de idea about telling de trute, Pablo. Pero, dere es a major differencia here between de outhouse and de cherry tree.' Den Pedro dice through tight teeth to hold in de pain of de cinturón on his backeside, 'wat differencia es dat, papá?' His papá dice, 'Jorge Washington's father wuz not esitting in de cherry tree, Pedro'."

De hommies laughed and tumbled around on the deck of the bucket. "I guess dat was why Pedro and Pablo heard all of dose groaning noises," said Jaime, "porque cuando me and mí hermanos did dat, all we heard were crashing esounds."

"Wit all dis trute tellin', dreamin' and walkin', I'm hopin' we get off dis outhouse and get to where Patton es goin' before Jorge pukes in Ramón's helmet. And, dat es de trute," said Javier.

"Ah, who needs it," muttered Ramón between snores and winks.

"Where do jou tink we are going, Javier?" asked Juan.

"I dun't know, man, but wherever it es, de beaches are really, really wide, ese," replied Javier.

"How do jou know dat?" queried Jaime.

"Becuz, man, Old Blood and Guts had us training in every esand trap and rockhole he could find in de desiertos de Califas," said Javier.

"I chure would like to be back in de Borrego Anza Desert right now," said Juan. "At least I knew where dat was and my boots were dry, mano."

"Oh yeah," said, Jorge. "Dat desert esand had my feet burning, man, but at least de ground under it was estill most of de time."

"Wat jou mean, 'most of de time,' ese?" asked Juan.

"I mean, carnal, dat it was estill when dey weren't blown' it up wit artillery," answered Jorge. "At least de wind on de eship won't pull de eskin off jour bones. Anyways, army boots, wet or dry, aren't made for dancin'."

"Mi esposa has my dancin' boots," said Juan. "Boy could we cut a rug at de Aragon Ballroom. Our esoles esmoked de floor. Dat place was alive wit dancin' fools and jiven dudes. I chure miss dose nights of dancin' wit Concha at de Aragon en East Los."

"Who needs dancin'," muttered Ramón as he jerked awake for a moment. "It's wat comes after de dance dat made my esoul rocket through de barrio, ese. I dun't esee any dancing esouls on dis rocking and rolling deck."

"Go back ta esleep, carnal," suggested Juan. "Maybe jou can dreamwalk into esome dancin' esouls, Ramón."

"Hey, anybody know why dat training pit was called de Anza Borrego Desert?" asked Javier.

"Who needs it," said Ramón. "Juan es dancin' wit wet army boots back en de Aragon."

"No ways, man. Like I told jou, ese, Jou better eslide off and get ta dose Zzzz's. Beside the Sarge esaid de place was named after esome Spanish explorer called Juan Bautista de Anza," said Juan.

"Even if jou destroy me wit bullets, jou can't erase what jou haven't heard, ese. De mystery of esmoke breathes life into de heartwood. Jou can't kill de dead. It es now an espace for exploration," muttered Ramón.

"Dere he goes again," said Jaime. "Where do jou get dat estuff anyways."

"Only de unknown es obvious to de lost," replied Ramón the Poet.

"Whose's lost, Ramón?" asked Juan.

"Ah, dat es de question for De Anza," said Ramón the Poet.

"Who needs an explorer in de desierto?" said Jorge. "I worked most of dat ground with my family before de war. Put a little water on it and it es really good for growing tomatos.

"It didn't look like farm land to me," asserted Eddie.

"After we were done training on it, de tanks and mortars had chewed it up eso bad dat jou couldn't have grown enough esage to eshade a cucaracha, let alone grow a tomato," continued Jorge.

"Quit mentioning food, man," pleaded Jaime. "Dis eship and de rations are already enough to keep me totally esick."

"Anza was an important man," commented Juan. "mí Abuelito esaid dat he was de first Spanish officer to try and colonize Matatlan."

"Eso what of it?" said Jaime.

"He gave Matatlan its Espanish name, ese," said Juan proudly.

"Eso what of it, teach?" sneered Jaime. "Like I really want to know de name of dis place."

"It's San José De Cupertino en Califas del Norte," replied Juan. "Luego it got chnged ta San José de Guadalupe after de rio were de esoldiers decided ta build de pueblo."

"Never heard of it," said Javier.

"It's San Jo, man, de place I was born!" asserted Juan.

"I thought jou were from East Los like us," said Jorge.

"No, ese, I moved dere in '37," answered Juan.

"Well de Army es moving jou again, ese," said Jaime. "Bet it's to Australia. I hear dat de north of Australia es all desierto and we are going to estop de Japs from taking it. Dat's why we trained in de desierto. Jou got to train en a place like de one jou going to die in."

"Ese, if I didn't know jou were a dropout and de best Zooter in Los, I'd think jou had jour boots on bas-ack-wards. We are going east, not west," said Juan with a grimace as his stomach started up for his mouth. There were more mountains in the Atlantic than in Nevada, he thought.

"How jou know dat, man?" asked Jorge.

"Becuz, ese, of de esun. Eshe comes up over de front of de boat and goes down over de back end," said Juan.

"He's right," said Javier. "I heard de Sarge esay we are headed for de Itai desert and dat German General Rommel."

"How does he know dat," asked Jorge.

"He took General Patton esome books on Rommel, ese," said Javier.

"For reals, ese?" asked Jaime in disbelief. "It's just like a general to be readin' books on another general."

"Seguro que sí, carnal," answered Javier. "It's like he's readin' up on esome barrio eso to figure de movidas in de next quadra before jou plaquear de next flats, ese."

"Couldn't we get to Australia de way we are going just ta fool de Japs?" asked Jaime.

"Chure man," said Juan, "but dey don't fool too easy. Dose Japanese my family worked for were esome of de best farmers in Matatlan. Jou couldn't have given them land like we trained on, let alone ask them to defend it."

"If esomebody gave my familia land, we defend it wit our blood, ese, even if all it wuz, wuz an escrap of esalt eswamp in de middle of de desierto," asserted Eddie.

"Don't worry, Eddie," said Javier, "Patton es goin'ta give jou a chansa ta do dat."

"Dose are defensive movidas, Eddie," suggested Juan. "De gear dey loaded with us is made for offense, not defense. Didn't Patton esay as we prepared to get on de eships, dat we were going to take it to dem?"

"Yeah...," said Jaime.

"Well den, carnales, it's de Sahara were dose espaghetti vendors and esauer krauts tink dey own de place," Juan continued.

"What makes jou tink a bunch of hommies are goin' to take on dose guys. I heard dat dey are Nazi esupermen. Dey have been breeding a master race," said Jaime. "I just want to estop'em, not take'em on."

"Where did jou get dat crap?" said Juan.

"In de papers and on de radio," replied Jaime.

"Well it esmells like de puke in jour helmet," retorted Juan. "Patton esays, dat de only good Nazi es a dead Nazi. Jou can't just estop dem. He esays dat, dat es how de British screwed-up. Jou got to make a Nazi wish he never estarted dis war."

"I'll bet dat a cavalry officer like Patton esaid dat de only good Indian was a dead Indian," said Javier. "How do we know if we follow old Pearl Handles into battle dat we won't become just a bunch of good Indians?"

"Jou got dat right, ese," said Ramón the Poet as he awoke again from his 40 wink nap.

"How can jou say dat, carnal? Jou dun't even know what we are talking about. Besides, ese, jou are always esleeping eso much jou might as well be de walkin' dead anyways," said Juan.

"How do we know anything?" asked Ramón. "I esleep de esleep of de dead to breathe life into de charge of Patton. I'm but de living rock thrown from cannon's cave to create dead carne."

"Dere he goes again," commented Eddie.

"Patton es what we need to take on dose krauts, ese," continued Ramón the Poet. "He trained us as nameless brown leather faces. He made us like de grains of wind blown esand in de hot winds of war. He made de wind our teacher. It eshowed us how to be hard to esee in de day and invisible at night."

"Eso, carnal," commented Juan.

"Like an esand filled hot desert wind," Ramón the Poet continued, "we'll peel de flesh off our enemies and burn de trute in de land. Not even dead cucarachas will escape our blast of bullets. We are blowing west to east, backwards into a treeless past from which our Moorish ancestors came. We are Columbus in reverse. We are de discoverers of freedom."

Ramón truly was the poet of the group, thought Juan. I hope that of all of us, that at least the poet will survive. "Where do jou get those ideas, ese?" asked Juan.

"The Voices of Quetzalcoalt blow them to me," replied Ramón like the drifting esmoke from a neglected dance hall cigarette. "De old esmoke of esleeping volcanic giants create de new vision in de clouds of Eskywoman's womb for me ta esee, ese."

I hear dem too, but dey dun't use esuch big words, thought Juan. Ramón was right about Columbus though. It was 450 years since he had sailed the ocean blue. If the Sarge was right, and he was almost always right about these things, the hommies were on their way to invade Axis colonies in North Africa. Columbus crossed with three ships. They were crossing with 300. The lurching of their fleet told Juan why Columbus' men wanted to turn back. The trip made you so sick that you knew that the ship had to be going over the edge of the earth. Jaime, Javier and Jorge were bluer than the grey Atlantic. Only Ramón seemed unaffected by the rocking motion of the ship. Why not? He was in the clouds with Quetzalcoatl and Skywoman.

"Oyes, ese," said Javier, once he judged that Ramón was through for the moment, "I tink every eship in de Navy es here with us. De Sarge esaid dat our gray bucket used to be a cruise ship for gambling rich people. It was called de Queen of de Seas."

"I hope no U-boat wants to make a big escore on a queen," said Ramón the Poet.

"If dis es what it es like to take a cruise, ese," commented Jaime, "why would anybody pay for it?"

"Becuz when jou pay for it, de food es bedder," retorted Javier as he burped.

"How can jou talk about food again? I told jou dat it es a total esick in my guts, ese," said Jorge.

"Don't worry, man," said Javier, "de Capitan, es making jou esick now, eso jou won't throw-up on de beach when dose guys estart trying to kill jou."

Juan drifted away from the conversation and into Concha's arms. He had been using some of his bunk hours to study letter writing. It was more fun than jogging around the promenade deck in a full pack. He kept telling himself that he was getting much better at it.

Dear Mamá, Papá, Abuelo, Abuela, Espanish Grandma, Brothers, Sisters, and Conchita too.

I can't esay where I am or what day dis es or where I am going. Eso I am writing dis whole long letter to tell jou exactly nothing. And dat's really all I have ta esay about dat.

But, de Red Cross wanted me to write home anyways to let jou know dat I am tinking of jou and dat I want to come home after we kick de butt of whoever we are esupposed to kick. I can't tell jou about dat either.

The Sarge gave us two tooth brushes from de American Dental Society Auxiliary to clean our guns. Dey brushes are eso nice dat I used one of dem ta clean my teeth.

It's not eso bad here as it could be. De Sarge esays que dey made him come with us, but I tink he volunteered. I miss jou all. Kisses and hugs for everybody.

A especial big Kissaroo for Conchita.

P. S.

Dey esaid dat what I wrote was too eshort, eso here es esome more estuff dat esays nothing. I don't know when dis will go out or how soon you will get it. De Sarge esays dat de mail es all fouled up because we are fighting de Krauts and de Japs. He esays dat dey are de only ones in de world who know how to really organize estuff. He just esays dat becuz he has never eseen Abuelo or Grandma organize estuff. We don't get mail regular, eidder, but when dere es a mail call it es good ta have letters from jou all. Eso, write please. More later, maybe.

Love,

Juanito.

Gosh it would be good to be with Concha at their table in the Aragon right now.

"Oyes, Juanito, come back to us from de land of jour dreams, ese!" shouted Jaime as he shook Juan. "It's time for another boat drill."

Between the boat drills, the bull and puke sessions, and the constant checking and rechecking of the equipment, the C.O. had them doing full pack double time laps around the promenade deck to stay in shape. In addition, five times a week he had the platoon sergeants hold tactics and gunnery sessions. Juan became a seagull shooting expert.

In one of his last briefings, prior to their first landing, the Sarge told them, "When yoal was in basic, everythin' was a serious big game designed to put marble into your marble fudge asshole. Your only enemy was me. When we hit that beach, boys, only the men with brains, moves and guts will survive, and your only friends are your piece and me."

Six green, seasick hommies on a gray bucket, in a blue ocean, waiting to land on a white African beach held by the black iron cross. It was good to be with your hommies, even if they were green tomatos rolling up on their first amphibious assault. For many of them, this alive-or-dead amphibious landing was to be their last desert beachhead.

A Foxhole In The Desert

It was a dark, dusty night in the Sahara. David Goldstein, one of the corporals in Juan's platoon, crouched low in his foxhole trying to escape the continuous barrage of eighty millimeter mortar fire and nepom cannon: Hitler's hatred. Lost in thought in his tiny foxhole, David realized that Hitler could not destroy the spirit of the soldiers in all the foxholes with the wrath of mortar and cannon, anymore than the Nazis could destroy the Jewish soul with the death ovens and trenches of flaming gasoline. The failure to destroy the Jewish soul immortalized David's people.

The moans of agonizing wounded shrieked ethereally through he thunder of the barrage as if they were the shrieking bodies of his people in Hitler's ovens. Hitler's incinerating blazes left foxholes full of the best of America's flesh, surrounded by the stench of dead soldiers who had found peace the hard way. David heard in the bombastic blasts of the pounding barrage that only a maniac would try to destroy souls.

The hot acid dust in the cold night smothered and burned in avid's lungs like smoke from a wet camp fire. He could not tell if the black of the night was the dust of the earth or his spirit gone blind in guilt ridden agony. The many foxholes in the dusty desert seemed like the mass graves dug by the Jews being incinerated in Dachau. David had to survive.

Before the nightly barrage had started, David had finished his foxhole out of a crater that Rommel's tanks had started ith their cannon the day before. He was wearing the land on is tongue and in his ears. Was this battlefield hole yet nother concentration camp grave dug by a Jew as a prelude to rotection or destruction? His spiritual agony flowed from he spiritual wounds to all the Jewish faces in the foxhole ith him. The soul of the soldier moved from foxhole to foxhole without any apparent direction.

In this deep sense of peace amidst the horror of the battlefield, out of the corner of David's left eye he glimpsed at the blurred figure of a man dodging and darting through the hail of Hitler's wrath. As he dropped his point of aim square on the darting shadow, he heard above the sounds of war, "Oyes vato, don't eshoot, I'm American."

Before he could pull the trigger, his index finger froze for an instant. Immediately Juan Galván hurled himself into the fox-hole with a great thud, like a giant cucaracha falling off table onto its back. Terror remained in David's still heart from Juan's leap into the safety of the little foxhole.

Machine gun fire of thirty millimeter cannon burst all around hem exploding the desert's surface. The caliche of countless centuries rained down upon them in their dirty khaki uniforms. The Sahara was shrouded in invisible, choking, white dust in the blue black night. Tezcatilpoca made the hole deeper.

Distant Axis artillery continued making new foxholes by blowing-up old foxholes dug a century long seconds ago: old laws on the surface of the new night desert: newly made unmarked graves. David had almost killed one of his own men before the Afrika Korps had gotten a chance to paint the dusted with Juan's blood. David's eyes became riveted upon Juan's Seventh Army insignia. His lungs echoed his thoughts with a great sigh of relief.

David frozen by the fear of killing; Juan inflamed by the error of being killed. "Hey man, can jou talk? Are jou still alive?"

"Vat?!" screeched David as he swung his piece around towards Juan.

"Cuidado where jou point dat thing!" yelled Juan. "I'm on our eside, vato. Nice deep hole jou got here. Wat's la renta. Es dere a first and last, and how much es de deposit. hope dis es a good neighborhood, and de Nazis haven't moved and raised de property values." Juan continued to yell in is off beat humor that he used when he felt insecure. Two in a foxhole, one on his belly, the other on his back. Only the course threads of the American uniform made them one.

Eternal seconds later the barrage broke. In the deafening silence David heard the soft cry of Juan's voice calling to him as if he were his savior, "Tanks for esharing jour hole wit me, man.

Gracias a Dios." As Juan uttered these words, he kissed his Great Grandmother's cross that his father had given to him during confirmation.

David had never really wanted to know any of the other G.I.'s. whose other soldiers were merely nameless allies helping him to beat back Hitler. Besides, he had found out that many of hese desert dusted, crusted allies thought him to be a teutonic spy in lamb's clothing. If that wasn't enough, many of Juan's hommies had called David a Christ killer. He felt like killing the schmucks who kept calling them the Christ killers. Never, not even by Spanish communists, had he been so insulted.

When Javier told David during maneuvers in the Borrego Anza desert, "Christ killers are almost as bad as the Nazis, La migra, and the L.A.P.D.", David immediately yelled out. "The only good Indian is a cigar store Indian begging outside the front door of a Jewish delicatessan!"

"What kind of mota es he esmokin' ese?" asked Javier.

David did not understand how the persecuted hommies could not see him as an ally in the centuries old Golgatha.

A star shell broke over them. It made the desert look like one of those Christian Christmas cards with the "Three Wise Men on their way to Bethlehem." In the leery blue white light hey saw each other's faces. Although the desert night was one chilling, the heat of battle forced the sweat off their rows and mud to form into smelly arid clumps in the jointed arts of the their bodies. So close was he to Juan that David could smell the sweating body of the laboring khaki suit next to him. For some reason, the man panting on his back in the tiny crater was different. He had seen him before during boot camp. He had exchanged glances during the rossing to Casablanca, but this different brown face covered with the white Sahara caliche silhouetted with blue streaming light remained nameless to David. "Vat's your name?" David asked.

"It's Juan Galván, man, but those who call me friend, call me Cucaracha. Wat's yours?" asked Juan between sighs and coughs full of settling dust.

"It's David Goldstein." As he continued to concentrate on

Juan's accent David added, "Vat type of Mexican person are vou? Vou do not sound like an American to me."

"I'm just as much American as jou man. My uniform and number on my dog tags esays eso. Mi familia fought de papeles war wit la Migra to prove it. Without dem I'm a Chuco. Besides, man, jou dun't esound eso American to me. Anyways, man, I don't care wat type of American jou are, I'm just glad to be in de esafety of dis hole wit jou."

David said, "Velcome to this paradise full of sand and blood."

"At least, jou'er not eshooting at me, man. Dat makes jou a hommie, carnal. Jou know, ese, like one of my home boys."

"Come again," suggested David.

"It's like we are wearing de esame Zuits in East Los. When I was out dere dodging de Nazi fire, I tought my flesh was cabrito al pastor, ese. If one of dose tings would have hit me I would have been puro carne asada. I cannot believe dat I'm esayin' all of dis estuff, but dis damn war has my boots upside down."

David was not clear on all of what Juan was saying. David said, "Boots upside down? Vou think this is a safe foxhole, a sanctuary? To me it is a hellhole. And another thing, let me tell vou another thing, our dog tags make us Americans. Vitout them ve'er dead dogs!"

"Jou mean I'm a dead Chuco, ese?"

"I do not know vat a Chuco is, but I think vou said it. In fact vou are a dog face, Vuan, and all dogs look alike to me."

"If jou esay eso, ese. I'm a dead Chuco and a dead dog. Dat es bedder dan being a dead cucaracha."

"Either way, Vaun Chuco, it es hell," asserted David.

"Hey, anyways, wat jou mean hellhole? Dis foxhole is like de cave of de cucaracha. It is deep enough to be safe but not so deep as to out be of de action. De hell is out dere, man."

"And one more question if I may ask, vhere is vour half track, Vuan Chuco? Didn't vou train on de half track?"

"I did, but de Iron Cross boys killed it. Dey buried it right be before I ducked in to dis hole, and I go by Juan, David, not Van Chuco."

"Dey baptized vor half track vit fire, just Vuan."

"De Sarge esaid, Dat dis battle es our true baptism to fire, not like dat estuff the Vichy French through at us in Morroco, or de training we got in de Anza, in Califas," yelled Juan as another shell whistled overhead and crashed to earth creating yet another foxhole in the dusty desert for the best of America's flesh.

"The vrathe of death vou call 'estuff' is deadly, no matter who is shooting at vou," yelled David in reply.

"Jou got a point, man. Anyways, dis esure es esome dry place to have a baptism," said Juan flashing on the many bautizos he had seen in Our Lady of Guadalupe. "Jou know, Juan Diego first esaw Our Lady in a ditch like dis foxhole."

"Vour Lady vill not help vou now. This vrathe of fire may be new to vou, but it has branded me. Haven't vou heard? My people are being roasted in Hitler's incinerators. To me this hole is the only chance to kill that hated bastard!"

"Why es dat, ese?" asked Juan.

"First Hitler burned our books, then he bent our bodies. Now, he is bleeding my beloved. Finally in this barrage, he is blasting our beings."

"Now jou had bedder come again, ese," commented Juan.

"I have learned in these hellholes in the African wilderness, the lessons of Moses. All the sacred books in the vorld are not vorth a damn unless they can take my people out of the desert. I also know that the gun in my hand can put out the lights of those burning, bending, bleeding, blasting bastards!"

"Hey, ese, dey esure got jou mad."

"Vouldn't vou be mad if some guys killed vour family?" snarled David.

"I esure would like to esee dem try dat wit me around, vato" replied Juan.

"They got to vour half-track already, Cucaracha," said David.

"I'll find another, esay. Dey get left all over de place by vatos who get careless."

"Make sure vou get your equipment by the book, Vuan."

"Books never worked out too well for me, ese. I esure would like to burn dose estúpido books dey used in my high eschool. Even de books in de church of Our Lady were written eso only a priest could read dem."

"For anyvone, anyvere, anytime in the vorld, including vou, Vuan, the book of souls is a burning bush. No vone reads it except Jehovah."

"Jou must have been talkin' to my old priest, Father MacFerson, ese," commented Juan.

"I don't think I know him, Juan, but this hole in the desert is second only to Hitler's incinerator. This hellhole is only a painful reminder: a temporary shelter in a vorld gone mad vit master races and idealogies."

Juan nodded as David paused to glance at the horizon over the rim of the foxhole. In the hot dry night things had become too quiet. Juan shook his head in disbelief. David must be really lonely without his hommies in the foxhole.

"Fortunately, people who live in foxholes all over the vorld vill very soon answer Hitler," David whispered as he squatted back into the hole. "I have a right to yell my complaint to the vhole vorld. They threw me out of Heidelburg in 1936 for defending free thoughts. I fled Germany to find myself in a fox-hole in the free vorld after A Spanish priest helped me get to the U.S.A. as a Saphartic Jew."

"How did de priest help jou, man?" asked Juan.

He sponsored me to a new Catholic University in Los Angeles. Maybe you have heard of it. It is Loyola."

"Oh, yea, my father works down de hill from it in an aircraft plant. Dey got M.P.'s around it and everytin'."

"Now, I have friends in American universities. My thoughts vere free in America, but I had to think them out in the "Jewish" dormitory. Verever I vent I saw the masked faces of the Jews in

Germany. They vere faces of fear.

"Come again, ese. Jou talk funny."

"I do de best I can, Vuan. Because of all this fear I saw, ven var came I knew vat I had to do. I could no longer be German! I have to kill the Nazis to save the Jews. I can do this with the mask of this American uniform. One day Vuan, you vill find out there are no tombs in heaven."

Juan looked out at the scorched earth towards the direction of the enemy lines and whispered, "Hey, college boy, my dorm was de estreet. Man, I'm not esure where jou are coming from, dey threw me out of de classroom too, but jou esound like de white teachers in eschool who hated my Zuit Zoot—and I didn't understand dem either. Man, did dey do a job on me and my Zuit."

"Then vhy are vou here?" David stated in disbelief. "Did vou not grow up in the U.S.A.?

"Eshure, carnal," asserted Juan.

"Then no matter vat vou think, America is the foxhole of freedom."

"Eshure, man. If jou esay eso. Jou'er the college boy. Jou don't know what it is like to be a foreigner in jour own país, ese!" said Juan while shaking his head from side to side.

"Vat are vou saying, Vuan?"

"Mi papá y tios were citizens born in de U.S. Dat didn't stop La Migra. Dey got deported to Mexico just before pay day and had to walk back to Matatlan. Took dem a year, ese.

"That's no big thing, Vuan. The Nazis deport Jews right after dey strip them of their dignity."

"It was a two-dousand mile walk trough deserts and mountains, ese. My father esays dat La Migra made esure dat jou had de freedom to leave without pay and estay gone long enough eso jour family would learn to live without a man in de house."

"Vat vou are saying sounds very strange to me. Nothing like that ever happened near U.C.L.A. or Loyola. Before vour teachers threw vou out of vour school didn't they tell vou vat America means to the rest of the vorld?"

"I tink dey had us in eschool becuz dey were esupposed to keep us off de estreets of East Los. U.C.L.A. es way out in West Los. My Abuelito esaid dat we only went to eschool to eat lonche, man. We always had de freedom to estay off de estreets, off de grass, eat our lonche, and keep out of de esight of La Migra, ese."

"I'm sorry for that, Vaun. This La Migra sounds like the Storm Troopers organized to deport my people from our land. This is not the America I know. Hear that, Vuan?"

"Hear what, ese? My ears are in mis zapatos from de eshellin'."

"Here comes some more mail from Rommel's supermen. Keep vour head down," said David as a cluster of star shells illuminated night into day setting the scene for another Christmas post-card from home. "Vat are vou doing, man, get back in here!" shouted David as he grabbed Juan's belt and pulled him back into their tiny hole.

"But de light, eshe eshowed me my hommie Ramón The Poet," cried Juan. "I tink dose Kraut bastards are killing esome of my esweet carnales."

"How can vou be so sure of this in the dust of the desert?" said David.

"I tink I heard him cry out por la Madre de Dios y La Reina de Los Angeles."

"I heard some of his poems on the ship coming over here. I didn't get all of vat he said but the vords had a good rythem to them."

"He's estill movein', ese. I hope he's O.K."

Don't vorry, Vuan. Even if they got him, they won't be able to kill his poetry," said David. As the heat of battle continued, mourning was a luxury for civilians.

"Here come de thirty-thirties again, ese. It's like dey're crop dusting with iron pellet pesticide. De air es eso full of guano dat my throat feels like one of the eseagulls I killed on de ship just crapped in my mouth. It's almost as bad as de manure Mrs. Marsh eshot at mis carnales in high school, ese," shouted Juan just prior to another deafening silence.

After a few anxious glances over the rim of the foxhole, David whispered, "Vat they should have showed and told vou in that school is that the U.S.A. is trying to save the vorld from destruction and rape by the Nazi's and Hitler's madness. Ve vill destroy the armbands to preserve our Jewish identity. If the Nazis vin this var, the Jew is lost forever."

"What does dis mean for jou, David?"

"Personally, I vill be their roasted lamb."

"What jou talking about now, man?" replied Juan imitating David's whisper. "I haven't had a good roast since my uncle buried a head for my wedding dinner."

"I'm not talking about a vedding, Vuan."

"I'm not eidder, ese. Boy, was dat ever a wedding night. Eshure wish dis hole was a wedding bed for me and Concha. Dat would really be worth defending."

"Vat's that new noise I'm hearing, Vuan?"

"I keep hearing motors, ese. Where are dose German tanks dat we keep hearing about from de Sarge? He esaid dat Rommel has got dis General Kesslering over here just especial for us, along wit a division of armor. Taking Tunis es not goin' ta be another Casablanca."

"Be happy ve don't see them, Vuan. Our grenades cannot be slung far enough to stop them before ve get a chance to defend ourselves," replied David. "I vant a chance to get at them. Our whole vay of life, vour little vife vou talk of, is vorth defending, Vuan," whispered David out the side of his mouth as he strained his night blind eyes for hints of enemy movement.

"What way of life? What would a Westsider know about de trucha of Concha mía. Beside, ese, all I know es dat I'm here because of my Zuit, man. It was come here or do time for I dun't know why. Dis American uniform dey gave me fits all esquare.

Dere es no suave to dese treads, ese. Dese drapes are only for dying.

"Vat are drapes, I do not see vou vearing a shawl?"

"Drapes are jour clothes, ese. De Sarge esays dis uniform es de American flag, but I wouldn't estink up a flag de way I'm grossing out dis American Army Zuit," said Juan as he took his turn glancing in the direction of the origin of the star shells. "Dose Iron Cross boys are up to esomething out dere. Dey must be in love with dis place to work eso hard at keeping it."

"The Sarge is right about the uniform being the flag, Vuan. It is vat makes vou and me vone. It is all of the armor ve got," said David.

"Armor," said Juan, missing the meaning. "Jou really tink dese zuits will stop a Kraut shell? Hey, jou got a especial blessing for jours? Or maybe jou got especial esweat. Jou estink like an outside barrio toilet on a hot Califas day. Jour uniform es eso crusty dat jou maybe escare away bullets. Anyways, what have jou to worry, man? I heard about jou guys."

"Vat you mean, heard about us guys?" said David expecting some anti-semitic remark to follow his question. "Not even a Jew tows the springs of Iliad around for a shower. Besides, vour uniform looks like brick blocks and smells like camel pies."

The ground near them erupted like a five-day old zit. Mutilated parts of the dead-dead were unearthed and deposited in with them. "Good comeback, ese. Jour are all right even if jou talk funny."

"Vou are the one vho talks, funny, Vuan."

At least my brick blocks are estill in one piece. Every eshell eseems to put more body parts dan people into dis hole. If dey kill de two of us, Graves Registration es going to tink we are eseven and a half guys," said Juan as a streamer of nepom blazed over their heads.

"Vuan," said David as he used his gun butt to shovel guano on the burning sand next to him. "Vat vou heard about me from the guys in the company?"

"Let me put out dis fire first, ese. If dose Iron Cross boys get any closer wit dat estuff, dey'll burn de estink out of dese flags we are wearing," said Juan following up on David's moves for smothering the fire on his side of the foxhole. "O.K., David. Mis carnales dicen que jou guys call joureselves de chosen few," said Juan. "Why are jou worried if jou are chosen people?"

"The problem vit being the chosen few, Vuan, is that the longer this var goes on, the fewer ve chosen get to be."

"Esn't fewer better? My teachers always esaid dat de problem with Mexican families was dat dey were too many, and getting bigger all de time."

David was about to seek meaning for Juan's statement, but the grinding of gears and the silhouettes of Goliathe's mobile iron cages carrying the armies of the iron cross told them why the barrage had lifted and the probing with thirty-thirty's had started. The many threads of the American uniform faced armor's indiscriminate nepom with only a few grenades. "I hope dat Eisenhower and Patton back at battalion know about dis kettle of fish," said Juan, "or de only esurvivors on dis line are going to be de cucarachas in de sand."

"At least ve know vere the iron cross tanks are, Vuan. The holocaust kills everybody," retorted David.

"I was happier when dey were fighting esomewheres else, ese," said Juan as he viewed the spectacle of a battalion of German armor crashing and plunging over the ridge.

Rommel's armor opened up with devastating accuracy. Millions of shells seemed to be directed at the foxhole. Only a miracle could save them from the wrath. "Ve'er lost!" screamed David.

"Dey are going to bury us eso Graves Registration will only have to use body bags. I hope dey don't put my parts in de bags wit other parts!" yelled Juan, as a mouth full of pulverized guano hit him right in the eyes.

"I vonder if I'll see the next sunrise from inside a body bag?" yelled David as a shell crashed to their immediate rear.

"Jou can't esee through a body bag, ese, unless jou got esome of them x-ray eyes. Jou got x-ray eyes, ese?"

They flattened out into the desert dust. Roasted guano fell over them. Flat on their faces before the might of the Reich, with fear in their knees. They began their prayers before their souls became doomed. Juan knew there was nowhere to run now. The dodging and darting were over for now. "Jesu Cristo, please forgive me when I pray to jou, I know where I'm going and dat es wit jou. Now I eseem to be always moving witout an esign posts in de tan oak forest of life. Only de dawn of jour wisdom can tell when I am dere. Let de armor of de cucaracha protect me. Señor, forgive me, or I am lost."

Somehow through the battle, Juan heard David murmuring, "During this time of doom I have obeyed you Lord, now is the time for you to come through for your chosen people."

In midprayer and promise, the shaking earth came alive with a new sound that thundered in on their strained ear drums. The black iron cages were stopped as if Tezcatilpoca saw The Lord of the dawn that reversed into the night. The screeching of Eagles and Falcons: incoming mail from the American and British armor zoomed over their flanks. In that precious moment Juan was sure that Jesu Cristo touched him on the shoulder. He looked at David who was still praying gratefully, "I know that even in this hellhole you vould not desert the souls of Vour chosen ones."

The little foxholes in the desert came alive with Seventh Army infantry fire as their division pressed the advantage their armor had gained. "If we have tanks, why do we have to chase deir tanks on foot?" Juan asked as he darted towards the exhaust plume's of the retreating Afrika Korps.

"Because vhile the tank takes the land, it takes infantry to hold it."

"Do you think we have beaten dem dis time, ese? I tink I can esmell de esea in de mud in my nose. We must be coming back towards de coast," yelled Juan as he started his well paced ducking and darting moves.

"They von't be beaten until my people are freed," screamed David. "Vat kind of dance are vou doing?"

"It's wat I call de Chivito Cucaracha. Estay low, duck and dart. De Itais and Krauts haven't learned how to eshoot at dese movidas yet, ese. Jou got people in Africa, ese?"

"No, Vaun, in Germany."

"Jou got a long ways to go, man. I hope jou make it, ese. For reals, I mean dat. Familia es important, carnal."

"Family is very, very important, Vuan."

"I hope my hommies can make it too. It looks like Ramón es movin' O.K. Estay by me carnal. My armor was just blessed. I tink jou are going to be lucky for me. De guano of de desierto has made us one."

"Vuan, vou are a strange duck."

"Call me Cucaracha, carnal. I only duck bullets."

A Beach Head In Sicily

Wave after wave of America's flesh was being washed ashore onto Sicily's coast. Seasick raw recruits and battle hardened desert rats on a beach in salty foxholes. The generals said the conditions were perfect for making a landing, but those conditions didn't prevent the Italian pill boxes and German armor from staining the Roman sand red with the blood of the allies. The sound of the sea, new waves of flesh and naval salvos pushed up their backs.

The Navy seemed to hit everything but the enemy pill boxes and machine gun nests. All of the hommies were body surfing with full packs on. Javier, and Jorge turned a white capped wave pink with the blood of Indian nations. Rogelio laid bleeding on the beach, feeling the blows of death like cucarachas Juan's father smashed off the walls of their chosita in the barrio. The brown rim of the cliffs and the natural caves the sea had made over centuries had been recreated into nests of fire that spit death down onto the dying hommies. The blue and white fertile corn of the barrio lay barren in the salt of the Italian beachhead.

Although his legs were still in the Sahara, and his stomach was on the bottom of the Mediterranean, Juan knew that he had to start up the cliff if he wanted to live. To stay on the beach was certain death, and the beach was no place for a cucaracha to die: the essence of Ramón's poetry pushed him on. His ducking and darting moves would carry their flags and poetry into battle. "David! Jou'er always yelling about ovens, well dese place es a bar-b-que pit. If we dun't move off dese Itai beach dey are going to make meatballs out of us.

"I'm vit vou, Vuan," called David.

"Have jou made dat Christ killer one of us, Juan?" asked Jaime.

"He fights good, ese," said Juan. "I'd trust him at my back anytime, anywhere."

"If jou esay eso," said Jaime. "I'll estay behind both of jou."

"Dose cliffs are on top of vou too, Christ profaner," said David to Jaime.

Man, dose cliffs aren't any worse dan a barrio fence, and believe me, I jumped many," said Juan. "At least here, we got friends wit big naval guns on our eside instead of La Migra with guns in our backs."

Through the battles of the Sahara David had come to trust the survival instincts of this cucaracha. He had a street savvy that no boot camp, drill sergeant, or Heidleburg professor could teach. "Vats your plan, Vaun? Vou are the vone that always is talking about the safety of the foxhole."

"I dun't esee any foxholes whoth esavin' on dis beach, ese," retorted Juan.

"My feet tell me not to move, Vuan. But, vou are right, if ve don't move soon, a red sea is going to close over us."

"From what, Red Esea, hommie?" asked Juan. "I'll bet dat esea was like un buche de agua compared to dis place. Dey gods already drank all the blood of de hommies dat dey are goin' to get today."

"No cultural dissertations, Vuan. Just tell me vat vou got planned!" yelled David over the blast of an exploding shell.

"Plan, jou dun't need a plan to do wat we got to do. Mi papá always esaid, 'Jou can't lift a bucket if jou are estanding in it.' Just do de duck and dart movidas I taught jou in de desierto, ese. We just do dose birds one at a time. Tink of dem just as big upside-down cement buckets."

"But, Vuan they are shooting at us out of those buckets," called David. "There's gott to be a smart vay to take those nests. Let's think before ve leap."

"Too much tinking freezes de feet, David. Besides it es hard to eshoot when jou are in a bucket. No Itai bullet will find us. Dey haven't made one fast enough to catch us, ese, once I get my boots to dance."

Juan bolted out of the hole like a chivo in rut. David followed without a thought. Juan always said those weird things just before he started to do something most people would call impossible. To others, Juan might be a heroic ignorant fool, but to David he was the Avenging Angel of the Lord of Hosts that could fly like a stone hurled from a sling when he wanted to. This assault on the cliffs above the beach was to be one of those times. David muttered, "I have gott to remember to tell this vato loco that there is a difference between blind faith and strategic wisdom."

Most of the other rats on the beach seemed content to lie and die there, as if that were their only alternative. This landing wasn't like the one at Casablanca, where no one told the French they were coming. This time the German Armour knew they were coming. Besides, who in their right mind would follow the moves of a loco chivito and a crusading Jew. Even so, others began to move, inspired by the uncanny success of this crazy pair.

Their sergeant had told them during their assault on Tunis, "The only way to kill a pill box is to approach it as if it were a loud mouth coward. Once there, stuff a grenade in its mouth."

The pill boxes reminded David of the Rabbi who told him, "If you take on a Goliathe, throw the stone to hit him between the eyes."

Juan's father always said, "Big talkers do much evil if deir guns aren't silenced real fast and real hard."

The Cucaracha and David speared into the cliff, stuffing, slinging and silencing each box one at a time. After the fourth nest, David said, "slow down, Vuan, vou don't have to vin this var all by vourself."

"Who's winning a war, ese? I'm just trying to estay alive. De blood of great and mighty warriors lives in me, carnal," Juan said with joy.

"Great warriors bleed too," retorted David.

"Throw jour espears at de enemy, David. I keep telling jou dat I'm on jour eside, ese," said Juan. "Besides, de way dose dead rats on de beach are cheering jou tink we're making a touchdown or esomething. Adelante, David! As my Abuelito would always esay, 'no time to estop now, we just got de ting rollin' good.'"

"O.K. vat's your plan for the nest emplacements, Vaun?"

"Just keep on de roll. Rolling cucarachas are hard to esmash. Beside mi Abuelo taught us to just keep on rollin' once jou got goin'. Abuelito knew what he was talking about, too. It took a lot to get tings rollin' when jou were wit him. I tink we pushed his carro more dan we rode in it. Let's take dat next nest from de left. We got more cover dat way."

"Vaun, cucarachas may have nine lives, but I only have vone. Vho is going to save my family if vou get me killed."

"No worry, ese. De estar and cross are with us."

On top of the hill next to the last pillbox that Juan had just destroyed. Juan's legs went one pillbox too far. His lungs were about to collapse. He started to stumble until he fell like a used dirty old washrag thrown on the side of the bunker. Gasping and panting, David collapsed next to Juan. As the salt from their sweat stung their eyes and their blurred vision cleared, their eyes were drawn to rose colored foam floating on the incoming surf. Bodies danced upon the waves like corks from a broken fishnet. Juan tries to move his arms to point at the eerie sight! He couldn't move. He tried to tell David but he couldn't speak.

Out of the corner of his eye he saw David's mouth moving but he did not hear anything. Juan's throbbing heart poured forth blood to beat back the violent wind of war. His shock held back his tears. The pride of the barrio, three of his hommies, poured their life upon the Sicilian sand and nourished the mother sea. Later the postman would deliver the pain to be shared by the families.

For the first time, Abuelo would tell him, "Jou're not a green tomato anymore, Cucaracha. Jou're sliced tomatos now." His bleeding for his dear friends brought Concha's image of his skull back to his heart. His right hand found the way to his grandmother's cross under his blouse. Christ's bursting heart told him that He was with in his pain. Zuits in body bags would cruise Brooklyn Avenue no more!

The Sarge pulled up in his 105 jeep and yelled, "Good job, Guano!"

"If jou esay eso, Sarge," responded Juan automatically as he tried to get to his feet.

"You did alright too, Rabbi." said the Sarge.

"Thanks, Sarge," said David. "All I did was chase Vuan up the cliff."

"Ya did the right thing, Rabbi. It's always good to have someone ya can trust at your back. Isn't that right, Guano?" asked the Sarge.

"I guess eso, Sarge," said Juan wearily.

"Old Pearl handles couldn't take his glasses off yous guys. He said if he had ten more like you that he could take this whole island in three days."

"Who needs dat?" asked Ramón the Poet as he walked up to the jeep.

"He said yous guys were real army," the Sarge continued. "He wants you ta have a couple of bronze stars. He says he's gona pin them on yous himself. I told him that yous two were real marble fudge and the bacon grease we needed to take Fortress Europe."

"I'm glad Old Blood and Guts es happy, Sarge," said Juan as the sun glint from the waves refocused Juan's eyes back down on the beach.

"Guano, your moves saved a lot of boys lives today," said the Sarge.

"Dat es not why I did it, Sarge," said Juan as he continued to stare at Rogelio's, Jorge's, and Eddie's corpses bobbing in in the white Italian surf.

"You and David jump on the jeep, battalion wants me to form a squad to set up an HQ on the ridge. Old blood and Guts is going to have the brass hats view the battle there as he leads it."

Juan turned his back on his carnales to get on the jeep. "I see them too, Vuan," whispered David. "I'm glad that I didn't know them better."

"I didn't have time to know dem well enough, David," said Juan.

No bullet was to find them that day.

A FOXHOLE IN THE SNOW

The Generals called it The Winter Line. The tourist posters Juan had seen before the war always made Italy out to be a sunlit paradise. A couple of those canvas posters would be nice to keep the freezing rain and snow out of the foxhole.

The long year since that dusty night in the Sahara had dried out the blood in many fine cucarachas. The stench of war and the dead eyes of faceless civilian focused in on Juan's sleeping soul. Even so the tree of life still coursed through his veins.

Juan came to realize that the third best thing about that year of dust and death were the lively heavy duty talks between David and the Cucaracha. The second best thing about that year of hot wind and brutal strife around the edge of an open foxhole was being whole enough to remember it. The best thing was being able to recall dancing with Concha at the Aragon as a safe and distant eternity away in another time and galaxy.

David was still fighting for the chosen few. His great anger had never subsided. On the other hand, Juan, a chosen one, had to fight to appease the anger of his gods. The flaw of perfection and the remnant of the chosen needed the time and space to regenerate the burned vineyard and the reversed inward direction. The flawless and the flawed marched together. The gods were not patient and the scorched earth was barring the thorny fruits of death and pestilence. Juan and David had to survive and win this war if the gods were to be regenerated or Elohimn to be praised.

The forgotten remembrances of shrieks and songs from a dimly lit childhood made distant by a forgettable war filled Juan's dreams with competing, converging voices: one voice said the Spirits are many; another voice said that God is the only way for the chosen many. Jehovah, the god of anger, wants the blood of the cucaracha to regenerate the earth, but in holding on to his Great Grandmother's cross he used a silver blade to conquer death, a denial he did not understand.

In the moonlit Italian Christmas, the soldiers on both sides hummed Silent Night as Juan captured a glimpse of the Resurrected-Regenerated Chosen One. The long line of battles north through Italy and the vision of spiritual silence helped Juan realize that souls were critical to reality. Even so on this cold moonlit night, he was glad that his Zuit was safe with María Concha. The fire of battle could not burn the Zuit as long as she was protecting it.

David had told him before the Gela beachhead in Sicily: "There are lists of names and dates in heaven. No use being afraid of death. Ve are dying from the time ve are born. In every var there is at least vone bullet out there vit your name on it." Juan was still making sure that he was at least one step ahead of that bullet.

Even a darting chivito in a green American uniform invited but defied the black German bullets. The generals had mapped out well established battle lines with yellow pins along the Italian Peninsula. The Germans kept up the defense 24 hours a day. The war on paper had turned into a slugfest with both sides swinging desperately to gain some advantage for a small piece of Italian real estate. The opposing wills of Patch and Kesslering attacked the moves of the chivito.

The foxhole was a target even at night. The firing of their weapons revealed them in the dark. Both Juan and David knew that to protect their shadows they had to keep them short. Shoot an duck was the order of the day. David whispered to Juan, "Vou can run away from a bullet even in the light, but vou can only run avay from vour shadow in the dark."

The white 1943, Italian Christmas day, was the pure icy cold heat of the winter turquoise sky. Gone was the Golden Sun of Matatlan. All that remained was the cold silver of frozen sunlit days and ice blue nights. The wind pierced through Juan's American uniform like a spear of steel. David and Juan were now in a day bright white Italian foxhole. While the slug feast of military giants made them buddies, the Roman countryside, with its catalogued historical monuments, had become the grey uncultured battlefield. Even in this void of civilized death, many of the monuments and tombs of the pock marked land held the voice of his Great Grandmother's silver cross.

Abuela was on his mind like a helmet on his head. He often

wondered around Christmas how someone who looked so Indian could say such Christian words. From what he had seen of war torn Italy his Abuela definitely had an Indian perception of the real world. Her "tragito" released in her the torn allegiance to two God/gods. She struggled with the big golden cats in the pits of her Coliseum. Christmas revealed her silver spirit. He could smell her cooking even in this frozen white foxhole. Abuela always added her secret ingredient, golden cooking sherry. When he helped her kneed the yellow maza for the Christmas tamales, he knew that she abused the sherry. Her Indian styled tamales were filled with raisins and nuts, not the hearts of Christian men. As the patrona she offered her golden sweat her entire life for her family by carrying the silver cross twice.

Juan could feel the warmth of her soft gravelly golden voice. When she was in the tamale making mood she saw the vision of the holy cucaracha, the meat of sacrifice in the tamales offered during the Christmas meal. Her seed was concealed in her mellowed smiling face, the mask of colonial Christianity. To her all her niños looked the same, saw the same, and reflected her spiritual seed. He knew when she caressed him that he was an embodiment of her seed. Juan called this her "Mestizo assembly line." "Otro tragito, mi hijito, we all need to be free on Christmas." In the limited safety of the cold foxhole, her voice made his soul cry as he kissed her silver cross. She wasn't safe this Christmas.

Abuela was solid, but the bitterness of death came visiting. Tío Augustín, her forty-five-year-old baby brother, had been crushed in a stamp plant that was making bomb casings. The angry gods of war killed him. He had been good at grape stamping - what a way for a maker of golden sherry to go. She would plant him near his grapes in Matatlan. Augustin had always been a quiet warrior. He never gave Abuela any static over her drinking. He never seemed angry at La Migra for deporting him, even though it took this U.S. citizen one year to walk back to Matatlan. Abuela had many tragitos that year. "Estay with me, Augustinito," Juan felt Abuela say, "I need jour machitlz."

"Vaun, come back to Italy. Vou, Jaime und I are the forvard O.P. (observation post). I think the Iron Cross Boys are making a move. Vat vou think?" "I tink I would like a quesadilla and cabrito al pastor esmothered in my Mother's salsa," asserted Juan. "An esteaming hot bowl of cocido de res, a Christmas tamale and an enchilada con lengua would be even better, ese. Comida fit for reyes."

"Eso, carnal," echoed Jaime. "In de cold frosty mornings around Planada in de winter time dere wuz notin' like a hot tamal y café con leche fresh from de cabra."

"Get serious, vou locos!" ordered David. "This is no time or place to open a taco stand. Save it for after the var. Ve got to get vord back to battalion about these movements."

"David, it's Christmas," said Juan.

"Yah, rabbi, listen to de man, here," said Jaime. "I'd even esettle for esome matza ball sopa if it had esome salsa in it."

"No day is holy to the Nazi, locos. Get vour brains out of vour stomachs," commanded David. "Christmas is nothing to a good Nazi. He can kill everyday of the year. Don't go soft on me now. The only good Nazi is a dead Nazi."

"Dat's what dey esaid in de movies about Indians, David," said Juan. "Dis war es teaching me dat Cuatemoc eshowed us de ways of jour Iron Cross boys. Dey esure fixed it eso my tío Augustín was a good Indian."

"I'm sorry for that Vaun, but ve are going to be dead too if vou don't get vour hearts out vour brains."

"I'm losing it, ese. Dat tío told me of tings dat are just now beginning to make meaning. I eshould have told him how important he was to me. His voice has been one of courage for me. His thoughts are part of what little wisdom I have."

"I'd had a tío like dat too, Rabbi," commented Jaime. "He got runned over when a crop dusting plane crashed on him near Weedpatch. I tink of him a lot when de krauts try and strafe us."

"Many of my foxhole nights have been filled with his power and songs, David," Juan continued. "He left a wife and three babies, man. I am de compadre to two of his babies. What am I really doing here, who are we helping? Everywhere we go we blow up de whole place."

"Vhere helping vour families stay free," suggested David.

"I can't help my family from dis hole, ese!" retorted Juan.

"I'm sure vour tío knows of vour love, Vaun. Tell me about these new revelations after ve make our report, O.K.?"

"Dey dun't eseem to be doing anything new, Rabbi," observed Jaime.

"Let's let the brass decide that, Jaime. Ve are the eyes of our division, not the high command. Listen to vour Abuelos on how to survive. Didn't vou tell me they said to feed vour roots and do vat vou had to do to survive."

"Sí, mon," answered both Jaime and Juan.

"Then let's get that report in," commanded David. "Jour Abuelos vould have vanted us to do that if they vere here."

"Ya vol, mein general," snapped Jaime.

"Quit dat," snapped Juan. "As usual he es right."

"Boy, how jou heebs estick together, Juan," said Jaime. "Jou two will make a lovely couple at a barmitzva."

"Jou bedder cut dat out, Jaime, or jou could be wearing a body bag full of M-1 shell fragments!" said Juan.

"Jou don't have to be eso esensative, Chivito," said Jaime. "I'm just a kidder. I dun't mean no harm."

"Dat's what de L.A.P.D. esaid when de forced me inta de army. Dey didn't want any harm to come to me eidder," commented Juan.

"I'll stay here to see if they step up their moves," said David while ignoring Juan's and Jaimes exchange. "I'll follow vou two to H.Q. in twenty minutes or less, depending on how fast they come at us. O.K.?"

The spirit of courage that walked Juan's father and tíos back to Matatlan after the deportation to Durango jogged Juan and Jaime back through the snow with the report to H.Q. Juan stayed behind Jaime all the way. Jaime wasn't sure whether he was running from the Germans or Juan. David followed as planned. The Generals used their report to catch Kesslering off balance and break out of the Winter Line. Abuelito was right again: "Death of a branch brings de strength of life to de roots."

LIBERATION OF ROME

So this was the land of the Caesares and the Popes. What a place to have a furlough during a war! Required relaxation and recreation in a structured Rome with no structure! A picture of pure destruction overlorded with his family voices, especially Concha's. He was without Concha and her warm dreamy ideas of love in the afternoon on a white sand beach beside the sparkling blue waves of the Pacific Ocean. The violence of loneliness in the winds of war blew stronger and stronger in his heart.

Day after day up the Appian way still more structured Rome with no structure prompted a vision of an empty picture book full of memories. A paper Rome with no soul: Juan's family in letters. A great emptiness filled Juan's heart with nightmares.

The tourist illusion was no more: a real living hell! The four horsemen of the apocalypse were slaughtering Juan's hommies again. No tourist brochure photographer had taken pictures of this Italy. Juan could not write in his letters home the agony of the blood soaked earth. How could he write such meaningful empty words?

The broken rutted road was littered with souls. On that road into Rome Juan saw a dead mother and daughter beside the road. The mother with one eye opened, face half down in the bleeding Roman earth—and the little girl with both dead eyes opened, staring at her dead mother. Christian eyes reflected devastation: such dead honest holy eyes. Juan respected them in their grief and honest hope of a better tomorrow.

Juan saw Mexicans and Cholos in the tanned faces of Italian field workers and Spanish eyes in the faces of dead Italian officers with tall shiny boots. Marble heads and headless truncated bodies filled the city. Armies became destructive littering, thieving, "picture taking tourists."

The forgotten shattered widows and windows parted burning bushes and burnt holes in walls to revive a glimpse and sustain a vision in David's and Juan's souls. Broken glass everywhere. Boggy roads littered with brave armies, aimless soldiers, cowardly deserters, converted enemies, maimed civilians, chunks of monuments, and exploding graves. The hospitals were bulging with agonizing moans of "wounded wounded" and the half dead. As he walked down the broken streets in blood and mud splattered boots, he ingested the horrific cost of liberating history from the idealogy of madmen. Juan became engulfed by enemies who wanted to be allies.

As Juan marched into Rome he could feel the persecution of enslaved and crucified Christians with its martyred Jews to glorify the Caesars! When Christ came to Rome he replaced the "Caesars" through the church hierarchy. Juan's painful heart burned like a Christ turned black on the cross full of grief for warring Christians: La Migra deporting the barrio off the planet.

Juan turned both his eyes skyward as his soul shrieked at God, "War is hell, a living nightmare for everybody; even for the enemy!" Not a sound passed his lips! Not a letter dripped out of his pen! Sleepless horror invading the farthest reaches of his being!

David Goldstein saw the nationalistic hatreds, sleeve worn summary sentences and Christ killing wounds of bleeding Christians, as if they were his family in Germany. His bowels of denial for leaving his family unprotected and helpless gnawed in the pit of his stomach, a seething stifled volcano of guilt. The Allies were saving everybody but his family!

Liberating a gentile people from their facist ideology did not save his family. An angry frustrated Jew on R & R concealed inside the culture of Latins: no sound, no word, no sleep. "Vat the hell are ve doing in Rome!?" he shouted at Juan as they arrived at their assigned barrack tent just outside Rome.

"We need de rest, David," said Juan. "If we keep going like we have been, we will run out of army before we get to Germany and a chansa to free jour people. De Sarge esays que fatigue kills even de best unit."

"If I have a choice between fatigue and extermination, I'll live with fatigue, Vaun," asserted David. "All that is important to me is the saving of my family from the Nazi killing machine."

"All people need esaving, David," replied Juan. "Mi Abuelo esaid dat Christ died for everybody, even jour family. De wounds we esee on de crosses of de church walls, which are everywhere in dis city, poured blood all over de world. We're not gods, David. We have ta do dis liberation one step at a time."

"Those steps are too slow, Cucaracha!" yelled David.

"My heart truly bleeds for jou and jour family, but it bleeds for dese people too, ese. A family lying face down in de mud is not de answer for peace, David."

"A moment for living is one luxury my family can't count on Vuan. I have a pater, mater, one brother and two sisters facing Hitler's final solution! The minute we put a foot in Africa, he started exterminating the living dead."

"Now jou Jews know a lot about dying, ese, but what do jou people know about living, David? Jou've never been killed over and over, bit by bit until now. Jou've never almost estarved in de fields of plenty until now."

"Vat are vou saying here, Vaun?" asked David. "Now jou are being such a tease. Are vou teasing me now?"

"No, carnal. I'm being real eserious here, man. Tink wit me on dis if jou can. Jou'er picking a flat of glorious estrawberries and not one of dem es for jou, man," Juan answered. "All jou get to do is esuck in de jellow powder dey espray on dem berries to keep de bugs off. Jou drool on de ground and jour bowels growl in jour ears all night. Eso jou dun't know what it takes to live, do jou? Jou defend de Jew way with jour God to make jou live on estone tablets."

"Everywhere ve vent, Vuan, dey are trying to kill us, Vuan! We are de vanderers of Europe. The day of the starving and persecuted Jew continues," asserted David. "And another thing vou must remember, Vuan. They think ve are the black death or something. Our home is the next place vhere ve are allowed to survive a few more years. Even our new Italian allies still see me as an enemy in an American uniform."

"Everywhere we went, de growers tried to work us to death,

David. For months at a time my home was the back of my Abuelo's pick-up. When we were out of work we were pests. When we were working dey dumped pesticides on us."

"Maybe I do not know a whole lot about how to live, but I have survived more than vou know, Vuan. In all of my vanderings I have kept my homeland in my heart!"

"My homeland es de place of my roots, ese," responded Juan. "We are foreigners in our own lands. My wife sent me a letter dat told me dat de esoldiers are raiding and raping mi barrio and de policía locks us up in jail for our own protection."

"Dat must stop, Vuan. This hatred of peoples must be ended by this var. I met a priest in Spain who taught me how to preserve my spiritual life."

"My Abuelito always esaid dat life es life and hate es hate. Jou can't keep jour meaning in pieces, ese. Killing any part es a killing to all, carnal!"

David and Juan's visions were different. Respect for each other as soldiers became their common battlefield as they shared their mutual pain and deprivation.

"Tomorrow morning right after chow, let's go visit de legendary site where de Roman pagan overlords crucified Peter, and other Christians." said Juan.

"Lead on my exploring Cucaracha," said David.

For the first time in the war, Juan felt his boots on right side up when he heard that Peter glorified his acceptance of Christ by requesting to be crucified upside down. Peter, who had denied Christ three times before the crucifixion of Christ, now refused in front of the whole world to deny Christ a fourth time. In his Zuit and uniform Juan sensed the denial of his soul. His Zuit and uniform were his tree of blood! At the shrine he turned his tear-filled eyes to David and murmured, "Peter the Jew, glorified Jesu Cristo. Standing here in my stinking boots I can't glorify basura!"

"Hitler still has us upside down, Juan. Do you know vat vou are fighting for now?" said David.

"I'm just a pile of garbage in a dirty, army green Zuit that the Sarge says es the flag of my country. What do jou want from me? I'm already on my knees, again, in a foxhole!" said Juan in his wretched anguish.

"Vat did Christ vant from Peter?" asked David.

"What Christ wants from jou too, man. He wants us to estop denying the truth."

"And vat does that mean to vou, Vuan?" asked David.

"The truth cannot be married to a lie, David."

"Then vat is that lie vou told vour mater about vour Zuit, Vuan?" asked David.

"Dat's between me and mi madre, David. Where es de eshrine for St. Paul?" asked Juan.

"Vhy do you vant to see another shrine? Hasn't this vone messed you up enough? Let's see some art or find a good place to eat," suggested David.

"How can garbage appreciate art?" asked Juan. "Besides, I'm not hungry for more Italian food right now, carnal. On top of that, I promised mi Mamasita and Espanish Grandma dat I go esee dese eshrines."

"Vat did vou promise this time, Vuan?"

"We make mandas in our family, David," answered Juan.

"I know vour soul is full of spirits, Vuan. Vou have them yelling in vour dreams ven vou sleep. But, I never pictured vou as ritualistically religious."

"David, I keep telling jou to talk in English, or at least in an English made for de ears of a Cucaracha. Nobody has estolen my esoul with a picture."

"I just meant that I never vould have thought of vou vanting to visit religious shrines."

"I'm not visiting them, I'm going to them for my Mamasita and Grandma."

"O.K. Cucaracha. Let's ask that priest over there for directions," said David.

"Padre, Padre."

"Qué quieres, mi hijo?" the priest said as he turned toward them.

"Oh, my Got! It can't be really him!" shouted David.

"Who are jou talking to, ese? A priest es a man, not a god," said Juan.

"I'm looking at my savior, Padre Diego," answered David.

"Esavior? Man, jou are weird. Have jou been at the jungle juice again?" asked Juan.

"Vuan, I met this priest in Spain. He's the one I told vou about. He befriended me and saved my life in 1936 during my flight from Nazi Germany. He got me a false passport so I could go to the U. S. of A. He risked his life for me and I lost track of him ven he was vounded by the Popular Front in Spain in the same year."

"Dey let jou in with a false passport, David?" asked Juan in disbelief. "Dey deported my Papá and Tíos for being citizens in Matatlan after de season was done. I'm glad La Migra let jou in, ese, pero dere es no justicia por raza y mi familia."

"Vat are vou talking now, Vuan?" asked David.

"Just dat dere es justicia and den dere es justice, carnal," answered Juan.

As the priest approached them, he said in broken English, "David, es dat really jou in de uniform of de Americanos?"

"Yes, padre. I'm so glad to see vou are safe from those vho vere trying to kill vou. Tell me vats been happening to vou?"

"Cuando jou left por de Estados Unidos, I left por de Vatican. My countrymen acted as if Dios was at fault for de economic and political problems of de world. Deir fear affected all directions and faiths in Spain. Who es dis with jou, David?"

"This is my ally in the search for truth, La Cucaracha Ultima," said David.

"La de Don Quijote o la de Sancho Panza," Father Diego said laughingly.

"What's de differencia, Padre?" said Juan, "Y me llamo es really, Juan Galván. Mi amigo David was referring to mi nombre en la calle."

"La verdad del nombre will make you insane or it will eset jou free, my young eseeker of de truth," said Father Diego. "It es truly a pleasure to meet esomeone who calls David a friend. It has been hard for him to trust his fellowman after what he and his family have endured on nuestra tierra. To which direction are you going in my esons?"

"Juan is taking me to see saints for his mater and Espanish grandma, but as usual his is lost," said David winking in Juan's direction.

"I'm not lost, David," said Juan. "I just dun't know where we are going at dis very moment. We were going to esee St. Paul, Padre Diego. Maybe jou can help me out on esometing dat has me going in circles."

"It would be a pleasure to help jou, hijo," answered Father Diego.

"Mi Mamasita esays que Paul knew of de estraight and narrow direction."

"Este amigo tiene mucha razón, David. Adelante," said Father Diego as they set off for the shrine of St. Paul. "What do jou know of St. Paul my joung friend?"

"Only de stories from catequismo," replied Juan. "He was a Roman Jew who witnessed for Christ. I tink many of his letters make for a lot of de New Testament. At least I tink que dat es what mi madre esays about him. Can jou teach us more, Padre?"

"I take it den, dat jou are Catholic."

"Why do jou ask, Padre?" Juan said as he pulled out his dog tags and Great Grandmother's silver crucifix.

"Not too many joung men admit to being Catholic dese days, jou are on a quest por la verdad, and jou are with David," said Father Diego as they neared the shrine.

"Well I'm Catholic. My niños made me be baptized," said Juan. "I made my first Holy Communión en Misión San Juan Bautista. I was confirmed in Our Lady de Guadalupe en Los Angeles, and I was married to Concha María in de esame Church en mi best tacuche. If I make it through dis war, María and me will have all our babies baptized in de Church. Mi madre y mi suegra would esee us dead first if we dun't do dat."

"It appears jou have tried to follow at least some of the Sacraments, mi hijo, pero what are dese tacuches?" inquired Father Diego.

"Dey are mis drapes, Padre, my very best Zuit of clothes," replied Juan proudly. "In my wedding I put dem before La Virgen and mi esposa for a double blessing. De priest even had a tragito de tequila wit me and my Papá when I espoke with him in de priest house right before my wedding to my beautiful Conchita."

"I take it dat María Conchita es el nombre de su esposa, Juan?" asked Padre Diego.

"Sí, Padre Diego," answered Juan.

"And es eshe part of our Holy Mother Church also, my eson?" asked Father Diego.

"Oh, sí, Padre Diego," said Juan. "Eshe had her quinceañera and everythin'. Mi Mamasita would not have allowed me to marry Conchita if eshe wasn't a virgin and a daughter of de church, because mi mamá had a big idea on how de wedding was to happen. We had de lasso and padrinos por todas de las cosas jou could ever imagine."

"Dat es all very interesting, my eson. Dere are esometings about jour wedding and quinceañera dat I would like to talk on later," said Father Diego as he rubbed and pulled at his chin with his right hand.

"Dat would be nice, Padre," said Juan as he glanced and smiled at David.

"Good, hijo, but for now I wish to talk about dis esuit jou were married in, Juan," said Padre Diego.

"Vhy is that so interesting to vou, Padre?" asked David.

"Dere are many references to esuits in de Holy Escriptures, mis hijos, pero Our Lord teaches us dat even wearing a blessed esuit, and following de esacred wishes of jour elders, y padrinos casorio por todo, does not make a man of God nor help him in de research por la verdad," replied Father Diego.

"I tink que I heard dis before cuando mi Mamasita esaid dat I did not do my faith justice en mi Zuit," stated Juan. "Eshe made me promise to visit dese eshrines for de good of de family esoul. Eshe esays dat eshe will be able to esee dem through my eyes when I return. Eseein' dem for myself has made me want to know more. Mi Espanish Grandma esays que I need to find all de trute I can in in dem."

"Only God can plant de trute in jour esoul and help jou to make it blossom and bear fruit, mis hijos," asserted Father Diego.

"Mande, Padre? I do not understand jour meaning for me," said Juan.

"Let me esee if de Spirit will help me open jour heart, Juan," said Father Diego. "You might want to listen too, David."

"I'll listen to vou as I always have, but my ears find it hard to think of a merciful God vhen I see the vrath of his judgment all around me," said David.

"It es not our place to esit in judgment of De Creator, David," said Father Diego. What es his wrathe as jou esee it through de glasses darkly, maybe a blessing para jou in His grand design."

"How do jou know dis, Padre?" asked Juan.

"David and Juan, I know dat Jesu Cristo es Love," replied Father Diego. "When anyone tries to destroy Him, dey can try to do it with hate and dey will fail. My esons, dat es de trute. We can see dis in de holy places in de Vatican. Entiendes?"

"Sí, Padre," said Juan." David nodded, but stared off to the walls they were passing.

"Jesus Cristo es faith and when anyone denies Him he fails, and dat es de trute," Father Diego continued.

"The meaning of that is not clear for me," said David. "Jews are the carriers of the truth and Law. That is their commission from Got. How can Christ the Jew be The Truth?"

"Jesus Cristo es more dan a Jew, David," said Father Diego as they turned into a spacious hall with a vaulted ceiling. "He es de only begotten of God. He demands obedience on a voluntary basis and if anyone succumbs to temptation, he fails. My esons dat es de trute."

"Then, vat is happening here in Italy and Spain to the Christ?" asked David.

"David, Jesus Cristo es trute," said Father Diego. "When anyone tries to destroy His Trute with de lie, he fails. And dat, my sons es de trute even here in de Vatican. Paul eshows us dis trute in his witnessing to de Romans and to all de Gentiles of de earth."

"How did he do dat, Padre," asked Juan who was trying not to get lost in this quiet, bold man's logic.

"Because he was a Roman, dey did not want to kill him. Dey wanted to change his mind in prison as dey have done to de Jews in Germany. But dat was when he wrote de Holy Testament. For dis dey beheaded, him, but de testament endured. And dat mis hijos es de trute. De Jew must be esaved. It es my work. I owe it to St. Paul, St. Peter and my most Holy Lord."

"Padre es dat not an estrange misión for a priest?" asked Juan.

"No, hijo mío, Our Lord esends us forth to witness to de whole world, not just de chosen few. He has chosen de Jews for an especial misión dat David just testified to," said Father Diego."

"Rosh ha Shanah," said David with reverence.

"Dat es right, David. Many Gentile nations tink dis means dat Our Father loves de Jews more dan other nations for dis, but dis es a lie married to de Truth. His love es universal. De Jews have a particular witness. God calls each nation at different times in history to be a particular witness."

"I disagree vit that, Padre Diego," said David.

"Let's examine dat by dis fact, David. My witness for Jesu Cristo es currently to esave Jews from de Nazis from within dese holy Vatican walls, even if it means putting my life on de line."

"Vell, as I told vou in Spain many vears ago, I do not follow vour motivation, vet I'm proud and grateful to note that vou are still doing this, Father," said David.

Turning to David Father Diego asked, "Can an Oak tree change its grain?"

"Mis tacuches estripes always follow de perfect crease," said Juan.

"Dat es not de trute jou are eseeking here, mi hijo," retorted Father Diego.

"My Abuelito says dat de Oaks of Matatlan have great roots," said Juan.

"Jes, my eson, dey great trute en life ground our faith in de caves and catacombs of our esuffering. Now jou are moving more toward de trute," said Father Diego.

"Padre, why must oppressors behead dose carrying de trute?" queried Juan.

"What es de meaning of dis new question, my eson?"

"Well, Christ did not demand the heads of anyone, only deir hearts and faith," said Juan. "But," he continued, "Herod took de head of Juan Bautista when he told him de trute, and Ceasar took de head of St. Paul when he told him de trute. David eshowed me an old old book in de library here dat has a picture of Cortez taking de head of Moctezuma when he espoke de trute."

"I tink I esee where jou'er going wit dis line of tought," said Father Diego. "Let me tink a moment to find an answer, and give jour question justicia. Maybe de frescos in de chapel will help."

"Vhy don't vou tell him vat happened to vou in Spain as a start, Father," said David.

"All right, I'll estart dere." Father Diego began as if he could still see the bloody event. "In 1931 de Republic overthrew the Monarchy in España. De Soviets supported de Republican government. In February, 1936, Espaniards jammed de polls to elect members to de Espanish Parliament: de Cortes. At de esame time de were killing de Jews in Russia. De majority of de eseats in de Espanish Cortes were won by de Soviet backed leftist parties: de Republican Union, De Republican Left, de Socialist Party and de Communist Party. Dey united to fight Hitler on one eside and de Roman Catholic church on de other." Father Diego paused for a minute to reflect on what were now painful memories.

"Are jou O.K., Padre?" asked Juan.

"It es alright, my eson. Dus, in 1936, an attach on church property occurred after de election of de Popular Front Party. During dat black period, de esatanic forces in España destroyed 160 churches and/or convents, killed 269 clergy, 12 bishops and 7000 religious. Pope Pius XI denounced de plot as an esatanic enterprise and blessed Franco's cause. He had no way of knowing Franco's agenda for de esuppression of de church. We all believed dat he meant good tings for us when he esaid, 'España eshall be an empire turned towards God.' De church beheaded itself for not eseeing a lie as de trute."

"What happened den, Padre?" question Juan.

"Den Franco invited Hitler into de country to experiment on de Communists with his master plan for Europe. All hell broke loose in de land. De false trute beheaded de nation. I had to flee to carry on my work of esalvation."

"Eso what es de meaning of dat long estory, Padre?" asked Juan.

"De esocialistas and de comunistas were trying to behead de Holy Mother Church, mi hijo," answered Father Diego.

"Following de direction laid out for us by God es not always de way our heads feel we must go. Yet, if we ignore de trute we behead ourselves. If we try to destroy trute in others we must behead dem."

"Vat truth is being ignored, Padre Diego?" asked David.

"De trute es dat God loves all of us, David!" retorted Father Diego. "When we tink dat God loves us and not any others, dat es when we behead ourselves. Dat es why I must work to esave de Jews. I cannot estop de Nazis from beheading demselves."

"Does dis mean dat we cannot choose one eside or de other?" asked Juan.

"God does not choose esides, Juan. Men do," answered Padre Diego. "When we try to justify dese facts on one eside or de other, we create what de dogmatists call history. To create an estructure of trute, all de esymbols and mytos, in particular positions or directions, can be used to esupport a culture and or idealogy. Look at de frescos on de ceiling, hijos. Dey tell de esame story."

"How es dat?" said Juan.

"De positions of each character in de estructure of de masterpiece es used to justify de culture," Father Diego answered. "De cultura represents de values and its ideological truths. Once interpretation begins de dominant keepers of de faith, historians or knowing esubjects become part of de event because in de process de idea becomes de esubject and de art becomes de object. Dis is de essence of 'historical realism', which es not de esame as 'actual realism' and 'truth'. De Herods, Ceasares and Cortez's of de world will eventually be beheaded. Franco, Hitler, Tojo and Mussolini will follow dis road. It es a matter of time in God's grand design."

"I hope you are right in this, Father, my family is depending on it," said David.

"Unless I have totally missed de teachings of Our Lord, I know I am right," Father Diego stated. "De position of trute es de crucial roll of ideas in de course of human events. Dis es historical and not empirical idealism."

"Ve need to move from the ideal to the real for now, Padre," said David.

"Listen esome more, David, before you move on to quickly," said Father Diego. "Dere are no eshort cuts to His trute. To esee dis we need to understand dat dis form of idealism has two masks, de metaphysical and epistemological. In de metaphysical we especulate with de trute and in de epistemological we esearch for it. De historians estudy art, prejudice and dogma to advocate deir points of view. Dey use dese two masks to defend demselves and advance deir points of view. When dey do dis, dey make war. Dey have to destroy de maskbreakers to continue in power. When de masks are revealed, de historians tumble as discredited dogmatists. Ah, here es de eshrine jou were eseeking. What do jou esee my esons?"

"I'm not esure, Padre. I'm estill back on de ceiling wit jour palabras grandes," said Juan in awe. "My father taught me a lección when I was esix. He esaid trust in yourself like de cucaracha dat estays alive by playing dead. At de esame time, he esaid, trust in jour familia like de cucaracha dat esurvives in de life of de familia. Dat es de alma dat no one can estep on. Only jou can estep on jourself. A cucaracha never esteps on itself."

"I'm not eshure how dat all ties into de trute jou are eseeking my eson, but it es good for me to esee what esurrounds me with new eyes. New points of view are good for checking possible masks. I'm glad we are here together," said Father Diego.

"I am glad to be here too, Padre." said David.

"Juan, to continue with jour answer, let us examine de trute presented to us in dis holy place. De very words chosen reveal de idiomatic position. Each in dier own way es a worship of God. Dey and de art dey provoke, only reveal His estrategic intent."

"Padre, con mucho respeto, I know jou are esaying many powerful words, but I need jour help to understand dis contesta bonita," said Juan.

Father Diego pondered for a moment as this was the first time in many years that he had had an opportunity to think through these thoughts as related to hungry disciples. "Let me try it dis way, Juan. Most often, cultural trutes and traditions are practices or life ways dat have been done eso long and eso often dat es de reason for doing dem are forgotten. Most of the artifacts of civilization are made dis way, like de art here on de ceiling."

"How es dat, Padre?" asked Juan.

"On dis ceiling we can esee dat as man's esymbols remove him from God, de need for Godly trute es increased. When we as Christians put ourselves on de line to get nearer to God, we need de trappings of man's esymbols less and less. All dat es important es written en de heart of man by God."

"Father," said Juan, "I tink I got everyting dis time except for de last two esentences. My head es estarting to come off. Please help me to put it back or I'll be like St. Paul."

"Dat es not esuch a bad place to be, my eson," remarked the Padre. Turning to David he added, "David, dis es a most persistent young man. Does he always keep to an idea eso estrongly?"

"I have come to depend on this trait, Father," replied David. "He has saved my life several times in this var. That is vhy I call him La Cucaracha Ultima."

"De good padre doesn't need to hear all of dat estuff, David," muttered Juan with some embarrasment.

"He does too, Vuan. Somebody I respect must know the truth about vou," asserted David. Then turning back to Padre Diego, David said, "Once Vuan really makes up his mind to do or learn something, he doesn't let go until it is his. I knew ve vere in for a session like this the minute he told me that his mother and grandmother vanted him to visit these shrines. Ven he is in the center of his thought, he alvays uses the feelings of others to start locating his focus. Please go on Padre, for I, too, need to learn of the truth from different ways."

"Then my inquisitive Cucaracha, let us continue to explore jour questions, and the place of jour cabeza," said Father Diego. "Culture and de trute or lie of it es man's jurisdiction, his creative efforts to esave himself, to esave others, to destroy himself and/or others. Dese are all creative efforts. What happened in 1936 in Spain and Germany are an example of dis. Eso are de beheadings you have mentioned. Dis eshrine also illustrates dis concepts."

"How dose it do dat, Padre?" asked Juan like he was understanding all of what was being taught to him.

It dose dat by eshowing dat if culture es dose learned solutions to de problemas presented by de environment, den cultural fragmentations are esimulations and masks of cultural reality. Cultural diversities are de basis of truth and reality. Dat es why we must work to esave de Jews."

"How is this related to the Jews, Padre?" asked David.

"De historian and ideologue cannot use cultura as a metaphor for civilization. In doing eso, dey become fabricators instead of creators. For example, ideas are not reality until dey are transferred into deir own peculiar and creative way to de actual artifact and/or event dat es part of de life way of a people. De creative effort gives value to diachronistic realities and not historical/ideological interpretation."

"Padre, otra vez," said Juan. "Qué es esta palabra, dia, uh, chronic, uh, uh, isatias? My Abuelo made art from fallen Oak logs, but he never called dem dat word. He made his carvings as gifts and rewards to dose he respected or loved."

"Your focus es excellent, my eson. De word es diachronicity. It means the actual events or cultural trute as dey occurred in time without any extra interpretation or fabrication. When jour Abuelo made his art he was being a humanist with a grateful heart. What es happening to de Jews in Europe es also a diachronistic fact. However, Hitler's interpretation of dese facts es his answer to history. He es carving on the Jews his hateful heart. To Hitler's interpretation I answer, theories of cultura and trute have no owners. Only God can own and create de trute."

"But, didn't ve already say that the Jews are the carriers of the Truth?" said David.

"What jou esay es de trute in de Old Testament, but if we estudy de tradition of de dispensation of grace we can esee dat trutes fall into two major categories. De first category es what de books in de Vatican libraries call humanistic. In dis way of tinking, esome concepts are considered esuperior to other concepts. Dis es called normative trute. If de concepts are equal in power, den de humanist deals wit activities. If de activities are equal in power den de humanists shift to definitions. De question for de humanist es where es de battle."

"What do all dose equations mean for me, Padre, otra vez?" asked Juan.

"What dat means, Juan, es dat de critical factor for de control of de minds and hearts of a people es de keeping de dominant intent. De red flag es a way to eshow esuperiority over de inferiority of a civilization."

"Are you saying that Hitler is a humanist?" David asked in disbelief.

"Exactly, my eson," replied Father Diego in his soft even tone. "He wants to be de esuperior humanist. In dis way he imposes his values on de whole world with de new Germany."

"Then vou are saying he is a civilizer," suggested David as he tried to make meaning of Padre Diego's logic.

"On de contrary, my eson. Hitler es a destroyer of civilization. Look at what he es doing to Europe. Hitler has masked his position of hatred with patriotic love. In de pain of dis reality he has fabricated a New Order dat hides concentration camps in beautiful forests. Dat es why dere needs to be de esecond category of cultural trute."

"And what is de name of dat category?" asked Juan while trying again to act as if he totally understood all that was being said.

"Dat category es called de anthropological point of view," replied Father Diego.

"How does it work, Padre?" asked Juan.

"In dis way of viewing trute and cultura, concepts are neutral to other concepts. Dey are just descriptors dat honor de culture and its basic trutes in and for demselves. Dis es de basic meaning of human life and de basis for what es of value. De books in de great Vatican Libraries have taught me dat civilization es de general process of becoming cultivated, fabricated and/or woven."

"Then vhere does persecutions and vars fit in, Father?" asked David.

"Let us go back to de chapel, David. Look at de ceiling, otra vez. What you ask fits in as part of a historical process dat occurs in cycles. Historical humanism es de estory of 'my life way es better dan your life way'. Or, 'my government es better dan your government'. Our civilized fragments are our cultural esolutions for basic truths in a particular context."

Juan was fascinated by this man who said things his Spanish Great Grandfather had said while bouncing Juan on his knees beneath the great golden oaks of Matatlan. Of course his Great Grandfather had used much simpler words but the pensamientos were the same. Why hadn't his teachers told him these things? Juan was about to ask for more clarification on the meaning of the term anthropological when David said, "No more questions for vou, Vuan, Father Diego has critical work to do. Father have vou any news of my family?"

"All I know es dat jour father and esisters are in Dachau. While this es very bad, at least it es not an 'extermination camp' like Bugenvald. I fear dat jour mater and one of jour sisters were killed in an escape attempt."

"Father, I do not understand your meaning," David said with agitation in his voice. "Vat are vou saying? How did my Mater die? Vat about my other sister?"

"Dat es all I can esay for now. To esay more would endanger dose I'm trying to esave with de help of God and de money of esympathetic Jewish bankers outside of Europe. Go in de Peace of God my esons. May He bless jour endeavors and use jou as His instruments of esalvation."

"Let's go back to the barracks, Vaun. I have had enough truth for one day. Ve can see more of St. Paul tomorrow."

"Maybe jou eshould go back to de barracks, David," said Juan. "I need to talk to de good padre a little more." Juan turned to Father Diego and with affection said, "God bless jour work, Padre, I wish I would have known a teacher like jou in 1936. I tink my life would have been very much different. I know mi Mamasita would love jou and mi Papá would feel blessed if jou entered our house."

"Gracias a Dios for jour kind words, my eson. God helps dose who desire de trute, to find deir way to Him."

"Padre, jou have opened many new paths for thought in my

mind, but for my esoul, es it possible for jou to hear my confession," asked Juan. "I have been trying to bury a great lie in my heart. In dis place and hearing jour words, I must get it off my esoul. I have got to put my mind at rest on dis."

"David," said Father Diego. "Please allow the time for dis, as death es a soldier's constant companion, and Juan eseems greatly troubled by esomething."

"I hear his need," replied David. "Although I haven't an inkling of vat this great sin is. Do vat is appropriate, Father."

"Den let us estep over here to de confessional, my eson," said Father Diego to Juan. "What es dis matter dat es eso troubling to jou?"

"Bless me Padre for I have esinned, it has been two years since my last confession" Juan began.

"And what esins have jou committed since your last confession?" Father Diego replied.

"In my last confession my heart was not contrite of dis, Padre, eso I didn't confess it."

"Continue, mi eson."

"In hearing jour words, Padre, I know jou carry Jesu Cristo in jour heart. Dis es good. David trusts jou and dis es also good. De chaplains in de army don't make me feel dis way. Dis es why I need jou to hear my confession. I would have told dis to tío Augustine, but he has died. My father would have only esent me to mi Mamá. Padre, be my niño. David knows of dis esin. Eso dose mi esposa, Concha. What es worse, I forced her against her esaintly desires to be part of it."

"Mi hijo, dere es noting dat de blood of our Esavior cannot overcome. Get out dis great esin eso we can find de esolution," said Father Diego.

"Padre, my mother told me to burn my drapes. To burn dem would cause me great pain. I lied to her and told her I did. I made Concha hide dem wit her wedding dress. Dis lie nags at me all of de time. I cannot go to my grave wit dis pain on my heart, Padre."

"It es good dat jou have gotten it out, Juan. Lying to jour madre and involving jour esposa in de lie is a terrible, terrible ting. Es muy terrible," said Father Diego.

"What eshould I do, Padre?" said Juan

"Can jou tell me about dese 'drapes'?" said Father Diego.

"Like I told jou before, Padre, dey are my Zoot Zuit o tacuche. Dey are a very especial Zuit of clothes dat are my identity in mi barrio. De eschool authorities expelled me and la policía put me in jail for wearing it. Yet, like I esaid earlier, I was married to Concha in de church in my beautiful Zoot Zuit. La Virgen lets me wear it in her church, but my mother won't.

"Jour mamá es right, mi hijo," said Padre Diego. "The Church es de bride of Jesu Cristo. Always remember Who really loves jou and Who owns de Church. It also esounds like dere es esome vanity en de wearing of dis esuit. To put vanity before jour God and madre es a most grievous ting, mijo. Dis too must be estopped."

"But Padre, dat trute es esmothering me in de pain of my mother's mask to God. Mi mamá, eshe es praying in trute for my life because eshe doesn't know of my lie. I cannot pray for her because I tink I am making her a liar before God. Please forgive me, Padre."

"Only Jesu Cristo has dat power, my eson. He es always with us, mijo. Pray, go on."

"Mi familia, especially mi madre, feels dat as long as I wear dis Zuit dat de people outside mi barrio will cast me out. Mi madre es afraid dat dey will kill me in it. Eshe only permitted me to get married in it becuz eshe wanted me married esince I would not be a priest for her."

"Espérate, mijo. Are jou now telling me dat jou denied de priestly sacrament eso jou could wear dis Zuit ting?"

"No, Padre, please dun't make it any worse dan it es already," pleaded Juan. "I got married en vez of being a priest. I told mi madre dat I would only marry if I could wear de Zuit and de church esaid it was O.K."

"And de Church esaid jou could wear it?"

"Yes, Padre, Father MacFearson let me and all my carnales wear our tacuches at de wedding."

"I tink I got it now, Juan. Pray, continue."

"I needed dem both through una trucha, but I can only protect me in mi familia with a lie, Padre. I have told de trute to de Virgen through jou. But I cannot tell de trute to mi madre o Jesu Cristo. What eshould I do? All of a esudden my boots are on upside down again with San Pedro on de cross."

"Jesu Cristo already knows de trute of jour lie, Juan. Why can't jou tell jour mamá, mijo?" said Padre Diego.

"Becuz mi mamá es praying for mi vida, Padre. If eshe knew de trucha, her prayer would only bring death."

"Do jou truly believe dis, mijo?" asked Father Diego with a puzzled tone.

"Yes, Padre. Eshe es almost as close to God as jou. Eshe would esay dat my lie to her es my denial of God. If I tell de trute only to Jesu Cristo I deny mi madre."

"Dat I understand, Mijo, but what es bothering jou."

"Because of dis, de gods will not allow me to have esons to fill my Zuit."

"That es blasphemy, mijo!"

"But, if I lose either one, Padre, I lose mi centro. I need to know what I eshould do. I feel dat I must espare my mother dis pain, but de pain of de lie es also heavy upon me because of Jesu Cristo."

"Mijo, do not deceive jourself. Dat es a pain dat no one can endure. Jou cannot rest until jou ask forgiveness from jour mother and then Jesu Cristo. Dis will be jour act of contrition. If jou do not do dis, dis confession es only a deceptive mask to God. No one hides from God. He will esee jou as jou are, not as jou hope to be. Esay three Our Fathers and three Hail Marys, repent and go in peace."

"O.K., Padre, but what do I tell mi madre?"

"Pray with a contrite heart, Mijo and de Trute will come to jou trough de Espíritu Santo," said Father Diego.

* * *

Laying on his bunk that night Juan saw the priest as a man separated from his people in Spain by becoming a cloistered witness in the Vatican hiding in the skirts of Mother church. Many of his parishioners were dying in Spanish jails for their witness. Juan realized that if Father Diego had stayed with his people they would have killed him to appease the state, but in his death he would have been true to his faith. Maybe this is what his Abuelito meant by, "Prisons of physical death and spiritual life."

Father Diego was a dedicated priest in the luxury prison of the Vatican. While he truly admired Father Diego and trusted him as a man of God he wondered if the Father could be judged as a coward and a sellout. As the night wore on and Juan struggled with the thoughts, confession and truths of the day he began to realize that this quiet man of God was on hold waiting for the death of a political order built on a "state religion". Juan had had the rare privilege of seeing life in death and the death in life through the eyes of a living priest with dead witnesses, the Jews and his parishioners.

For Juan, his Zuit in Concha's bridal box remained hidden. With his Zuit he owned his own identity; without it, others owned him.

In the dim moonlite of the barracks, Juan pulled a pencil and a folded sheet of paper out of his right rear pant's pocket. He had taken up the habit of carrying a short pencil and paper just in case his number came up and he wanted to get a quick note off to Concha.

Concha mía,

I have eseen many tings here in Africa and Europa. Eso many tings here are old and dead without a desire for continuing. De crosses of dis land are upside down and many of us are dying on dem. I have met a wonderful priest and he esays dat I eshould tell mi madre dat I didn't burn my Zuit. Dis must be done eso if I buy a plot here in the ground of our European ancestors, I can go wit a clean heart.

I have decided dat it would be good if jou did dis for me. Dis way jou can be clear of de lie too. I tink my greatest worry is dat I had to esoil jou wit dis lie. My good buddy, David, esends his love too. We only go to museums and churches, eso we don't esee any women and bars. Thanks for jour letters. Dey tell me what I am here for even when dere eseems to be no reason for all dis killing.

Love, Juan.

"Wake up, David, I have got to eshare dis estuff I have been tinking wit esomeone," whispered Juan.

"It is three o'clock in the morning, Vuan. How about telling it to one of vour dream valkers?"

"Dey aren't here in dis barracks, David," replied Juan.

"Can't it vait until breakfast, Vuan?"

"No it can't. Besides jou are awake anyway," said Juan with a smile in his whisper.

"O.K., so vat is it that can't vait until breakfast, Vuan?"

"I've been tinking of all de tings dat Father Diego esaid. I know dat mi Mamasita es lighting candles for me to have met esuch a man."

"I've been thinking of him too. I vonder vat else he knows about my family," said David.

"He esaid he couldn't esay, ese. He would have if he could. I just know it. Jou know, man, in another time, I would have thought dis priest to be a loser. In leaving his people and denying his witness I tought dat he had denied his espiritual identity to preserve his physical identity. However, after eseeing Peter crucified upside down, hearing Father Diego espeak those bold words, and jour estory of how he got jou out of Germany at the risk of his own life, not to mention de risks I tink he es estill taking for both Christians and Jews, I have changed my mind. I esee dis priest as an underground living witness dat es transporting Jews to Palestine and Christians to Switzerland. We were with greatness today, David."

"Father Diego was right about vou, Vuan. "Vou have a rare

gift of focus."

Out of the darkness of snoring thunder, yelled a voice, "Pipe down yous guys. This is an army barracks, not a sorority dormitory confessional."

"Good night, Vuan."

"Good night, David. I'm really glad jou let me call jou friend."

As Juan drifted into the dream walkerless sleep admist the unharmonious snores of the restless barracks, he heard Concha singing, "It is a sin to tell a lie, but it hurts even more to tell a liar's truth."

THE RIVIERA

The French Riviera: Juan's last beachhead in Europe. The aerial blitz by 2500 planes left the play ground of Europe's idol rich looking like a cratered lunar landscape: burned out story book villages, ugly beyond belief. For Juan, the beautiful testimony of the Flyboy's precision, made it a relatively easy beachhead. Only half as many of the newly arrived hommies died coming ashore as they did at Anzio even though Anzio was a surprise and this landing wasn't. Or, at least that's what the Sarge said.

Body counts on a beach. Not as many black wreathes would be added to those already hanging in barrio windows. What a way to measure the ability to "kick a Nazi butt."

Juan's travel itinerary in the Seventh Army would have been a great trip if he were a tourist. The embarcations and the transport to each new stop on the tour weren't so bad once you filled your helmet with puke. It was the landings that were the killers.

First, Casablanca with its flying rugs, dancing Arab girls, and Arabian nights replaced by Stuka bombings and bliztkriegs. Second Gela, land of the Sicilian cult, wonderful pasta and Mt. Etna replaced by hell bent panzer divisions and flame spitting messerschmidts. Third, on to Sorrento, home of box standing balladeers and rail sitting lovers usurped by pill boxes and eighty-eights on rails. Fourth, Anzio a hidden romantic beach that opened the bloody road to Rome. Fifth came Corsica, birth place of Napoleone Bonaparte: the great soldier, now a dead tourist. Sixth, what a tour at Toulon. Beautiful beach villas and wine growing villages billeting soldiers of mighty nepoming armies.

The G. I. "tourists" danced north through the Rhone valley to gay Paris. The travel posters of Italia and France became the propaganda of a prewar fantasy. None of the posters said come here to a anonymous mass funeral in the land of the wine drinking, swimsuit modeling, sports car driving, gambling rich.

Juan had expected Europe to look really old and wise, but the old buildings in East Los and Matatlan were older and wiser. Europes falling buildings and villages aged Juan and provided more street wisdom. The Sarge commanded, "Move it, move ya marble fudge fuckin' wise guys. Ya ain't goin' ta get any older sitting on these marble floors. Pull up yer belt real tight. I don't want any red balls hangin' out of lost pants. Stop shittin' around. I don't want any of my brownies browned out with their pants down. Ya can't do the Can-Can on yer can, brownies." The Sarge had taken this tour in the First War. The only time the raw mouthed tour guide became tongue tied was when he was around women.

Everywhere in France the G.I.'s saw the wreckage of four years of exploitation and occupation. All the "Frenchies" shouted for joy as they passed through the rubble of quaint fortified towns and fortified villages. The "Frenchies" were like cocks full of fight now that the G.I.'s bled and bled to liberate them.

The roads and paths were muddy, but the G.I.'s. had no time to stop and enjoy the tour. The Red Ballers supporting their arrow head like effort could hardly keep their vehicles fueled. By day the allies advanced; by night the gas trucks made fuel dumps. David was happy with their progress, but he would have run day and night if the support columns could have kept up.

The Sarge had told them that an army ran on its stomach. For once the Sarge was wrong. This army ran on oil.

"Even de 'K' rations taste like dey had been eshipped to us in oil drums, Ramón," suggested Juan.

"Jous got dat wrong, man. If dey had come in oil drums, Patton would have put dem into de tanks of de tanks!" snarled Ramón the Poet.

"Tanks for drumin' dat into me," retorted Juan. "I esaw me an idol half track with a flat in de last mine field we passed. If we could liberate a tire and get to dat swastika boobie trap we could ride more dan we are walkin'."

"Do ya tink de Sarge will let us do dat, Juan?" asked Ramón the Poet.

"I ain't askin' de Sarge, hommie," answered Juan. "Besides de Sarge es always tellin' us ta use our initiative. Ain't he?"

"Vuan, I think that vou are taking his advice just a little too far," suggested David.

"Tink how far and fast we could move if we had dat half track, David."

"Let's get it, Vuan. Vou find us a tire, Ramón."

"Jou got it already, Rabbi," said Ramón the Poet.

"How are we going to get it out of the mine field, Juan?" asked David "We can blow a road with Enrique's bazooka, ese."

"I was afraid vou had some violent idea like that, Vuan. Do vou tink he vill let jou do dat mit his bazooka?"

"Enrique will do anythin' dat gets him off of his feet, ese," said Juan with a chuckle.

The hommies pulled it off and once again rode in style. "One good ting jou can esay about de Nazis, David, es dat dey build excellent vehicles."

"Remember this is a vehicle of death, Juan," answered David.

With their own blitz Patton and Patch trapped and surrounded 350,000 German soldiers before they could regroup in southwestern France. The hommies' Nazi half track feasted on the parts found in deserted vehicles. Juan drove as fast as the spearhead spare parts could move. The tractor mechanic no longer walked. Dirty oil stained finger nails were less painful than bleeding feet.

Prisoners of war bring death to armies faster than dead soldiers. Those first weeks in France Juan and David spent more time herding defeated Germans rather than shooting them.

"Who da thought, David?" said Juan. "De Cucaracha—a vaquero in France riding a Benz built Nazi horse—herding de sonabitches from de Reich."

"Vatch out for their Teutonic horns, Vuan. They won't be hogtied until we stone Goliath. I've looked in their eyes. They are defeated, but not beaten. Let's not forget they still believe in their cause. If ve get careless they vill imprison and kill us."

"Jou always tink de worst, David. Dey're just blank white faces to me. Most of dem look like de L.A.P.D. I like knocking dese guys off deir motorcycles and getting medals for it."

"Vuan, cocky soldiers make good targets. Aren't vou learning anything from the vay ve are beating these Nazis?"

The cocky Cucaracha stood up tall in the half track, quickly took a Kraut bullet in the shoulder and passed out. He saw Paris with a sling. The Eifle Tower looked like it had its arms shot off. Notre Dame stood like an empty warehouse with beautiful windows and empty pews. His Mamá had written to him to see it and light a candle, but the lights in France were out. The candlesticks and the altars were missing. Like Juan, France wasn't dead, but she was muddied, hurt and in great pain.

Juan was a fast healer. So was France. At least now they were really taking it to the Nazis. Any sandlot quarterback knew that the invasion of France was like crossing the fifty-yard line and the liberation of Paris was like taking the thirty-yard line as the Allied team headed for victory. There would be no punting now. The Vestval, the twenty-yard line, meant putting the game on the line for the Germans. The throb in Juan's shoulder told him that the enemy still believed fanatically in its cause. The German winter was a new real wall time-out that prolonged the agony of war.

Juan could hear David better, now that the throb in his shoulder rounded off his corners during David's interrogations. Captured soldiers revealed a knowledge of unknown horrors buried in the Fatherland. David wanted to stop the interrogations and move on. Next stop Germany. The scenery was beautiful. So were the girls, although none of them could compare to the golden glow of his Conchita. Too bad a war was on. One day when he got the time and space he'd have to write Conchita about all he had learned, but today it would be a short letter. All he had to say was,

Dearest Conchita,

I miss jou, babe. I haven't got any new pictures to esend jou. War es hell. I wish we could be cruising wit de hommies in our short.

Love, Juan.

Cyrano De Bergerac was dead. He lost his nose for words in Juan's letters. Only his sharp sword remained. Concha's bridal box remained hidden.

FOXHOLES IN THE WESTVAL

Each night a new foxhole took them further east towards the Westval of Germany. Juan and David in their German built, barrio modified half-track blitzed the blitzkreigers. Both sides mercilessly used up sons, husbands, and fathers to defend their positions.

Patton and Patch used the flower from Juan's barrio to prevent tomorrow from belonging to Germany as if there was no tomorrow!

Day after day the Third and Seventh Armies, spearheaded by the Sixth Armour Division, pushed faster, faster, and faster: today reserved for the fighting warriors; tomorrow, for the memory of the dead left behind in the muddy trenches of distant battlefields: Juan and David forever feeling the loss of buddies in each of their victories.

With the birth of each new day, the beautiful French and Belgium country side blocked the deliberately forced footsteps of the surviving allied soldiers with fortified farms, fortified villages, and fortified towns towards the gateway of the Westval. The Third and Seventh U.S. Armies became possessed with entrapping the Germans before the Belford Gap, to open a hemorraging flood gate for both sides. While both Patton and Patch hated and lamented the destruction of their troops, both loved the sight of retreating and surrendering, do-and-die Nazis. Patton's and Patch's desire for speed and power drove the allies to "out-blitz" the damned blitzkriegers. Only the constant waiting for supplies and green replacements slowed down their advance. For David, Patton and Patch weren't going fast enough towards Dachau, the dastardly concentration camp. His worries and frustrations continued to multiply all day and night of each passing day.

His flower of Germany, cut-off in a camp of thorns!

For Juan each day of war devastated and exhausted his inner force in the desperate convulsions of the bloody battlefield.

Each day Juan tore apart the enemy; each night he tried to mend his heart. The wound of hatred were so deep that those scars would take a lifetime to heal. The victories only masked his nightmares!

Everybody kept on fighting; nobody rested. The soldiers fought others from without and themselves and their fears from within. All the voices on both sides tragically cooperated in each others reverberating echos of death that kept rebounding in their hearts.

To David, to stop and rest during each restless, ground rattling, and sky rocketing night committed desperate Third Reich Jews to death and destruction.

To Juan the devastation of war exhausted the forces caught in the desparate convulsions of the nation wide battlefield. Everybody kept on fighting; nobody got any sleep in this campaign.

Each new group of muttering beaten German prisoners hinted in angry German at inklings of the atrocities beyond the Westval: slave labor camps, biological experiments, deportations, relocations, and even death camps. David's German enabled him to eavesdrop upon the true hatred of the vanquished. When the Seventh Army Victors got on German soil he would make Germany pay with its vain goose-strutting pride.

The remnant of the do-and-die German army slugged and swung wildly and desperately at the inevitable might of the crushing Allied blows. The dying ember that fueled the Nazi hatred forced its whole being at pushing the Allies back into the sea. When the Allied planes were grounded by fogs and storms in the Parisian Plain, the power of the German military might and war strategy crushed and bulged the overextended lines of the Allied forces. Only the superwill of the Red Ball Express staffed with rejects and hommies allowed David and Juan to suppress the crazy will of the "Alleged Supermen." Patton and Patch saw the ingenuity and resourcefullness of the hommies and rejects, but they missed the superwill of David's sling, the Redball's spear, and Juan's obsidian bat. Together, they were a rapier puncturing and pushing a coiled snake back into its pit.

David's finally felt as if he were pruning the vineyard. Nepom was too good for the SS fanatics. "Only Gotterdamerang is hellish enough for these damned Jew killers!" screamed David as he squeased off a rifle grenade into a German bunker. Only beating the clock ticking death in Dachau could satisfy David.

A backward glance at the spiraling road to the Westval filled Juan's eyes with images of racing broken full trucks containing supplies, slicing through mud bogged trails littered with dead snakes and hommies. Only the ripping out of the heart and tearing out of the fangs of the German juggernaut by shoving a grenade down its throat up close and very earthly pleased the battle fatigued and calloused Juan.

The countdown continued to race in David's mind: no wall could pen the wail of the murdered Jews. Not even the Westval.

The mournful howls even pulled and directed Juan's feet. The dichos in his soul read the spiritual placas.

To Patton and Patch the blood of the nameless American dead solidified victory; for David the blood paid the price of redemption, purification and satisfaction for the foolish Hitlerian blood thirsty madness. For the Spanish Juan, the dead American soldiers became rotting meat that shed blood to sanctify the purity of thought, while the German dead soldiers became a polluted blue blood: the death of Hitler's propaganda in hell. For Indian Juan, the bodies of the soldier, both German and American, were floating fools who allowed the spirits' forces to drink their blood away from home soil.

Blood rimmed, snow filled foxholes are good pre-requisites to insure a vivid dreamscape. A real fantasyland of horror mixed with war and peace, thoughts and memories. Abuelito, Abuela, Mrs. Post, Concha, Papá, Mamá, Benjamín in the Marines in the Pacific, his sisters and his unborn children, Spanish Greatgrandma, Spanish Grandma, Don Castillo, Greatgrand Father, Sarge, and Albert E. Waugh, the statistical man and the father of Mr. Education, melded into the devastating vail\vale\veil of war singing in peaceful voices of remembrance and soothing whispers of fantasy. Pits, caves, and trenches colored red were filled with blacken trees. If either Juan or David got killed, a branch would die on their tree of life, but all their trees would continue to grow.

"Hey, David," yelled Juan between bursts of machine gun fire, "I tought jou esaid dat dis trench warfare estuff with de infantry caught in de middle was old fashion fighting and dat dis new mechanized estuff was esupposed to do away with it."

"I guess ven vou get down to vo is going to own a piece of territory, Vaun, it still gets paid for vit da blood of da foot soldier," replied David.

"Esince it looks like we're planted for de night, I'm going to try again at takin' a few Zzzz's and dream of Concha in her white veil and me in my Zuit. Es dat ok with jou, David?"

"It's O.K., but sleep fast. This Army is in a very big hurry, Vuan."

With all haste, Juan fell into a deep restless dreamscape. Concha in her veil vanished in the fast dream of war. The Zuit went up the spout of an unwashed chimney of a snow filled desert barbeque. Both Hitler and Patton blasted at a pyramid to the rhythm of the song "This is your land, this is my land." in a spirit's land of all earth. The pyramid and the foxhole for David and Juan was next to the Great Pyramid of Tenochtitlan. Hitler and Patton didn't even see nor acknowledged this pyramid where Juan kept yelling that they should stop so he could move the foxhole and pyramid out of the line of fire. "My dream walking Abuelo is climbing himself towards the Forces of Light while jumping the craters created by the artillery fire."

As Abuelo climbed his space, each step in Juan's ladder became whole. But even with a whole ladder, Juan could not climb out of the foxhole fast enough to get to the step before the strength of Abuelo ebbed. As the Force Light entered his heart the pyramid turned to gold and Abuelo was united with Teotl in the fire of life. Abuelo beckoned to Juan with a smile as he felt the strength of the moment but, he also warned Juan to cherish only the ladder that must be stepped upon in the appointed time. Then Abuelo flashed into the pyramid like a jade comet with a turquoise tail, hurling inward/outward to the womb/tomb creating the fire of life. At last he was beyond the wilderness of mirrors and steel. The family's earth was redeemed once more in the regeneration of his soul: springs of living water replenished.

Father Diego appeared admist the exploding shells flying through white angelic clouds, but he did not disturb the fire of life while yelling at Juan, "Come back with me, Juan, jou are in the realm of blasphemy!"

"But if I do Padre I lose my Abuelo. Everybody es eshooting at him. Even de Great Spirit is doing it as dey are lighting up out Abuelo's heart."

"Go to the Padre," said Spanish Grandma, "he speaks educated Spanish and English. At last those pochismos are going up in flames."

"Jou must climb de ladder to jour center to find it," said his Papá from the foxhole. "Circle in the flame of the Spirit to put jour center into the mouth of voiced focus.

"How can I do dey centro ting if I'm flying around de centro, Papá?" asked Juan in the confusion of a truthful dreamwalk.

"Be de perfect flaw, mijo. Jou must estep on jour past to own joureself. Dis can only be done wit jour voces. Dis keeps jour history alive in jour dreams. If jou dun't estep on jour past jou will estep on jourself. A pyramid es un estep ladder up to Teotl. If jou join him jou will be on an estage from which de Voces de Luz watch out for de respect of man."

"But, Papá, I have to help David esave his family!" yelled Juan.

"Always protect jour tree, Juanito," replied his papá. Abuelo's flame has secured our roots. Jou are de Papá of de familia now."

Juan jerked himself awake. At least Concha still loved him. She had moved deeper into his heart. In the voice of her living love his tree always continued. She nourished the roots of Matatlan.

The trees in the Westval were different from the trees of Matatlan: longer shadows, shorter dreams; two is one and one is two. They made short dream shadows long in the snow. Sequoya's forest camped out of season in a frozen fog.

The heavy German armour in the snow hemorrhaged the resources needed for victory: trees and history shattered like shrill, grating, strident voices grinding to a screeching halt: humanity forever shrieking. The Battle of the Bulge raged more wildly than Juan's dreams as the last offensive gasp of an over-matched martial player on the stage of wartorn Europe. No time left to bury the dead: "sleeping trees in the snow."

"Hey, yous grease balls and beaners. The brass is looking for guys who speak German. Do any of yous gunbutts spreken Hun talk?" asked Sergeant Jess Milner. "Hey yous, butthead, Corporal Goldstein, didn't 'I-Corps' use yous to interrogate Krauts back in Paris during R&R?"

"Yah, Sarge," replied David.

"Then report to HQ immediately, Rabbi. There are sergeant stripes in it for yous, and take that Mexican taco vendor with yous for a guard. There are corporal stripes in it for him, too. On second thought, mobile HQ is moving so fast that if yous stand here, it should be here in 15 to 20 minutes. The radio just reported that Patton, Patch, and now Bradley have just encircled tens of thousands of Huns in the Colmar pocket. Our forced marches have worked."

The exhausted troops cheered!

"Well!, said Juan sarcastically. "I didn't know jou and me getting estripes would make dese carnales cheer eso loud."

"They are cheering the strippin' of de Krauts, not the strip-ing of vour arm, Vuan, Ve are ready for a first and one on the 'Siegfried Line'. Next: a touchdown in Gotterdamerang," snarled David like the Sarge.

"Dat's cool, David. Didn't jou tell me dat Siegfried was de warrior dat used de magic esword of trute to cut down de false gods?" asked Juan.

"Yah, and vour dat svord, Cucaracha." replied David. "Here comes mobile HQ."

"Why am I de esword?" asked Juan.

"He who believes in the quest for truth, like Siegfried, is the sword that encircles and casts out the evil in the vorld. Ve have saved thousands by forming a ring around the best of the SS. Only the Home Guard of old men and children are left."

"Eso, Sergeant Profit, what do jou tink es next?" asked Juan.

"Wagner, Hitler's poetic idol, wrote Hitler's death varrant a hundred years ago," answered David. Vuan, vou are my magic sword to change Herr Hitler's magic crown into rust on an iron cross. That is vhy ve now riding vit Die Valkeries straight into the land of Vahalla."

As they climbed into the trailer that made up Mobile HQ, David whistled the horn call from 'Siegfried's Rhine Journey:' A victorious tune of sad remembrances.

"David, only a Jew could whistle in de middle of de war," said Juan shaking his head in disbelief.

"That's right, Vuan, if ve didn't vistle in var, ve vould never vistle at all," retorted David.

While Juan stood guard, David collected strategic information that sped the defeat of the Nazi war machine. As part of his collection of facts, David began to assemble a framework of information on the Jewish remnant. He found out that by 1939, very few Jews remained in Germany itself. The desperate Jews had no problem leaving Germany, but they faced barriers of gaining entrance into other countries. The children of Jews taken over by the German state as "True Aryans" always remained as "free captives."

The Jews continued to move from the frying pan into the fire in the nation the German Army occupied. The "Jewish Problem," the herding of Jews to slaughter for the "Final Solution," was employed in the occupied areas: "Work shall make you free" became "Work shall kill you!"

Until 1940 the Jews had been forced to emigrate. However, starting in late 1940 and all of 1941, all Jews were shipped to reservations called "Ghettos" in Poland regardless of nationality. As Himmler's "Final Solution" became effective on 10/04/43, a special force called the "Einsatzgruppen" was formed. "Herd the Jews into a ditch and shoot all of them down!"

Then came the death vans, the gas chambers and crematoriums of Auschwitz and Bugenvald. In Auschwitz alone, the Nazis gassed 3,000,000 Jews. In other concentration camps some were injected with typhus to provide serum for German troops. Others were killed by starvation and disease in forced labor camps. And still other became fuel in the cremetoriums.

These facts wrenched in Juan's and David's bowels. David's face became an ashen blue white.

The German Army used the few surviving Jews as laborers in occupied areas. They trusted them as Germans and hated them as Jews. The Weirmacht viewed live Jews as useful hostages in prisoner exchange negotiations. The interrogations taught David that the Jews were the bronze, iron and golden ring of truth that the more he heard, the more he feared.

Juan watched the field interrogations David conducted. He appreciated David, known to most of the company as "the Rabbi" or "the Christ Killer," as one who could see into the inner workings of the German mind and read the meanings between the lines. To Juan, David's Jewish identity, that the Germans thought that they had destroyed, survived in a white hot, cold analytic zigzag fashion.

David cloaked his personal soul in small lies that were big barriers for the German soldiers. David became a master at hiding his Jewish soul to reveal the hidden atrocities within the German big lie. David told Juan that as long as the Nazis were killing Jews the reality of the Jew still existed.

Protecting to kill sounded like the Indian reservation starvation to Juan. On a reservation Hitler would try to rip the heart out of the Nation.

The interrogations confirmed that once the Jews were exterminated, the prisoners of war were next. In fact, there were unconfirmed reports stressed that the SS had already begun to exterminate the Russian prisoners. Juan and David used the information they acquired as HQ's immediate motivation to push-on beyond the Siegfreid Line into the heartland of Germany and cut down on the number of killing days that the SS had to finish the Final Solution.

In moments between interrogations David began started to confess the ugly nightmare of his own personal and familial experience in the holocaust. "In 1938, Vuan, I had tried to bring out my vhole family from Germany, but my mater vould not leave vitout my little brother Hans. Because he looked Aryan, in 1936 the SS ripped him out of my mater's arms and made him a Hitler Youth. Later, ven I got to the United States I tried to get entry visas for his sisters, but I could not raise the funds for their bonds or reveal myself as an illegal alien. As a last resort, in 1939, my pater took the remnants of our family to Poland to escape the big lie. To get legal citizenship in the U.S. I volunteered for the Army in January, 1942. By this time my family, except for my younger brother Hans, vas imprisoned in the Dachau work camp. To protect himself in the SS, Hans did not use his connections to get the family out of Germany before the Final Solution."

"I can understand Han's mess," David. "After all, once de Zuits were made 'illegal public dress' in California, I got in deep mierda with de cops. Now Concha has written dat many of de vatos locos in de barrio are burning deir Zuits to please de cops."

Once during the interrogation, right after the capture of a German SS Panzer unit, the blood drained out of David's face and his cloaked Jewish soul surfaced. Juan intently looked at David who was staring at a Jew who had become German against his will to escape the fate of the German Jews in Dachau. David stood face to face with Hans: the former escaped Germany to save the Jews; the latter escaped Judaism in Germany to save himself.

"Hans, it is vou, my baby brother. Vat are vou doing in that SS uniform?"

"Vou, the servant to the Jew," said the German prisoner turning towards Juan, "Tell the Jew my papers prove I'm a true German. Not an eresatz American pig vit a German accent."

"I know it is vou, Hans," retorted David.

"Only if vou recognize vour death. Troll, crawl back into vour cave."

"Do jou want me to fix dis guy's chips for jou, David?" asked

Juan.

"I can handle it, Juan" said David with an icy calm in his voice.

"I can take him out in a way dat it will look as if he went in his esleep," commented Juan.

"The servant of the Jewish pig barks but can't bite," scoffed the German prisoner.

"Cuidado, asshole! Jou are a knats eyelash away from Vahalla!" yelled Juan.

"Jew, I still hear vour mongrel dog barking in broken English."

Juan level his gun at the head of the prisoner. David waived him off.

"Let us continue vit the interrogation," said David regaining his composure. "This man vou have just called a dog is my brother, Juan. This is a brother our mother would still die for. Hans, if vou are dead then the rest of the German family is dead."

"Vat do vou mean, Jew vit a heathen dog?" asked Hans.

"The Nazis tried to kill the Jew in the German and vound-up killing the German in the Jew, Hans!" exclaimed David. "Vou, above everybody else, are living testimony to this truth."

"Don't worry, David, dis man couldn't be jour brother. He's all gunbutt and no gun. He es not enough of a man to lick-up his own shit!" yelled Juan.

"Quiet, Vuan. I need to find out vat Hans knows. Do vou know if our family is alive, Han's?" asked David hoping for some glimmer of Jewish humanity in Han's eye.

"My family, the Weirmacht, vill show vou the vay to the Atlantic Ocean, pig!"

"Next," yelled David he motioned to Juan to escort the prisoner out of the tent.

A very frustrated and furious Juan returned to the tent. He

looked straight into David's eyes and yelled, "David, why didn't jou let me do esomething to dat Nazi mierda, man?"

"Vuan! My fine young Chivito! Hans is one of vour cucarachas that stepped on itself!" retorted David. "As vou say, he can no longer dream his past; he has lost his Jewish voice; his Nazi boots only leave broken stars in the snow. Hans has cut of his own head."

"Gee, David, all of an esudden I feel a great pain for jour brother. I esee his silenced voice, but I can't hear his heart or the rivers of lies in his veins. A cucaracha with dry blood esticks in the wettest of throats. A calavera just estepped in the grave of mi familia."

"Vat does dat mean, Vuan?"

"Mi Abuelo dice que a calavera with dry blood can't dream. It can only walk in de forest of esouls forever looking for itself with no eyes."

"Hey, Sarge," blurted out Corporal Satchette as he shoved his way into the interrogation tent. "Do ya wan chure mail before chure next Kraut? I gots a letter here from da Red Cross for Corporal Beaner here."

"O.K., Satchette," replied David, "but next time Corporal make sure ve are not in the middle of something before vou come blasting in here like da Vizard of Oz."

"Whatever chue says, Sarge," said Satchette as he tossed Juan the letters and dashed out of the tent saying, "I don't know if this Army thinks I'm da blinken pony express with nothin' ta do but deliver the mail at its convenience. Don't they know dat I...," In coming mail from the German artillery drowned out the rest of Satchette's little talk.

"Ve'er not going to interrogate for a vhile, Vaun. It seems like the Nazis vant us to be in varm foxholes tonight," said David. "Let's get out of this tent before it becomes our tomb."

David and Juan dashed out of the tent into the black night of the Bergen Forest and the blue white flashes of the battle. The Cucaracha's latest move was to duck an cover near a tree instead of diving into a foxhole.

"Let's stay out of de foxholes tonight, David. Last night's barrage taught me dat a shallow foxhole or shell crater es a grave in de forest. Dose 88's kill doble in de forest. Let's be tall thin shadows next dat big fir."

"Vat are vou talking from now, Vuan?" asked David as Juan pulled him toward a large Arden fir.

"In de desierto or on a beach when an eshell hits de ground, de fragments fly up and out. Laying sprawled on de ground dere makes jou a esmall target. In de forest when an eshell hits up in de trees, de shell fragments and splinters de size of lances rained down upon de ground with esuch force dat many of de G.I.s sprawled as taught in training will be pinned to de earth. David, learn from de plants around jou. Being in harmony wit other living tings nourishes jour roots, ese."

Just as they instinctively hit the dirt near the large fir tree, the interrogation tent got pasted by an 88 round. "I tink dat dat one almost had our name on it, David," yelled Juan.

"It did, Vuan, I think I got a piece of the tent stuck in my boots.

"For reals, ese? Let me check it out before jou move. Jou need a new pair of botas, ese, and jou are going to have some very sore feet, but noting looks broken, and I don't see any blood."

"Just liberate me a pair of boots and spare me the medical analysis, Vaun. I don't vant any of those MASH boys to know of this. I must keep on vit my vork, Vaun. Every little piece of information I get brings me that much closer to liberating my family."

"Size eleven, ese?" asked Juan.

"That's close enough, Vaun. In fact, make them twelves if they look new. I'll need some dry socks too," replied David.

"I'll be back in a flash," said Juan as he dashed off in search of boots in his now famous dodging chivito style.

David thought that Juan was the perfect requisition officer in an army were forms out numbered equipment and supplies. Juan had liberated their entire interrogation kit, including a jeep. For Juan the Army was one big store designed to help David and him fight the war. David never asked where the items came from. All he knew was that Juan would take good care of their needs in a tight squeeze. Before David could get the blitzed boots off, Juan had returned.

"Hey, ese, jou estill an esize twelve? I found a brand new pair next to esome vato who won't be needing dem anymore," said Juan as he helped David get the rest of his burned boots off. "In fact, ese, all dat was left of him were his legs De rest of him was just one big eshish kabob, carnal."

"Don't tell me these are dead man's boots, Vaun."

"O.K., ese, I won't tell jou dat," Juan said with a boisterous laugh.

"That's not funny, Vaun," said David.

"Jou want dat I eshould be crying, ese. Dis es wat jou need to feel bedder? Besides, once we get dese botas on jou, ese, dey will be live botas, man."

"What are vou jiving about now, Vaun?" asked David as he reached to check out his feet.

"Mi Abuelo always use to esay que 'Botas are only dead if de vato wearing dem es on de way to de happy battlefield in hell.' Let's get dese new dry socks on jou. Mi Mamá would be proud of dese socks. Dey are handknitted Argyles, ese."

"Vere did vou get these socks, Vaun? They have more color to them than my feet."

"Dun't ask, ese, unless jou really want to know," said Juan. "I almost kept dem para mí. Besides if jou are worried about de colores, jour feet will catch-up to dem in a couple of days. Jour feet look bad even in de dark, ese."

"Just get these socks and boots on them before they svell-up, Vaun," commanded David.

"Whatever jou say, ese. Anyways, David, tings are looking up, ese. Dis vato who doesn't need dese botas was near a jeep with a couple of tents and a B.A.R. in de back dat had a 'take me' esign hanging on dem. I figured dat meant de jeep too, since ours was esmoked wit jour botas."

"I think that if vou vere in charge of the var, Vuan, the opposing sides vould be all fighting vit each others' veapons."

"Ese, if I was running dis war, it be over."

"That sounds good to me too, Vaun."

"Now dat jou got jour new boots on, David, let's take our new jeep out of dis hellhole before de Nazis esmoke it too. I got to find me a place where I can read dis mail dat es burning a hole in my pocket. One of dem es from de Red Cross."

"It is probably one of those notes to remind vou to vrite to vour mater, Vaun."

"Like I have de time to write anybody in dis hellhole. What de tink we doing over here anyways, pissing in our boots? I'll read the one from my brother first. Look at dis, ese. His letter looks like Swiss cheeze, man."

"The censors do that so the Krauts won't know what's going on if they capture our mail, Vuan."

"He fooled dem anyways. He tells me he es in de other war fighting de Japs."

"Where does it say that, Vaun."

"Right here, ese, where he esays dey got him wearing his cross upside down. Dat means he es in de South Pacific under de Southern Cross. He and me made dat an esignal before I came over here. Now for dis Red Cross note." Juan proceeded to tear open the nondescript letter. "Shit, man, dis de worst, ese. Look how de tell jou dis kind of news."

"Vats vrong, Vaun?" asked David as Juan handed him the letter and got into their new jeep. "I'm sorry, Vaun, I know from vour stories dat vour Grandfather was a very important person for vou."

"Tanks, David. Mi Abuelo already told me adiós in my dreams." Juan fought back the tears of his anger as he started up the jeep. There were still so many things that he needed to ask Abuelo. They started down what the map said was a road towards the Kraut lines. The knowledge of the smoking letter in Juan's hand could not hold the fact that Abuelo an excellent dream walker knew the dream path.

The barrage let up. David and Juan came to a fork in the road and stopped. To Juan, forks in the white world of Europe were always a bad sign: broken treaties without end. "If Abuelo was here, he would know which branch to take," mumbled Juan to himself.

"It is about time jou locos got here wit dat gun," yelled a voice from behind a wall. "We've been waiting por jou about an hour and dey are about to make dere move in dat next grove. The Capitan, he esays we gots to hold dis check point, or we lose de whole company. In our espare time we are esupposed to clear dat mine field" said a sergeant as he approached the jeep. "Hey jou're not Martinez, boy. Who are jou?"

"Cool it, ese. I was just about to ask jou what a nice home boy was doing so far from de barrio," said Juan in a half laugh.

"How did jou get Martinez's gun, ese?" asked the sergeant.

"He told me back at de taco stand up de road dat esince his arms and legs weren't no longer connected to his cabeza, dat I was to borrow it for de rest of mi vida natural, ese." The road burst into flames. The voice with the questions became instant charcoal.

"Get on dat gun, Vuan. I'll drive us off de road. He doesn't care who ve are anymore," yelled David.

Juan aimed into the field at the source of the flames. The B.A.R. spit death and revenge. Stray bullets began taking out mines. A star shell burst overhead revealing German infantry and tanks coming down both roads. David maneuvered them in behind the stone pasture wall. "Cover me wit de gun David and pin dat infantry. I'll eslide down de wall and take out de lead tank on each road wit dese grenades esomebody left for us behind dis wall."

"No need to a hero, Cucaracha," said David. "Stay here vit me."

"I got to take out dose tanks, ese. Dat'll force de Krauts into der own mine field."

"Let's get the hell out of here, Vaun. There's no way we can do this."

"Jou never met mi Abuelo, David, or jou wouldn't esay dat. Beside jou can't run on dose feet and we just got dis new jeep," yelled Juan.

"Do vour thing, Vuan," said David. "I'll back vour play."

Juan ducked and darted up the left fork. He took out the lead tank with a grenade up the panzer's belly. David pinned the infantry in the trucks with bursts of fire from the B.A.R. Juan ran back to the fork and hurled two grenades at the lead tank on the road to the right of the fork. The right side track broke and the tank twisted to a stop. Burning snowsuit clad Krauts ran into the mine field to fine Gotterdamerang. Juan crawled back to David's position behind the wall.

"Wat took vou so long, Vaun?" asked David as Juan returned from the blazing shadows to the now bullet ridden jeep.

"Hey man, dat first tank must have had full gas tanks. It blew-up all over de tank behind it. I'm not going to get jou any-more new equipment, ese, jou don't know how to take care of it. Just look at my beautiful new jeep. Besides jou let dem put a new hole in my leg, man. I told jou to pin dem down."

"Are vou O.K., Vuan? It's hard to pin down a whole column wit vone gun, Cucaracha."

"Just tie me off while I keep dese Krauts looking for cow pies and mines in de dark, de hard way, ese!"

"Too bad vou are married, ese," said David. "The vay vou complain, vou vould make some poor schmuck a real nasty vife."

"Just tie me off, ese!" yelled Juan. "Now neither of us can run."

As David finished the tourniquet, a mortar shell rearranged the stone wall and all but buried the jeep. "Look at dat, ese, dey are trying to build us a new bunker." David would not hear that or any other comment for about two days. Seeing the blood run-ning out of David's ears, Juan yelled as he stared down the hot gun barrel at the on rushing hoards, "Dun't worry, carnal, jou are one bloody Jew dat de Nazis will bleed for. "Help me, Abuelo; esave mi carnal."

"De Matalanes rule las voces de la familia, Eshot-gun. Dun't forget to keep jour barrel clean. Look estraight into de unloaded barrel y las voces will fill jour ear full of toughts with de tunder of de trute."

"But, Abuelo, I miss jou already."

"Dis es good. Keep jour aim true. De more jou miss me de more I will be found in jour heart."

"But, Abuelo, how am I to find my way without jou to guide me?"

"Jou are not listening again, my little Eshot-gun. Jour way will find jou. Dey are coming to jou. Estay centered. Dun't look for it or at it. De more jou try to find it, de esmaller es la chansa of getting on it."

"But, Abuelo..."

"Teolt's esmoking mirror and earth espears are jours. Use dem Cucaracha."

"I only esee de gun's spitting flame and Kraut bodies flying on clouds of exploding earth, Abuelo."

"Good mijo. When jou would esee me, de earth would eswallow jou."

*   *   *

The C.O. told Juan and David two weeks later in the field hospital just before their release that they had held that crossroads for almost eleven hours before battalion relieved them. The only good thing about being in the hospital was that it allowed time for some more of their mail to catch-up to them. In the pouch was a letter from Concha.

Dearest Juanito,

By now you have probably heard that Abuelo has died. He was killed in an explosion in a defense plant. The Army won't give us any details, but we will keep trying to find out

261

what really happened. We are all praying for you. Before he died Abuelo asked me to send you a note telling you dat he had a dream where you were walking with holes in your legs and your hands were full of blisters like the time you burned them on the manifold of the old Ford. If you are wounded again, Chivito, you had better tell me. I don't like hearing it from the Red Cross.

We received a letter from the priest you told us you had met in Rome. He seems to be a wonderful man. He sent your Mother a medal. She put it with the one you sent her. I wear the one you sent me constantly. I won't take it off until you come home. On the matter of the Zuit, with Abuelo dying and all, I haven't found the right time to do it, Chivito. So, you will just have to stay alive so you can tell her yourself.

I love and miss you so very, very much. Please write more. Even your short lousey notes are gold for me.

Love,

Conchita.

Dearest Concha,

The night I was notified about Abuelo's passing I got hit in both legs. So, his dream was right. Fortunately, my wounds were only what the doctors call 'flesh wounds.' So I'm healing-up just fine. You have probably noticed that this letter is not in my usual bad hand. The nurse that is taking care of me and David is doing the writing. That's because like in Abuelo's dream I got some burns on my hands. I guess the gun I was using over heated and I burned myself when I moved it a couple of times during the night. But, I don't really remember that happening. The Nurse says that the burns aren't real bad and that I should be able to take off the bandages in a couple of days. Maybe she will help me write more soon.

Love,

Juan.

P.S. Mrs. Galván: Juan doesn't know it yet, but everybody around here says that he and his Sergeant are some kind of real heroes. I'm sure you are going to be reading about him in the papers real soon. Oh, he's also the worst patient I have ever had. It seems that all he and his Sergeant want to do is to steal a jeep and get back to the front lines.

Nurse Allenfield.

"I hear you boys want to be released, post haste," said a Captain wearing the citation cords of the general staff.

"Jou got dat right, Captain, Sir," said Juan showing off his best smile.

"That goes for me too," said David.

"I know that a lot people and the press from 'Stars and Stripes' have been asking you boys a bunch of questions, but I have a few more before I can release you back to your unit," said the Captain.

"What's one jour mind, Captain? We'll tell you whatever we can," replied Juan.

"Corporal Galben, what I want to know is what the hell you and Sergeant Goldstein were doing on that road in the first place."

"We were just trying to find H.Q., Sir."

"I guess ve got lost," said David.

"Are either of you qualified on the Browning Automatic Rifle?"

"I am not, Sir," said Juan. Are jou qualified on one, David?"

"Captain, I can honestly say that I never actually used a B.A.R. in combat conditions prior to that night," said David.

"How did you guys get that gun and all that ammo?" asked the Captain.

"It was just sort of on a jeep dat was willed to us by dis guy named Martinez, Captain," said Juan.

"Who is this Martinez? Is he part of this action too?"

"I don't think so?"

"I don't know if you two clowns realize it or not, but you are bonafide heros. General Bradley, himself, has asked me to get the particulars on what you did."

"All we were trying to do, Captain, Sir, was work out a way to estay alive," said Juan. "I had a couple of holes in my legs and David's feet looked like borched from where esome eshrapenal had burned off his boots."

"Ve didn't do anything special, Captain. They just kept coming at us and ve kept loading and firing the gun," said David. "Ve'er just lucky dat dose tanks blocked de roads and our gun didn't blow-up."

"Didn't you two heroes get the order to pull back?"

"We didn't have no radio, Sir, Captain, Sir," said Juan. "Even if we did my Sergeant here gets all of our vehicles eshot-up real good. Eso, we could not have left dat position even if we had wanted ta."

"Well be all that as it may be, you two, single handedly stalled an entire German Armour Column with its supporting infantry for eleven hours. We estimate that before your position lay seven hundred German dead. You appeared to have systematically destroyed four panzer tanks, two fuel trucks, five personnel carriers and six supply trucks. The major in the relief column that came up behind you kept looking for the rest of your company. Can you tell me what happened to them?"

"We didn't have no rest of our company, Captain, Sir," said Juan. "Sergeant Goldstein and me are part of the H.Q. interrogation unit. David here was just trying to take a couple of prisoners."

"The General thought it was something like that. He said he had seen Sergeant Goldstein's name on some intelligence reports."

"Sergeant Goldstein is there anything that you would like to add?" asked the Captain.

"Not really, sir, except that it was Corporal Galván that did all the stuff you mentioned. All I remember vas him taking out a couples tanks vit some grenades ve found behind the vall vhere I crashed our new jeep. Vuan did it all. I vould also like to know ven ve can get back to the interrogations of the German prisoners. That vork is so very important to me. Ve need that information to justify our thrust to Munich and Dachau instead of Berlin."

"You don't need to worry about that, Sergeant Goldstein," said the Captain.

"I must complete my interrogations to complete my report for the general staff. I know the German mind. Ve got to stop that genocidal Nazi var machine."

"The people at home need heroes, boy, and I think you are being elected," said the Captain.

"Begging your pardon, Captain, Sir. I don't tink que I am any kind of hero. I was just trying to estay alive," said Juan.

"I already heard that soldier, but now that I have verified the accounts found in the Major's report and recommendation, I think both of you went way beyond the call of duty," said the Captain.

"Vat does that mean?" asked David.

"I think both of you will be up for the Congressional Medal of Honor. I'm going to send in my recommendation immediately. The Generals want the Army to move on this. It has truly been an honor to meet you boys."

"Captain, Sir, I truly appreciate the honor the Army wishes to bestow upon me, but vat good is it ven the heritage of freedom is being exterminated in Germany?" asked David anxiously. "Please let me finish my report."

"I'm sure that can be arranged, Sergeant," said the Captain as he left their room.

"Ve got to figure a way to get out of here, Vuan."

"I'm wit jou, ese," said Juan. "Besides, I dun't want to espend El Día De Los Magos in no hospital, even if dat nice Nurse Allfeel was feeling me."

"Get vour mind vhere vour heart is, Cucaracha," said David.

Juan liberated another jeep. This time he made sure that it didn't have a gun mounted on it. It took the Army two weeks to find them at the Mobile H.Q. The Army not only gave them the Medal of Honor, but it also gave David a battlefield commission and Juan, his Sergeant's stripes. The generals read David's report and decided to thrust towards Munich.

The new lieutenant and sergeant were reassigned to a newly formed combat unit.

WAREHOUSES OF THE DEAD

The Bavarian countryside remained beautiful. The fertile green valleys and the snow capped Bavarian Alps had escaped the vengeance of thousand plane raids that had been aimed at cities like Munich, Liepzig, and Dresden. While the naked eye could not discern the ten-foot deep fire purified furrows that contained the flower of Germany beneath freshly plowed fertile mountain fields, the crystal clear air and the pastoral sounds of Beethoven blowing loudly on the ice cold mountain wind exposed the horrors of secluded forced labor death camps: God given strengths and belief hiding deaf human frailty. Souls listening for the triumphant chorus of truth without hearing it!

The Ode to Joy glistening in fast falling mountain streams and fast rising clouds.

The killers of the Third Reich falling under sky riding Die Valkeries marched into the glorious Bavarian countryside. These skilled killers assaulted a massive and extensive industrial complex ten miles northwest of the once fairy book styled architecture in Munich. The taking of this fort would be easy: conquest without G.I. risk and loss. The walls of the factory complex were no longer defended even though the smoke stacks were still blazing a black acrid smoke as the furnaces glowed with work. The gun implacements had all been reversed. Only the search lights beamed outwardly.

The strong marching G.I.'s relentlessly pressed towards the complex through rubble strewn, devastated villages and cities filled with the corpses of combatants and civilians beaten into submission through armed liberation. The horrors of their advancing strident tide of war did not prepare David and Juan for the liberation of living souls creeping and groping in dead bodies amidst the unmarked mass graves of pulverized, rotting humanity—the remnants of ancient nations and ideologies.

Dachau, dark windowless buildings full of pieces of walking skeletons with tattooed numbers over the veins of the forearms.

Jews with prophets and no shadows. Gentiles with no profits in ruin. Political dissenters and nonconforming religious believers smashed with the great lie preached as the truth. Death dealing forced labor set them all free.

Goliathe stoned himself by torching the vineyard and graneries. The Talmud and Mein Kamph lying side-by-side in the open graves of a rotting nation whose flame had been extinguished before it was able to sanitize it sins before the conscience of the world.

In staying neutral the Jew had lost physically but won symbolically as the chosen few. They had tried to outlast Hitler as many, but only a very few survived. Out of six million, only a 100,000 remained.

As David and Juan opened the factory doors, their full moving shadows extended into the human void of bodiless souls. Staring, frightened by their strong military posture, the gray forms of former talents shrank into small corners amongst the stacks of rotting corpses and fecal filth in the warehouses of death. They made the silent shuffling sounds of scurrying, starving termites exposed to a bright light. Juan and David were that light in the dark, but their light could not liberate the dead. That work had already been done by the reaper.

Juan stared into the endless hall and puked. Not the puke of a seasick cucaracha, but the puke of a wrenching soul being assaulted by the unbelievable horrible reality that confronted all of his senses. The churning magots in his guts poisoned his tear clouded vision. He could feel the witness in the apparent priestly sellout of the Talmud and the Bible in ash laden ditches of calaveras. He turned slowly toward David's devastated pain and sighs of tearless distress between the wretches of his stomach.

"Dis is de madness of the German esoul inside out. David, de incredible effort dat it took to do dis is what destroyed de madness of Hitler's war machine."

"Vuan, give me a break! As Peter upside down on the cross, I don't vant to hear vour folk philosophy now. I'm so sick I don't think I'll eat for veeks. I'm going to make the Nazis pay for this. They owe us justice! Some how, some vay the prophets vill profit from even this!" David decried.

"I got to talk, mon, or I will bust a gut!" yelled Juan.

"Vou can't be a Jew, Vuan, until you are stereotyped as a Jew by the whole vorld!" asserted David.

Juan started carrying the moaning, fragile living calaveras into the light. Living masks of black ringed eyes and blue ashen faces dangling on whithered gray bodies stared up at his well fed brown face. The calavera moans almost had a lyrical pastoral sense contrasted to horror and obliteration of the few. Opening each new door added horror for Juan and became an ode to joy for the remnant. The march song of Germany had changed from the goose step of Gotterdameran to the Freida of Beethoven and Goethe.

The cucaracha walked slowly and carefully among the living dead. Juan remembered the cucarachas in Abuela's kitchen. A cucaracha disgorged its bowels to tolerate the gases of death.

As David searched amongst the remnant for clues to his family, he saw all the Jews upside down on Peter's cross in Rome. This was the ultimate Gentile madness. The reality of the sins of fathers being visited upon their children made meaning as he found small tiny bodies among the adults. Hatred in Dachau knew no age, nor sex.

"Are vou here, Herman Goldstein?" yelled David in German.

From one shed of the living dead to the next, David searched frantically. Juan with a snap shot of Herman Goldstein in his left hand chased David down the long rows of five stack bunks. David had come too far to lose the blessing of seeing his living sacred family.

"This is what Father Diego in all of his dedication to the truth could not tell me," mumbled David to himself. If I had only known, I would have not been able to wait for what now seems as an eternally slow march from Toulon," he continued as he took another body out into the light.

Every minute meant life to many of the few in these warehouses. He asked each gaunt face for Herman Goldstein's bunk site. With each new trip back into the shed he continued to call out for his father.

To protect each other, the remnant used numbers tatooed on their wrists. Names were forgotten. One of the remnant said he thought there was a Herman in the next shed.

"I cannot stand this anymore, Vaun! Trying to find my family here in this pit of death is like digging in the ashes of hell. Got has turned his back on us. Ve are on the far, far, far side! What did we ever do to Gott to deserve this? Herman Goldstein, are you here?"

"David, mi carnal, God es with us in dis work, trust me. De family jewels must be protected. It es jour placa on de wall. I tink my Zuit taught me dat."

"Who can Got be vit in this pit of death, Vuan?"

"Father Diego esaid," Juan replied, "dat St. Paul taught dat God es with dose dat are eserving Him. My Grandfather esaid, 'God is in de hearts of all good men. His works are expressed trough deir deeds'. Dat es what keeps dem in a good road."

"Vat service are ve rendering here, Vuan?"

"We are esetting jour people free, ese. Isn't dat what jou been telling me all de way from Morroco to Tunis, to Italy, to France, and now to Germany?"

"Free from vat? Look at their boney bodies and gaunt faces, Vuan. Cut the crap, Vuan! Go free my dead sisters and mother. Liberate my brainwashed brother. Hitler intimidated us. Then he poisoned our children one by one. And if that wasn't enough, Hitler stoned my people vit frozen ashes of death!"

"Come on David, help me find jour father," consoled Juan. "I can hear his voice. He es in dis next row. I can feel it in my botas."

David had followed Juan so many times before over the past two years that in spite of the pain and disgust that was clutching at his throat, he had to follow now. He continued his search for the living, down the row of broken humanity. The going was painfully slow as he carefully lifted the living from under the dead, but where was his father? Would God only let him serve the priestly function of guidance and liberation?

Desperate groping gray ashen fingers at his laces. "Goldie my boy, is it really vou?" called a voice from the shadows with hoarse, choked effort.

"My Gott! Vou are alive!" Found among the lost. Joy and anguished melded together in a blanket of guilt and mission. "Help me Vuan! Come and see! Gott is not dead!"

"Did jou really find him, David?" asked Juan.

"Oh, yes my cucaracha, he vas never lost! Pater let me move vou into the light," suggested David as he squinted his eyes to see through the shadows to the gaunt skeleton reaching out to him.

"There is no need for that now, my son," answered David's father as other living skeletons shuffled towards Juan and David. "Gott has preserved and saved me in this deathhole, just long enough for me to pass on the shroud of truth, 'gasp.' "

"That is not necessary yet, Pater," asserted David as he stooped to cradle his father's frail light figure.

"I saw vour sisters, Ruth and Rebecca, my perfect Lambs, gassed. They vere silenced for protecting our inheritance."

"I don't understand, Pater, I..."

"Because Hitler could not buy our vineyard, he tried to bury us," 'sigh...Gasp,' "but, seeing vou, my son, proves that the dying vines in our vineyard have strangled Hitler, 'gasp.' "

"Pater rest for a moment."

"There is no time for that now. Vou are my living vine. I heard that vour mother was shot vhile trying to smuggle in some dried milk for a starving baby."

"Please rest, Pater! I cannot bear to hear anymore."

"Let me complete my covenant. Then there vill be much time to rest, my son. Our vineyard is alive in vou. Vou are Gott's promise to me," 'sigh...Gasp,' "our spiritual truth has protected the sons. Goldie, please forgive vour brother, Hans. He never had vour choices."

"I hear vou, Pater."

"Then also hear this, Goldie. Ve paid for vour salvation, 'gasp.'"

"Vat do vou mean, Pater?"

"Ve have protected the vineyard, Goldie. No matter vhere the family is, it's home. Even a cemetery in this damned Dachau, 'heaving... sigh... Gasp!'"

Only David knew that Han's inheritance had been stolen by the "Big Lie".

"Goldie," David's father continued after a gut wrenching period gasping and coughing, "Please, please, always protect our vineyard. Our lineage," 'gasp,' "Our life! Be fruitful and prosper, my precious fruit of my loins," Dr. Goldstein sighed between death rattling gasps.

"Vour loins are my loins, Pater. Vour vords are sacred vit me," David said through tears of strength.

"Promise me that you vill finish vour studies in law and find vour brother, Hans, David," said his father.

"Considerate it done, Pater."

"As I die here now, for the first time in many, many years I am free, Goldie."

"Vou can't die now, Pater, now that I just found vou!"

"Vou can't rewrite vat has already been vritten in the book. Vour mater taught that, Goldie, 'gasp.'"

"Please stay for just a vhile longer, Pater!" said David as his tears flowed freely.

"My eternity is beginning, Goldie, vit my last earthly breathe, my blessing is double for vou, 'sigh.'"

"And for vou, too, Pater," murmured David as his father's frail body went totally limp. "The Vestval has crumbled in my father's death, Vuan," said David, turning to his brother in strength. "Jericho has fallen again. The goosestep and zuit strut are not necessary for spiritual life!"

With warm tears on his cheek, Juan pondered what he had just witnessed as he felt the right hand and the warm breathe of his Abuelo on his left shoulder. "Tink, my little Eshotgun. De familia must esurvive. I live to protect and feed it. I'm de root. Jou are de branch. De root of de oak es deep. When it es estrong de tree es powerful!"

Juan looked deep in David's piercing and painful stare. "What does my Zuit have to do with de death of jour father, David?" said Juan, as he moved his eyes down to the tattered lifeless form in David's arms.

"Not vone thing, Vuan. Our appearance is not honor. Our suits and uniforms are not respect. Our tattered lives vit great love are better than any general's uniform. Ve come into life naked, ve only die clothed if ve die vit dignity and respect." David looked upwardly as he raised the frail tattered body of his father and shouted to his God.

"Gott! Vit all my heart and soul, I offer to Vou the best dressed man in the whole vorld!" Search lights beamed outwardly.

HONOR IN DEATH

The gagging allied soldiers carried the old and new dead to the pits. The horrific stench overpowered and engulfed the smell of puking Americans trudging through the sins of a Nazi reality being buried: Siegfried's Funeral March. In the first days of the Bavarian spring, the Jews had been forced to dig their own graves by their Nazi tormentors. Had the allies come a week later, all that would have remained would have been the empty barracks of an unnamed labor camp. The freshly plowed fields of the spring Bavarian planting would have secreted the evidence.

There was no telling how many layers of rotting, burned and scorched skeletons were already buried there. David lowered his father's body into the horrendous unmarked grave where the walking numbered forearms with lifeless staring eyes said, "The remains of your mother and sisters should be in the ark of this place." No salute could remotely begin to pay the honor already done by this spiritual army. Juan witnessed as David marked the place with his boot: 7x7x7.

"Deir witness will light our feet once we get used to de esmoke of dis place, David. Now I know de honor I owe my father for walking out of Durango on guaraches of maguey. We will honor dem as long as we never allow dis to happen in any form again."

"That is all vell and good for vou, Vaun. Vour light is till alive."

"A living death es harder dan death itself. It honors life as no other witness, David. Dat es wat jour family has proven here and es wat we can never forget."

"Things like dis are so hard to remember that ve forget dem to stay whole, Vuan."

"Remembering where jou have been brings honor to where jou are, David. Mi Abuelo taught me dat and lived many a death. Dey killed him and his children and grandchildren. Dey even tried to kill his dreams. But he said dat death honored life by making birth possible." Juan marked next to David's 7x7x7, a 20x20x20.

Dearest Conchita,

A few eternal months ago, I wrote in one of my letters that I didn't really know why we were over here. Even den I knew dat we were fighting because some crazys were trying to purify de world for deir own kind of madness. These past ew days I esaw de real heroes of dis crazy war. I met one face to face who esacrificed everyting o protect us all. Even jou, Concha.

I know dat you probably heard about de medals dey gave me. I won't esay dat I'm not proud to have dem, because I am. But, if I live to be a hundred, I will never be able to forget these past few days. I will never forget Tio Augustín, Abuelo, and David's father' esacrifices. I will always remember dem as de bearers of my medals dat I have earned and won.

I remember Abuelo esaying that an estarving man can't eat poisoned estrawberries. My Dad esaid dat, 'estrength es born out of de ashes.' Dis place they call Dachau will be dat for our people, too. To me, Hitler es already eating his poisoned estrawberries, carnala mía."

Now I know that St. Paul told de trute when he esaid, 'If God es with jou who can be against jou.'

I remember when I was taking my first holy communion at de church of San Juan Bautista, I esaw a little esign esaying dat 4,000 Indios are buried in a mass unmarked grave on de eastside of de church. As I looked at dat place, I esaw only little crosses with no names.

What I esaw here in Dachau brought dat esign back o me. It tells me why my Great Grandfather hated de Gachupín, even though de blood of de Conquistadores flowed in his veins. He esaid dat de Gachupín killed 27 million Indios to take de esavageness out of our land. But like Hitler de gachupín estepped on himself with his own espurs.

I am learning in dis place dat 27,000,000 Indios died to prove de moda of España was pure. Out of dose ashes rose our mestisaje."

I am learning here dat it eseems to be esomething dat groups of humans do to other groups of humans to prove dat dey are bedder, or dat dey own de trute

Dere was dis German crazy man who was de principal of my first grade eschool. His name was Mr. Waugh. He taught me two things. God put lovers of torture on earth to make de rest of us tough and dat for each jerk-butt lover of torture es esomeone or esomething esent up by God to estep in and estop de torture. For me dat is my papá. I guess I had bedder estop for now. I guess jou probably dun't want ta get dis kind of ledder any-ways, but I had to tell all die estuff ta esomebody I trust with my heart, or I would bust a gut. I know if I didn't ever know it before, Concha mía, dat jou are dat somebody I trust with all of me.

Love,

Juan

PARADES AND HONORS

Juan flew home in January, 1946, from France in a chauvinistic Liberator loaded with secret files and liberated art work for "friends" of the Army in Congress. The best part of the trip was eating the pine nuts and corn nuts Abuela sent him in his Christmas package from home. A Nor'easter rained like fire upon the Liberator for most of the trip. He could only see Ursa Major as they flew over the English Channel. The uniformed jaguar had devoured the giants in the earth by both day and night. Cortez was returning to eat up the streets.

The bomb bay doors where strapped shut to prevent the destruction of the cargo: bowles full of hidden stolen enemy treasures rather than treacherous bombs to be vomited upon the enemy. Juan the liberator was traveling with "liberated" goods: some of the plunder of Europe flying home to the victorious. "Esome of the victorious rich who had never fought had found a way to make a personal profit from a war," said Juan to himself.

"Did you say something, Sergeant?" asked the navigator.

"Would jou like esome pine nuts, Sir?" asked Juan. "My Abuela sent dem to me last Christmas."

"No, thanks, Sergeant. I've have to concentrate on our course for the moment. I would just like to add that it is a real honor to transport you back to the good old U.S. of A."

"What are jou talking about, Sir?" asked Juan.

"We all read about Captain Goldstein and you in 'Stars and Sripes,' Sergeant. You two were really something else. The radio stations we are monitoring from New York City say that they got everything but the golden carpet laid on for your homecoming. The brass wants the whole world to know about your arrival."

"Gosh I hope not," said Juan. "All I want to do is get home to my wife and family."

"That may not happen for a while, hero," replied the navigator with a laugh. "The brass wants to show to the American public what they paid for. And, Sergeant Galbens, you're it."

"What do jou mean?" asked Juan.

"All I know is that we have orders to taxi up to the V.I.P. area to let you off. Your coming home with all the rest of the trophies, Sergeant Galbens. "How does it feel to be a trophy?"

"I don't know, Sir," replied Juan as he tried to avoid the conversation. "I never thought of myself as a trophy before.

"Well think about it Sergeant, because you are going to be paraded like one."

"I don't want to talk about being a trophy," said Juan.

"Do you mind if we talk a little about something else?" asked the navigator. "I find that it helps to pass the time on these long flights."

"O.K. by me, Sir," said Juan. "What do jou want ta talk about?"

"Well," said the navigator, "there is something I always wanted to ask one of you heroes.

"What's dat, Sir?" asked Juan.

"What's a real hero really like?"

"Dat question makes me feel all hollow and lost inside," answered Juan.

"Why's that, Sergeant?" asked the navigator.

"When someone tells me someone dies is he suppose to be resting? I am not so sure. Can anyone tell me when a person dies where the beginning of the heroric dream walker begins and ends? Is it the mass and the flowers on a grave or a medal filled, flag draped coffin?"

"What are you talkin' about, Sergeant?" queried the navigator while checking Juan's oxygen supply.

"To me when loved ones die, nothing remains in my heart: no feelings, no memories, and no flowers on deir graves," Juan continued. "I am still wearing de esame boots. But I do not know which way to walk."

"You don't need to walk, Sergeant. We're flying you there," said the navigator with a smile.

"That may be, Sir, but what does flying have to do with de ashes of true heroes?" asked Juan.

"What!"

"When I see the ashes, I cry," said Juan. "I have a seen a lot of ashes in dis war. My family is all over the earth, but others have told me dat dey are resting here with me. Today I am a hero. Something raised above de ashes of war. Others tell me I am a hero but they only see my medals. But if I do not put them on my uniform, I'm just a dogface. Jou esay I am a trophy, but where are de trophys for all dose unplated unsung heroes who died to protect de esong ofdeir trutes?"

"Do you really understand all the words you just used, Sergeant?"

"Not totally, ese. But, I hope dat jou and I know dat I'm espeaking una trucha here, Sir. My voices have always been faithful to de trucha, even when I can't esee de direction dey are pushing me. Jou mentioned my carnal, David Goldstein. Let me tell jou about dis real hero. Ever since David volunteered for the army, he promised himself to liberate the Jews. He always told to me dat Hitler had created a horrendous song with de "Big Lie." David esaid dat Hitler had done in loyalty for de German Jew and espat on deir rituals and esongs. Dis hero, David, left Heidelberg to esave de trute from being lost. If he didn't do dat and leave all dat he held dear, he esaid dat his song would have been destroyed by Hitler's honesty and hatred of de Jews. His little brother, Hans, didn't get dat choice. Hitler made him a Nazi hero. Yet, de choices his brother had made had to be a lie. When his brother became an SS he lived the 'Big Lie.' But to de German, Hans was a hero. My Abuelo said dat for a hero, desertion of de espirit only helps dose who would flaw demselves. For jou, Sir dat's a hero who's a fool. Es dat a real hero for jou, Sir?"

"I'm sorry I asked, Sergeant. Could I have some of you pine nuts now?"

"Esure, Sir," said Juan as he leaned forward to pour out some nuts into the navigator's outstretched palm. "Since jou are dey first to ask me what es a real hero, Sir, let me tell jou esomemore about Capitan Goldstein. He esaid dat he always felt like de Greek estudent in de Gospel written by Luke. Dat estudent was eseeking de truth, for he believed dat trute would bring happiness. And just like dat heroic estudent en Luke, trute didn't bring him happiness, it brought him confusion."

"What happened then, Sergeant?"

"During many esleepless nights in de foxholes, David had worked trough de real tings in his life dat had made him be willing to give up his precious family to protect de trute of who he is. Dis made him a hero por me. But in his guilt for deserting his family, he felt dat he was a Judas and not a Jew. But as his boots oozed trough de feces he felt dat what he was trying ta preserve was de mask for his esoul rather dan his Inherited Esoul. Now I ask jou, Sir, how could a heroic esoul live in de dung of dis hell on earth?"

"I don't know," said the navigator while wondering if he could quietly open the bomb bay doors and lose this hero with a big mouth.

Not knowing this, Juan kept trying to answer the navigator's original question. "Dachau revealed de 'Big Lie' as de truth full of hatred and courage. It proved dat heroic trute and de heroes who carry its song do not deal only with de romantic search for knowledge and reality, but also with de screwed-up, lying realities dat mocked de trute. So den I esay to myself, where es de real hero in all dat."

"Whatever you say, Sergeant," said the navigator. "All I know now is that if I don't plan our final approach, we will be in for a heroic swim in the Atlantic."

*   *   *

Promised big shots on parade: medals on the chest: politicians and would be politicos making hay in the dark while Tenochtitlan burned. Juan was rich and powerful in his Medal Of Honor, but poor and sick in his soul. He had sacrificed five years of his first creation for the boisterous silence of unexpected parades and laudations without substance. David was still fighting for justice in Nuremberg Germany: a deer chasing the hunters. The brass had even made David a Captain to prove they weren't anti- Semitics.

The squadrons of rumbling returning liberators from the east were arriving in the winter of alleged victory only to be shoved into the desert in unheard storage. The clay feet of marching wooden soldiers had no heart time to praise God and regenerate the sacred earth. Only the vanquished were being forced to bend their knees. The presence of empty praises offended the God/gods. Juan had finished his pine nuts and started to eat his corn nuts while pondering the reality of honored substance: "Remember who loves you best, Chivito Cucaracha," said Abuela.

The contract of obligation had already been assigned in the blood spotted, rainy battlefield east of Metz to the rhythm of near and distant artillery. The gift of honor flowered on a mid-winter sunlit day in Washington D.C. at the foot of the Capitol Steps surrounded by tasseled generals and hay makers. "Newsrealers" with cameras grinding and flashing joined the cacophony of bands playing. Medals awarded by dignitaries and the chosen political few to the rhythm and heart beat cadence of a deliberate Star Spangled Banner. The rich parade of color and music consumed the poor honored soldier: "Remember who loves you best, Chivito Cucaracha."

A great snorting iron horse smoked and thundered from parade to parade. Everyone wanted to be seen with a real hero. The train took him from Union Station to Union Station. No buffalo impeded their progress.

Hoards of uniformed, card playing, smoking, former hon-ored and not honored service men crowded the railway cars like packed pigs headed for the stockyards. Westwardly they rolled in a rhythmic dissonance.

Juan couldn't wait to see Concha and his family. Yet, he feared that meeting more than an incoming 88 round.

As the great metal steed steamed past middle American and skirted the bedrock of the continent, Juan felt the tears of his honored great grandfather upon his soul. "De gabachos tought dey loved our land when dey cut down dey trees, blew up de montañas, esilted de rio, burned de grasses, and belted it with steel. Dose generals tried to put bullets on our chest to get medals for deirs. We were esacrificed to dey earth to make possible deir frontier espirits. Now dey use de giants in our earth to feed deir boilers. De espíritu of de acorn es all dat I can pass unto you, my eson."

Juan traveled the land with the conquered and conquering "heart clash."

"What a way to espend jour days of glory," said Juan to a uniformed stranger on the train.

"What days of glory, Medal Winner. There is no glory being a dogface gunbutt from Fort Dix," said the stranger in the uniform.

"I just hope my old lady has the house fumigated before I get home. With her, there is no telling what 4-F trash she has had parading through my house," replied the nodding uniform behind him.

"I just hope I still have a home. About the only thing I know right now is that both of the rails we are riding appear to be going in the same direction," said the uniform that spoke to Juan originally. "You got a home, Mex?"

"I tink eso," replied Juan as if the rails he was on were going in different directions. The rhythmic pounding of the steel wheels seemed to say, "Coronado had to eat his horses to survive. Crazy Horse died rather than starve."

The rippling ribbons of silver steel glistened on the earth like golden chevrons on his arms. The golden acorns were smashed upon the tracks.

"Don't worry mihito. Juan remember who loves jou de best," murmered Abuela to the rhythm of the tracks.

Honored in Los Angeles at Sixth and Flower. The homage of office scrap paper snowed on his glorified, ribbon filled chest. One disguised barrio hero exalted by a short parade in a big new smooth riding white convertible with lots of fuel and a police escort to take him to city hall. Everybody gave a hero in uniform esteem, even when he was an unseen Zuit Zooter in a dress army uniform.

Juan wearied of parade makers honoring themselves with speeches. Why wasn't his family at the train station? Why weren't they at City Hall? Hadn't anyone asked them to be in the parade? Ritualistic homebound homeless homecoming.

"We are proud of you, soldier," said the mayor. "You are living proof that Hollywood isn't all fluffy glamour, tinsel and celluloid."

"I wish I had been the first to pin this medal on you," said the Chief of Police as he ritualistically repeated the awarding of the medal with a key to the city. "This a real honor, soldier. We need more citizens of your caliber. The whole city is at your feet."

"You can't have honor and respect without both personal and group identity," Juan thought. "I'm not even from this dump and all its tinsel."

Juan got the key to the city that couldn't unlock doors. Movie starlets with cheese cake bodies smiled and gave him wreaths and kisses. Everybody was watching. The eyes of the world were listening on their radios. Nobody was seeing. The witnesses with hollow victories were honoring themselves. The bands were playing, confetti everywhere.

Today Juan was everybody's hero, but yesterday's news: Juan in his uniform on parade. The illegal barrio Zuit was in a box in the closet.

Smoking buses and jalopies with limited fuel jerked and jolted Juan to his mother-in-law's chosita in the barrio: surprise homecoming. Nobody was home in the barrio. Only Juan wasn't working. "Hey ese, what jou doing on dose esteps. Jou don't live dere," yelled a young child as he skated past Juan. "Where did jou happen from, señor?" said the child on his return trip.

"I just got home from de war, niño," said Juan.

"Then I guess jour are not my Papá."

"Why do jou say dat, niño? If I had an estrong niño like jou he would be about jour age."

"Mi Mamá has big medals like jou got. De prettiest one has a big purple ribbon on it."

"I'll bet jour mamá es real proud of jour papá, niño," said Juan.

"I guess eso, Mr. Man. Pero, mi mamá cries a lot when eshe looks at dat medal."

"Why es dat, niño?" asked Juan without thinking.

"Mi Mamá dice que mi Papá es never coming home."

The silk pine tree in front of the chosita looked like it stepped on itself. A good cucaracha would never had done that. No wonder Papá had moved back to Matatlan. Abuelo would have laughed at this scrawny rootless imitation struggling to see the sun through the Los Angeles smog. Juan was glad Abuelo was buried in Matatlan, even though it would be a while before he could visit the grave.

Juan decided that while he waited for Concha to come home, he would walk to St. Joseph's and light a candle to Our Lady to honor her for bringing him home to his family.

THE APRON

In March, 1946, Juan mustered out of the service. He kicked around for about eight months looking for work. His daily search in the want ads for employment told him that wanted him. A "normalizing society" had very little need for foxhole diggers.

Before and after a war, heroes never needed new furniture to feel status. Before the war Conchita loved cruising the boulevards with him. All he needed was money in his pockets and a steady job: all she needed for status was his last name. But now she was more interested in buying furniture and clothes. His mustering out pay and back pay had its limits. She sorely missed his dependent's allowance. From her "patrona looks" at the breakfast table, Juan could only fight the "good husband" battle with a "good job" or else, he could wind-up as another piece of old furniture.

As a husband, the aprons boxed him in. She had him on the horns of a dilemma in a no win situation. He had thought his marriage, courage on the battlefield, and love for María Conchita served as proof of his manly intentions. The chest of his Eisenhower blouse had three bronze stars, two silver stars and cluster, the purple heart, ribbons for four campaigns, and the Congressional medal of honor for his heroism at the Bulge in Luxumberg.

However, when he wanted to try on his Zuit, the employers didn't want it and his Mamá would find out. Concha would see to that. Now the blouse and the metals were folded neatly in a box that was on top of the box that had his neatly folded Drapes and cracked wedding boots. "How can you wear an honorable Zoot Zuit when the carnales are still blood stains on a beach in Italy?"

To wear the Zoot Zuit now would be to step on the memory of the barrio. "A cucaracha can't estep on itself, Eshot-gun, without eshiting in its nest, mijo," said Abuelo.

"When are you going to wear your Zoot Zuit again, Juan?" asked Concha in one her letters when Juan was still in Europe after the Armistice. "I'm getting tired of hauling it all over L.A. just to keep your memories alive, querido."

In another letter she had told him, "I found a record of our song in the Discorama. You could put on your Zoot Zuit and I could wear my black sequined, Betty Grable dress and we could dance to our song right here in our own front room by playing it on the new record player I got today at the furniture store."

When the subject came up after he finally arrived at her mother's chosita, he said, "I want to wear my Zuit, Conchita, but if I do wear it, de carnales will die within me and de carnal in me will die with dem."

"Don't lie to me some more, Juan. Just put on your Zoot Zuit and let's dance!" Concha suggested. "That always made you feel good before the war."

"I just can't, Concha."

"Then why don't we just burn that Zuit Zoot like your mother wanted you to do in the first place?"

"Why don't you go burn dat new record player with dat old record on it?"

"Stay on the point, Juan. You can't erase the memory of a song even if you scratch and break the record. I can't say the same for your Zuit. I played this record over and over when you were overseas."

"Here's a broken record for jou, Concha. I'd go back over dere with David in Nuremburg eso jou can play jour memory fantasies."

"Big talk, Small Wallet!" snapped Concha. "I thought you said they wouldn't let you re-enlist."

"They won't even take Audie Murphy back with his Congressional Medal of Honor and battlefield commission. De Army es only keeping perfect soldiers after a war. All dey wanta do now es to esave tax dollars and make generals fat on new defense contracts for weapons in de next war."

As the mustering out allowances diminished Concha continued to make all the payments on their things out of her earnings. Juan went from the perfect soldier chivito to the imperfect sponge, but who said finding a good job would make him the perfect husband.

Before the war he voluntarily put on the Zoot Zuit for protection and identity with a specific group in the barrio. To Juan, uniforms worn during peace time were protective aprons, but in these times of conflict, those uniforms became target/tag-me signs. His mother saw the Zuit as negative peer strings and as a target sign for the LAPD. For Juan, the American uniform was involuntary. So was Han's Nazi uniform.

The search for the identifying shield or placa led to the Zuit and the stern plate for the Niña, Pinta, and Santa María on the deserts of Califas. The Zuit was Juan's coat of arms and his group identity. However, it could not serve as his personal identity. The same held true for his army uniform. The Zuit had tagged him for the draft, and the Eisenhower blouse with its medals tagged him for a hero. Even in a box the strings attached to those aprons controlled his reality and fantasies, especially when forces beyond his control had a hold on the strings. Spiritually, Concha was definitely beyond his control.

Cuatemoc's decorative shield never protected him from Cortez's technology and Cortez's shiney sword never protected him from Cuatemoc's spirit. The badge of courage made Juan a target: a courage that led to the movidas and street smarts for survival.

Juan felt that he had become a crying clown on a string in front of the curtain of aprons on the stage of life. The bills of domesticity, Concha's distance, and the coming of a baby all discounted his efforts and made him less a man. He had not signed up for this assault on his manhood when he waited in line for the marriage license and then took his vows before the priest in the church.

The strings on the apron of marriage kept pulling on him like bad letters from Hitler: the mail delivery of frozen nights in Eastern France. When he did lay in bed at night after doing the monthly bills, it seemed as if he were still on his back in a frozen foxhole. Concha kept pulling the strings towards the inner stage under the arch. The tighter her hold, the greater the chance that he would fall off the stage. That would give everyone a big laugh: the making of a fool.

It was lonely out on that apron. The footlights of marriage hid the orchestra pit of the hommies and good times with the vatos. The orchestra of skeletal hommies conducted by Ramón The Poet was constantly playing, "It Is A Sin To Tell A Lie."

The desire for personal dignity that he learned from David put him in the audience as an observer of his own song. In life he was the observer, not the player: a soloist in silence wearing an apron while eating salted peanuts and corn nuts in the balcony of life. He heard the tremulos of scarred vatos playing the overture to his song in the pit, trenches, and sewers; he saw conductors and directors yelling interpretative instructions for the notes from a stand in the dark; he felt his family players on the well lit stage of family life singing his battle hymns as broken warped records as directed before Juan could tell them which song they were to play. He introduced a wailing echoing song after the last curtain came down for the night in a darkened theater minus its audience. He observed himself playing silently in the empty darkness.

He had heard from his hommies and father that the male was number one tether in the house. But every act of Conchita said he was at the end of the tether instead of the controller of it. All the members of the family put the kids and themselves first. He was only important as an apron and meal ticket. Without a job he was a joke: an empty Zuit, a folded uniform, with all the right moves and nowhere to go.

The whole institution of marriage was compromising his manhood. Even the Zuit and boots it started in seemed less important. Those drapes and the alleged burning of the drapes placed his identity on the margin of the incinerator. Hitler's incinerators moved him to a marginal position in the realities of his Zuit and relationship to his wife. Four years of war and separation had driven many wedges between them. The stage was full of closed curtains, but no dialogue. Conchita was not the sweet young thing he left. Waiting for the mail each day, hoping to hear only good news, and most of the time sensing the fear of the coming of the next letter had hardened her. While Juan was no longer the one dimensional Zuit in a box seat next to the incinerator in the pit, she wanted more than the Zuit had to pledge and play.

The cold box for the pen stripped Drapes formed a black cage to protect the remembrance of good times, hommies, cruising and a normalcy of a romanticized pre-war illusion. Those symbolic pen stripped bars also represented to Juan, the gulf that time and war had created between his soul and Concha's. The Drapes only served to obscure meaning and heighten tension of blind actions in the routine of post war readjustments.

Concha used to admire him in his Zuit. Now she blossomed as a mother at the risk of her office job. With each passing month she acted more and more as the new patrona in his life. Since Concha became pregnant, she acted like Xochilinzti smoldering upon a pile of kant wet diapers. She was working for some 4-F who had made money off the war that Juan had fought. She told Juan, "I would stay home more if you had a job that really meant something and would give the family some dignity. Even my 4-F boss has a dignified job."

He felt small and empty when Concha looked at him with dead eyes of accusation and asked, "Why can't you provide us with all the things that other families seem to have. We are at a standstill. Juan, you are not moving fast enough. Let me rephrase that. You are not moving at all. Do you expect a job to find you?"

"Querida, jou sound like a Sarge I jused'ta have. He never thought we were moving fast enough either, even when it meant marching into the gates of hell with only your guts for protection," Juan retorted.

"Well, my house and bed are not the gates of hell, Juan. You're not in the army now my little hero," she snapped. "You don't even act as if you want to adjust to a normal life. I'm not sure you even want to be home."

"I'm glad to be home all right," Juan responded. "It's just dat dis es not what I tought home was going to be when I returned, querida. I did a lot of growing in de service, but it's not de growing dat jou and de 4-Fers tink es useful to what jou call a 'normal life'. I'm esorry to be a disappointment to jou. I guess jou were a war widow too long. I want to kiss jou but de room es too full of jour negative vibes. Maybe jou don't want me to be home at all!"

"You know that's not true, babe. I'm sorry too, Juanito. Are we so different now that we can't connect like we used to?"

"I'm not sure we ever connected in de way I learned how to connect to people in de war. Jou can really get close to a guy in a foxhole surrounded by incoming mail. Maybe it's me dat's different."

"You sound different, babe. Even your accent has changed to sound more gringo," said Concha. "Maybe if you worked at losing it all together, you could find a job."

"I'm not the Pachuco who left here, querida. I've eseen things dat a person shouldn't know of. I've eseen de hoards of walking calaveras and the birth of de dead. I've eseen forests full of body parts looking for body bags. I've buried parts that had no body. I learned what it meant to live upside down on a cross, both with and without my patron saint. You can't know of these tings because jou were living de good life of the war widow."

"What do you know of the 'good life of a war widow', you self pitying, introverted jerk!" she snapped. "The last four long and lonely unglorious years without you were no picnic for me, either, hero."

"Right, that's my point, querida," he replied. "The counselors at the V. A. say, dat all dis estuff we are blurting at each other has changed our directions and goals."

"Beautiful, Juan. What does that mean to you?"

"As for me, querida, like my sweet poet, Ramón, use to esay, 'I just want to esleep a esleep without estages and hommie calaveras until the morrow of the tomorrows.' Then maybe I'll start to think about rejoining the world of your dreams dat I fought four years to esave.

"What did you save for us, Juan?"

"Who knows, Conchita."

"When are you going to find out, Juan?"

"Do you realize, querida, I can't even sleep through an entire night without checking the perimeter of the house twice. Haven't you noticed everytime a car backfires I want to dive into the sidewalk."

"Was it rugged, babe?"

"Was what rugged?"

"The war, babe."

"Jou don't really want to know what it was like. None of jou civies really want to know anything about it. Jou all think it was like a John Wayne movie with the flags a-flyin' and planes a divin' in living technicolor with happy endings. Esomehow jou all eseem embarrassed that jou weren't there doin' de dyin'. Even my family don't want to know."

"I really wanted to know about it, babe, but you wrote so little."

"Stop calling me babe, querida! Where did jou learn dat term? Did you get it in some dive with your 4-F boss?"

"What are you saying, War Hero?" she retorted. "Somehow everything that is not totally to your liking is labeled '4- F' by your lousey attitude."

"I dun't have a lousey attitude, Concha, and jou know exactly what I'm saying. You dress and walk too esmart to have learned it all from reading the pages of Life Magazine," he snapped back.

"That is an ugly thing to say, War Hero!"

"Well at least what I really feel is out, and it's really how I feel about things in dis house, Concha," he said feeling some sense of relief.

"Look, Juan. Things just didn't come to a skreeching halt just because you were off somewhere being a war hero. I never wanted you to go off to that war. I died each time the postman brought a letter to the house."

"Jou know I didn't go because it was my life's ambition to fight in a war, Concha. And, if de postman's arrival escared jou eso much, I guess dat es why jou wanted me to write more."

"Don't blow smoke at me, Juan. Your criptic letters are not what scared me, and you know it. I was glad that the men of the other women at the plant were dying. I felt it improved your chances of returning home whole. But all they have given back to me is a jittery old burned out lazy dead hulk with a bunch of pretty medals pinned to his chest!"

"To those guys who blew all for mom and apple pie, those medals they gave me are a really big thing. Especially the Congressional Medal of Honor. The Army even wanted me to come back to the States and parade it at a Victory Tour during the war, but dat meant making speeches and I just wanted to get de war over."

"But you were a hero, Juan. There is no denying that."

"I actually felt guilty that I got medals and others who fought just as hard as me died. I wasn't tryin' to be no hero, querida. I was just trying to stay alive. Over there it was kill or be killed. The question of how or when didn't eseem to matter when de bullets were flyin'."

"Well, goodie for you, Juan. I'm sorry you didn't get dead, Juan, if that is what you really wanted."

"I didn't say that, Concha."

"You didn't do or say a lot of things, Juan. You didn't have to listen to your mother crying for you and Benjamín when he came home in a body bag, or when your uncle and abuelo were killed in the explosions at the aircraft plants. The grief in that house got so bad, I had to move out.

"You should have estayed and helped out, Concha."

"I was brought up in a home that war deprived of a father. I lived with that grief all through my childhood, Juan. I didn't want you to go. You didn't try to stay. I wanted you to leave a new life in me, but you wouldn't. I tried to tell you that night at the Aragon. I decided not to tell you because it sounded unpatriotic at the time. Promise me that if we have sons that you won't put me through the hell your mother has had to endure these past four years. What's wrong, Juan, you are shaking like a leaf."

After a long pause filled with the chattering of teeth and stuttering grunts Juan slowly and haltingly said, "Whenever I, ah..., I can't work..., work esomething out I get de/the eshakes, real..., real bad." He shuddered again as if he were naked in a tub of ice water. "D/That's why I..., I haven't gone ta/to see my parents. I'm afraid d/they'll esee me like d/this."

"Have you had them before?"

"Sure I have. It's not..., not just an allergic reaction to j/you, you know."

"Get serious, Juan. When was the last time this happened?"

"D/The day I mustered out I..., I came here ta/to a locked a... an apartment. Jou were nowhere por mi, querida. I got esome shakes d/then on the estoop, but I just tought it was a cold coming on."

"What did you do then, Juan?" she said softly.

"I went to visit the grave site of mi tío. He was always able to walk in my head and help me work things out. But when I got dere at the grave, I got..., got dese shakes eso bad that esome G.I.'s vis..., visiting d/the graves of esome buddies and d/the cabbie helped me get to the V. A. for esome pills. I estayed dere for four days. I told dem not to call jou. I wanted to meet you the esame way I left j/you. Dat es why I called and told you dat I was just getting out and dat I wanted you to meet me in front of de Aragon."

"Why didn't you tell me this before?"

"I didn't want to worry you, querida."

"Your life is not a Zoot Zuit you can hide in a closet, Juan. Don't treat me like you are treating your Mother. We all have a right to know these things so we can be part of each other and help each other through both good and bad times. You don't have to be Don Quijote for me, Juan."

"That's nice," said Juan, not realizing the power of her words. "D/the Docs over at d/the V. A.," he continued, "esay d/these shakes will wear off once I get adjusted to home. But if I'm like a lot of the other guys I know, these shakes are going to get a lot worse before d/they get better."

"When did they really start, Juan. Tell me. I really care. I need to know of your pain. Please open up to me," she pleaded.

"They started in a foxhole in the Bulge, Concha. David told me that es esomething the Docs call battle fatigue. You know, it's when you eseen eso much death d/that de fear of eseeing more es worse than de fear of dyin'. At first I would freeze only for a few seconds and the sound of a bursting shell would bring me out of it. The time dey put me in for the Congressional Medal of Honor I did esome estuff during a time when I thought I was totally frozen."

"So what did you do, Juan?"

"I can't even tell you what act of bravery I did that got everybody eso excited, Conchita. If it wasn't for David, I wouldn't have estopped advancing on the German positions even after I cleared that mine field and fried about a hundred Krouts. I was just kill crazy at de time."

"So what is freezing and shaking you now, Juan?"

"I keep eseeing their escreaming burning faces esurrounded by the walking dead of Dachau in my dreams. Sometimes I wake up on the couch at night escreaming the esilent escream I felt in my foxholes."

"Is that why you don't come to my bed?"

"That's part of it, querida."

"What's the other part, Juan?"

"It's your bed, querida, not our bed"

"Sorry, Juan."

"So am I. You know, querida, I felt esafer in dose foxholes than I feel in your bed. And that is even funnier than it esounds because esometimes your partners in the foxhole were corpses."

"It doesn't sound funny to me, Juan."

"Well it es because jou can't believe how esomething dat could make jou feel eso esafe, could esmell eso bad. In case jou don't know what it es like in a foxhole, Concha, imagine being in a phone booth wit four ugly women who haven't bathed for at least a month and who think your hole is a toilet. What am I talking about, de filth and stench of de place, jou can't even begin to know de half of it."

"Keep going, Juan. Don't shut me out. I need to hear this."

"O.K., jou asked for it. Believe it or not, Conchita, after awhile jou get used to death all around jou. It es pretty esickening. De odor of death es unbelievable. De esilence of death es as deafening as de 88's in a barrage. De foxhole of safety becomes a grave of frozen lines in de hot esun. Yet, esomehow, eseeing jour amigos and compadres of de week laying around with gaping wounds, or in pieces with blood espurting and oozing from dem, makes jou want to live even more dan jou can believe."

"Is it like that all the time, Juan?"

"Well, de battlefield es happening all over de place. Especially in a big eshow like de Bulge. Esometimes it es right on top of jou and de rest of de time it's just a boring job of esuffering and estaying alive. Jou are escared to death one minute and laughing just because jou are estill alive in de next. Jou are not even able to imagine what es happening even a few hundred yards away from jour position."

"Can't you see what is going on?"

"Believe it, querida, nobody es even looking to find out what's happening even if dey could in de dark and dust or mud, depending on if jou are in de forest or de desert. In de Bulge I just kept shooting at everything dat moved. Esometimes jou don't even know who, or what jou are eshooting at. Jou just hope jou are quicker and deadlier dan what es eshooting at jou."

"How do you keep going through all that, Juan?"

"Jou just do, Concha, because even wit all dis going on, jou are glad jou are in de army, because de civilians, many just babies, are eso hungry dat dey are trying to eat jour escraps. De armies eat or destroy everything dey see. Another reason es dat out dere, missing in action, meant dat dere wasn't enough body parts to bury. Den, after de heat of de battle, and de end of d/the d/thunder of death, jou were just glad to be alive."

"What were the Germans like, Juan. In the newsreals they looked so vicious."

"When jou are eshooting at dem, Conchita, jou tell jourself, que life es cheap to dem. Den when jou take dem prisoner and esee how dey related and cared for each other, jou know dat dey are fighting for de esame razón jou are. Dey just want to estay alive too. Dey get just as beat-up as we do. Dey hurt just as bad. Dey were hard to kill once dey began to have faces."

"Then what keeps men fighting if they know what you are telling me?"

"Querida, jou don't think of dis stuff during the fight. Jou just hear words like what Patton said, 'It is not our duty to die for our country, but to make them die for theirs.' Der are dose damn shakes again."

"I'm here now, Juan. Maybe my holding you will help."

"No. Don't touch me. It will stop. The Doc says dat I got to make dem stop by myself."

"Then get it out, Juan. You are right. I had no idea it was like that. But, how could I know. All we got here at home was the censored newsreals."

"I really don't want to talk about it anymore. You may care, but you cannot understand what I'm feeling, querida."

"You keep underestimating my capacity for understanding, Juan. If you'd just keep it going maybe I would understand you more, even if I don't get all of it."

"Querida, I fought four years for some restaurant owner who won't serve me a piece of pie because I'm a Mex. That's the kind of crap that put the Jews in Dachau. I also found out a couple of days ago down at the V.A. Service Center that the mother of one of my compadres in Bavaria, Frank Ono by name died in a concentration camp about a hundred miles from here. He lost both legs in the service to a country that was killing his mother because she had slanted eyed Japanese ancestry. He saved my life when he lost those legs. You can not believe the bravery of the 512 Artillery unit. When David and I worked with them we knew they would do whatever had to be done. Can you believe that we were ordered not to tell anyone about the Japanese Nisee being part of the liberation of Dachau. It's like they didn't want anyone to know that the American Army used the sons of deportees and internees to liberate the German concentration camps. Esee what happens when I talk it out. Th/de shakes are estarting again."

"It's O.K., Juan. Those shakes you have are like a tree bending to get rid of the dead wood. Just keep on letting it go. If you try to hang on to this poison it will shake you to death."

"I'll bet th/dat would suit y/jou just fine. D/then jou could be out with th/de Gabacho 4-Fer j/you call a boss."

"That comment is so ugly and beneath your ability to think things through, Juan, that I'm not even going to believe that you said it. You have got to be less negative about things, Juan."

"It es time d/that jou do a reality check, querida. When I was in a foxhole, hitting a beach, or charging up a mountain, I knew that I could count on the guys with me and d/that th/dey were counting on me. Th/dis went on even if I had no idea who th/dose guys were. As long as we were together, we were a team. We had a common objective. Now I'm on my own and I know I've got to make a move, but I'm not sure what moves to make."

"Come on, Cucaracha. There are a million moves still left in you, Chivito. Just get started and it will be just like old times," suggested Concha.

"Th/tings are just not like old times, Conchita. Nothing here feels familiar. Things look a lot th/de esame, but everything es really upside down. Mis carnales are all dead. My Zuit must estay in a box."

"Maybe that's because old times were four very very long years ago, Juan," she said with a softness in her voice that he hadn't heard for four years. "I cannot replace your hommies for you, Juan. When you went off to war I dreamt of how it would be when you came home and I feared you would not return.

Front windows in the barrio were full of black wreaths around gold stars. At one time in 1943, we all felt that none of the carnales were coming back. Now that you'er back you are not the man I dreamed of. I guess what we were will never be. Maybe that is good. At least we are together."

"Th/dat's th/de worst part of de pain, querida. Even when I'm with jou I'm lonely."

"Grow up Juanito," said Concha in what was to become her motherly, matriarchal voice. "You have both of your legs and two good feet. Why don't get off your butt, get a job, and stand-up like the man I was proud of."

"Th/dat's easy for jou to esay, Concha. I'm de one with de accent and de eshakes. Can't jou esee me as a bus driver or an estreet painter?"

"There lots of other jobs you are qualified for, Juan," Concha asserted. 'I see 'help wanted' signs in a lot of store windows."

"Esure dere are, esposa. I even got a job for half of a day pumping gas."

"What happened to that job, Juan? This is the first time you mentioned it."

"I got fired because the twenty-two year old, gabacho, 4-F manager thought I was going to blow-up the place and his daddy wouldn't be happy with that."

"So now you are unemployable, Juan? Just walk into those stores and tell them you are a G. I. and they should take down their 'help wanted' sign and hire you."

"Look, I told jou th/dat jou wouldn't understand, Concha. I guess I don't fit in anywhere just jet. I'm back from th/de war with almost everyting normal, yet I feel d/that esomeone or esomething has estolen four years from me. I just don't know where to estart to get tings back on track. I'm not even esure if d/there ever was a track. Even if I find d/the tracks I'm not esure which one I eshould take."

"I don't want to sound phoney, Juan, but let's start right here at home."

"Estart with what?"

"With us, Juan."

"Thanks, querida, but I'm not ready for dat just yet."

"Why not, Juan?"

"I don't know. I'm just not ready yet."

"Well, when will you be ready, Juan?"

"I don't know dat either."

"That's too bad, Juan!"

"Why, querida?"

"Because the only things you seem to know positively is that you aren't really ready to begin to pick-up the threads of civilian life and that you don't know when you will be really ready."

"Dat's de trute as I esee it, Conchita," affirmed Juan with a nod of his head.

"Just remember, Juan, you didn't become a soldier overnight. You can't expect to become a civilian over night, but things won't even start to happen until we make a start. Let's make it tonight, Juan. Don't let our life together become a pipe dream."

"I really want to estart, querida. I want to esmoke d/the peace pipe with y/jou, but I need to get th/de smell of th/de foxhole out of my head first."

"Try not to take too long, Juan. I don't want to be talking a year from now about losing five years out of our lives."

*   *   *

The next day, Juan started to go through all of the whoops the V. A. staged to find a good job. Finally he got a job wearing overalls and an apron. They called him a sanitary engineer. It was hole and pit digging work. The V. A. had found him a "part" digging holes all night in the sewers beneath the great sleeping metropolis of East Los.

The job had no dignity. The rats were his audience. He did not want it, but it was work and a pay check. The check, overalls, apron and work made him a player again. There was no place for a Zuit Zoot in the sewers nor on the stage.

But, Concha's apron strings did not go away. As the children got older and the number of children increased, the apron got thinner and heavier around his neck. Concha was spending even less time with him. She seemed more involved with the religious instruction for the children, than the spiritual nourishment of their marriage. Her small apron was plastered with rigid religious ritual. It was so short that it rarely extended to cover him.

David kept telling him that he was wasting himself in the sewers, but an apron in a big black rubber apron seemed safe in the waste and slimy filth of the sewers. Even the sewers were full of hidden illusions and quiet untold dreams. Why should he come out onto the the street of minimum wage clerking sales jobs? Even a promotion in the sewers was a step up to daylight and the gutter.

Sweeping the cluttered stage of streets eluded to sweeping the barrio clean of aliens. La Migra pulled the apron strings and tried to sweep the barrio. Juan's indigenous family hung by a thread. Most of Juan's co-workers were aliens. It seemed that keeping America clean was a dirty job that only aliens could do. The job was so dirty that Juan had to wear a canvass apron over his protective rubber apron and overalls.

For Juan the two level set sewer aprons became involuntary. They protected him from a few of Concha's complaining ambitions while attacking his dignity.

"Hey, Johnito," the foreman called out to Juan from the safety of his truck, during a noon break.

"What can I do for jou, Mr. Johnston, Sir," said Juan as he approached the truck.

"Yous are one of those Mexes that speaks the lingo and English too, right?"

"Jes, sir, Mr. Johnston, Sir."

"And yous are polite for a Mex. I like that. Besides, they tells me that yous are a Mex-Vet. I'd a gone too but, I have this trick football hip that means that I'm only good at sittin' down thinkin' work."

"I esee de sittin but can't find de tinkin," thought Juan to himself.

"I have my eye on yous," continued Mr. Johnston. "A new rulin' has come down the from City Halls that your wetback buddies has gots to start working on their citizenship if they wanna keep their jobs. The City is concerned that with this McCarthy stuff, too many alien commies cleaning the streets would be a security risk if the Ruskies tried to invade us."

"Th/dey can't be eserious," said Juan in disbelief. "I just espent four years of my life fighting a war d/that esupposedly estopped d/that kind of thinking. Anybody d/that has to wear an apron over d/their apron and overalls to do d/their work isn't doing d/the job in order ta be an esecurity risk, Mr. Johnston, Sir."

"I wouldn't says that too loud, Johnito. Yous boys are just one sweep away from South of The Border Down Mexico Way, if yous gets my drift. That's a why I want yous guys to start a citizenship class. Yous might wanta learnta fix up your accent too, so yous can be ready for a job like mine if and when I moves up the ladder of white success."

"Thank's for the tip, Mr. Johnston, Sir," said Juan with a smile while he reflected on the quality of Mr. Johnston's English.

"I saw in your personnel folder that yous completed some classes at City College. I like a Mex who knows his place, but tries to better hisself. Were any of them classes you took down there, on how to be an American?"

"Yes, Sir, Mr. Johnston, Sir," said Juan biting back his anger. He really wanted to tell Mr. Johnston where he could stick "them classes," but he needed this job and maybe it was a chance to get the dust and slime off his boots, jump out of the pit, and get the apron off for a little while. So he said, "I took both Poly Sci 1A and B, Mr. Johnston, Sir. "

"I don't know if that psychology stuff will be of help," replied the Foreman.

"Sir, th/dose courses are about government, th/de passing of laws, th/de Constitution, and estuff like th/dat," said Juan.

"Oh, good, good. Just testing yous with a little joke there, Johnito."

"Sure, sure," thought Juan. "Th/dis guy must be a councilman's brother or esomething. How could anyone eso dumb drive a foreman's truck and work without an apron?"

"Then it is settled," continued the foreman. "You can start tomorrow during your lunch. If things work out, then yous can do sessions during your break times. The experience will be good for yous. Who knows, I'm up for promotion and I'll be recommending to Mr. Gunther who I think can keep these wetbacks in line."

"Sir, will there be any extra in my pay envelop?"

"Look at it this way, boy. Yous and your buddies don't havta keep an appointment with the immigration boys. Do ya hear me, boy. That appointment is only a nickel away. Do yous get it, Johnito?"

"Yes, Sir, Mr. Johnston, Sir." Juan was dying to tell this moron that he was a Congressional Medal of Honor holder, but he thought that telling this person that would stink up the medal. "Will I have any materials to teach from, sir?"

"I'm sure that a bright Mex like yous will think of something, and I'll put in for five dollars petty cash, so I can travel down to the Federal Building and get yous some of those citizen booklets Gunther told us about in the foreman's meeting this morning. Of course the booklets are all in English. Yous read English, Johnito?"

"Yes, Sir. I learned it by reading the manual on how to clean guns and throw grenades," replied Juan. How much more of this Cracker was he going to have to stomach during this lunch hour!?

"That'sa real good, boy. Yous can translate them for your buddies, then. I'd do the class myself, yous understand, but I thinks those wets will take it from yous better. Besides yous gots the lingo down. Right?"

"Yes, Sir, Mister Foreman, Sir. If jou esay eso, Mr. Johnston, Sir."

"Johnito, I likes your attitude. You's my kind of boy. If you weren't a Mex, you'd go far in the Sanitary Engineering Department."

"Right into the fart department," thought Juan.

"But likes I said," continued the foreman, "I'll put in a good word for yous anyways. I always says, do someone a good turn when he does you a good turn, even if the boy's a Mex. I'm not prejudice like the other foremens."

"You need an apron just to stand near a racist like Mr. Foreman Johnston, Sir," Juan thought. The worst of it was, he was right. The other foremen were worse. They would have used their buffalo nickel and called La Migra.

*   *   *

Juan teaching a sailing in the desert with aprons for sails and stern plates limited the winds of knowledge and prevented the mind from the erosion of thought.

The four years he had spent with David during the war had opened Juan's eyes to the power of learning. He could still see David marveling over some book or piece of art when they liberated those towns in Italy, France, and Germany. Three and a half years in the eroded tunnels under a city helped him realize sewers were great places for cucarachas and excellent eroded sites for catacombs. If he were going to do the things he wanted to do for his family and Conchita, he would have to start using the skills that David had taught him. This citizenship class might be just the thing to get him started, even if all his pupils were wearing aprons.

As he lay in bed that night, checking out the meanings of Mr. Johnston's phrases, he pondered on how he was to begin teaching this new class. He recalled a question and answer session with Mrs. March, his pigeon breasted, smock wearing, U. S. History teacher at Central High. She said, "Guon, are you ready for a quickie quiz today?"

"Chure, teach," replied Juan. She thought that her 'quickie

quizzes' kept the trouble makers in line.

"Then, please name some of the important generals in the history of this fair country of ours."

Juan responded, "Let's see teach, uhm, der was, der General Electric, uhm, der General Dynamics, uhm, der General Foods, uhm, der General Motors, uhm, y der General Telephone."

"Very good, Guon," said Mrs. March. "You have showed your talent for eroded imbecility once again. Sit down and write one hundred times, 'I will not lie to the class, General George Washington is the father of my country.' Then you will come in after school and clean my room until it sparkles. Look me in the eye, Guon. Have I illuminated that dim mind of yours with my intent?"

"Yes, Madame teach, Mrs. March," Juan said as he saluted General March and continued to stare at the floor. He hated being called Guon worse than writing lines. Anyway, since the George Washington bit was one of her favorites, he already had about 75 of them written. In addition, cleaning her room to her specifications, was no big thing. He already had it sparkling from numerous other after school sessions. If he really went far as a sanitary engineer, he owed it all to good old Mrs. March, Madame Teach, and her historical Grover Cleveland-cleaning techniques like in and out sweeping of corrupted eroded class-rooms. Like General Washington, Mrs. March never told a lie.

"I wonder if eshe has dis year's crop of babies (as she called her students) writing dose esame tired lines," he said aloud to himself. "If eshe wasn't esuch a bulldog, eshe would have been funny."

"Who are you talking to now, Juan?" asked Concha in a half awake voice. "I need to get some sleep. If it is your voices again, keep them to yourself. Don't forget to give Chavela her three in the morning feeding."

How could he forget. Concha was more consistent at remind-ing him about that feeding than Mrs. March was about writing lines that proved to her that General George Washington was the father of her country. Now that he thought on it, George was always a general, and not the president, in Mrs. March's class.

Mrs. March missed her calling. She should have been a wonderful sergeant. She taught just like Sergeant Milner. She ran her class exactly like that sergeant ran the boot camp barracks in Pittsburg. They both taught as if learning was God's punishment for spics.

The Sarge always called him, Guono. But he always framed Guono with, "Hey, Greaseball, Guono. How's My Brown Butt Soldier Boy." That was the only difference between Mrs. March and him. She just said, "Guon, you are an eroded imbecile." In high school he thought that an imbecile was something you found in the feeble farting sewers. At least she didn't call him a feeble menso like his junior high school teachers did.

Except for David and the two days with Padre Diego, only Mrs. March and the Sarge had taught him anything. How different each pair's style had been. With David and Padre Diego, Juan had learn to inquire, probe and learn by doing. With Mrs. March and the Sarge, it was, "Do it or die!" Whether you learned anything or not was irrelevant. With these four as models how should he start to teach his pupils? It was their lunch hour. Who wanted to learn about General George Washington on their lunch hour. "Maybe I eshould estart de lección by taking off my apron," he muttered.

"Leave it on, Chivo," muttered Concha in a half sleep. "Chavela might throw up on you. Don't forget the feeding, Honey. Turn off your voices and go to sleep."

Maybe if he could show Mister Johnston, Sir that he was more than a feeble minded, dumb Mex, he could start a real in-service for the department and get rid of the apron all together. Then maybe Concha would say his job had dignity. He would start the session with the importance of the U.S. Constitution in sewer worker's daily lives. That should be a topic important enough to interrupt a lunch. Maybe he should have Mister Johnston, Sir, tell them about the buffalo nickel and La Migra. That would definitely stampede their attention.

"Honey, don't you hear the baby crying?" said Concha. "She's hungry."

"But it es only dos y media de la mañana, Conchita mía,"

answered Juan wearily.

"Get out of bed and feed her now, Juan. She only knows that she is hungry. She can't tell time yet. Get to her before she wakes up the whole house. Mamá needs her rest, and so do the boys. We need to keep my mother happy, Juan. She is helping out a lot. If she quits on us, I'll have to stay home, and if the boys get sick one more time this year I'll lose my job."

"Honey," Juan said as he got out of bed, "I dun't tink que jou know what time it es eidder!"

"What do you mean by that remark, Juan? Forget your feeble answer. I need to get some sleep. Just move it and feed Chavela."

"I'm putting on my apron, honey," Juan said sarcastically.

"What apron, Juan?"

"Never mind, querida. I'll take care of everything. Go back to esleep."

"How can I sleep with the baby crying and you making weird remarks? You had better start working on that accent if you want to get ahead."

"I already work in a head, Concha," retorted Juan.

"Are you going to feed the baby or not, head cleaner?"

"I'll feed Chavela, dear. Y/jou will have to answer jour own questions. I have a class to teach tomorrow," he said as he put the bottle into Chavela's hungry little mouth.

"Class, what class?" asked Concha.

"It es nothing important, querida. I'm feeding th/de baby, eso go back to esleep."

"Why do you have to wait until the middle of the night to start up with the remarks, already?"

"Because, dearest, d/that es when Chavela gets me out of bed and jou estart making like a midnight drill sergeant with a clean mouth."

"Nobody likes a midnight smart ass, Juan. O.K., are you going to tell me about this class thing, or is it just another one of your voices from that dark stage in the bowels of Matatlan?"

"Th/dey are voices from th/de Caves of Matatlan, querida," answered Juan.

"Are you going to tell me or not, Juan?"

"Jou have all d/the answers, darling, jou fill in d/the blanks."

"That should be easy, Juan. Talking with you lately has become one big, empty blank."

She had hit her stride now, he thought. As long as she kept jabbing he knew that there was still a spark of life in their marriage. "I love you too, querida. Good night."

"Don't forget to burp the baby."

"I'll put my apron on first. D/that way, even if I get de eshakes I won't mess me up," said Juan with a silent smile.

"Good, night, Juan," Concha said wearily and deliberately.

"I estill love jou, querida," said Juan hoping to stir a little romance in the beautiful form laying on the bed.

"Good," Concha said. That final 'good' told him that all he was at this moment was a tattered apron about to be thrown-up on. He'd tell the aproned crew about the buffalo nickel and La Migra himself. Then he'd start the class.

*   *   *

Juan tossed and turned all night with George Washington driving a truck load of nopales while chasing La Migra in Concha's apron. Even Abuelo got into the act. He kept dropping golden pyramids off of Skywoman's turtle to direct the generally misdirected nopal truck. "What dis troka needs es un eshotgun que tiene huevos!" shouted Abuelo.

"Watch your mouth, viejo," chimed in Spanish Grandma.

"Pero he's not looking to where he es goin', vieja!" responded Abuelo.

"The principle is to go where you are looking, not to look where you are going, suegro," answered Spanish Grandma.

"You can't dance with a partner when all she is, is a word in the wind," blew in Sequoya.

"Dun't worry about generales and la Migra, mijitito," asserted Abuela. "Dey didn't have dere nopales today."

"De needles of nopales have cured de sweettooth of more than one cabrón," asserted Don Castillo.

Juan decided to annouce his new job responsibilty to the whole family at breakfast. He even got out of bed early to make sure that neither Concha nor her mother beat him to the making of breakfast.

The first to notice the aroma of his famous huevos rancheros was Little David. As his fine young son staggered into the kitchen he squinted towards Juan with sleep filled eyes and innocently asked, "Daddy, how come you wear Mommy's apron more than eshee does?"

"It's she, Little David, not eshe. J/you Dun/don't want to talk all chueco like me, eson. If you help me maybe we can both get it bedder."

"O.K., poppy, but it's better, not bedder, and why do you wear Mommy's apron so much?"

"Because I cook more dan j/your mamá, David."

"I wish you cooked as good as her, poppy. What's dis green stuff in de huevos rancheros, poppy?"

"It's well, not good, David. The green estuff are nopales. I opened a jar Abuela sent us for Christmas. Eat them. They will make you estrong."

"I know your comida will keep me well, poppy. Some of it even tastes good. It's just dat it is eso sloppy the way you make it that Grandma Francesca makes me wear an apron when I eat it."

"Wearing an apron is a fine thing for a man to do if it protects you and de familia, David."

"Th/den why don't you get one of your own, poppy?"

"If I had one of my own it would feel permanent, David."

"You mean it would make your hair curly, poppy?"

"No, mijo, that is a different kind of permanent. I'm talking here about de permanent like you get when you make cement for a patio."

"You mean like forever, poppy?"

"That's pretty close to what I mean, mijo, but when I wear your mamá's apron I know that it will be on me for only a little while." "If wearing an apron is a good thing for a man to do, poppy, why do you want to get it off so fast?"

"Eat your eggs, mijo, before they get cold. Did I ever tell you dat jou ask real good preguntas?"

"You tell me that all de time, poppy, right after you estop answering them."

"It's stop, mijo. Not, estop."

"I know that, poppy, but you still didn't tell me why you want a temporary apron."

"I want it that way because your mamá wants it that way, mijo."

"Dat's not what she told me, poppy."

"What did she tell, j/you, Son?"

"She said that jou should help all the time with the cooking, washing and cleaning since you are doing that under the city all day anyway."

"Not anymore I won't, mijo. They are going to make me a teacher for some of the time."

"Does Mommy know that, Daddy?"

"She will know it soon enough, mijo."

"I'll go wake her so I can watch you tell her, poppy."

"Your mamá needs her rest, mijo. I'll tell her in my own time."

"Do it when you have her apron on, poppy."

"Why should I do that, mijo?"

"You said that it is good for a man to wear an apron for protection, poppy."

"You are esmart little, David."

"It's smart, poppy. I getting even smarter because I am eating Abuela's nopales with an apron on."

"If you esay eso, David."

"Mommy says that you will always work under the city as long as you talk like a cactus eating sewer rat, poppy."

"When did eshe esay dat?!"

"The other day when you were late and Grandma Francesca was over here to help Mommy make my dinner."

"The reason I'm late some nights is because I'm goin' back to eschool to learn what I didn't get the first time I went to eschool, David."

"I'm going to learn it all right the first time."

"Good for you, David. Go wake up your mother while I get her breakfast."

"Don't put nopales in mommie's eggs, poppy."

"Why is that, David."

"She's smarter than you already, poppy".

"Who told you that?"

"Grandma Francesca."

"I'll go wake up your mother, David. She and I need to have a little talk."

"Can I watch, poppy?" asked David innocently.

"Not this time, mijo."

"Are you really going to talk with Mommy or are you just goin to make a speech like you do to the neighbor's dog?"

"What are you talking about now, mijo?" asked Juan as he sat down in wonder on the chair next to his son.

"Well, Grandma Francesca says she knows what you are goin' to say like a book."

"What else does she say?"

"Well, Grandma says that all you know how to do is make big speeches that smell like a dirty bathroom."

"Grandma Francesca sure has a lot to say, mijo. Is there anythin' else I should know, David?"

"Well, Mommy and Grandma says that you talk to them as if they were dogs, and..."

"That's enough, David. Sometimes big people esay tings like they don't mean them in fun, mijo."

"It's things, poppy. Not tings."

"D/this time j/your mamá will have to discover all about my great big promotion all by herself. I wouldn't want to wake her with the howl of a dog."

"I heard that, Chivito Cucaracha," called Concha from the bedroom.

"You see, mijo," said Juan loudly, "women can always hear what they want to hear. Their mothers train them in this skill from de time they are only ten minutes old."

"Why do they do that, poppy?"

"Eso they can keep the aprons on their men from long distances."

"Why would they want to do that, poppy?"

"This answer is one I want to hear up close and personal," said Concha with her big mamá voice as she entered the kitchen.

"Not in front of the boy, Conchita," said Juan in his little boy voice.

"He might as well know the lay of the land from the point of view of a sewer worker who lives in the house of a professional woman," asserted Concha.

"Do you understand what your mother just said, mijo?" asked Juan with a voice that searched for his son's support.

"Not really, poppy."

"You will know what eshe es esaying one day, if you are lucky enough to marry a fine handsome, strong woman like your mother," said Juan with a wink of his left eye in David's direction.

"If you say so, poppy. I have to go caca because of your nopalitos, poppy."

"If you have to go, mijo, jou haveta go," said Juan imitating one of his father's favorite phrases.

"Now what was it you wanted to talk to me about, Juan?" asked Concha as Little David ran out of the room like someone was about to light his after burner.

"I've got to go to work now, honey. I haven't got the time to make espeeches for jou."

"What does that mean, Juan?"

"Ask your mother, Concha. Little David says that she knows me like a book," said Juan as he gathered up his lunch pail and moved towards the back porch door.

"Take off my apron, Juan. If you wear it on the bus all the men will howl like dogs at you."

"I love you, too, querida," said Juan as he pulled off the apron and slid out the back door of the house.

CITIZENSHIP CLASSES IN THE SEWERS

"**H**ey, Johnito, I got that promotion I was telling yous about. Now I can gets one of dose new Cadillacs."

"That's nice, Mr. Johnston, Sir. Have you been able to get any of those materials I requested for the classes on citizenship?"

"I'm still workin' on that, Johnito. These things takes time ya know. I've been hearin' good things about that work you're doin', and the Mexes seem pretty happy about the classes too."

"I need to have esome more to tell them besides the reality of the I.N.S. and George Washington, Mr. Johnston, Sir."

"Well tell them about how the Draft Board works. I'll bet they would be glad ta know that they can serve this country just like any other citizen can. Maybe they could learn English in the Army."

"I was thinking more along the lines of tax preparation materials and vehicle code booklets and stuff like that, Mr. Johnston, Sir."

"Well, along those lines, Mr. Gunther said it would be a good idea for you to take some more of them there night classes like yous use ta take. I hears that they got the fall '52 classes open at LACC."

"I don't know if I can afford to do that right now with Concha being with child and all."

"God, boy. Can't yous Mexes leave your women alone at night?"

"What are you saying, Sir?"

"You Mexes are just one big old baby makin' factory."

"We are making up for the lost time during the war, Mr. Johnston, Sir," said Juan as he looked at the foreman's huge frame and tried to imagine how a woman could have sex with Mr. Johnston, Sir.

"Well if yous get off your little woman for a couple of minutes, Johnito, as a vet yous could use that G.I. Bill thing to pay for your tuition."

"Thanks for the tip, Mr. Johnston, Sir." David had once told Juan how he had used his G.I. bill to reenter Loyola Law School in 1948. He had also heard that there was a veterans' counselor at LACC. "I'll look into that tonight after work, Sir."

"I likes your attitude, Johnito. Take fifteen minutes off early to go do that. While yous are there, see if yous can find some of those materials you need. Has the army called up your number for this Korea thing? My sister's boy got a draft notice yesterday."

"I haven't heard anything other than the recruiting commercials to get us WW II vets to re-enlist, Mr. Johnston, Sir," said Juan.

"Well if they draft yous again, I won't be able ta tell them that yous are essential to the war effort or anythin' like that ther, Johnito."

"If you esay eso, Mr. Johnston, Sir."

That night Juan called David after he had picked-up some registration information at LACC. "It's too late to get into a four year school for the fall," said David, "so take a class at LACC to help vou vit those sewer level citizenship classes they have vou conducting. Get that V.A. counselor to help vou apply for a scholarship at one of the State Colleges. However, you may have to leave L.A. to get that scholarship."

"I thought about applying to U.C. in Berkeley, but I dun't tink Concha will like that, David, especially with the new baby coming and everthing."

"Ve have a whole semester to vork on her, Vuan. Couldn't vou vork out something vhere her mother could help vou out?"

"I hate feeling even more obligated to my Suegra, David. She already does a lot for us."

"Using up your G.I. Bill is a now or never thing, Vuan. Ve got to get on the move. Vou aren't getting any younger. Concha alvays seems to listen to reason."

"I've got to put together a package that keeps our costs at a minimum, David."

"Since vou have family in San José, vou might think of applying there too, Vuan."

"Good idea, David. I hope jou are right on d/that bit about Concha, ese. It esure would be nice to get out of th/dose sewers and into de daylight."

"It sure sounds good to hear vou say that, Vuan. I think vou are vasting vourself in those sewers and vor accent in English is getting better."

"Jours, isn't, ese," said Juan with a laugh. "I think that jou are right about d/that wasting angle. D/that is the angle we got to use with Concha, David. Her ambition for me makes her think I'm wasting my time in de esewers too."

Juan applied everywhere. He was even accepted in a "probationary status" at UCLA as a special admit. Most of the admissions rejection sheets informed Juan that while his City College and Army service record were excellent, his high school grades didn't not show any academic promise. One V. A. counselor at Long Beach State called Juan to tell him that because of his high school transcripts that he might do better if he applied to a trade school.

Only San José State College sent him an acceptance notice along with a small scholarship that covered tuition and books as well as a dormitory allotment. Concha decided with David's and Spanish Grandma's help that the package offered by San José State was too good of an opportunity for Juan to pass up, she knew she needed her job in L. A. for the family's economic well being.

Francesca made a big scene about how she was going to sacrifice her church life she could allow her daughter, Concha, to support her speech making, shiftless husband, play at going to school. "I love my grand babies, daughter, but I just don't know why you let that dreaming, shaking sewer rat waste your life," said Concha.

Concha constantly worried about how she would carry on in their East Los chosita with their six month old baby and two other small children. She felt like a wife without a husband and a mother without a father, while being locked into the role of a working mother and supporting daughter.

Ramón the Poet, whose blood sanctified the beaches at Anzio, yelled across the waters to Concha's walking nightmare, "It is better to be the head of a rat, than the tail of a lion! Among the carnales, your Juan is the king of the cucarachas, not the slave of a lioness."

"Why must I live through four more years of lying the truth to make a rat into a real hero again?" asked Concha through the vailed mist of nightmarish love as her wedding dress danced by itself in the sewers of Juan's dreams.

After six months of living in an agonizing indecision, Concha finally made up her own mind that her being married to a sewer rat for the rest of her life was worse than losing Juan for extended absences to take advantage of the scholarship to success of full citizenship at San José State College.

"Your song of the one headed double horned mystery is solid, Conchita. But, the sweat of the Sun still has to play the golden tune. Reach out with your whole flute to preserve the silver silence of this rosy melody. In the light of the dark moon sing the truth and get your apron wearing rat, out of the zoot sewers forever," whispered Ramón.

Sequoya whurred laughter at the poet through the dew/frost of the rosy rising dawn, "The seeds of the tallest tree lay on the hard mother earth covering the golden song of the soft pink roots. The heartwood beats within the solid core of the tree, but the porous bark covering that heart character must retain the apron of the tree."

When Concha returned home from the bus station at Sixth and Flower she plugged in her Orthophonic RCA Victor hi-fi, set the turntable a 78 rpm, carefully lowered the arm to the shoulder of her favorite record and listened to their song once again. "Once again I must tell you I'm sorry, it's a sin to tell a lie. Millions of hearts have been broken, just because these words were spoken...." Concha stared away into the the space of the pink wall where on hung Juan's Medal of Honor.

VOICES IN THE CLASSROOM

Scholarships sailing backwards in the Valle de Matatlan assailed Juan's meger confidence. "Isn't this place the most friendly place you've ever seen?" asked the blond next to Juan as they waited for the New Student Orientation to start.

Juan turned to the student and smiled. The blond turned to the person sitting on the other side of him and said, "George, I wonder if this old guy sitting next to me understands English."

"Why is that, Hans?" asked George.

"All he does is smile at me when I talk to him."

"Ask him if he speaks English, Hans."

"What language should I use?" asked Hans.

"How many do ya know, Hans?"

"Just English and a little Spanol," answered Hans.

"Try the Spanole," suggested George.

"Ablo Asted English or Spanol?" Hans asked Juan.

"Are jou talking to me?" asked Juan.

"Allright, ya speak the lingo. Have ya taken the English placement test yet?"

"Jes I did," answered Juan.

"Wasn't it the worst?" asked Hans.

"How do jou mean?" asked Juan.

"Me and George flunk it cold. Almost everyone does. How did you do?"

"I passed it," said Juan with other smile.

"Can ya believe what I just heard, George?"

"What are yous talkin' now?" asked George.

"This old guy, a foreigner, no less passed the bonehead English exam."

"So what ya telling me, Hans? Everybody knows ya have to go to a school in Europe ta learn English good."

Hans turned to Juan, "have yual been ta Europe, mister?"

"I spent three jears in Europe," answered Juan.

"Figures," said George. "Where are ya livin' now?"

"In Hoover Hall," answered Juan.

"Yous in the new Brick Dorm. We'ens are pledging Acacia. We'er here on football scholarships."

"That's nice," said Juan while wondering if George and Han's were nephews of Mister Johnson, Sir.

"Good morning group," blared the P. A. system. "Don't we look already to go for it, big time, Spartans? Let's stand and salute our beloved flag." The students said the pledge.

"Welcome to San José State, freshmen. I'm Dean Keeman. I'm here to help you unlock the doors to the mysteries of a college education at San José State."

Juan discovered at the San José New Student Orientation why, even with a G. I. Bill and a G. I. Forum scholarship the colleges and universities of the Southwestern United States had been reluctant to admit a Mexican American applicant. According to the keynote speaker, Dean Keeman, the colleges were only admitting the cream of the cream. The orientation was supposed to make him feel welcomed, but it only served to make him feel like a round peg in a square hole. Juan, a scholarship student, had to prove himself to the college just to have a shot at the academic union card.

The gift of a Mestizo scholarship didn't necessarily make him a worthy present to the field of higher education. He was just a bone thrown to appease the papooses. Appeasing the gate keepers of English by passing the English bonehead examination brought Juan under suspicion instead of acceptance. The Forum and the Veteran's Administration could only make a federally funded institution honor and respect the scholarship, but they could not force social and institutional acceptance.

When he met with his faculty advisor at San José State, a Dr. Piston, Juan was told that his achievement in the Army and junior college were all the College had focused upon to start with. Dr. Piston continued his explanation by saying, "Your acceptance was also influenced by the insistence of the V. A. You know that the new Mexican soldier group called the G. I. Forum has made the V. A. work at getting Spanish ex-soldiers into College even when they aren't qualified."

What had actually made the difference and gotten Juan his scholarship in the first place was his combined score of 1492 on the Scholastic Aptitude Test that San José State College use as an entrance examination. Juan was the new Cristobal Colón sailing the Scholar Ship stern first against the wind into the roots in the shade of knowledge. The fact that the forum was willing to back Juan with a scholarship showed a community support most students did not have.

"But, I want to make it very, very clear to you, Mr. Galeban, that all that did was just get you into the college," stated Dr. Piston emphatically in a condescending manner. "It will be your job to see just how long you can keep us from throwing you out."

"Thanks for such a great opportunity," said Juan, hoping that his advisor did not catch the sarcastic double meaning of his remark.

After his little talk with Dr. Piston, Juan realized that he really didn't get to select his university or college. To use the scholarship he had to leave home, attend a Land Grant college and live on campus in a pinto dorm. The college regulations were so written that if he didn't live in approved housing, he could be removed from the college.

During orientation week Student Services had picked out his housing. The college housing authority practiced de facto segregation. It put Juan in the "restricted" floor of the nonrestricted dormitory of San José State College. Juan was on the dorm floor that housed the Black "jocks" and foreign scholarship students. He was living in a dormitory barrio with exceptions to the rule.

Through the "housing allowance" the institution owned his life for a pittance. While his days were full of learning Anglo-Saxon version of reality at San José State College, he frequently hallucinated in the evil segregated isolation of the dorm. The dream walkers continued to chew on the his heart. The crowded dorm jammed with strangers filled his heart with loneliness. Nobody sounded or looked like him.

He was in an academic "boot camp." But at least in the Army's boot camp most of the recruits were Juan's hommies. In the service he could see the enemy; in the college the enemy blinded him with the rhetoric of democratic academic life. In addition, while Juan felt joy at being back in Matatlan with his padrinos and padres, he missed his East Los comadres and compadres. Being far away from Concha and his children reinforced his remembrance and guilt.

For Juan, San José State College next to downtown San José in the center of Matatlan, appeared like a stonewall of nameless faces to be vaulted. The wall became full of doors, many marked with signs that read: "Danger: Enter At Your Own Risk," "Do Not Enter" and/or "Forbidden". The wall revolved with the swinging doors hitting Juan in the face and ass simultaneously. The multiple entrances in the wall became a maze into the assimilated, plastic world of the Anglo that sparkled and glared with illusions and materialistic traps.

"No smoke here," said Abuelo. "The heart of Matatlan is full of concrete."

"No respeto o honor either, brother-in-law," retorted Spanish Grandma. "Don't let their double-hinged swinging doors strip you of your self respect, Juan."

"The college is just trying to help me express myself. They want me to develop my reflective powers, Abuelos," replied Juan.

In his freshman year Juan was only scores in a series of grade books. Each new course was an experiment in retention and maintainance of a surviving grade point. The enslavement to a numerical standard of 3.0 or better seemed more important than the knowledge base. Only when precisely placed in the mouth of God, did the drawn sword of truth hold his focus. As he sat in each new class the pitard of reality kept poking at his unshielded hands. Lectures, papers, and exams, bled all over his face: burning vanities swinging in a bell curve: stuck in the middle of an edge, with nowhere to go.

"Reflective mirrors are transparent walls designed to cage and divert jou, mi hijo," said Father Diego. "You can't bank on salvation in a gilded cage. Another man's word is not your own, my son."

"Don't worry, father, I won't steal any words," replied Juan.

"The theft of your soul by false prophets is an affront to God my son," replied the priest.

"I'll keep my eyes open and stay out of their cages, father."

"Angeles have fallen for less than that, Juan," asserted Father Diego. "Your Grandmother and I will keep praying for you."

"Thank you, Padre"

Concha's apron, Mr. Johnston's apron, the American Army uniform, the Zoot Zuit, Abuelo's blue pick-up, Spanish Grandma's wash boiler, and Abuela's sherry bottle had all been cages: Juan's domesticity, revolt, survival, conformity, freedom, purification, and "escape." All these protective rituals tightly held his identity, roots and friendship.

To Juan the new college cage became a pretense of academic protection in an old cage falling off his father's kitchen table. He could trust very few in the lying-truth of this new cage of pseudo-inexperienced knowledge without an honor code of a dear friend: respect, dignity, and pride. The Scholar Ship sailed without the Friend Ship.

Dearest Conchita

You have no idea how I miss you. I miss the shelter of you arms. When I was away from you in Europe, I always missed your love, but after the talks we had in our bed in your mother's house in East Los, I now miss the companionship and friendship of your presence.

I found a night job up here driving a tow truck. It's a big

white 2-ton Ford. I'm hoping with this new job that I will be able to save enough money for you, the kids and your mother to take the Daylight up here to San José. My mother says that she can set us up a space in my brother's old room for us. She hasn't done anything with it since he was injured in the Pacific.

Benjamín is still over at the V. A. Hospital in Palo Alto. I've been over to see him a couple of times. It's just a short bus ride from my room at the college. He is doing a lot better now. Benjamín has asked to see his nieces and nephews, so maybe we can all go visit him.

Thanks for your note about the kids. I'm glad they are behaving well for you and your mother. As for braces for David, let's discuss this when you come up here. I think I have found us a house near my parents on Rocky Mountain drive. It is also near my Abuela's house.

The house has a flat rock roof and the latest in large casement windows. It's east of White Road outside the flood areas of Ruby and Penetencia Creeks. The house has a lot of possibilities for additions and has a rent with an option to buy.

It already has a vet loan on it, so I won't have to use mine or qualify for the home. The couple who own it now just want out. We can get it by assuming their payment of sixty-five dollars a month. It has a big backyard for David, Juanito, María, and Diego. Abuela says that Abuelo left me some money to help me get a house. We could use some of it to fix up this place.

Write me soon, because this kind of a deal doesn't wait for long.

Love, Juan.

While he was excited by the possibilities and opportunities of a college education, somewhere in the back of his mind he felt that the great buildings full of ancient content draped in the flags of new and better innovation could not match the power of a cave filled with his Grandfather's thoughts: the battlefield of harmony for the mythical Mechicá. The clash of powers became necessary for Juan's evolving personal identity. On the battlefield of university learning, the conflict led to separation, specialization and isolation. On the other battlefield of Concha's apron he was still a puppet dancing on a string.

So many of the labs and lectures seemed to present truth, yet everywhere on campus were signs that restricted freedom. Even the Library restricted thought exchange in the stacks of moth eaten, dusty, mildewed silence. "No Parking" here, "No Standing" there, and "No Talking" everywhere. With Concha the restrictions were stated in commands like: "Get a real job," Get a second job," "Get a job that will pay enough for me to stay home." With Concha there was no thought exchange. Even so, Concha and the kids coming up at the end of the semester excited him.

Dear Juan,

What do you mean by looking at a house without my permission. It sounds like you have it all planned for me and the children to move up to San José. Wear your own aprons, planner. That "some money" from your abuelo to fix "some of the house" doesn't sound like much of anything to me, Juan.

Moving like a house on fire without me will only lead to ice in your pants. Know this, Juan, no hot desires on your part will melt that condition either.

The children are doing great here with my mother. They are very happy with all of their little friends and the neighbor's puppies. My mother loves her house and I like my job.

I miss you too, especially when I put on the apron you wore to feed María Chavela. The train ride sounds nice, but staying in your mother's house sounds a little cramped, even if it is for only two weeks. Why don't we meet in Yosemite or something.

Be careful what you write, Juan. The children want to come up and see their tío and abuelitos. Send that money for the tickets immediately. You don't know how to buy things at a discount. The bank has a program that will help make the money you are sending go farther.

Love, Concha

Answering one of Concha's letters was tougher than answering test questions. He felt that he could write what he wanted as long as it was what the professors wanted to read. With Concha, no matter what you wrote, she didn't want to read it. The 3.0 grade point depended on his answers to the professors. However, his freedom to think was being enslaved by their feeding him facts, skills and figures for a degree. He wanted them to develop his intellect, soul and spirit.

With Concha, the test was over and if he wouldn't do some extra credit work soon, he would return to the fart department.

Dearest Conchita,

I'm glad to note that you are coming up to San José. I'm enclosing the money for the tickets, as you requested. It should cover yours and the kid's fares. I just didn't have enough to go around to bring you mother too. You will have to dig up the money for your mother's fare.

My Abuela said she will watch the kids for a couple of days so we can have sometime to ourselves. The Yosemite idea sounds great. Papá says that we can borrow the family camping equipment.

Maybe we can look at some of the properties I have been looking at in San José.

If the bank can transfer you up here, then my sister says that she can babysit the kids. If you need any further information write soon. Don't forget to write down the schedule for the train trip and send it to me.

Miss you a whole lot. I love you more and more everyday.

Love, Juan

In late May Concha called to tell Juan that she, their children and her mother would be arriving by train at 5.00 P.M. on the second Friday of June. She also told Juan that San José Savings, an affiliate of Golden Community Savings, had offered her a job interview at the Main Branch in San José. Concha's mother stayed to East Los.

After a joyful trip to Yosemite, Concha interviewed for and was offered a job at San José Savings. They rented a house with an option to buy. The family was was reunited at 777 Rocky Mountain Drive in East San José.

Juan continued to be the working student, the grateful husband and above all the very active father.

He kept his night job with the towing company. However, the scholarship committee extended his allotment to cover only his tuition and books. Out of each overtime pay check he set aside funds for Concha and him to go out to the Tropicana Ballroom. He watched his children afternoons and Saturdays.

Abuela and Juan's sisters all pitched in with the babysitting. The whole family caravaned back up to Yosemite for two weeks in August.

*   *   *

During Juan's second year at San José State College, he began to understand the power of words even though David and Spanish Grandma had always told him that the power of English depended on the verbs. During a rare rainy day on the campus in one of those tough, thought provoking English 1B lectures on how to use alliterations, the tall, tan, tense English professor presented, and provided highly specialized techniques to produce alliterative poetic and prosaic effects for prospective writers. The course outline, or green sheet, instructed the students that the theme for the week was titled Remembrance and Thoughtfulness.

As an illustration for this assignment, the professor used "Remember the Alamo," the war cry of Texicans in 1836. Juan did not agree with the professor's version. Juan changed his title to the simple majestic phrase: "Remember my Abuelo."

Juan wanted to write about a real professor, his Abuelo. He, also, remembered his own version of World War II which paralleled the Alamo: Remember the troops, who ate like in-winter sheep, fed during the severe storm, a respite from the stench of death and the worries of war. Juan had an excellent memory. He remembered but did not relate very favorably to Mrs. Post's sacred 1492.

In the voices from Matatlan he heard timely universal wisdom. In other voices of authority and authoritative figures, he heard masked wisdom. Juan used the universal voices creatively to authenticate his identity. For him the voices of time created the reality in his soul's inner life. The imaginary historical characters that the English professor described were certainly real to some of the students, but to Juan they were merely empty shadows marching to a different battle cry as their voices preserved the revered revolving rotunda of historical echos of unrevealed time, tradition and thoughtlessness for others. The professor had his ships sailing on the California deserts in every direction, again. Scholarship weighted down in the white shining silicate sand outweighed friendship, swordsmanship and craftsmanship.

Juan remembered that somber December 22, the day his Abuelo had climbed the pyramid ladder to a regenerated earth. He, also, remembered the night he received the terse, terrifying telegram: the sudden shock, the sinking sorrow and the smothering solitude. The family was there in spirit but without the patting of the hand on the shoulder, without the "siento mucho," without the velorio, and without anyone to console his crimped head and crumbling heart.

On that shell filled, crater making, bone chilling, and fog frozen night a chivito with a heart of iron broke down. He wept without tears, as he saved his grief for that day full of personal petition, prayer and peace. For Juan, that solemn intellectual night of spiritual survival, his emotions erased errors while his heart hearkened the humility and honor of home. At his desk in the "shadowless" classroom of pseudo technicality his hand shook vigorously as his pencil portrayed his personal prayer.

As Juan read his essay three days later, the class cheered for his old hero and reserved their praise for the new star. The staring stereotypes snapped at Juan's non-Shakespearan approach. But Spanish Grandma came to her Juanito's aid: her green eagle eyes staring into the distance, flying through a jarabe tapatío, snapping her fingers, showing her insolent teasing skirts and pounding her zapatiados and jotas on the wooden floor beating the exciting rhythm that twirled the hearts of those who dared to laugh at her family in the barrio.

Spanish Grandma revived the requerimiento, her own battle cry for the salvation of souls. In that somber and sacred moment, she bore the cross; she bathed in spiritual waters; and as she bent her knees to petition for her friendly adversary, Abuelo, she blessed as the jarabe tapatío ended but as dancing eyes glorified Jesu Cristo and prayed, "Abuelo, may your soul rest in peace. Thank you, Jesu Cristo."

The cross and the blood belonged to every repented sinner: those in the Alamo, those in the barrio, and those in every familia. The irascible Spanish Grandma's index finger and courageous heart sculptured the Abuelo down and up to the winking of his eyes. As the Abuelo moved from his plasticity, he tore the pages of the mechanical writer as he said, "A piece of art no viene de la basura. Viene de mi barrio, de nuestro barrio, del barrio de mi Abuelo, de su corazón, siempre de su corazón. Remembrance and Thoughtfulness: Mi Abuelo. Juan slowly walked back to his desk. Only the essence of stunned silence remained as the successful professor smiled.

* * *

During his fourth semester Juan took a general education requirement on European History (4B). This course continued to heighten his awareness that his voices were his cultural roots. He realized during the course that the voice he selected for his authenticity determined the direction of his cultural values. His first awareness of the need for authenticity occurred in Dr. Jenks' 4B lecture on the WW II African and Italian campaigns and the holocaust. No text book reading researcher could tell him about Dachau, for Juan had opened the sheds of the living dead. Yet, whenever he tried to relate his actual experiences to the course content and assignments he was told, "Mr. Galván, you have a unique point of view that is very interesting but not scholarly in its presentation. You need to learn to perform in an academic and scholarly fashion."

Another "A", but his point of view sandbagged again. It seemed to Juan that the barrio and reality from a minority point of view were not worthy of academic pursuits unless there was a federal grant in it for the Anglo American social scientist. Underpowered, underfunded caged ships loaded with sandbags full of misspent federal dollars.

When Juan started thinking about taking college courses in earnest he discussed the matter with David. "Remember, Vuan," said David, "The 'afikoman' of the seder has been turned into an Easter egg hunt in the United States by the inability of the dominant vestern European culture to see through the use of cultural perspectives, the apparent bastardization of ancient/contemporary lifestyles. Ven vou enter upper division courses, vou should expect more of that. To the idealist, a university searches for the truth. However, many times it advocates the status quo to gain influence needed for its survival. Sometimes, as in the case of Heidelberg in the '30's, it advocates a partyline that destroys its ability to search for the truth."

"It's hard to believe that could happen here, David."

"It happens here, Vuan. It is just more subtle. Therefore, this process can be even more dangerous here. Nobody talks of it much now, but look how vomen and minorities have been treated in the university. It is a great example of how the university defends the status quo at the expense of those the power controlling group vishes to exploit."

"David, it can't be all that bad."

"It doesn't look that bad on the surface, Vaun, because of the subtlety of the series of masks employed. It is only vhen vou start to examine the legal decisions and pleadings before that it become apparent."

"Was it your Heidelberg experience that turned you on to those subtleties, whatever they are, David?"

"They could have started me in this direction, but it vas some vork I did during my first year of law school at Loyola that really opened my eyes. I found that around 1875, collegiate coeducation was a combination of conservatism and the beginning of the gender revolution in the United States. In a novel titled, *An American Girl and Her Four Years in a Boys College*, Wilhelmine Elliot, a part German girl, is described in masculine and feminine terms to 'accept' her as a member of the college. Even so, the story is full of situations vhere the male students just don't know how to treat her for fear of trespassing the feminine domain. Because the number of vomen vas so very small, and the fashion allowed so restricted, the vomen vere not much of a threat to the men on campus."

"What's the point, Herr Abogado?"

"I haven't got there yet, Vuan, I'm just starting to lay the foundation for my case."

"Do you talk like this to everyone, David?"

"Only to vou and my fiancee, Naomi. In vour case, Vaun, I do it to nourish that tiny acorn that is rattling around in vour head and begging for fertilization."

"Very funny, David. And your girl, Naomi, why do jou do it to her?"

"Because she says she likes it."

"That will change once she gets that ring you have put on her finger through your nose."

"That may be true, Vaun. I guess that means that I vill just have to extend the period of engagement. Now, back to the case I vas building for vou. From 1890 to 1915, vomen vere beginning to enter professions, to become active in politics and to participate in the political reform movement. The suffrage movement gained most of its energy at this time. It is precisely at this time that the vhite Anglo Saxon Protestant male began to feel threatened. To counteract this threat, men started to separate extra-curricular activities and encourage the development of black and vomen's colleges. This also vas the time vhen the 'Spanish schools' vere started. However, the separation vas not equal. Vhite men continued to get a greater share of the resources and faculty interest. As vomen's influence gained momentum, some of the universities started a backlash: they started using quotas and entrance standards that favored vhite Anglo Saxon Protestant males to control the number of vomen and minorities entering their hallowed halls of learning. Stanford was one of the pioneers in this backlash movement. Cal,

Illinois, and Visconsin, vere vell known for these biases."

"How did this happen on a individual basis, David?"

Vell, Juan, that part is hard to say, but men continued to separate the vomen through their idioms and descriptions at Cal.
The men called the vomen students the 'pelicans' and named
the campus humor magazine, 'The Pelicans.' This magazine is a
frequent vehicle for satiric comment on gender relationships on
campus. Vomen and minorities are dehumanized by this strategy."

"But that's no big deal, David. Satire is a always used in the
funnies."

"Look, Vaun, the same type of satiric dehumanization was
used on Jews in Heidelberg as the Nazis gained power in the
'30's. The political agenda is hidden and masked in humor that
plays to your existing prejudices vhile creating new ones vitout
raising any objection in the victim."

"Are you calling me a victim, or are jou back in Heidleberg,
David?"

"I guess its both, Vuan. After Loyola I got into Bolt Law
School at Cal and saw vat I am telling vou on a first hand basis.
Vomen and minorities are virtually laughed out of the school
before they even get a chance to enroll. I only got in because I
vas on a research grant that the University vas interested in. At
Cal, the Pelicans have become synonymous with old maid school
teachers like the one in the novel, *The Terrible Miss Dove*, because
no self respecting college man vhould vant to marry a career
voman. Vomen are just supposed to stay home and have children and keep a cute little house for their lord and master. This
not right, Vuan."

"As a man married to what jou call a 'career woman,' I can
tell you that there may be some truth in why they are hard to be
married to, David."

"See how you would be trapped by satirical logic and sub-
scription to a form of academic discrimination that is also used
against you. Even if vou get into the University they vill separate
vou out in an approved house that only has minorities in it. That

is just one of the vays to keep the Vhite race pure, even in the 'land of the free'. And just in case vou are wondering about how that university thinks of Jews, ve are also considered as 'non-vhite' and vill either be put in our own 'restricted house' or in vit vou and the black sport scholarship athletes."

"I don't believe that can be going on in a university. Jou must be reading more into it than is really there."

"I really wish vou vere right, Vaun. But George Orwell in his book Animal Farm said that vhile all the animals vere created equal, 'some animals are more equal than other animals.' Vat the university is doing vit both vritten and unvritten policies, vit the unvritten tradition actually being stronger and more enforced than the vritten, is to implement activities and screening devices that defend the status quo were in that the vomen are supposed to stay home and have children and the minorities are to function as a menial labor force. Those minorities and vomen who are 'allowed' some opportunity to succeed, are only 'allowed' to succeed to the level vhere they act as overseers and first line managers for the groups they represent."

"I'll say one thing for your argument, David, I can see why they funded your project and it sounds like the summation to a civil rights court case."

"That's two things, Vaun, and I vish I had the physical evidence and the money to take an actual case all the way to the Supreme Court."

"If I know you as I think I do, David, you'll find that evidence and take it all the way."

*   *   *

In Anthropology 1A Juan thought he would find out about his shared heritage as if it were both boots, but when he discussed some of Dr. Corni's lecture material with his father, Juan found out that the professor had his boots on upside down. David was right. The status quo presentation for social stratification was big and bold in the course content. In the lectures the professor implied that Indian chief Seattle is not an Aztec were not relevant: "Their scholarly achievement could not fill one boot." To prove his point the professor assigned the students to critic the testimony of Chief Seattle. That weekend Juan drove into the hills above Matatlan (San José) to hear the weeping of the trees, straining the fog to rain on the ground, protecting the roots during the drought: the voice of the Redwoods or sequoias, the loss of innocence, the remembrance of the dead, the little girl in Rome, the babies in Dachau.... These memories compounded by the hissing, moaning, wailing, whirring (whoooo) voice of the forest trapped him at the base of the pyramid of life, unable to go up, unable to stay. He could not discern Sequoya, the Indian tree; Cuatemoc, the eagle of the smoking mirror, and Seattle, the keeper of the bones and the sky from Abuelo.

Juan decided to use Indian criteria to critique Chief Seattle from the vantage of the mountain top instead of the tombs of the library stacks: Chief Seattle's morgue. The more he read Seattle's speech the more the words of Luther Standing Bear a Lakota chief thundered in his ears:

The white man does not understand the Indian for the reason that he does not understand America. He is too far removed from its formative process. The roots of his tree of life have not yet grasped the rock and soil. The white man is still troubled with primitive fears: he still has in his consciousness the perils of this frontier continent, some of its fastnesses not yet having yielded to his questing footsteps and inquiring eyes. He shudders still with the memory of the loss of his forefathers upon its scorching deserts and forbidding mountain tops. The man from Europe is still a foreigner and an alien. And he still hates the man who questioned his path across the continent.

But in the Indian the spirit of the land is still vested; it will be until other men are able to divine and meet its rhythm. Men must be born and reborn to belong. Their bodies must be formed of the dust of their forefathers' bones (1876).

Standing Bear's voice told him that the title of his paper should be "Seattle: The Keeper Of The Bones And The Sky." Juan pondered as to how he could present a critique of these two Indian scholars in a manner that would have merit to the Indian and European. He needed to show that Seattle's heartfelt speech spelled quality scholarship. He used their position that:

We know that the white man does not understand America because for the European the land and its occupants are enemies to be conquered. As a stranger the European came during the day to make his promises, but as a stranger during the night he took the land away from all and justified his act by calling this land America. With that name the European stole the title and deed to the land as if man could keep God, for God is always in the earth and the stars. In the rending of the veil the stranger and Indian lost their understanding of each other. With his titles and deeds the European continued to ravage the indigenous heritage of the land.

For Juan, the mestizo, this was the truth of his paper, but only partially true for him. Abuelo consented to the position of his boots: heels together—toes pointing in opposite directions. The Zuit could no longer cover his loins with justification.

Thus, Juan wrote his assignment:

The thirty-one broken treaties between the U.S. and Mexico attest to this reality. With the Treaty of Guadalupe Hidalgo, the textbooks said that the Mexican and Indian in the conquered territories were to be made Americans. But the U.S. Senate expunged these promises on March 10, 1848, and replaced them with the 'act of Congress language' found in the Treaty of Paris of 1803. This language promised that we could remain at the wish of Congress as aliens on our own land. Seattle understood this critical awareness associated with heritage and identity when he stated in 1854, 'When the Great Chief in Washington sends word that he wishes to buy our land, he asks much of us.' To me his sacred land which is our heritage, whether we call it the vineyard, the earth, or heaven cannot be be sold. Moreover, the Great Chief in Washington is not our father or we his children.

Spanish Grandma said that no national chief had the right to act as God. For once Abuelo agreed because the chief hadn't earned his pyramid. An apron was not the badge of a chief.

We need to perform our quest as honorable keepers of the earth's heritage by maintaining our environment. As Seattle stated, "The air is precious to the red man, for all things share the same breathe.... The white man does not seem to notice the air he breathes. Like a man dying for many days, he is numb to the stench. But if we sell you our land, you must remember that the air is precious to us, that the air shares its spirit with all the life it supports."

With his inquisitive eyes Juan could see from Mt. Madonna that the keepers were fouling their air in Matatlan with iron ponies on artificial rubber tires. With his nose he could smell the broken promises.

Scholarship does not come from garbage no matter how many degrees are lavished upon it. I learned in Dachau that every time the truth is imprisoned and the vineyard is ravaged, that there is little merit in the life way that is built upon it. Everyone shudders with the memory produced by the heat of unfounded criticism and the icy stares of false evaluation. Seattle's prophecy is becoming a certainty. He stated that: 'Whatever happens to the beast, soon happens to man. All things are connected.' The current generation's failure to acknowledge this truth makes us all foreigners and aliens to the spirit of our land."

Abuelo, Sequoya and Cuatemoc smiled. The guardians of destiny were protected. Seeing them satisfied, pleased Spanish Grandma.

Remember that to merit a place in a heritage each one of us must seek to become dust on the web of life while not dusting off the spirit of the web. Seattle keeps urging us that, 'Man did not weave the web of life he is merely a strand in it. Whatever he does to the web, he does to himself.' In keeping with this remembrance, I took an investigative trip through the Chesbro basin to Mt. Madonna, the place where my grandfather taught me the meanings of Seattle. His memories are still flowing in the sap of the tree. His tree has not been girded. As an irrigator, he never made his pipes into a tree. The crystal clear springs of Chesbro reflected the blood of his ancestors and consequently mine too. The voices of my Abuelo and Seattle murmur in the creek to let us know that 'the ground beneath their feet is the ashes of our grandfathers.' To heed Seattle's words makes us worthy of his scholarship: the keepers of the bones and the sky."

The Golden "A" at last.

Back in the foxholes of the Sahara, David had told him that the American universities were one of the foxholes of freedom. Had David wanted to find this freedom from the Nazis so bad that he saw rhetoric as truth? The campus did everything but put numbers on your wrist, Juan thought. Admissions and records, financial aids, and many of the support staff treated him like a dog tag. He had to stand in line for everything.

Heidelberg was supposedly a bastion for knowledge and truth, but even in the Sahara, long before Juan's effort to acquire a collegiate education, David had realized that Heidelberg was a place where David could search for the truth as it effected him directly, as well as a place where a selective type of truth was propagated to enhance the status of the chosen.

"Hello, Dave. It's the line standing, book burrowing, dog tag wearing cucaracha calling, seeking respite from the stained glass windows of surrealistic learning and knowledge," said Juan with the black humor that had become part of their communication style.

"Vat are they teaching vou at that place, Chivo," replied David. "Except for vour voice, vou sound like those prosecutors at Nuremberg. They used hyperbole almost as well as vou do."

"Hyperbole, shmerbole. I'm not sure what I'm learning here. One thing is for sure, I'm learning how not to teach, carnal."

"I thought that, that is vhy you vent to that school. They vere supposed to make vou a real teacher. Don't vou vant to be a teacher anymore? Vou like teaching in the severs? Do vou vant to go back into the ground?"

"Foxholes under a city are no fun, ese."

"Vou vanted to get that apron off, right?"

"More than ever, ese," said Juan. "It's just dat the harder I try to develop the truths that the voices of reality direct me to, the more the faculty of the university seem to point to illusions as truth. The funny part is that the tools of knowledge I am gaining from the courses and their related readings, are helping and motivating me away from the rhetoric in my class work instead of towards it.

"Chivo, vou are ducking and darting again. Vat are vou really getting at?"

"That is how I feel, David, like a Chivo underfoot, being fed whatever garbage happens to fall off the table of knowledge. I'm full, but hungry. Stuffed, but empty."

"Vat do vou think is happening to cause this feeling, Vuan?"

"I think that the university provides most students the freedom to assimilate. Yet, for me, the process of assimilation is not the choice as it is being presented. In fact, I think that it is not a choice at all. It is only the illusion of choices. Jou can say what jou want as long as it is what they want jou to say. I think that is why so much of the things I am hearing here, seem to be a little off center and/or out of focus."

"Get avay from the rhetoric of complaining, Vuan. Get back to focusing on vour voices. For me, I saw the hand vriting on the valls of Heidelberg in 1936. I found out that the ideology of the university vere set upon falsehoods and the prejudices of the majority vere stronger than the search for the truth. Vat are vour voices telling vou about this?"

"I remember my Abuela talking to my Mother and Father about this. She talked about being medio y medio. I think she felt caught between her Christian and Indian values. The Christian values trying to separate and the Indian values trying to integrate. In addition, she felt caught between the Mestizo synthesis of the Christian and Indian spiritual values and the shadow process of assimilation towards a society that wanted to strip her of those Mestizo spiritual values. She often spoke of how we were losing our heritage, She said, 'Our hearts are being cut out and sacrificed on the altar of greed and profit with little or no benefit to the seed.' When she talked that way, I saw the image of the golden cucaracha impaled on a silver shaft."

"Vat is the meaning of all that to vou, Vuan?"

"I'm not sure, David. That is why I called jou. Jou are the only person that I can talk to, on some of these things. My Abuelito is gone and my dad thinks that the university is a place where those who can't work go and play at working. He thinks I should go back to the sewers and get back into a real job. Jou taught me in those foxholes we shared that sometimes the only way to figure out the maze of the heart is to talk it through until the voices are clear."

"I did that? I did not know that vou vere getting that out of our talks, but I'm glad for it. I guess I do talk things out. I remember that time vou forced me to talk at Dachau and how much it helped."

"Funny jou should mention Dachau. I remember it every time I smell and see the stacks in the library. The ideas are alive, but many of the people that are using them are dead. I read in one of those books that they burned almost all of the Indian books in the name of Christ. All the books in the library aren't worth the paper they are printed on unless they preserve the cycle of reality for the living. Why do ideologists feel they must burn books?"

"They think that by burning the important books, that they are burning the threatening and illuminating ideas in them. I have come to realize that is vhy ve burn, exploit and destroy people too."

"That's really good, David. If it's O.K. with jou I will try and use it in my next term paper. It's better than a lot of the stuff I hear around here. Some of the books and articles seem to be written for the dead."

"Read them anyvay, Chivito. Use all the ideas ve discuss. Test them out on those ears. Vou might just sing life into them. There are many lessons to be learned from garbage. Vasn't that vone of vour Grandmother's favorite sayings?"

"Jes, David, she loves that dicho. But sometimes, David, I think that if I stay here in the university too much longer, I'll be walking dead in my boots."

"Are vour boots still on, Vuan?"

"I really think they are, but sometimes I think they are walking by themselves, ese."

"Then find vone of those directions vou said vour Grandfather talked about and follow it. If they are as true as vou say they are, then it may take a little advocacy for vour position, but vou vill profit in the end. The passagevays of diachronicity are opened for those who have the influence to control the direction and benefits of such a truth. San José State and U.C. Berkeley are no different than any other institution that takes pride in denigrating the poor man who is forced to survive on the vrathe of grapes and starve on poisoned strawberries. These downtrodden are mentioned in vone or two pages of each book ven ve are in luck. On the other hand, the few chosen heroes of the elite occupy the rest of the literature. Strategize and be the downtrodden's advocate, Vaun."

"Gracias, Herr Abogado."

"Vour sense of humor vill take vou a long vay, Vuan, if vou don't offend those vho vant to see vou dead. Vou vill find the dust and mildew in the library has the same purpose as the ashes in Dachau. They are only partial truths, but they are the part of truth that forms the foundation for renaissance. Vou pointed that out to me in that horrible moment before I found my Pater."

"But the ideas in those books are enslaved and starved as were the Jews in Dachau, David. How can I set them free?"

"By staying true to vour voices, keeping an authentic focus, remembering Dachau, the severs, oppression, and vour Got. Keep vour goals simple. Be the champion of the diachronicity that is left out because the ideological elite vho create their version of history are not members of 'the civilized society.' There is simplicity in truth. I find that out everyday in my vork vit the law."

"Ese, jour words are like manna for my soul."

"Manna can be boring, Vuan. Moses had a hard time vit that one for forty years."

"I'm not Moses, David. I'm Quetzalcoalt upside-down on the cross."

"Right vou are, Don Quijote."

"I guess I have an intellectual challenge then, David."

"Right, Vuan. Vou are an exception to their rule. Vou have

been permitted the rare opportunity to stop them from coming into gather the harvest that is rightfully vours. Vou are being faced vit the same valls to learning I faced at Heidelberg. The difference is that forces vou face, are masks more cleverly fashioned than those created by the Nazi rulers of Germany."

"Dave, I don't see what jou are saying here. What masks are jou talking about?"

"The hidden agenda of apparent assimilation that is forcing the reality of dissimilation. The university acts like it vants vou to become part of the system, but it is really giving vou the tools to reject the system. If vou fall into the trap, the university vill use vour 'new found truths' to condemn vou and push vou out of vour chosen field. For anyvone vho hears the diachronic voices, the university can be a bottomless pit instead of a foxhole of freedom."

"Then what do I do, ese?"

"Recognize their masks as traps and use the voices of diachronicity internally to keep vour focus. This vay vou can play their game and quietly subvert them vit their own facts vitout revealing vour position. If vou do this, vou vill educate vouself in a vay they do not intend. It vill also help vou find vour personal purpose and identity."

"That is what I needed to hear, Carnal. Thanks for being there for me, David. I'll give it my best shot. Got to run now. Say hello to Naomi for me. How are the newlyweds doing, David?"

"Thank vou for asking, Vuan. My new wife, Naomi, is glad ven ve talk. It saves her from listening to my lectures. Now that ve are married she does not have time for them, but I have kept that ring on her finger anyvay."

"Boy has she ever got you snowed, David. You don't even know when your nose was pierced."

"Careful how vou talk about my nose, ve are sensitive about any discussion of that type, Vuan. Besides, she is sensitive about our telephone bills," said David as he laughed at his stereotyped comments.

"Not so sensitive that a beautiful women can't pierce your

stereotyped nose without your knowledge, David," said Juan with a chuckle. "Remember, David, jou always told me that jou were a stereotype because jou were a Jew."

"My talking to vou, helps me see so much, amigo. Don't let anyone look down their noses at vour ability and vit. Auf wieder-sean, Vuan."

"Adiós, carnal."

The classes in the college kept turning the clock backwards and forwards, melding in Juan's mind the words of David, Father Diego, and all the voices of Matatlan. Walls made tall and wide with stacked notecards fluttered heavily down upon Juan's head. Silent notes blown forcefully from the stage of lectured brass discourse: facts as fiction, fiction as facts. He wasn't even sure why he had received the Golden "A" from "Dr. Trumpet" himself!

In the large lower division classes almost everyone was just a "hey you face" to most of the professors. As the classes in the junior year got smaller and more intense, most of the professors, especially those in his major that had him more than once, learned the student's names.

By mere accident he had blinded the thought enslavers with reality and confused the confounders with their apparent facts. As he established his major during his junior year he continued to blaze the mesitzo trail in boots faced in the right direction but pulled on the wrong feet.

Through no accident Concha was promoted to headteller, but it meant that she had to move back to Los Angeles with her mother. She took the kids with her. Juan couldn't afford the loneliness of the little house on 777 Rocky Mountain Drive even though they had assumed the title to the house. The small rooms of the house became large and empty by his family's absence.

To fill the void Juan allowed his baby sister and brother-in-law to moved in with their kids. After two months Juan couldn't handle the noise of children that weren't his. He rented his sister and brother-in-law the house for seventy-five dollars a month and moved back into the dorms as an assistant resident advisor to tutor the jocks and foreign scholarship students. He continued working for the towing company and started working three hours a day as a teacher's aide.

As he started his senior year the tear sodden friend ship was left at the dock once again. The scholar ship, piloted by the skilled that "there face" as in "that there student" wearing ill fitting tractor boots, faced the "right direction."

Voices In The Domitory

The three years that Juan had spent at San José State College had not changed any of the campus housing policies. When Concha left for Los Angeles his status went from an independent married student to an undergraduate that had to live in approved housing. Juan became the resident advisor on the dorm floor that housed the Black "jocks" and foreign scholarship students: exceptions to the unwritten all white rule.

The reemergence and rebirth of his regenerated childhood memories in Matatlan emphasized sal si puedes, an imaginary melting pot that isolated Juan. The "restricted dorm" assaulted and really separated Juan's cultural identity from his barrio like the walls of Dachau isolated the Jews from German society. His half-cubical cubicle in the dorm became an asinine isolation cell, a remote island, in the midst of censored cultural identities and accents. Only his Scholar Ship crossed the moat. Residence in the scholarship dorm labeled his "homo erectus" face like a swastika stamped armband in Heidelberg: the root of European jawbone: no skiljaw.

As part of a speech course he was assigned to talk on his heritage. He again stumbled upon speeches given by Luther Standing Bear, a Lakota Chief who had to renounce his citizenship in the Lakota Nation to become a U.S. citizen in order to regain ownership of his sacred land and "maintain his traditions".

As he read the words of Standing Bear he saw the power in the voice of Abuelo saying, "Are jou really going to write dis speech, Juanito? De professor has his boots upside down. Only de pyramid of life is de pyramid of knowledge. Traditions regenerate la tierra. If jou put a pyramid upside down it will fall on jou. De old ones say our heritage is de way of de Elders. To tell of it is to have de pyramid fall on jou."

"Then how can I give this speech and get another golden "A," Abuelo?"

"Esearch for de revealed meaning of jour roots, Juanito. Give de espeech on dat. Den jou will find de way to put de professor's boots on right side up."

As Juan laid in his bed in the red brick pinto dormitory he felt alone. He thought that by now he would have adjusted to this reality, but he could not escape the evil of the isolation. The artificial civilized voices Juan kept hearing in the university choked Abuelo's tree and the forests of the Matatlanes with the smog of industrial progress. They uprooted the life giving orchards and covered the fertile earth with asphalt and match box track houses. The book shelves of the dorm and college libraries were full of ideological titles: trees without substance: La Llorona, weeping like a great Tan Oak, creaking, snapping, and popping acorns, poisoning the ground to preserve sacred cows and missing roots. The voices of his ancestors were not used to the artificial atmosphere and environment of the brick dorm. Juan was blind to King Lear's madness: suffering over these empty shadows; one, in the library; another, in the dorm;and still another, in the sculpted woods of the campus. King Lear wrapped in Mr. Education shouted at revealing Abuelo beneath a Hunan Meta Sequoia.

Juan feared falling asleep as the nightmare of the golden "A" started to recur: Abuelo, at the top of the pyramid screaming, "Be where jour tree is, please dun't esplit de trunk! Jour tree is on de side of de hill. De fire of false knowledge will try to scorch de fruit. Jour tree must survive. Its roots hold de shaking earth out of de valley of death. Wherever jou go, jou are. Everyting in jour espace has a voice. Listen to nature with jour eyes and heart."

"How do I do dat, Abuelo?"

"If jou listen to de thunder of de falling upside down pyramid, de earth will vomit jour roots!"

Juan, could see himself at the pyramid's treeless, shaking base, falling through the rootless cracks: all voices degenerating the earth, forever. Father Diego, hurriedly came and dragged Juan to Golgotha for the salvation of the sinner; Spanish Grandma, pruned the deadwood off his tree. Juan awakened in a smoldering bed, cut in half slowly from head to toe by a nightmare that sucked the breath out of his earth. Dream walking always taught him that magic was the essence.

No foxhole in the darkest hours of battle shrouded him in danger like his asinine half-cubical cubicle at 3:00 A.M. The prayer blanket was cast upon the smoking fire. Everyone was exposed: no prisoners taken. The sun was regenerated.

The crowded dreamscape in the synthetic forest of brick and mortar screamed at his mind's eye with windward and leeward voices of prophesy and doom. Somehow he knew that if he were to be become a success at the college's table of knowledge he would need to knit magic into reality. The oak and the sequoia had to become one forest to survive in both the windward and leeward sides of the smoking mirrorfaced mountain.

In the dream of the mirrored mountain he looked into the mirror in his Zuit and heard the voice of his wife, the voice that was not the echo that thundered after the screech of any incoming 88. It was the still small voice of guilt and doubt. She let him know that his mirror reflected smoke. Yet the voices he heard beyond those of his wife prevented him from falling into the narcissistic syndrome. In their authenticity they became distractive creators that destroyed imitation.

At the foot of the windward/leeward mirrored mountain he saw himself screaming silently, "Great Great Grand Fathers, hear my voice that I might hear yours and the voices of our God/gods. I have survived the wrath of ideological hatred and come through the prejudice and intolerance of my time; yet I am not fulfilled and I cannot fulfill. Truth allegedly surrounds me. Those who love me, truly support me. Yet, the quest for the unique tree alludes me because of the smokes and fogs. I cannot find my place and focus."

The dream mountain glowed red with the desire of his quest. He gave chase and Concha tripped him in her womb. His dream walker cried again, "Quetzalcoatl, Lord of the Dawn East and West, I move from one direction to another without design. I'm stuck in the inward center between North and South. I am blind to the pattern. That which is written for me is a blur. Where is the truth in my life? How can I be the resurrection and regeneration from the ashes of oppression if I cannot focus on the authenticity of my purpose?"

Sliding down the faceted golden pyramid ablaze with the energy of the molten dawn, the Great Lord said, "Dream Walker, focus not on the 'I', for it is blind like snakes in a "lightless" cave. Focus on the open eyes of Teolt and climb with me out of the barranca of your decaying bowels. The truth for you is in the eyes of Teotl."

"I am not focusing just on me, Great Lord," asserted Juan. "I can already see the truth for others. I can see David's 7x7x7 at Dachau, Concha in childbirth: a mirrored reality, Abuelito ascending to you as 20x20x20, the poetry of Ramón: Ash Wednesday and holy smoke staining a European beach red, the learning of those about me, and the roots of the great Oaks of Matatlan. But for all this support and vision, while soul is a vibrant root, my spirit is a lonely blur that alludes my grasp."

"It is good that you can see others, Dream Walker, but that is not the lesson of the Smoking Mirror."

Juan's bed was soaked with the sweat of his search. The green of the unique tree reflected yellow and blue. The near felt far and unfamiliar. He sat awake with the thunder of silence in his ears. He got out of bed to quench his choking thirst. He changed the sheets and wearily returned to the land of talking trees and smoking glass. As he moved towards the beginning of the dream walk path he heard Spanish Grandma calling in the distance, "Abuelo was delerious as he whispered to me between gasps, 'Where is my Juan the fruit of my lions?' I answered him that you knew his heart."

"What did he say to you then, Grandma?" asked Juan as he drifted off the path in her direction.

"As Abuelo was gasping for air, in his very weak voice, he said, 'Talk to Juan through me, suegra. Juan, Juan I have the answer of the Carpenter and woodcarver for you that you asked me about at Mt. Madonna.' He sighed and died at that very moment. To this day I do not know what he meant," said Spanish Grandma with a mournful voice for a loss that could not be replaced.

Juan comforted Spanish Grandma, "He is with your husband, now."

New voices started to whirl in his mind as he continued to moved back towards the dream walker's path. "Welcome to the western windward side," whirred Sequoya. "The plumed Serpent whispered your presence. Are you still lost in the forest, Yellow Dust? May the winter rains and summer fogs cool and water your roots. May the splash of the creeks end your reflective smoke."

"Sequoya, I know of you through my Abuela's tragitos and Abuelo's dichos. I have heard you in the mouth of mis padres, Concha and David. I have smelled your sweet freshness in the smoke of battle. I have felt you in between the lines on the pages in the library."

"I felt jou too, Small Walker, but your feet are soft on their bottoms," whirred Sequoya. "Combat boots have knocked you off your path. You are trying to see beyond the light of focus given to you."

"Sequoya, I missed you in the rituals of Rome, in the foxholes of death in the Westval, in the roads of destruction from the Sahara, in the warehouses of summary death in Dachau, and in the sewers of undetermined poisonous waste beneath East Los. If I am walking in the dreams of my Grandfathers, it is now time for you, Great Lord Sequoya, to touch me."

"It is not enough to have knowledge of the world to be unique in our tree, my Walking Yellow Dust. To pollinate your seed the touch must make us one. I must dwell in you and you in me. In the forest of life, this pollination will fertilize the windward side as it has done from the ending of the beginning ended times. Let us walk on the smoke of your mirror in the seed of you spiritual birth."

"But that is all an illusion, Sequoya."

"All light is an illusion, dreaming Small Walker."

Juan awoke lonely in his communal quest with the hidden and revealed voices. He felt a desperate need to communicate with fertile roots. The dream journeys made him worry if something was wrong with Concha and the kids. Concha continued to stay in L.A. His only contact with her and his children continued to be a weekly three-minute phone call. He had already used up that allotment this week, but the dream made another call necessary.

"Hi, querida," said Juan with anticipation of a lonely, long-distance touch. "What's happening with jou and the kidos? I miss jou guys so much."

"Not much is happening other than the usual old things, Juan," said Concha in a tired voice. It was almost as if she did not appreciate his call. As if, he was interrupting her life. "Little David wants to talk."

"Hi, Daddy, when are you coming home. My friends say you are dead in Korea."

"Then who do jou think is talking to jou now, My Little Cucaracha," said Juan with a laugh.

"You could be a record. My mommy plays a record with your song on it all of the time. My grandma says you can do amazing things with a record."

"Well, I'm not a record, son. Are jou being a big boy and helping mommy with jour brothers and sister?"

"Yes, daddy. I'm helping her so she won't be so tired. I think she misses you almost as much as I do, daddy. When are you coming back so my friends can see you?"

"If I come it will only be for a short time, son. I hope you, mommy and your brother and sisters can move up here at the end of this school year," said Juan.

"Does mommy know that, daddy?"

"Let me tell her, David."

"O.K., daddy. Bye for me. I love you daddy. Mommy, daddy wants to talk to you," Little David called out.

"I love you and miss you, son," said Juan sadly.

"I love you too. Here's mommy. Bye for me."

"He sounds good, querida. What's happening with the other

children?"

"The same old things, Juan. If he sounds good it is because mamá does a great job with them."

"I miss those same old things, querida."

"I'll bet," she said. "If I had an opportunity to get away from here I sure would."

"I keep telling you to come back up here with me," said Juan.

"Does that mean moving my mother too?"

"How can we afford to do that?" asked Juan.

"That is the point, Juan. If I can't bring Mom, who is going to watch the children. I didn't like the way your sisters watched them. Everyday I had to call the whole barrio to find out who was watching them. Besides, where am I going to get a job if I leave this one? They don't have any openings right now in San José. Didn't you rent our Rocky Mountain shack to your sister?"

"Yes, querida and I have been sending you the extra seventy-five dollars she pays us in rent."

"That's nice, I never liked that house anyway. It was too small and too close to your mother's house. So do you have a proper house for us, Chivito?"

"I could put in for married student housing. A lot of the G.I.'s are using it."

"I saw those fire trap projects. I grew up in that type of housing, Juan and I promised myself that my children would not have to live in that type of environment."

"I'll look for an apartment," said Juan. "I'll see if my housing allowance can be transferred to it. I'm also looking into one of those No Down Payment/Low Interest G.I. Loans."

"Make sure the house and/or apartment is big enough for mamá to live with us. She said she is willing to move up there with us to help with the child care. All she needs is a room for herself. She has been really lonely since my papá died and this would help me by taking care of the household while you're playing with your books."

"I'm not playing, Conchita," asserted Juan.

"Whatever, Juan. Oh, and while you are out looking for ways for us to move to your precious Matatlan, be a good boy and find me a job that is better than the one I have now. I'll need it to make the payments on that low interest loan you keep telling me about," Concha said.

"Could jou take some vacation time and come up here by yourself?" Juan asked. "I'll line up some job interviews on campus and around downtown. We could also look at some houses and/or apartments like we did before."

"I'll look into it, Juan, but Mr. Jackson has several rush orders and an inventory to do. He has me working overtime and we need the money. Thank God, Mother is here to help with the children. When is the next time we will see you?"

"I do not know, querida," said Juan with a sigh. "I may be able to get a job as a summer school aide. That would look good on my resume when I apply for a teaching job. That means that I couldn't come down until August."

"That is four months, Juan. I hope all of this is worth it. We have been married twelve years and we have only lived together seven of them."

"I feel that way too, querida. Quit that job and come up here," pleaded Juan.

"We need my job, Juan. We need it to maintain our family's stability. I could not leave the babies with anyone besides Mother. Sounds like you are planning to stay in San José permanently, Juan. I noticed that you took your Zuit and botas with you."

"Why not, querida? How about my mother doing our child care?" he responded as a small light appeared at the end of the tunnel.

"Did she say she would watch them? Has she moved to a better part of town?"

"That part of town was O.K. for me to grow up in and besides it is close to the college."

"If that part of town was so great, how come you turned out

to be the great pachuco."

"I picked that up in East Los, Concha, not Matatlan. Besides you liked my pachuco ways when we married," said Juan.

"That was then, Juan. This is now. I want my daughters to have more options than I had. When I was sixteen you could knock me over with a flashy car and well creased pants. You had that and more, Juan but now I want even more. So, I ask you once again, Mr. Macho, how come you packed up your boots and Zuit and took them with you? I thought you wanted me to keep them with my wedding dress."

"I want them here waiting for you, querida."

"What for Juan," said Concha grinding her voice just enough to inform him of her frustration. "I may have to wear the pants in this family, but I've no desire to wear your Zuit and botas to do so."

"You can have the pants, querida, but I want to be more than an option in your life. Mi Abuelo always said that all we need is enough light to illuminate just three feet of our path at anyone time."

"We'll see what we shall see, Juan, but you have to know where the path is in order to get on it. Did your Dream Walker tell you that too?"

"I think my three minutes are up, Concha. I love you, sweetie," Juan said.

"Don't give me that sweetie stuff, Juan. You don't even have the nerve to answer my question, Chivito. Three minutes worth of long-distance verbal combat, once a week, does not a marriage make," she said sarcastically.

"I know, querida, but I love you, miss you, and want you."

"Forget the want part, Juan. No more babies until you get a good paying job and a house I can live in with joy. Good- bye, Juan."

"Give me a kiss, dear," Juan said in his little boy voice.

"You get your kiss when you come see us," Concha said in her big mamá voice.

Even though the phone call finished Juan's dream walking for the night, he danced a lot in the Aragon while gliding down the streets of Rome and Paris. Near dawn he was trying to figure out the connection when he realized that someone was knocking at his door: one more evaporated fantasy.

As Juan opened the dorm room door the gravelly voice of Spanish Grandma said, "Buenos días le de Dios, hijo. I have brought you some clean clothes. Have you been a good boy for me? I think you have lost some weight. When have you last had a good home cooked meal? Your mother is asking for news from you."

"Nice to see you too, Grandma. You should have called me so I could have met you at the bus to carry this load. Almost nobody ever comes to visit me."

"You know that I do not like using that phone. It is so disrespectful and impersonal. The phone company is just trying to separate you from your money. Besides, a somebody is visiting you now."

"But there is no need to be carrying heavy loads of laundry on busses, Grandma. I have a car."

"Cars are for the lazy nobodies and spendthrifts. I'm not an invalid yet, Juan. It is time I inspect this den of inequity and disrespect that nobodies live in. I have a crucifix in my purse, mi hijito, that would look nice right there over somebody's bed. I also have a small statue of somebody's patron saint. He cares for everybody."

"That's nice Grandma. How did you find my room?"

"Don't patronize me like your Abuelo did, Juan. It is easy to find a nobody in a building where everybody lives. The nice young man at the desk told me how to find everybody. He even offered to have some other nice young man carry this load of laundry up the stairs to somebody's room, but I told him that his job was to mind the front door. I think they meant well, but I won't give into the temptation to be frail."

"I think I like your style, Grandma, even if it makes me feel like a nobody bullfighter with very little class."

"What do you know about Spanish style, Juanito! If you had on a pair of red shorts and you saw a charging bull, what would you do?"

"I'd use them to fight the bull, Grandma."

"While you are wearing them?"

"No, of course not. I would take them off."

"That is one of the things that worries me about this place. They are teaching you to be a nobody."

"What do you mean, Grandma?"

"Naked bullfighters don't have any style."

"I wouldn't be naked, Grandma."

"Are you trying to tell me that you are into Abuelo's dobles with two pair of under shorts?"

"Well at least I'd have on my silver crucifix."

"What would that mean to a bull, Chivito? Besides that's another thing that is worrying me about this place, Mr. Nobody."

"What's worrying you, now, Grandma?"

"When I deliver laundry to the University of Santa Clara to one of my comadre's sons, at least they have crosses on the buildings. Here the buildings are just red brick without dignity. Between the pochismos your Abuelo taught you and this godless place it is difficult to have a style. Have you been saying your prayers like your mother and I have taught you?"

"Well sort of, Grandma."

"You rode with your Abuelo too long in that rattle trap pickup of his, mi Hijito, Juanito Nobody. Be honest with me. I saw two young men with Bibles heading down Tenth Street near San Fernando. You should follow their example."

"They were probably on their way to the Morman Temple, Grandma."

"Well at least they are following through with their beliefs,

Juan, even if they are misguided nobodies."

As Spanish Grandma opened his closet to look for the demon rum and get nobody's dirty laundry sack, she made note of the Aztec Calendar hanging on the inside of the closet door. "I see you have your Abuelo in your closet, Juanito."

"I have the Bible you gave me last Christmas in my desk drawer, Grandma."

"It is difficult for anybody to read a Bible in a drawer, Juanito! I can see by the book titles you have on your shelf that this college is working hard on your mind and cares very little for your soul."

"I have to read them to get the 'A's' you have always encouraged me to go after, Gramdma."

"'A's' don't make you somebody, Juanito. Those Greek philosophers and Roman artists like Michealangelo were gross men. They were very much into nudity. Of course that probably wouldn't bother a nobody bullfighter. It is good to temper their teachings with His Truth. I don't care how round your world is, Juanito, God is still the center of the universe. Why don't you leave this sin city and move in with the family like the good boy you are."

"I have to stay here in in the dorm as part of my scholarship. Besides we can only stay in approved housing."

"Is this a college or a prison for nobodies? Who do they think they are that they can approve or dissapprove somebody's house. I don't see crosses in these rooms and you are telling me that because they are in the rooms of our house that it isn't good enough for anybody to live in?"

"I'm not sure that is what approved housing means, Grandma."

"Then what does it mean?" she asked.

"I'm not really sure of that either, Grandma."

"For somebody with so much intellectual ability, Juan Bautista Galván, you can be very ignorant when it comes to the important things in life. You can't hide that pin up over this bed. No wonder your wife and mother are so worried about you and your wandering morality in this world of Greeks bearing evil gifts."

"What have mamá and Concha been telling you, Grandma?"

"That is for me to know, Juan, for I know what I know. Don't pay too much for your education, Juanito mío. You are here to fill your mind, not empty your soul. Don't you have a room-mate?"

"Yes I do, Grandma. That's his pin up you saw."

"Then, where is your roommate, mi hijito."

"He had to go home on some family emergency."

"Is he Spanish?"

"No, Grandma. There are only 25 of us on this campus out of 21,000."

"Are there any Spaniards in this dorm with you?"

"The only other Raza in this dorm is a guy on the second floor named Rafael Menendez. He is the son of some wealthy Peruvian Banker who stays in the dorms to practice his English."

"Living in the dorms hasn't helped your English, Mr. Pocho."

"Grandma, we have the Newman Center on the other side of campus," said Juan ignoring her comment. If you would like we could go over there this morning for early mass and some coffee and donuts. I have the time and I could introduce you to Father Largente."

"That would be nice, Juanito, but a cup of coffee and a hole filled donut is not the same as holy communion. I would rather stay here and say an Our Father with a somebody."

They said the Our Father together. "I feel better now, Juanito. I'll take this laundry and return next Thursday."

"That is a week away, Grandma."

"That should give you enough time to learn the Our Father in perfect español. He is perfection and deserves no less than that from us. He is our Tree of Life. Seek Him, Juan. He will find you. Remember that Jesu Cristo is the Garment of Salvation and the Cloak of Justice. In his garment you are blessed. Remember who loves you, Juanito."

"Thanks for coming, Grandma."

"Thank you for listening, Juan. Our tree prospers. He will multiply our fruit."

Dearest Conchita,

I went to my senior interview today to check out what I needed to do next fall. Much to my surprise I found out that because of the classes I took in Los Angeles City College, my four unit veteran's credit, and a summer class here and there, I will be able to graduate this June instead of next January. I am enclosing the money for train fare. On the radio they are advertising group rates and calling it the Daylight Special.

Miss you and the kidos a whole lot.

Love,

Juan

THE UNIQUE TREE

The day was hot, even for the last days of May in Matatlan. Juan had just rented his robe and cap at the Spartan Student Store. On his way back to his car in the college parking garage on Seventh Street he stopped near San Carlos Street in front of a converted fourplex. In 1957 the building served as the office space for the Spanish Department. His load of books and boxes slipped ever lower on his perspiring arms. The boxed robes of tradition felt like another Zoot Zuit in a box. He set the box and books on the ground in an order that appeared to make them more transportable. He felt like a burro carrying this load. "I guess there times when even an educated man has to be a burro," said Juan as he smiled and laughed to himself.

From his kneeling position he made note of the young college students running to their finals. If he entered graduate school the running for finals would continue for him. "I sure don't look forward to that," said Juan as he continued his dialogue with himself in the shade of a small tree. As he stood up to continue his walk to his car, Juan observed a big yellow East Side Union High School District (ESUHSD) Crown bus that had been disgorging a field-trip load of new recruits on the curb. Seeing the students jostling each other and calling out nicknames fascinated him. Since he had a few moments to spare, he decided to lean against the strange shaped tree. The small one foot wide trunk and exposed surface roots of the young tree made him feel safe. While the short tree provided only enough shade for his head, it covered his backside. The spot felt comfortable.

The parked yellow bus from the school district commonly known as Barrio High School in Matatlan only had Anglo American students and staff on it. Juan approached the adult who seemed to be in charge of the field trip and said, "Sir, are these seniors from James Lick High School?"

"Yes, they are," replied the educator with pride as he assisted the bouncing, bubbling pink faced students off the bus. "Are you our campus guide?"

"No. I don't think so," answered Juan. "I am just curious and puzzled to see so many shining white faces getting off an Eastside Union High School Bus."

"Why is that?" asked the educator.

"I would have thought that some Mexican American students would be on this trip with you," replied Juan.

"Well, they are on their own field trip today," said the educator. "The few who get this far are touring San José City College. The vocational courses offered there are more suited to their academic abilities. A trip to San José State would probably be a waste of time for them, but you probably would not understand the reasons for this, you being a foreign student and all."

Juan was absolutely stunned by the counselor's assertion. "What makes you think I am a foreign student?"

"Well I pride myself in being able to recognize educated people from other places and nations," replied the educator.

"That is really interesting, sir. Where do you imagine that a person like me would come from?" asked Juan.

"I would say, from your refined and careful academic English that you are one of the oil-rich Arab exchange students that are appearing in ever increasing numbers at this college."

"My Grandma thanks you for noting the quality of my English," said Juan, trying not to smile at the ignorance of this educator.

"I take it then that your grandfather had an English woman in his harem," stated the educator. "I have heard about things like that. I really enjoyed the musical, *The King And I.*

"May I infer from your comments that you object to foreign students coming to American colleges?" asked Juan trying to probe the depth of the educator's prejudice.

"No," replied the educator. "In all candor I think that as long as there is room for you and one of my students from here is not kept out of this college because your country is sending you to learn of the superior business practices and democratic institutions we have developed here in America, it is O.K. for you foreign students to attend American colleges. Of course, I would also hope that you foreign students are not a burden to our taxpayers and that your country is paying full tuition. Besides, a selected few foreigners provide our students the opportunity to have a controlled mingling in a learning environment in order to broaden their attitudinal and academic horizons."

Juan was about to ask the educator what he meant by the phrase, "controlled mingling," when the educator said, "Excuse me while I make a few announcements to my charges."

The educator turned to the four other adults with the group and said, "Let's spread out to gather in the herd. We don't want to lose anyone until they graduate." As the other teachers started compressing the students and counting heads, the educator cupped his hands around his mouth and shouted, "May I have your attention, please. It appears that our guide is a little late. So, I will take this opportunity to welcome you all to my alma mater, San José State College. I was just discussing with this foreign student the opportunity the college is developing for you to get an international flavor in your educational endeavor. When you meet a student like this nice young man here, it will probably be the first opportunity for most of you to see a person from another culture. I know that I have counseled most of you to take advantage of every golden opportunity you are given. We will start our tour of the campus as soon as the guide gets here. Until then stay close to the bus. Remember at all times that we are guests here. Please keep your activities down to a dull roar."

As the educator turned back to Juan he said, "Would you like to say something to our students. It would probably help pass the time for them and give you an opportunity to speak in front of a large group."

"I welcome the opportunity to speak in front of a large group. You see the campus has chosen me to be the class valedictorian for this year's graduation at Spartan Stadium. I just picked up my robes. However, I don't think your charges are ready to hear what I have to say."

"My, my, how times have changed here at the campus," said

the educator swinging his head back and forth in wonder. "When I went here in the early forties, foreign students were not allowed to be class valedictorian."

As Juan turned back to his load of books and boxes in the shade of the tree, he thought to himself, wouldn't you know it, on top of everything else, this educator is a "4-Fer." Then he muttered just loud enough to be in ear shot of the educator, "They still aren't."

"Then how are you the class valedictorian?" asked the teacher stepping forward into Juan's space.

"Because, Sir, I have a 3.5 grade point overall average at this college and a four-point in my major. Besides my essay on 'Golden Opportunity' was considered the best of the valedictorian proposals in a blind reading. The committee tried to have my speech read by the person with the highest grade point but I did not allow that. A minority group in the committee supported me fully because of academic integrity."

"How interesting," said the educator.

"In addition, sir, I have been on the Dean's list every semester. Moreover, I'm a Congressional Medal of Honor holder and I was born about a half mile away from where you allegedly teach everyday. In fact, most of my ancestors for the past six generations have been born in that location. Thus, I feel that I must at least welcome you, as an uninvited white guest into my house." Where did those words come from, thought Juan to himself.

"I'm sorry I misstook you for an educated Arab," replied the educator as he stepped back out of Juan's space. Are you one of those new, revolutionary, separatist, Chi-Chi-cainos I have been hearing about."

"I would have said no until our little talk here," replied Juan. "But I guess what you just said gave birth to, no, awakened the Chicano in me. I want to thank you, sir, for giving me my mission in life by setting me free. At last I can see my unique tree. It is small, strange looking, and poorly watered, but its survival power is strong."

"I wish I had more time to talk to you, young man," replied

the educator. "We were looking for a speaker for our school staff Mexican sensitivity inservice day. In thirty seconds or so, could you please tell me what you Chi-Chi-cainos really want."

"Well," replied Juan, trying not to laugh at the racist stupidity of this educator. "You have probably been reading about the freedom riders in the South."

"Yes I have and I think it is a crying shame what they are doing to those poor unfortunate Negroes, I mean blackies in the South. I think you should be able to ride on whatever part of the bus you want."

Not even Mrs. Post, the kindergarten protector of Christopher Columbus and her sacred history would have believed the tunnel vision and uninformed bias of this educator, thought Juan. "That is an interesting idea regarding individual freedoms and personal rights, Sir."

"What do blackies riding on a bus in the Old South have to do with what you Chi-Chi-cainos want?"

"Well, sir, to use your example, while the Blacks don't want to ride in the back of your bus, at least they are on the bus. The Chi-cainos as you call them, are not even allowed on your bus. You are guilty of either drop kicking or pushing them out of your school. The remnant that somehow survives this process is sent by you and your patronistic attitudes off to City College in pursuit of second class vocations and dead end careers."

"For a young man that has been given the opportunity to speak for his class at commencement, you sound as if four years at State have missed their mark. If you stay with your rebellious attitude young man, no self respecting educator or college graduate will listen to you," replied the educator as he dismissed Juan with his eyes.

"You may be right on that, sir. But all I can think of as a retort for your prophesy is that life has taught me that those who live in the silent dark lie of freedom in chains cannot hear the bright trumpeting truth of bondage unfettered," said Juan in glorious pedantic academic English to the educator's retreating backside.

The tree grew strong in the light of the truth. It would be a great oak bearing the red fruit of the California Holly. It was a Mestizo tree: one yet two: deciduous yet evergreen: a symbol of eternal regenerating immortality: an adorned cross of salvation.

Spanish Grandma winced at how well Juan used his "perfect English" to cross swords with "The Man." "Only draw blood and the sword if it is in harmony with the regeneration of the moral order," murmured Sequoya. "Don't dishonor the sword and scabbard of your tree on the back of a dishonored man," the murmuring voice sang.

"An honorable sharp sword held by a righteous man in a scabbard is twice as powerful as a dishonorable sword drawn by an evil man," declared Father Diego.

The concrete sidewalk buckled under the pressure of the of growing roots of Juan's young tree. The tour for the white elite from the Barrio marched off in the hot Matatlan sun tripping here and there on the buckled sidewalk. Most of them acted like they had no reason to be on the field trip except for the fact it was what a white senior from the barrio was supposed to do. Spanish Grandma could tell from their giggling English that the knowledge they hoped to gain here wouldn't save their souls. Abuelo smiled at the cracks in the cement.

Juan looked at his tree once again. Abuelo said he would know it when he saw it. Juan hugged the tree! The young bark was course and strong. The smell of the cool and rich Matatlan earth exuded through its pores. "Thanks for being here for me. I would never have thought I would find you here!" he shouted. "Gracias a Dios! I can't wait to tell papá about you. I promise you this upon the spirit of my ancestors, I'll return to you one day." The tree stirred in the warmth of the day. A green leaf dropped upon Juan's head as an acknowlegement of Juan's pledge. Juan bent over, picked up his load, placed the leaf inside the box containing his cap and looked for his car in the garage.

DAYLIGHT'S ARRIVAL

"Hi, Concha, is everything ready for you and the kidos to come up to the commencement?" asked Juan.

"I guess we are as ready as we ever will be, Juan. It was really difficult to get the time off to come up to this event."

"It is supposed to be something special, querida."

"My boss's son graduated from USC last year and he said that sitting in the hot June sun in a football stadium to hear a bunch of boring speeches was proof that he really loved his son."

"I haven't told you yet, Concha, because I wanted it to be a surprise, but one of those boring speeches is going to be mine."

"That's nice, Juan. Who did you write it for?"

"I wrote it for me, Concha. I'm the class valedictorian."

"You have got to be kidding, Juan. You can't talk for two minutes without one of your herd of voices having to make a speech too."

"I've written out the whole thing and two of the professors in the Speech and Communication Department have been rehearsing me. They say that I'm really quite good, querida."

"Watching you make a fool of yourself in front of a whole stadium will make the trip worthwhile, Juan."

"Thanks for the support, Conchita," said Juan in his valedictorian voice.

"You'er welcome, Juanito," said Concha in her big mamá voice. "I thought that a remark like that would keep your chivito cucaracha brain scurrying for perfection."

"When are you going to tell me what you really mean, Concha?"

"I always tell you what I really mean, Juan."

"Do you have the tickets for the Daylight, querida? I wish I was riding it with you."

"What are you up to now, Juan? Surprises interest me very much. I'm sure that this is the start of a very interesting story."

"Over the summer I have an opportunity to work on a graduate demonstration project in a migrant program with Dr. Abernathy Wilson. We are going to use the community centers in the migrant housing camps as classrooms and provide schooling for children who have never been in a classroom, and ..."

"Hold on, Chivito, how much money are we going to realize from this great opportunity?"

"Well it is just an opportunity, not a job, querida."

"When are you going to get a real job, Juan? I can't buy groceries for the children with certificates of graduate opportunity. And another thing, Chivito, how can you be the valid-dick-torian and you can't even get a real job?"

"Well I still have my tow truck driving job, Concha. And, Dr. Abernathy says that there is a real shortage of teachers. With this work and two more semesters, I'll have my General Teaching Credential and some units towards a Master's degree."

"Now listen, Chivito," Concha started in her big mamá voice, "take the wax out of your ears before I put the towing chain around your neck and hook you all the way to personnel! I didn't let you go San José State to school for the rest of your natural born days."

"Please don't come off like a ball and chain queen! You wanted me to improve myself and I doing it! So why are you complaining?"

"Which one of your voices is speaking for you now? Your words smelled in the sewers and I understood. Now one of those voices smells, period! We have invested and invested in you, Juan. My mother says that it is about time that our investment bear some dividends besides children."

"I can smell opportunity even if you can't, Conchita!"

"Have you got wax for brains, Juan? Have you got a real job

yet?" Click!

Juan waited five minutes to make sure that the "mechanical problems with the phone line" had cleared. "Hi, querida."

"Diego, there is some more of that static on the phone line again," said Concha.

"Can't you hear me, Conchita?" called out Juan.

"There must be some wax on the line."

"Are you and the kids arriving tomorrow on the Daylight?"

"Are you riding back to East Los with us on the Daylight?"

"Since the tickets are already paid for and I have two weeks vacation coming from my tow truck job, I'll go back with you for two weeks."

"Then expect us at 6:00 P.M. tomorrow, Juan. I want the kids to see you graduate and mamá has planned something for you with your mother. Just remember there will be no extras for you, Chivito, until we are on the train heading for East Los."

"What are extras, mommy?" asked María Chavala.

"They are apron strings for your father," answered Francesca.

"I heard that, Conchita!" said Juan. "What is your mother teaching our children?"

"If you were here more, Juan, you would know the truth. We will meet you at the Cahalan Station in San José."

"I'll be there, Conchita." Juan wanted to say more, but decided that the less he said the better. "Bye, querida." "Adios, Chivito Cucaracha."

*　　*　　*

The big orange locomotive steamed, clattered and squeaked into the station slowly. The children waved at Juan as their car passed him on the platform. They already had their hand luggage and toys in hand. The train stopped as the red caps placed the boarding stoops by each car exit.

There were hugs, and kisses for everyone. The children

wrapped themselves around Juan's legs. Juan couldn't move. Concha just shook her head. "They really miss you, Chivito," she said.

"The kids are going to have to ride in the back of the tow truck, Concha. The car broke down today. My boss lent me his truck to get you home to Abuela's. I'll take it back tonight after we eat and pick up the car for tomorrow."

"I keep telling you, daughter, this man you call a husband is not much good for anything besides making you fat," said Francesca.

"I know that, Mom, but I love him something awful, anyways!"

Juan loaded the truck. The three older children were thrilled to be riding in the back, beyond Franceca's mal ojo and Concha's long reach. After six miles of sporadic urban sprawl, they arrived at Abuela's house. A very anxious Abuela and her golden sherry smile greeted them with warm abrazos. "Your mother has evertin' ready for jou and jour hijos, mijo." As Abuela winked at Juan, she gave Concha a big abrazo. The family talked late into the night in anticipation of the big day.

At four A.M. the next morning Juan got up and went into the backyard shed to do a final rehearsal of his prepared speech, but the words would not come. He then spent the next three hours writing and rewriting a speech entitled "Golden Dichos."

After a nice breakfast, full of excitement and bantering the whole family loaded into cars and caravaned to Spartan Stadium. When they got there the orchestra was playing Sir Edgar Elgar's "Pomp and Circumstance March." Juan made sure the family had good seats. Then he ran to the stage for last minute instructions.

THE COMMENCEMENT AT SJSC

" Graduates, Faculty and Honored Guests: I am proud and honored to have been selected our class valedictorian. This honor humbles me. I will always give honor to those who have so acknowledged and recognized me with this gift: the privilege of being our class voice and your valedictorian. This opportunity ranks in my life with my marriage, Congressional Medal of Honor and the sacred voices of wisdom that have always nourished me. But, there is more to appreciate here than the fact of our graduation and this valedictory honor."

"I am truly amazed to be speaking as the representative of our class. I never expected to be here, partly because I never thought I would ever get to go to college, let alone finish high school, and partly because in the most remote portion of my dream walking, I would have never contemplated finishing a degree. I am the first in my family to attend let alone graduate from this institution. Yet, being first here has made me last in my barrio. My grandfathers taught me that a true leader is always last."

"In preparing for this speech I had a really long intellectual and academically oriented oratorio filled with the usual pep talk and reminiscences of the years we have spent here at San José State. My speech was entitled "Golden Opportunity." I felt responsible for the preparation of a litany of suggestions for our futures. My speech had as its central theme, living out partial truths. It was to emphasize that the professional roles we have trained for here at San José State, only partially prepared us. Today, as we are about to receive our degrees and celebrate our accomplishments, we are jointly respecting our accumulative efforts."

"We are due hearty congratulations. From the bottom of my heart I wish all of you the very best in all our lives that are advancing towards us: the harmony of our merit and soul. Yet for all of our degree verified education, we will have to prepare yet another part of ourselves to be whole human beings."

"Most commencement speeches seem bent on convincing us that the union of our education to the work place will meld us into the self actualized individuals we seem to value in our society. But all of that preparation reminded me of one of my Abuela's favorite stories wherein a Portugues fisherman opposes the building of a light house on the grounds that, "De lighta housa, she lights; de fogga horna, she blows: But de damma fogga comesa justa de same." I decided that if the farewell light and horn of plenty is being replaced by the incoming fog of the real world we are commencing upon, then we need the wisdom of the ages instead of the platitudes of the moment."

"Then, when I picked-up my cap and gown yesterday, an encounter with a racist high school counselor occurred that made me realize that most commencement speeches missed the concept of, comenzar. I realized that to begin something, you must know where and who you are. There was truth in my Spanish Grandmother's words when she said, "Remember, Chivo, pick your spot carefully. You can't lift a bucket if you are standing in it.""

"I wish all my ancestors could be here today. We owe a lot to those who have paved the way and sacrificed so much so that we can be here. Thus, instead of my prepared speech, I want to leave you with the voices of my ancestors and other precursors. Many of them never went to school. Many of them could not read nor write their own names. None of them published. They spoke little, but said a lot. Some of my earliest memories and recuerdos stretch my soul with quiet but heated discussions of substance at the adult dinner table: the celebration and personification of emotive words spoken through and from timeless living souls."

"Some people acted as if my ancestors were ignorant fools. It is true that I often had to stay home from school to translate for many of my old ones. Yet, I learned more wisdom of living from them than any other single source of knowledge. As a group they are the most educated humans I have ever been allowed to meet. They are my tree of truth."

"What they taught to me I will be forever learning. The new voices of heart and soul, my spouse, Concha and our four children, are constantly providing precious reflections and refinements on the words of my precursors. Pre-dawn fishing for breakfast and lunch from the canals banks of Matatlan taught me that the light reflected by a carefully placed bucket was double bright."

"Over the years when I ate and learned at their tables they set forth on different occasions a series of heartfelt dichos that I will be forever applying. Thus I have written a short speech entitled "Golden Dichos.""

"Know where you have been to find out where you are going."

"In your life search process, if you forget your gods, you are a brave fool."

"The Earth sustains us so that we can be part of its constant regeneration."

"When you forget the purpose of regeneration you fail both the gods and yourself."

"You are either fertile or fertilizer."

"In total humility we must confront the Teotl in the center of our souls."

"If you remember your gods in denial, you are a coward."

"If you deny your God you are unfaithful."

"If you remember your gods in conversion, they will be one with you and your future, past and present."

"If you believe in your God you are one with Him."

"When you ignore the needs of your soul space you will lose your spiritual focus."

"Remembering the soul space maintains the spiritual focus."

"Staying focused sustains the soul."

"Salvation of the soul is God's focus."

"7x7x7...the perfect creation. 20x20x20x20...the perfect regeneration. Document your lineage."

"Know how to protect both the sacred and profane of your heritage."

"Your last step in your past is your furthermost point in your future."

"The true Mestizo creates a unified existence from disparate elements."

"A unique tree maintains and finds the soul for the singular group by preserving your soul."

"By these words, my illiterate yet sabio ancestors were always trying to teach me that as something ends, new life is born; with every slammed door, a new one opens. While this seems an easy lesson to learn, many of us here today will probably die not tasting of its fruits."

"A wartime soul mate, who saved my life many times then and since, suggested to me a fool proof way to begin learning this lesson by developing a criterion for picking out a career or some graduate pursuit. At one time in my junior year I thought about pursuing a career in law. When my soul mate found this out he asked me if I knew the difference between a dead skunk and a dead lawyer. Seeing the puzzled look upon my face, he told me that the difference was that one was a rotting stink and the other was a rotten stinker. I asked him which one was which and he told me that only lawyers would be able to adjudicate the answer. I told him that I didn't get it and he then told me not to pursue a career in law."

"The lessons I have learned from the battlefields, sewers and schools in my life has confirmed that survival at any cost is not survival: wisdom to heed. By virtue of this commencement we students have finished our spring planting and are starting the summer of our lives. What we harvest in the fall and set aside for our winter depends upon the decisions of commitment we now make. From this point of focus our tree will either bear fruit or whither like a blossom blown in the hot wind of Matatlan. Chivitos cucarachas, remember who loves you. May you fare well."

"My ancestors thank you for listening."

"My ancestors thank you for remembering."

The normal clapping that follows a traditional valedictorian's speech sputtered and then crackled like a radio on high volume seeking a distant station. Then the delayed ovation grew and grew until all were on their feet. Tears flowed freely, but true comprehension was yet to come. Sequoya said, "You moved your branches gracefully. The wind did not even feel your sword." Father Diego replied, "The Truth will always set you free."

The commencement speaker, Dr. Abernathy Wilson decided to scrap his speech too. Following the practical wisdom of 450 years worth of ancestors was just too hard of an act to follow. Instead he commented on Juan's speech by saying, "Maybe the heat in the stadium is getting to all of us. Mr. Galván has given us the key of truth to unlock the doors to our futures. The keynote of this commencement is the Quest for Truth, but I learned something new here today. By his speech reflecting the power and wisdom from our combined heritages, the unfamiliar hidden voices and beliefs of our present have been revealed. This college should be proud of this class and its valedictorian, for by his speech and your applause the faculty and staff have received a new charge. We will all be a little different as we leave here today. We will no longer be able to ignore the voices of wisdom brought before us by Mr. Galván. Respect for the cultural heritage of each one of us and the humanity we represent is now our challenge."

After the handing out of diplomas and the closing prayer the crowd dispersed.

"Great espeech, Juan," said papá. "For once jou have truly espoken en truchas from jour esoul. Por me I tink dat jou are not of jour Zuit anymore. At last jou are estardin' to make jourself un hombre entre nosotros. Jou have made our familia very proud!" Juan moved into his papá's and mamá's embrazos and felt his unique tree and glowing voices hugging him.

Others moved into the space to congratulate Juan on his speech. Concha and the children broke out of the crowd of well wishers. "Mamá and papá want us to go to your Abuelo's house for the family celebration," said Concha. "My mother and Abuela have prepared a feast for us. Let us not keep them waiting Mr.

College Graduate. You have already kept us waiting for four years."

"Let us enjoy this moment, querida."

Juan noticed Spanish Grandma standing behind his parents with one of her rare smiles. As he walked toward her with thanks on his heart, she reached out to him and silently hugged Juan while placing her favorite rosary around his neck. Then she hugged him tightly again.

"Thanks, Grandma," said Juan softly.

"My Don would have wanted you to have it!" she replied with intensity and a tear in her eye.

Concha tapped Juan on his shoulder. "Juan its like we all have graduated here today! We are so proud of you!"

"It is I who is proud of all of you!" he replied with tears in his eyes.

All the voices, Concha, Juan and the children embraced each other as one great tree with very deep well nourished roots in Matatlan. The hidden voices remained poetically undisturbed.

GLOSSARY

abuela . . . . grandmother

abuelo . . . . grandfather

acerca . . . . about

agabachada . . . try to be white

aguila . . . . eagle

aleman . . . . . . German

Alviso. . . . . town north of San José

ancho . . . . wide

ancianos . . . . . ancient ancestors

andele . . . . let's move out or on

antiguas. . . . . . old, historical times

aqui . . . . here

árbol . . . . tree

arroz . . . . rice

asento . . . . acent

ayer . . . . yesterday

bandidos . . . . . bandits

barrio . . . . neighborhood

basura . . . . garbage

besitos . . . . caring kisses

bien educado . . well brought up

bigote . . . . mustache

borranca . . . . . gorge, canyon

bosquejos . . . . sketch, outline

botas . . . . boots

brazos . . . . arms

bueno . . . . good

burra/o . . . . . . donkey

burrito. . . . . . . food, meat or beans wrapped in a tortilla

caballos . . . . . . horses

cabeza . . . . head

cabrito al . . . . barbecue goat pastor

cabrones . . . . . damn machos machos

caca . . . . manure

cajita . . . . little box

calavera. . . . . . skeleton

calcos. . . . . shoes

caldo . . . . soup

Califas . . . . pocho for California

callate . . . . be quiet

calle. . . . . street

campo . . . . pocho for camp

canción . . . . . . song

canerias. . . . . . caneries

capulli . . . . neighborhood

carnales. . . . . . pocho for brother

carne asada . . . roast beef or steak

cariño . . . . lover

carniceria . . . . meat market

celoso . . . . jealous

cerveza . . . . . . beer

chale . . . . down with

chamacos . . . . little boys

chansa . . . . pocho for chance

chaparral . . . . scrub oak and grease

charriada . . . . round up festival

chichis . . . . breast

chivito . . . . little goat

cholo . . . . new arrival

chosita . . . . pocho for small house or shack

chueco . . . . twisted

chuco . . . . short for pachuco

cinturón . . . . . belt

cocido de res . . . Mexican soup served at Christmas

colonia . . . . neighborhood

comadres . . . . sisters and god mothers

comerciantes . . merchants

comida . . . . . . food

comunidad . . . community

contestar . . . . . answer

corazón . . . . . . heart

cosa . . . . thing

criollos . . . . Spaniards born in N.W.

cristianos . . . . . christians

Cristobal . . . . Christopher
Colón   Columbus

cruz . . . . cross

cuando . . . . . . when

cucarachas . . . cockroaches

cucuhi . . . . boogie man

cuento . . . . story

cuidado . . . . . . be careful

cumpleaños . . . birthday

curandera . . . . folk doctor

curanderismo . . traditional Indian health practices

de coro de . . . . the love of your
camarada   friends

de veras . . . . . . really

derecho . . . . . . straight

desierto . . . . . . desert

diablos . . . . devils

dicen . . . . they say

dicho . . . . saying of phrase

discorama . . . . record store

doble . . . . double

drapes . . . . a suit of clothes

educado . . . . . educated with class

El Dia de los . . January 6th
  Magos

el rey . . . . the king

el chingón . . . . big

embrazos . . . . . embraces

empanadas . . . turnovers

en coche . . . . . in your car

en vez de . . . . . instead of

enemigos . . . . . enemies

entiendes . . . . do you understand

equis . . . . the letter "x"

escuela . . . . school

espíritu . . . . . . spirit

esposa . . . . wife

esposo . . . . husband

Estados . . . . . . United States
  Unidos

estómago . . . . . stomach

feliz . . . . happy

fidora . . . . pocho for hat

flaco . . . . skinny

frijoles . . . . beans

fuerza . . . . force

gabacho . . . . . . white man

gachupines . . . Spaniards

ganas . . . . desires

gente . . . . people

gobierno . . . . . government

grupo . . . . group

guaraches . . . . Mexican sandals

güeros . . . . light skinned
  people

hace . . . . you make

hacendados . . . hacienda owners

hay lo watcho . pocho for I'll
  see you later

hembra . . . . . . pocho for woman

hembras . . . . . women

hombre . . . . . . man

huevos . . . . eggs or testicles

humanidad . . . humanity

ingles . . . . English

interesante . . . interesting

invierno . . . . . winter

janilla . . . . girlfriend

Jarabe . . . . dance of
  Tapatio   Mexico

jardines . . . . . . gardens

jefe . . . . chief

juventud . . . . . youth

Kiva . . . . holy pueblo
  temple

La Conquista . . . Invasion of
  Mexico by Spain

la migra . . . . . . immigration
  officers

la tarde . . . . . . the afternoon

la reina . . . . . . the queen

lección . . . . lesson

lechuga . . . . . . lettuce

lengua . . . . tongue

limpia . . . . clean

lisa . . . . pocho for shirt

locura . . . . crazy mask
tapatio

lonche . . . . pocho for lunch

machista . . . . . male in

machitez . . . . . wisdom

maestra . . . . . . teacher

maguey . . . . . . cactus for rope
and tequila

malcriado . . . . bad shout

mañana . . . . . . tomorrow

mandas . . . . . . commands and/
or promises

mansanilla . . . . plant for herbal
tea

manta . . . . fat,lard

mantillas . . . . . shawl

mascaras . . . . . masks

maza . . . . corn dough

me llamo . . . . . my name

menso . . . . dumb

mentiras . . . . . lies

mestizo . . . . . . Indian/Spanish
mix

mijito . . . . my little son

mijo . . . . my son

moda . . . . way, style

montañas . . . . mountains

mordida . . . . . the bite or bribe

movidas . . . . . . moves and
manipulation

muerte . . . . . . death

mujer . . . . woman

mundo . . . . . . world

mytos . . . . myths

nalgas . . . . buttocks

noche . . . . night

nopal . . . . plate cactus
prickly pear

nosotros . . . . . us

novia . . . . fiancé

nuestro . . . . . . ours

oficina . . . . office

ojos, ojitos . . . . eyes

olla . . . . jug

oro . . . . gold

pachuco . . . . . Mexican-American
youth 1940-50

padrinos . . . . . godparents

padrinos/as . . . godparents

pais . . . . country

pajaros . . . . . . birds

palabras. . . . . . words

panaderia . . . . bakery

papeles . . . . . . pocho for papers

papitas. . . . . . . fried potatos

patrona . . . . . . ruling woman

payaso . . . . clown

pendejo. . . . . . stupid

pensamiento. . feelings

piedras . . . . . . rocks, stones

placas   your brand or
                sign

placita . . . . plaza

plaquear . . . . . to paint your
                sign on the wall

plata . . . . silver

pochismos. . . . word made up
                of Spanish and
                English

pocho . . . . culture mix of
                Mexico/U.S.

polecia. . . . . . pocho for
                police

ponte abusado . . be smart

preguntas . . . . questions

prieto . . . . dark

promesa . . . . . promise

pulque. . . . . . . juice of the
                maguey

puro pedo. . . . bullshit

quadra. . . . . . . squre, block

que quieres . . . what do you want?

querida . . . . . . my love

quesadilla . . . . tortilla with
                melted cheese

quinceañera . . 15th birthday

ramflíta . . . . . . pocho for old car

raza . . . . race

razón. . . . . reason

recodatas. . . . . records and
                documents

recuerdas . . . . do you
                remember

repleats . . . . . . double back
                folded pleats

requerimiento . . requirements

respeto . . . . . . respect

ropa. . . . . clothing

rubio . . . . blonde

rucas . . . . pocho for
                girlfriend

sabio . . . . wise

sacerdote. . . . . priest

saco . . . . sport jacket

sacramento . . . sacrament

sangre . . . . blood

santos . . . . saints	triste . . . . sad
seguro que si. . surely	troka . . . . pocho for truck
sesos . . . . brains	trute . . . . pocho for truth
siempre. . . . . . always	ultima . . . . the last, highest, ultimate
siento mucho. . . feel very much	un buche de . . a drop of water agua
soldados . . . . . soldiers	
somos. . . . . we are	vato . . . . pocho for guy
suaharos . . . . . tall barrel cactus	velorio. . . . . . . brave
suave. . . . . smooth and sophisticated	verano. . . . . . . summer
	verdad. . . . . . . truth
suegra . . . . mother-in-law	verdadera . . . . a truth
sus . . . . yours	verdes . . . . green
tacuche . . . . . . pocho for finest suit	viaje. . . . . trip
	vida . . . . life
tacuche . . . . . pocho for outfit	viejo. . . . . old man
temprano . . . . early	voces . . . . voices
tia . . . . aunt	wachate. . . . . . pocho for be careful
tiempo. . . . . . . time	
tierra. . . . . land, earth	zapatiados. . . . dance steps
tijeras blancas. . white scissors	zapatos . . . . . . shoes
tio . . . . uncle	zuit . . . . pocho for suit
toreador . . . . . bull fighter	
tragito de . . . . shot of tequila tequila	
tramos. . . . . . . pocho for pants	
trapos . . . . rags, clothing	
tren . . . . train	
trensas. . . . . . . braids	

Other books offered by Chusma House Publications
ORDER NOW!
Order Form

No. of Copies:

_____ **SOLDADOS: Chicanos in Viet Nam,**
narratives by Charley Trujillo **$12.95**

_____ **CANTOS,** poetry by Alfred Arteaga........................**$7.95**

_____ **CARING FOR A HOUSE,**
poetry by Victor Martinez **$10.00**

_____ **UNDOCUMENTED LOVE,**
poetry by José Antonio Burciaga..............................**$12.00**

_____ **IN FORMATION: 20 Years of Joda,**
poetry by José Montoya..**$17.95**

_____ **DOGS FROM ILLUSION**
A Viet Nam war novel by Charley Trujillo **$11.95**

_____ **HOW TO MEET THE DEVIL AND OTHER STORIES**
Short stories by Ramón Sánchez **$11.95**

_____ **VOICES OF MATATLAN**
A novel by Felix Garcia Jr. and Randall C. Jimenez **$13.95**

Name _____

Street _____

City _____ **St.** _____ **ZIP** _____

Also send $2.45 for 1st copy shipping & handling plus $1.75 for each additional book-make checks payable to Chusma House. Allow 2 to 3 weeks for delivery.

Write to:
Chusma House Publications
PO Box 467
San José, CA, 95103
(408) 947-0958